MURDER *at the* ROYAL BOTANIC GARDENS

ANDREA PENROSE

KENSINGTON
PUBLISHING CORP.

www.kensingtonbooks.com

For the Word Wenches
Sisters-in-Writing and dear friends
*Nicola Cornick, Christina Courtenay, Anne Gracie, Susan
King, Mary Jo Putney, and Pat Rice*

*Thanks for always being there with hugs, sympathy and
cyber chocolate in those moments when I'm convinced that the
dratted manuscript is never going to make it to the light of day.*

MURDER *at* *the* ROYAL BOTANIC GARDENS

PROLOGUE

The floral fragrances—a symphony of subtle sweetness—swirled with the earthier scents of mist-damp leaves and the nutrient-rich soil. The gentleman closed his eyes for a moment and drew in a deep breath.

The essence of Life. There was nothing more beautiful, Josiah Becton mused as he stood very still in the shadows and let the warm air caress his cheeks.

Moonlight flickered through the soaring glass-paned walls of the magnificent conservatory, its silvery softness twining with the gold-hued glow of the lanterns hung among the exotic greenery. The faint sounds of a string quartet—was it Mozart or Haydn?—floated out from the assembly room attached to the rambling structure, the lilting notes punctuated by discreet laughter and the crystalline click of champagne glasses.

It was all so . . . elegantly civilized, this international symposium of botany scholars and wealthy patrons of science, gathered at London's legendary Royal Botanic Gardens in order to share their knowledge for the good of mankind.

Becton slowly released a sigh. "But I am far more at home in the wilds of the world, where the flora and fauna have not yet been disturbed by the footsteps of men. Exploring . . . searching . . . learning . . ." His words trailed off as he meandered down the brick pathway, delving deeper into the vast assortment of specimens gathered from around the globe.

The music gave way to the whisper of the leaves and the drip of water feeding a section of succulents from the West Indies. His steps brought him to a smaller room that housed the treasures brought back from the islands of the South Pacific by Sir Joseph Banks, the noted scholar and adventurer whose tireless efforts over the years had established the Gardens as the leading repository of botanical specimens in the world.

"Ah, the South Pacific," murmured Becton, bending low to examine the lush colors of a tropical flower. "Perhaps the Antipodes should be my next destination. Granted, it is so very far away . . ." A twinge of regret pinched at his chest.

So little time, so much to know.

"I see you are admiring the efforts of Sir Joseph." Fronds rustled as a gentleman slipped past a cluster of leafy brake ferns.

"He is an inspiration to all of us who believe the natural world holds unlimited potential for improving the lives of all people."

"Ah, but you, too, are an inspiration, Mr. Becton."

"That's very kind of you to say. But such praise is undeserved. I'm merely a curious traveler who is happiest in the solitude of the jungles or mountains." He quirked a wry grimace. "I've always been far more comfortable with the company of plants than people."

His companion chuckled. "I fear that a passion for science makes all of us odd fish."

Becton smiled.

"Your work has always been quite special—ye heavens, your solitary journeys have taken you where few others have managed to go! Everyone here is eagerly awaiting the lecture on your explorations through the northern reaches of the Spanish Empire in South America, and all your fascinating experiences. The sense of wonder . . ." His companion allowed a pensive pause. "And discovery."

"Yes," agreed Becton. "As a fellow man of science, I know you understand that such opportunities can simply take your breath away."

"Indeed, indeed." A muted rustle of well-tailored wool. "Come, I took the liberty of bringing along some champagne. Let us raise a toast." His companion offered him a glass. "To discovery!"

"Thank you, sir, but no." Becton waved away the wine. "The marvelous botanical specimens here are intoxicating enough."

"Nonsense, my good fellow. You have crossed the ocean from America to be here for this grand occasion. Surely, that calls for celebration—and the effervescence of champagne!"

"Alas, the years of traveling under constant adversities like heat, cold, and pestilence have taken their toll on my constitution. My physician forbids the use of strong spirits."

"Sparkling wine is hardly strong spirits," protested his companion. "A few sips to acknowledge the spirit of collegial friendships that have brought us here, from near and far, surely can do no harm."

The lantern's glow danced over the cut crystal coupe. Becton watched the tiny bubbles beckoning like myriad diamond-bright points of fire.

"Quite right," he agreed, taking the proffered glass. "With so many dark forces at play in the world—war, disease, hunger—we must celebrate the light of knowledge and the hope it brings for the future."

"To scientific triumphs that will change the world," said his companion with a beatific smile.

Glass kissed against glass, setting off a sonorous ring.

"A lovely vintage, don't you think, Mr. Becton?"

"Yes, I—" A sudden, strangled cough cut off his words. "F-Forgive me, I seem to be . . ." He reached out a hand to steady himself on one of the display pedestals, only to feel his knees begin to buckle.

". . . Feeling unwell," he gasped as he slumped forward, spilling the rest of his wine. A fierce pain spiraled through his gut, drawing a guttural moan. Everything was turning black as Hades. His head was spinning . . .

His companion plucked the glass from his spasming fingers. "It's all right," soothed the man's voice. It sounded very far away. "All your mortal aches and pains will soon be over."

Another drunken lurch as Becton felt himself sinking, sinking into darkness . . .

A thud echoed in the muffled crack of terra-cotta pots as his thrashing arm knocked several specimen plants to the stone floor.

"Rest in peace," murmured his companion, crouching down beside the American explorer's still-twitching body. "Your discovery will live on—I promise you that." His voice was solemn, but betrayed not a ripple of remorse. "Though it won't be you who reaps the rewards that will come with its fame."

The gentleman waited for the final death throes to cease before shifting the crystal stems of the two glasses to one hand and beginning a methodical search of Becton's waistcoat pockets.

"*Eureka!*" He smiled as he extracted a small brass key. "Thank you for making this easy."

The display room was once against quiet as a crypt, the moist air undulating through the fanciful silhouettes of the plants as they settled back into a peaceful slumber. Rising, the gentleman smoothed the wrinkles from his trousers and disappeared into the gloom.

A bevy of footmen, resplendent in their royal livery, circulated through the crowd, discreetly ringing handbells to signal that the gathering in the conservatory's reception room was coming to an end and the guests were to exit and make their way along the graveled walkway to the nearby Kew Palace, where a gala supper was soon to be served.

"The bells are quite unnecessary," said one of the governors of the Royal Society, the illustrious scientific organization that had created the symposium. "Once the pop of champagne corks ceases, everyone will quickly understand that it's time to move on." He waggled his brows. "I understand that a very fine claret and German hock are to be served at the banquet. After all, man cannot live on the fruits of knowledge alone."

The quip drew a round of chuckles from the small circle of scholars standing with him.

The governor gave a courtly wave toward the brass-framed glass double doors. "Shall we proceed, gentlemen?"

Other groups were also beginning to drift toward the exit, still engaged in lively scientific discussions with frequent terms in Latin echoing amid English, French, and German.

"Has anyone seen Mr. Becton?" asked the leader of the American delegation, after sweeping the room with a searching look.

"I believe I saw him wander off into the main conservatory, Dr. Hosack." A vague wave accompanied the answer. "It looked like he might have been heading for the section that houses the South Seas specimens collected by Sir Joseph Banks."

Hosack smiled. "Becton tends to lose all track of time when distracted by plant life. I had better go fetch him. He's absent-minded enough to forget all about supper."

"We'll come with you," offered a pair of Royal Society members. "It's easy to lose your way if you're unfamiliar with the twists and turns of the walkways."

The three of them set off, but no sooner had they passed through the first display when a shout of alarm shattered the stillness.

"A physician!" came the panicked cry. The thud of boots echoed like gunfire against the night-dark glass panes. "Help, help! A physician is needed!"

"Ye gods." Hosack started to run, only to skid to a stop as he rounded a turn and came to a fork in the walkway.

"This way!" One of the Royal Society's members grabbed his sleeve and pulled him to the left. The lamplight turned jumpy as they raced down the narrow slate-flagged path, setting off a dance of jagged shadows.

"Help, help!" A gardener burst free of the gloom, his face tight with fear. "A gentleman has collapsed near the South Seas specimens and I . . . I think he ain't breathing—"

Hosack gave the fellow a hard shake. "Take me there— quickly, man, quickly."

Drawing a steadying breath, the gardener nodded and turned around.

Palm fronds slapped at their coats as they shouldered through a cluster of tropical trees. And then the lush vegetation gave way to a display alcove filled with tiny treasures—

A body lay sprawled on the paving stones, half shadowed by the marble pedestals.

Dropping to his knees, Hosack touched a finger to his friend's throat, but one look had already told him that he wouldn't find a pulse.

"Damnation, he's gone," he muttered, feeling a sharp stab of both anger and regret at the unholy bad luck of the Grim Reaper's choosing Becton at this, of all moments. "Why now?" he added in a whisper, just loud enough for his own ears.

A brusque cough. "My condolences, sir," said one of the Royal Society's members. "I heard mention that your friend had a bad heart."

"He did suffer some troubles while in the wilds," acknowledged Hosack. "Though of late, after proper medical care, he was much improved."

"I'll go alert the head watchman and arrange for the body to be moved to a more . . . appropriate place until a mortuary wagon can be summoned," came the reply.

"I'll stay with you, sir—" began the other Royal Society member.

"That's not necessary. I'm no stranger to death." Hosack sat back on his haunches. "I 'd rather you go along with your colleague and inform the rest of the American delegation of the unfortunate incident—discreetly, of course, as I've no desire to ruin the evening for the other guests—and help them organize their carriages for the trip back to Town. I don't imagine Mr. Becton's friends will be in any mood to make merry tonight."

"Very good, sir," they responded, and quietly withdrew, taking the spooked gardener with them.

"Damn, damn, damn." Smacking a fist to his palm, Hosack added a more colorful oath. Becton had hinted that his presentation at the symposium would reveal a momentous discovery—one that might indeed be called a miracle, for all the lives it would save.

And now?

Hosack sighed and shifted his gaze . . .

A puddle of liquid gleamed in the flickering light of the lantern hung on a nearby stanchion. Strangely enough, the surrounding flagstones were dry as dust. He stared for a moment longer before inching forward and leaning down for a closer look.

The whiff of grape-scented alcohol tickled his nostrils. Wetting a finger in the spreading rivulet, he touched it to the tip of his tongue.

Champagne.

Frowning, Hosack looked around for broken bits of glass. *But where is the crystal coupe?*

A conundrum—and one that seemed to defy logic. As a rational man of science, that bothered him. Ignoring the chill seeping through his trousers, he remained on his knees, crawling around to search beneath the display cases.

Perhaps the gardener had picked up the coupe—though it was highly unlikely that the delicate glass could have survived the fall. Or perhaps . . .

His thoughts were interrupted as a harsh, burning sensation suddenly had his mouth on fire.

Stirring a wash of saliva, he puckered and spit. *Holy hell—what the devil is going on?*

Hearing the sound of approaching footsteps, he quickly blotted up the rest of the wine with his handkerchief and stuffed it in his pocket before crawling back to his friend's corpse and studying the half-open lips, now frozen in death.

A bad heart be damned.

Unless he was much mistaken, the tiny telltale flecks of white powder indicated it wasn't the Grim Reaper's blade that had cut his friend's life short.

The mortal blow had come from some earthly hand.

CHAPTER 1

Lady Charlotte Sloane passed through the arched entryway of the grand drawing room and then paused. Wishing to compose her emotions for a moment before joining the crowd, she moved over to one of the massive urns flanking the double doors and pretended to be admiring the artfully arranged flowers. All of them were spectacularly rare blooms chosen, no doubt, to remind the international gathering of botanists that no other repository of specimen plantings could hold a candle to the treasures of the Royal Botanic Gardens at Kew.

Hip-hip-hurrah for the British Empire, Charlotte thought, though a small smile softened any edge of sarcasm. The Gardens were known for sharing their knowledge, as well as seeds and cuttings, with scholars from all over the globe, so while botany wasn't one of her passions, she appreciated the importance of what they did.

Her gaze lingered on the floral arrangement, memorizing the profusion of colors and textures—

"That look in your eye worries me." Her great-aunt Alison, the dowager Countess of Peake, finished making her way through the receiving line and came over to join her grandniece. "I do hope you're not planning on lampooning this gala gathering because they've cut a king's ransom worth of exotic blooms from their hothouses."

Working under the pseudonym A. J. Quill, Charlotte was one of London's most famous—some might say *infamous*—satirical artists. She had earned quite a reputation for exposing the misdeeds and scandals of the high and mighty who moved within the highest circles of Society.

And yet, now I've become one of them.

Her conscience still wrestled with the decision, though she had vowed that it wouldn't dull the point of her pen.

Repressing a sigh, Charlotte murmured, "I do, on occasion, give credit where credit is due. I admire the good work that is done here for science and medicine, and the public appreciates an uplifting story as a change of pace from the revelations of peccadilloes and corruption that are their daily bread and butter."

"Wrexford will be pleased to hear it," answered Alison dryly. "I imagine he would feel a little guilty for inviting the fox into the henhouse, so to speak, if you were to savage his scientific friends and their grand symposium."

The mention of the Earl of Wrexford sent a shiver of awareness down Charlotte's spine. That she was, in fact, the notorious A. J. Quill was a well-guarded secret known only to her closest friends.

Of which Wrexford was one.

Actually, he was far more than a close friend, she reminded herself. He was now her fiancé.

Both of them were still getting used to that fact.

"Are you perchance nervous about being here tonight?" demanded the dowager, after lifting her quizzing glass and subjecting Charlotte to a thorough scrutiny. "You look a little green around the gills."

Charlotte dismissed the suggestion with a low snort. Granted, it was her first appearance at a gala party since the announcement of the impending nuptials, and she could already feel the prickle of surreptitious stares . . .

"I merely dislike being ogled."

"You can't blame them for being curious." Alison's sapphire eyes took on a glint of amusement. "Wrexford has a reputation for possessing a hair-trigger temper and a rapier tongue. They are likely trying to decide how much steel you have in your spine, and whether to place a wager in the famous betting book at White's that you'll cry off before the wedding."

A pause. "The odds are apparently seven to five in favor of his being jilted."

"Ye gods, people should have better things to do with their mathematical skills," muttered Charlotte.

"Raven and Lady Cordelia will no doubt be interested in working out some sort of incomprehensible equation to calculate how to beat the odds and make money on placing a bet," mused the dowager.

Raven, the older of the two street urchin brothers Charlotte had taken under her wing, was showing a remarkable aptitude for mathematics—and it was flourishing under the tutelage of her brilliant friend, Lady Cordelia Mansfield.

"Please don't encourage such an idea, even in jest," she replied. "I would rather not have to pen a satirical drawing on the scandal of an adolescent running a gambling consortium for the gentlemen of the beau monde."

Alison snickered. "I daresay, the little jackanapes would soon be richer than King Midas. He's exceedingly clever—"

"*Too* clever at times." Charlotte repressed a wince. Thanks to Wrexford's sleight of hand—she hadn't inquired too closely on just how he had managed to create a family tree that was merely smoke and lies—she was now the legal guardian of the two boys, whom she loved as if they were her own flesh and blood.

But motherhood, however unconventional, was a constant challenge.

"He is," she added, "reaching an age when I fear we will likely begin butting heads over rules—"

The approach of a portly gentleman, whose curling silver hair was beginning to recede from his craggy brow, caused her to fall silent.

"My dear ladies, though I know we doddering old scholars aren't nearly as alluring as these exotic blossoms, I do hope I can tempt you to come join us by the refreshment table."

"Ha!" Alison exclaimed, waggling her cane. "You can't claim to be doddering until, like me, you're forced to use a stick for support, Sir Robert . . ." She flashed a wink and lowered her voice to add, "So you don't run the risk of falling on your arse."

The baronet, an old friend of the dowager, and a noted expert on orchids, chuckled as he offered Alison his arm. "Allow me to ensure no bodily harm comes to you." Another laugh. "Though I daresay, a gathering of botanists is the least likely place for any violence to occur. We tend to be very gentle souls."

Charlotte held back a smile. *No wonder Wrexford prefers chemistry over the study of plant life.* His temperament tended to be a tad more volatile.

Some unkind individuals might even call it explosive.

"And may I offer my congratulations on your upcoming marriage, Lady Charlotte. Lord Wrexford is much admired by all of us as a brilliant man of science." His lips twitched. "Though I think he considers botany to be a rather boring field. But, of course, he's too polite to say so."

"*Wrexford?* Polite?" Alison let out a snort. "Ha! Over my dead body."

"Dead bodies?" Another scholar, his face already flushed from several glasses of champagne, came over to join them. "My dear Lady Peake, let us not talk of such unpleasant subjects at such a festive occasion." He gestured for a footman to come over and offer his tray of sparkling wine to the ladies and Sir Robert.

"Rather, let us toast to knowledge and discovery," he said, lifting his glass.

"And to the coming nuptials of Lady Charlotte and Lord Wrexford," added the baronet.

"I daresay, one discovers a great deal about human nature when one dons a leg shackle," came a voice from out of nowhere.

For a big man, the Earl of Wrexford moved with surprising stealth.

"Oh, fie, sir." Alison rapped her cane against the earl's shin as he came to stand by Charlotte. "Not everyone is used to your sarcasm, and might misinterpret your words as less than complimentary to your bride-to-be."

"If I've said something disagreeable to Lady Charlotte, I expect she'll let me know herself." Wrexford looked at her through his sin-dark lashes. "With more than a mere *tap-tap*."

The glitter of his green eyes sent a shiver of awareness down her spine. On their first encounter, her initial reaction had been loathing. *And fear.* He could have ruined her life as London's most important satirical artist with one flick of his aristocratic finger. Instead, he had proposed an unconventional partnership in order to solve a dastardly murder—one in which he was the prime suspect. To their surprise, a grudging friendship had developed.

Strange how she now couldn't imagine her life without all the subtle textures and colors his presence wove into the very fiber of her being.

"An exchange of frank opinions between husband and wife

seems an excellent way to ensure matrimonial harmony, Wrexford," replied Charlotte. "Even if those opinions don't align."

"Just so, my dear." He shifted his stance, the soft wool of his coat now touching her bare shoulder. The drafty room suddenly felt a little warmer.

"Matrimony!" The flush-faced scholar waggled his bushy brows. "As a noted chemist, you have a great deal of experience in working with dangerous substances, so I imagine you will be able to prevent *that* experiment from blowing up in your face, ha, ha, ha."

"Indeed, I'm quite confident that I know what I'm doing," said Wrexford in a silky tone that immediately sobered the scholar's expression.

"Of course, of course! I did not mean to question your . . . er, judgment, sir . . ." Hemming and hawing, the scholar backed away to join the crowd around the punch bowl.

Charlotte didn't blame him. Wrexford didn't suffer fools gladly.

"Mr. Throckmorton has clearly imbibed too much of the Royal Society's fine champagne." A distinguished-looking gentleman dressed in an azure-blue swallow-tailed coat grimaced in apology as he came over to join them. "Allow me to express my felicitations in a more traditional manner, milord. And might I request an introduction to your fiancée?"

The ritual of polite pleasantries began, and was quickly expanded as several other gentlemen scholars and their wives drifted over to express their good wishes.

Wrexford, noted Charlotte, was behaving with admirable restraint. Such trivial socializing bored him to perdition, and he usually ended his part in it by saying something egregiously rude.

However, the talk quickly shifted to safer ground as one of the scholars brought up a recent lecture given at the Royal Society on minerals—a subject that greatly interested the earl. "Now, it seems that Sir Humphry Davy tested the hypothesis by performing a chemical analysis . . ."

Charlotte allowed her attention to wander as Wrexford shifted away to join the gentlemen discussing the technical details. The drawing room was growing more crowded as the guests made their way into the palace from the conservatory. The lilt of foreign languages—French, German, Spanish, Italian—twined with all the different accents of English, creating a lively buzz. The swirl of the Continental fashions, with the colorful sashes and fancy medals highlighting the various styles of cravats and waistcoats, couldn't help but catch her eye.

Already she was composing a drawing in her head—

"Charlotta?"

She spun around, her eyes widening in surprise. "Marco!"

"Why, it *is* you!" A tall, slender gentleman, with curling black hair and the fine-boned features of a Renaissance sculpture, flashed a winsome smile. "And looking lovelier than ever." His gaze quickly took in her elegant gown and the lustrous pearl necklace—an engagement gift from Wrexford—nestled at her throat. "How is Anthony? I'm sure his career is flourishing here in London. He's an immensely talented—"

"Anthony passed away several years ago," she interrupted. "As you might remember, his constitution was delicate, and the return to a cold, damp climate proved injurious to his health."

"I'm so sorry." Sympathy pooled in his hazel eyes. "Please accept my condolences."

"Thank you—but let us speak of happier things," said Charlotte. "I see your star has continued to rise in the firmament of Italian science."

She and her late husband had met Marco Moretti while living in Rome. The Florentine scholar, who, like all their acquaintances, was dancing on the razor's edge of poverty, had been finishing his advanced scientific studies at the university. But his interest in art and literature, as well as politics, had led him to join their bohemian circle of painters and poets . . .

All of us barely scraping by, surviving on lofty dreams, maca-roni, and cheap wine, reflected Charlotte.

Moretti gave a self-deprecating shrug. "I've been lucky enough to write several papers, which have attracted a bit of attention, and I'm quite excited to have been invited here to present a lecture. It may even lead to an opportunity for advancement and recognition in my field of study—as well as a secure financial future." Another shrug. "As you know, teaching pays but pittance."

"That sounds very promising," she said.

"I hope it will be so," replied Moretti, his voice holding a hint of longing. "There is a new scientific society about to be formed, one dedicated to discovery. Its patron is a worldly, wealthy man of science who is very generous in funding research, and he's expressed some interest in my work."

A flicker of curiosity lit beneath his lashes. "And what brings you here, Charlotta? You were very skilled in botanical drawing. I still have several sketches you made of wildflowers growing around the ruins of the Coliseum. Are you helping with making a visual catalogue of collections here at the Royal Botanic Gardens?"

"No, I've not kept up my drawing of plant life," she answered. "I'm here because my fiancé is a noted man of science here in Britain, and is a member of the Royal Society."

"Ah." Moretti smiled politely. "Felicitations on your upcoming remarriage. Your fiancé sounds like a very admirable and interesting fellow."

"He is." Charlotte looked around and spotted Wrexford some paces away. "Come, allow me to introduce you."

She started to squeeze through the press of guests, but just as she managed to circle around a trio of chattering Germans and approach him, a gentleman slipped free from the crowd and touched the earl's arm.

"Lord Wrexford." It was said in a discreet murmur, but Charlotte heard the note of tension in the speaker's voice.

The earl did as well, for she saw him stiffen as he looked around. She recognized the man as Lord Bethany, the secretary of the Royal Society, and one of the organizers of the symposium.

"Forgive the interruption, sir." The look of alarm in his eyes belied his smile as he drew Wrexford aside. "But might I ask you to come with me to the conservatory? There's been an . . . unfortunate mishap."

Mist swirled through the evening gloom as they hurried down the walkway, the vapor giving a ghostly sheen to the angled silhouettes of glowing glass and brass.

"Why fetch me?" demanded Wrexford, once Bethany had finished his account of the gardener's discovery of Mr. Becton's corpse among the exotic specimens.

"I confess, I'm not entirely sure, sir. But Dr. Hosack was insistent that I bring you to him, and as he is head of the American delegation, I felt it my duty to accede to his wishes, given the circumstances." The secretary grimaced. "Political relations are strained enough between our two countries without any bad feelings arising over any imagined snub by us in dealing with this incident."

The sharp crunch of their steps on the gravel seemed amplified by the peaceful quiet of the surrounding gardens.

"But I only know Hosack by reputation," mused the earl.

"Apparently, he knows of *your* reputation, too, milord."

Keeping his temper in check, Wrexford held back a sarcastic retort, even though the allusion to his previous murder investigations made no sense. From what Bethany had told him, the man who had dropped dead had a history of ill health, and there was no reason to suspect foul play.

They walked the rest of the way in silence, Bethany quickening his pace, clearly anxious to complete his good deed for Hosack.

The American doctor was waiting in the main foyer of the conservatory, the lantern clasped in his hand illuminating the grim set of his face. Several other men were standing together in the far corner, conversing in muted tones. At the earl's entrance, they looked up and stopped talking.

"Thank you for coming, Lord Wrexford." Hosack gave a gruff nod of greeting.

"Might I ask that you conduct your meeting with the earl as quickly as possible so that the mortuary men may be permitted to remove Mr. Becton's mortal remains to a more appropriate resting place?" Despite the chill air, Bethany's brow was beaded with sweat. He took a moment to blot them away with his handkerchief.

"As I hope you can appreciate, sir, the Royal Society would prefer that the untimely demise of your colleague doesn't overshadow the mission of the symposium," he continued. "We have brought together all these international scholars—no easy feat in these uncertain times of war and strife—in order for them to share their knowledge and discoveries with each other for the good of all mankind."

"I couldn't agree more with your goals, milord, and I applaud the Society's impressive work to make the world a better place for all," replied Hosack. "I simply wish to solicit Lord Wrexford's opinion on something before my friend's remains are disturbed."

"I still question why—" began the earl, but a quick mute appeal from Hosack caused him to leave off with a shrug. "However, I'm happy to comply with the doctor's request."

"Then, of course, I have no objection," conceded Bethany, though his expression remained troubled.

"I'm very grateful to you, Lord Wrexford." Hosack gestured toward the corridor leading to the rear section of the building. "Please come with me, sir."

The lush greenery and flowering specimens soon enveloped them in a heady perfume of sweet and spicy scents. Moonlight scudded over the skylights, adding a pearly glow to the bright flicker of the hanging lanterns that dotted the walkway. Leaves whispered softly as they brushed past the delicate fronds of a *Ravenea rivularis.*

Hosack led the way through one of the display rooms before slowing and coming to a halt behind an arrangement of potted *Theobroma cacao* trees. "I know how irregular my request must have appeared to you."

"It did, indeed," agreed Wrexford. "Seeing as I don't know you from Adam."

"But I have heard a great deal about you, sir . . ." For just an instant, a glimmer of amusement softened the look of distress in the American's eyes. "From Gideon Tyler, a friend from my time spent studying in Scotland."

Tyler was a man of many talents, two of which were serving as both the earl's valet and his laboratory assistant.

Alas. An oath hovered on the tip of Wrexford's tongue. Another was a penchant for grossly exaggerating the ghoulish exploits of their previous murder investigations.

"Tyler's tales ought to be taken with a grain of salt," he responded, now having an inkling of why his presence had been requested. "I imagine the sudden death of your colleague has come as a shock, sir. But most such incidents, however unfortunate, have nothing to do with foul play."

"Under most circumstances, I couldn't agree more, milord. I'm a physician, and thus am no stranger to death," answered Hosack. "I simply hope you'll bear with me and agree to have a look at the scene. Tyler speaks of you as a man who sees things with a sharp-eyed clarity, unclouded by emotion. So I would greatly value your objective observations."

A reluctant sigh stirred the air. "I've come this far. I might as well have a look."

They resumed walking. Wrexford liked that the doctor didn't

feel compelled to fill the silence with meaningless chatter. Hosack moved purposefully, his footsteps tapping a brisk tattoo on the stone flagging as he led the way through several more turns.

Up ahead, through a low archway, Wrexford saw that extra lanterns had been positioned near one of the display pedestals.

"This way, milord," murmured the American, cutting around a potted arrangement of brightly blooming *Bougainvillea glabra.* The cheery fuchsia hue, noted Wrexford, seemed oddly out of place with the somber tableau behind the plants.

A body—Mr. Becton, he presumed—lay sprawled on the stone tiles, the black of the scholar's evening clothes melding with the crisscrossing shadows cast by the surrounding displays.

Hosack stopped and touched the earl's sleeve. "Before you go any closer, sir, please take a moment to look carefully at the scene."

Wrexford replied with a brusque nod and then focused his attention on the small swath of space.

One of the pedestals looked askew, and a few small terracotta specimen pots had fallen, scattering crumbs of earth and burnt-orange shards across the slate . . . all confirming the scenario of a man seized with a sudden spasm and toppling over to the floor.

What am I missing?

Puzzled, Wrexford edged around for a different perspective. Hosack struck him as a steady, sensible fellow, unlikely to see specters where there were none. Still, nothing unusual caught his eye. Narrowing his gaze, he probed the nooks and crannies near the corpse before lifting his shoulders in a silent signal that he was ready to move on.

The doctor didn't ask any questions, but merely gestured for the earl to join him in crouching down beside the body. Becton was lying on his belly, with his face twisted to one side, one sightless eye staring up at the flickering lantern flame overhead. It was, noted Wrexford, a shade of blue that reminded him of a smoke-tinged sky.

Charlotte would know the exact name for it.

Flattening his palms on the tiles, Hosack angled his head and dropped his cheek to within inches of the dead man's visage. A moment slid by, then another. Wool rustled as he shifted back and made room for the earl.

"And now, I have one last request, milord," said the doctor, rising and adjusting the beam of the lantern. "Please take a close look at Mr. Becton's mouth."

Wrexford leaned low—low enough to feel the coolness of the flagging rise up to prickle against his chin. At first, he saw nothing other than the usual signs of death—a slightly protruding tongue, the lips surrendering their color to a waxy pallor . . .

Then he spotted the white crystalline grains dotting the corners of the corpse's half-open mouth.

"Any idea what that substance might be?" he asked.

"I was hoping you might tell me," came the dry reply.

"It could be any number of things, depending on what medicines your friend was taking—"

"That's just it. He wasn't taking any medicine. His symptoms had greatly improved, and we had both agreed several months ago that he could stop taking the distillation I had created for him." A pause. "And there was nothing in it that would have formed such crystals."

"It's odd, I grant you," said the earl. "In the course of his storytelling, I'm assuming Tyler mentioned to you that I've a friend who's very skilled at coaxing secrets from the dead."

"He did, milord."

"And so I take it, you wish to have the mortuary wagon take Mr. Becton to my friend's surgery, rather than the local morgue."

"I would be exceedingly grateful," answered Hosack.

"Very well." Wrexford rose and dusted his palms on the front of his coat. "Though I counsel you not to let your imagination run away with you. There are any number of innocent explanations for the grains. Perhaps he ate a pastry beforehand, and they are merely bits of sugar."

"I realize that," answered the doctor. "But I suspect that he drank rather than ate something. There was a puddle of liquid on the stones when I found him. It looked to be champagne."

"That's hardly surprising," replied the earl. "In fact—"

"Yes, but if he was drinking champagne when he died, what happened to the glass?"

The question gave the earl pause for thought. "Actually, I can come up with several very logical answers to that." He took another look around the alcove and saw nothing further to explain the American's suspicion of foul play. "I confess, I'm puzzled by why you're so ready to assume that your friend's death wasn't from natural causes."

Hosack drew in a troubled breath. The wagging leaves overhead deepened the lines of worry etched around his mouth.

"That's because I haven't yet told you about the revelation Becton was planning to make at this symposium."

CHAPTER 2

Charlotte found herself glancing yet again at the entrance to the drawing room, and wondering why Lord Bethany had sought out Wrexford's assistance.

The reason couldn't be a pleasant one. Bethany looked as if he had just seen a ghost.

"... And what is your opinion of the artist's latest exhibit, Lady Charlotte?" asked one of the scholars' wives.

Drawn back to the moment, Charlotte quickly improvised a reply—never mind that she hadn't a clue as to which artist was being discussed. Certain platitudes were never questioned. "Quite interesting," she murmured. "His technique shows some new developments, but I'm not quite sure I like his use of color."

The others all nodded sagely.

Alison, who had brought Sir Robert over to join the circle, gave her a quizzical look and waggled her brow in warning to pay attention. After all, the whole point of the evening was to begin playing the role of a countess, one that required poise and politeness, no matter how excruciatingly superficial the situation . . .

The thought made her innards clench.

"It seems we are all being asked to move on to the dining salon." Sir Robert offered his arm to the dowager.

"I'll follow along shortly," said Charlotte, making an abrupt decision. She touched a gloved finger to her topknot and made an apologetic grimace. "I fear I have a hairpin coming loose, and wish to visit the ladies' retiring room to have it fixed."

Polite murmurs sounded from her companions as she turned in a rustle of silk and exited into the center corridor. But rather than turn right and head to the rooms housing the amenities for the guests, Charlotte hurried in the opposite direction. She was familiar with Kew Palace and the grounds of the Royal Botanic Gardens from several earlier visits. Just ahead, a side portico led out a walkway that wound down to the west side of the conservatory.

Ignoring a startled footman, she let herself out into the night. The air was chilly, but it was the sense of foreboding that raised a pebbling of gooseflesh on her bare arms.

Has Hawk somehow strayed into trouble?

Raven's younger brother had become fascinated by the natural world. *Rocks, plants, insects . . .* An involuntary smile touched her lips. Mice and snakes were also part of the little menagerie he had created in their back garden, much to the disgust of his sibling. Wrexford had encouraged the boy's scientific interest. As had the earl's valet.

Indeed, it had been Tyler's idea to invite Hawk to accompany him here to the gardens earlier in the day. The valet had offered to help the symposium committee arrange some of the special exhibits within one of the smaller buildings surrounding the main conservatory, and had suggested that Hawk, a budding botanical artist, might enjoy the opportunity to sketch some of the specimen plantings in the outer hothouses.

Given the importance of the event, she had expressed reservations about the idea. But Tyler had convinced her that Hawk's presence would create no controversy.

But boys being boys . . .

Quickening her steps, Charlotte took a shortcut across the grass, ignoring the damage the moisture and mud were doing to her elegant shoes and gown. *Silks and satins be damned.* In truth, she was far more at home in the breeches and boots of a street urchin, prowling the city for the hidden secrets that helped her expose the wrongdoings of the rich and powerful.

A wolf in sheep's clothing, she thought. *A soon-to-be very wealthy faux sheep.*

The west door of the conservatory was unlocked, allowing entrance into the section housing conifer specimens from the northeastern states of America. The pleasant fragrances of pine and balsam, however, did little to settle her unease. Spotting a trail of lantern lights through the needled branches, she hurried down the path to her right.

After passing through several deserted galleries, she heard voices from up ahead.

Wrexford's was one of them.

Charlotte hesitated for a moment, then decided to plunge on. She might as well kill two birds with one stone and learn what bumblebroth was now bubbling around her eccentric family.

Wrexford looked around at the feathery sound of her slippers moving over the dark stone. She didn't recognize his companion.

"Has Hawk gotten into some mischief—" she began, only to stop short on spotting the corpse sprawled on the tiles.

Her throat tightened. "Dear God." She was no stranger to dead bodies. There was no need to inquire whether the poor fellow was still alive. "What happened?"

"We are still debating the exact cause of death, my dear," replied Wrexford. "One of Dr. Hosack's American colleagues was discovered a short while ago as you see him. Hosack is convinced it's murder. I'm less certain, so we've just agreed that Henning should have a look at the deceased and see if he can give us a definitive answer."

Turning back to the doctor, he added, "Allow me to present my fiancée, Lady Charlotte Sloane."

"My deepest apologies, milady. I'm so sorry that you had to experience such a ghastly sight." Hosack flushed, looking terribly uncomfortable. "Along with the horrifying mention of murder."

Charlotte calmly met his gaze. "No apologies are necessary, sir. My sensibilities are not easily shocked." A pause. "Wrexford will assure you of that."

She surveyed the surrounding area, noting there was no sign of a struggle. Nor was there any obvious sign of injury. But much as she wished to get a closer look at the body, Hosack was a total stranger . . . and she was here tonight as a prim and proper soon-to-be countess. The poor man would likely swoon if she got down on her hands and knees in all her finery.

Clenching her teeth, Charlotte felt a pang of regret at the loss of her anonymity. As a mere nobody among the countless nobodies living in London, she had possessed a great deal of unfettered freedom.

Her new life was promising to be far more complicated.

"Dr. Hosack, please forgive me," she murmured, turning her attention from death to a more pragmatic matter. "But will you excuse me for drawing His Lordship aside for a few moments? I need to have a private word with him in the adjoining gallery."

"Y-Yes, yes, of course, milady," stuttered the American. "I–I apologize again for—"

"Actually, Hosack, I believe we're finished with our examination, so why don't you return to Lord Bethany and tell him he may allow the mortuary men to proceed," suggested Wrexford. "I'll remain here to make sure they understand that the body is to be taken to Henning's surgery." The muffled chink of coins sounded as he patted his pockets to find his purse.

"That makes perfect sense, milord." The doctor looked greatly relieved. "I'm—I'm very grateful to you."

"It's the least I can do for you and your friend," replied Wrexford. His smile at Hosack belied the look in his eyes as his gaze swung back to her.

Damnation. Preoccupied with her own worries about the evening's festivities, she had neglected to tell him about Tyler's invitation to Hawk. It hadn't seemed important . . .

Wrexford waited until they were alone before uttering a low oath. "What did you mean about Hawk? Granted, mischief goes hand in hand with the Weasels—"

"Weasels" was the moniker he had bestowed on the boys during their first encounter, when Raven had stabbed the earl in the leg. That little misunderstanding had long since been forgiven. However, the name had stuck, much to the amusement of the boys.

"No, no, they are innocent of any troublemaking." At least, she fervently hoped that was true. "Tyler invited Hawk to come sketch in the outer gardens while he assisted the organizing committee. I'm sure the two of them have returned to Mayfair by now, but the fact that you were summoned by a very serious-looking Lord Bethany had me alarmed."

"I think we can rule out the lad as a murder suspect." The earl's expression relaxed somewhat. "Though McClellan would claim that he and his brother slay every rule of cleanliness."

"Muck also goes hand in hand with the Weasels," said Charlotte, greatly relieved that Hawk was not involved in the evening's troubling incident. But as for Mr. Becton's death . . .

"Did Dr. Hosack give any reason for why he thinks foul play is involved?" She glanced again at the supposed victim and the shattered specimens scattered on the floor.

"He suspects poison."

"Hmmm." She crouched down beside the corpse and took a close look at the man's face. "The white crystals at the corners of his mouth?"

"Yes." The earl waited while she inched back to examine the lifeless fingers, then offered his hand and helped her rise.

"It could be something innocent," mused Charlotte.

"That was my thought as well."

A pensive frown pulled at her lips. "At first blush, the circumstances seem to indicate a death from natural causes."

He then moved around the body, studying the details again before replying. "So they do."

The thumps and clatter of the approaching mortuary men forestalled any further discussion. "I think it prudent that you stay out of sight." Knowing Charlotte was familiar with the conservatory, he added, "I suggest you wait in the study room, where the collection of botanical art is kept. It's close by and the door affords a measure of privacy. I'll come fetch you when I'm done here."

Charlotte nodded and quietly melted away into the shadows.

Lud, what a coil. There was, she conceded, a certain irony to having a murder mar her first appearance in Polite Society since her engagement. Their good friend Basil Henning often accused her and the earl of deliberately tripping over dead bodies.

An unfair observation, though it did seem to happen with frightening frequency—

"Psst! M'lady!"

An agitated whisper from within a thick screen of foliage yanked her from her musings.

Spinning around, she quickly crouched down and parted the dark leaves, revealing her ward's dirt-streaked face. "Good heavens, Hawk! What are you doing there?"

"I . . . I—"

"No, no—never mind an explanation now," she interrupted. "Just come along with me—quickly and quietly."

The boy obeyed in a flash, clutching his sketchbook and a fistful of colored sticks of chalk to his chest.

"This way," she murmured, placing a hand on his shoulder and guiding him toward the conservatory's study rooms. To her relief, the lanterns along the walkway to that section of the building were unlit.

The door to the art room was locked, but Charlotte plucked a hairpin from her topknot. After a few deft twists of the metal, it opened with a soft *snick*. Drawing it shut behind them, she led Hawk over to a study table set by an exterior window looking out onto the herb gardens. The night sky was cloudless, the twinkling of the stars amplifying the whisper of silvery moonlight coming in through the glass panes.

The pale glow caught the look of apprehension on the boy's face. "I-I'm sorry. I know Mr. Tyler told me to stay in the section containing the bromeliads, so I wouldn't disturb any of the scholars. But he's been gone for an age, and there wasn't anyone among the ficus trees . . ."

His lower lip began to quiver. "I didn't think it would do any harm. I was quiet, and w-wery careful."

Hawk's pronunciation always turned a little shaky when he was nervous. Feeling her heart clench, Charlotte gently smoothed a tangle of hair back from his brow. "You did nothing wrong, sweeting. However, there's been an unfortunate incident in another part of the conservatory, and it's best that we stay out of sight while the proper authorities deal with the matter."

Hawk squirmed in his chair. "W-What sort of incident?"

Alas, both boys were far more familiar with murder investigations than she would have liked. Still, she saw no reason to mention the dead body.

"Wrexford will come fetch us when things have calmed down," she replied. He had let his sketchbook slip onto the table, but it appeared that his hands remained tightly fisted, though they were now resting in his lap. Seeking to reassure him that he had done nothing deserving a scold, she asked, "Did you discover some new and interesting plants to draw?"

"There will be an extra few guineas for you and your men if the body arrives at Henning's surgery before dawn," murmured Wrexford as he passed over a handful of coins.

"Oiy, milord." The driver gave a tug on his greasy forelock

as his two helpers loaded Becton's canvas-wrapped corpse into the back of the mortuary wagon. "Never fear, we won't hesitate te rattle a few bones te get there quicklike, heh, heh, heh."

"Then crack your whip and get your wheels rolling," replied the earl. The Royal Botanic Gardens were in Kew, a long drive from the heart of London. Given the less-than-official order he had just issued, it was best that the trip be completed under the cover of darkness.

He watched the wagon jolt off into the gloom, then turned to Hosack. "I think you should join the gala dinner, sir. One of the footmen informed me that Tyler is still somewhere on the grounds, so I'll have him wait here and bring you to my friend Henning's surgery, once the evening's festivities have come to an end."

"I'm profoundly grateful, Lord Wrexford."

"Well, there is an old English adage—*Be careful what you wish for*," responded Wrexford.

"Yes, I know . . . I know. It would have been expedient to ignore my suspicions. But it would have been wrong." Releasing a sigh that trailed off in a ghostly vapor, Hosack stared into the shadows. "Not to speak of being cowardly. Becton could be oddly reclusive. And secretive. But he was a dear friend. I couldn't in good conscience turn a blind eye on the evidence."

"I pray you're mistaken," muttered the earl.

"So do I, sir." Another sigh. "So do I."

A breeze rustled through the nearby trees. The leaves, already turning brittle from the first hints of autumn, gave off a mournful crackling.

Hosack blew out his cheeks and inclined a small bow before turning to the path leading up to the palace.

Wrexford remained where he was, feeling a chill slither down his spine which had nothing to do with the nighttime drop in temperature. Though this death did not involve him or those he held dear, he knew all too well how murder—if this, in fact, proved to be one—had a way of reaching out and entrapping innocent victims within its tentacles.

Damn the devil and his legion of demons.

He would have to stay sharp and be ready to cut off any threat that tried to come close.

Somewhere in the grove of trees, a branch cracked. Pushing aside his mordant thoughts, the earl turned around and set off to reenter the conservatory.

The main entrance foyer was deserted, and the agitated current of shock had settled back into the usual aura of quiet tranquility. In no mood to appreciate the lush sweetness of the air, Wrexford batted aside a leafy vine and started down one of the side paths, intent on taking a shortcut to where Charlotte was waiting. The way looped through a tall cluster of holly specimens, and as he emerged from the jagged shadows, he saw he wasn't alone.

Someone was sitting on his haunches and peering into a tangle of sword-shaped leaves.

A frustrated mutter floated above the ruffling greenery. "Where the devil are you?"

"Ye gods," muttered Wrexford. "I pray you're not looking for a lost Weasel."

Tyler looked up with a start. "He's not lost. He's simply . . . not where he was told to be."

"Which was where?"

"The adjoining gallery," answered his valet. "I've checked there, and then decided to widen my search."

The earl told himself there was no reason for alarm. It was late, and Hawk had likely been here for hours. He had probably fallen asleep somewhere in all this cursed greenery.

"How long did you leave him alone?"

Tyler gave a guilty grimace. "The head of the committee asked for my urgent help in setting up a scientific display in the pagoda for tomorrow's reception. Some of the instruments had been damaged in transit, and it took longer than I expected to repair them."

Wrexford swore under his breath.

"Hawk had his sketchbook and a sack filled with refreshments prepared by McClellan, including his favorite ginger biscuits." A defensive note crept into the valet's voice. "He assured me that he was quite happy to sit and draw until I returned."

"Weasel!" called Wrexford.

The only answer was the muffled echo reverberating off the glass.

"We can split up and make a methodical search of this wing—" began Tyler.

"No, first we need to fetch Charlotte. She's waiting in one of the study rooms."

Tyler quickened his pace to keep up with the earl. "I thought the two of you were attending the gala banquet."

"As did I. However, your friend Dr. Hosack had other plans for me."

The valet now looked thoroughly confused. "You're not making any sense. Is something amiss?"

"Other than the fact that you left the boy alone in here with a cunning killer on the prowl?"

"*What!*" The color leached from Tyler's face. "I'm well aware of your peculiar sense of humor, milord. But that's an unkind jest. As if I would ever knowingly place either of the Weasels in danger—"

"It's no jest," interrupted Wrexford. "One of Hosack's colleagues was found dead a short while ago, and the doctor is convinced it was murder." He ducked beneath a canopy of palm fronds. "However, you're right—it was an unfair cut. I apologize."

"To the devil with anything other than finding Hawk. You go on—I'll keep looking."

The earl grabbed Tyler's sleeve. "It's best not to run off helter-pelter. We're almost there, and among the three of us, we can map out a methodical search."

A grunt conceded the logic of his words. But a sidelong glance showed that Tyler's clenched jaw was rigid with fear and remorse.

Damnation. The evening was meant to have been a celebratory occasion—the first public appearance for him and Charlotte as an engaged couple. That it had taken such a pernicious twist seemed . . .

"Wrexford!" Charlotte shot up out of her chair as he and Tyler entered the study room.

"Thank God you're safe!" exclaimed the valet on spotting Hawk. He drew a shaky breath. "Though I should birch your bottom for disobeying my order to stay in the display of bromeliads."

"There's no need to ring such a peal over his head. No harm was done," said Charlotte. "He simply wanted to try his hand at drawing a different specimen."

"Oiy." The boy hung his head. "I only moved to the adjoining display room, and I was wery, wery careful not to allow myself to be seen by any of the guests."

"None of the scholars were supposed to stray from the main galleries. And as it was getting dark, and the committee needed my help, it seemed there was no reason why he couldn't wait here in the conservatory," explained Tyler to Wrexford.

"But one of them *did* stray into the side galleries," chirped Hawk. "However, I wiggled deeper into the grouping of potted plants when I heard him coming, and kept wery still—even when the glass he hurled into the specimens hit me in the head."

The boy made a face. "It's *him* who should have his bottom birched. He damaged a valuable *Asplenium ruprechtii* from the wilds of the Orient."

Wrexford felt his muscles tighten. A quick glance showed Charlotte had fisted her hands in her skirts.

"A gentleman threw a glass into the plantings, sweeting?" she asked.

"Oiy."

"Can you show me exactly where this was?" the earl demanded.

"I ain't—I'm not—telling a faradiddle, sir," answered Hawk, a note of hurt shading his tone.

"I'm not suggesting you are, lad."

"Poison," said Tyler, quickly making the connection. "You suspect the killer used poison?"

The boy straightened from his slouch, his eyes instantly coming alert. "Are we investigating another murder?"

"*We,*" replied Wrexford, "are doing no such thing."

Charlotte shifted, throwing her face into shadow.

"I'm merely collecting any pertinent objects that may help us ascertain why one of the guests collapsed," he finished.

"What does *pertinent* mean?" asked Hawk.

For a moment, the question hovered in the air, a tiny ripple of ice in the velvety warmth.

Wrexford bit back an oath. He had no doubt that the little imp of Satan knew *exactly* what he had meant, despite his attempt to hide it within a fancy sentence.

"It means *relevant*," explained Charlotte. "Something that may relate to the subject in question."

"In other words—" began Hawk.

"In other words, take me to the glass, Weasel," snapped Wrexford. "*Now.*"

The boy slipped down from his stool—a little *too* enthusiastically, he observed. Like moths drawn inexorably toward a flame, both Hawk and Raven had no fear of flying straight into the maw of danger. He would have to have a talk with them about tempering their devil-may-care actions.

Especially as they would soon be an official family, not merely individuals linked together by love.

Love. A word that had never come easily to his tongue.

Funny how it no longer stuck in his craw . . .

The brush of Charlotte's shoulder drew him back from his musings. He fell into step behind her, and it took only a few minutes for their little band to weave its way to the spot in question. Hawk disappeared into the dark foliage and quickly emerged triumphantly with the cut crystal champagne coupe.

Such a deceptively delicate object to serve as a messenger of Death, mused Wrexford as he took it and held it up to the moonlight.

From the look on her face, Charlotte's thoughts seemed to be marching to the same drumbeat as his own. She stared at the glass, but said nothing.

After wrapping it carefully in his handkerchief, he tucked the evidence into his coat pocket. "Did you perchance get a glimpse of the gentleman who tossed the coupe?"

Hawk hesitated.

"Just remember, sweeting, it does more harm than good to allow wishful thinking to color your answer," counseled Charlotte. "I know you're very observant. But it was dark and you were intent on remaining hidden. If you saw nothing, you must say so."

The boy squeezed his eyes shut.

Wrexford clasped his hand behind his back, willing himself to remain patient.

"I peeked up as I heard the steps coming closer, but only for an instant," said Hawk. "He was moving quickly, so I didn't see his face, though I could tell he was tall—nearly as tall as you, sir."

"Excellent," murmured Charlotte. "But more important, you did very well to keep yourself hidden."

The earl nodded, but after allowing a sliver of silence, he couldn't help adding, "Nothing else?"

"Wrexford . . ." Charlotte shot him a reproachful look.

Hawk's face scrunched in thought. "Sorry, sir," he said after several long moments had slid by. "I—wait! I *do* remember one other thing! As I ducked down, I heard his shoe catch on the edge of a tile. He muttered a word under his breath—it might have been an oath, as he sounded wery angry."

"Did you catch what he said?" asked Tyler.

"I'm not sure," admitted Hawk. "It started with a T . . . it sounded like . . . t-toll . . . toll-patch."

Wrexford looked at Tyler, who lifted his shoulders in a shrug.

"Does it help?" asked Hawk.

"Hard to say, lad," replied Wrexford. "Until we know for sure whether a crime has been committed, we ought not create specters out of a mere puff of vapor."

"*Where there's smoke, there's usually fire,*" murmured Tyler.

"Be that as it may, I intend to ensure that all of us stay well out of reach of any flames." He turned abruptly, causing the wrapped glass to hit up against his hip. "Come, there's much to be done before this cursed night is over."

CHAPTER 3

"Hold yer water, laddie," muttered Basil Henning as he turned from the stone slab in response to Wrexford's query about what the examination of the body had revealed. "My guest here only arrived a quarter hour ago. I've hardly had time to cut off his clothing, much less open his chest for a look at his heart, as per your request."

Charlotte followed the earl into the surgery. They had made good time getting here, despite the stop to leave Hawk in the capable hands of McClellan, her housekeeper. She flinched as the surgeon sloshed his scalpel in a pan of water and turned back to Becton's corpse. Though she had a strong stomach and had seen all manner of gruesome murders, there was something particularly unsettling about a mortuary slab, and the indignity of an individual being reduced to naught but a piece of meat.

"Before you get to his heart—and I do think it worth having a look, to ascertain whether it was damaged enough to be a threat to his life—did the driver pass on the other part of my message, which was to have a look at the corners of his mouth?"

"I may be getting old," groused Henning, "but I'm not yet

deaf." There came another clatter of metal as the surgeon switched from a scalpel to an odd-shaped instrument that Charlotte didn't recognize.

"Or blind," he added. "Of course I noticed the white granules. My guess is, it will prove to be a potent distillation of foxglove. Most apothecaries offer it, as it's often prescribed for a weak heart."

"Could a large enough dose be fatal?" asked Wrexford.

Henning let out a rusty chuckle. "I daresay, a good many well-off country widows could answer that for you. From the gossip I hear among my colleagues, it's more common than you might think for an elderly husband to be hastened to his grave by a wife with some knowledge in the plants that grow in a typical English garden. Especially if the fellow is a crotchety old devil."

"I stand forewarned," murmured the earl.

"Have no fear, Wrexford," said Charlotte. She had backed up a few steps, finding the sharp scents of the dissecting room were making her stomach churn. "Gardening is far too ladylike a hobby for me."

He smiled. "If you wish to put a period to my existence, I imagine you'll simply pick up your penknife and cut out my liver."

"Actually, I'd counsel using a longer blade, Lady Charlotte," called Henning. "It would be a lot less messy." He paused to roll up his sleeves. "Bloodstains are hell to remove from your cuffs."

Charlotte didn't dare try to identify the noxious streaks he had left on the none-too-pristine linen.

"Might we leave off discussing *my* demise and return to that of the unfortunate Mr. Becton?" suggested Wrexford. He took the champagne glass from his pocket and set it on the crude table beside the surgeon. "This was found in the conservatory.

I've reason to believe it contained whatever substance Becton drank just before his death."

After inspecting the inside with his magnifying lens, Henning blew out his breath. "There are definitely the dregs of a foreign substance. I'll perform a few chemical tests, but as I said before, I think we'll find Mr. Becton was dosed with foxglove."

"Hmmm." The earl pursed his lips. "Given the company he was in, I'm surprised it wasn't some more exotic poison."

"Sometimes the simplest answer is the correct one, laddie."

Rarely with me, reflected Charlotte. Complexities seemed woven into the very fabric of her being. And the threads promised to begin stitching ever more intricate patterns as she made yet another elemental change in her life.

"Are you feeling unwell, my dear?" Wrexford fixed her with a searching look. "You're looking a little pale."

"I'm just a bit fatigued," she replied.

The lamplight shivered as a draft rattled the glass globe, setting off a scudding of shadows. Still, his gaze held hers.

"And I confess," she added softly, "the idea of a murder investigation at this particular moment in our lives is a little daunting."

The wedding was less than a month away . . . Her innards gave another clench. And a meeting with her long-estranged older brother was looming, one that was fraught with questions of whether a family reconciliation could ever be achieved.

"There's no reason for us to be drawn into a murder investigation," said Wrexford. "Becton's death has nothing to do with us."

And yet murder had an insidious way of twining its way into their lives.

"Perhaps not us personally," she responded. "But given the venue and the occasion, A. J. Quill can hardly ignore the crime and its ramifications."

Wrexford's expression altered, but in the uncertain light, she couldn't read it.

"And please don't suggest that I can choose to conveniently turn away from it." Charlotte couldn't keep a brittleness out of her voice. "A tiny side step here, a small turn there, and before you know it, one's moral compass has lost all sense of direction."

"True north is etched indelibly on your heart," he replied softly. "You'll never lose your way between Right and Wrong. And I think you know by now that I would never, ever ask you to compromise your principles."

She closed her eyes for an instant. "Oh, fie, Wrexford—it's not *you* I'm questioning. It's myself. There are so many complications to consider, and I can't help but worry—"

The clatter of a carriage pulling to a halt in the narrow street beyond the yard's outer walls interrupted the exchange.

"Uncertainties are always part of life. We shall deal with them as they arise." Wrexford caught her hand and gave it a squeeze as Tyler's voice rose above the squelch of steps in the mud.

The warmth radiating from his touch steadied her shaky nerves.

"In here." The door opened with a rusty groan, admitting the valet and his companion.

Henning inclined a gruff nod after Tyler introduced the doctor. "I've heard good things about you and your Elgin Botanic Garden in New York, Hosack. It's always a pleasure to meet a man with enlightened ideas on medicine."

For Henning, a radical thinker who had precious few good things to say about any practitioner in the field, that was high praise, indeed.

"Mr. Tyler tells me you have some very progressive ideas as well. I look forward to some interesting discussions. But first . . ." Hosack's gaze darted to the shadowed slab and the dark silhouette beneath the canvas shroud. "We've more pressing matters to address."

"I've made a cursory examination of your friend, and Wrexford gave me a champagne glass found at the scene . . ." Henning proceeded to give the American a summary of what he had discovered so far. He then gestured to a heavy oilcloth apron hanging from a peg in the wall. "If you care to join me, we can begin a closer scrutiny, and decide what measures are necessary to satisfy all our questions about Mr. Becton's death."

"Thank you. I was hoping you would permit me to take part in the proceedings." Hosack began stripping off his evening coat. "Becton was a brilliant scholar and a loyal friend. It's both my duty and my desire to ensure that whoever snuffed out his life is brought to justice for the crime."

"Come, my dear." Wrexford kept hold of Charlotte's hand. "Let us leave them to their work. I'm sure we would both welcome a wee dram of Baz's Scottish malt."

"I'll join you shortly," murmured Tyler, whose scientific curiosity stretched far beyond the boundaries of chemistry. "They may require someone to hold the lantern for them."

She didn't argue. Fatigue had wrapped itself around her, twining with the weight of the other worries stirred by the events of the evening.

They crossed the short path to the back stair leading into Henning's residence, a small stucco-and-timber building with a sagging roof. Its angles had slumped, causing it to lean drunkenly against its neighbor. Wrexford lit a lamp by the doorway and moved to the sideboard to fetch a bottle of whisky. The oily light revealed the usual cluttered chaos of their friend's residence. Papers and books shared a seat on the threadbare sofa with a pile of laundered shirts. Charlotte cleared a place for them to sit before moving to the tiny kitchen, where she stirred the coals to life in the stove and set a kettle of water on the hob.

Wrexford handed her a drink when she returned. He had

kindled a fire in the hearth, and yet the flames did little to warm the chill from her bones. *"Slàinte,"* he murmured, touching his glass to hers and then downing half of the amber spirits in one swift swallow.

Charlotte took a small sip, welcoming the whisky's fire as it slowly burned away the sour taste of death lingering from Henning's surgery.

"Bloody hell." Wrexford grimaced and promptly downed the rest of his whisky. "My apologies. This was hardly an auspicious start to our round of engagement parties. I had hoped it would be an enjoyable evening for you, with interesting fellow guests and thoughtful conversation, rather than the usual bland banalities."

He ran a hand through his already-disheveled locks. "Instead, we spent it mucking around within the dark underbelly of humanity."

A corner of her mouth quirked upward. "Never say you don't know how to show a lady a good time."

Unsmiling, he turned to refill his glass.

A very un-Wrexford-like reaction. Which stirred a frisson of alarm.

"Is something preying on your mind?"

A soft splash, and then a winking of tawny sparks skittered across the plaster wall as the earl swirled the spirits.

Oh, surely, he wasn't thinking . . .

"I should have told Bethany that I wasn't free to assist with an unfortunate incident in the conservatory. I saw you were about to seek me out, and yet I went with him." Wrexford drew in a measured breath. "That was a mistake."

"A mistake to follow your conscience?" she asked.

Finally a twitch of his lips. "I don't have a conscience. I tend to act on ill-tempered impulses."

"Bollocks," she uttered. "You spoke earlier of a moral true

north. Your heart is unerringly drawn to that same point on the compass."

"There are times when one should temper idealism with pragmatism in order to protect—"

"Protect *me*?" Charlotte sighed. Ah, now they had come to the crux of the problem. "Lud, Wrexford, our relationship has never been ruled by conventional strictures or expectations. I think we both might expire from boredom—or frustration—if we tried to stifle who we are." A pause. "Don't pretend my impulses don't drive you to distraction."

That drew a chuckle. "What a pair we make."

"A well-matched pair," she murmured.

"Like two finely crafted dueling pistols?" he quipped.

Thank heaven his sense of humor is back. "You have to admit, we are always primed to shoot off sparks."

"True." He took a swallow of whisky. "But that doesn't mean we can't take care to avoid being singed by every challenge that rears its ugly head. Let us leave this to Griffin." They had met the Bow Street Runner when Wrexford was the prime suspect in a grisly murder. Antagonism had turned to respect—and then to friendship. Griffin's taciturn demeanor hid a clever, methodical mind and he proved to be a valuable ally in their subsequent investigations. "If the higher authorities look to be ignoring what he turns up," continued Wrexford, "A. J. Quill can always stir public sentiment in order to keep pressure on them to solve the crime. But I don't see any reason to allow ourselves to be personally drawn into the conundrum of Becton's murder."

That made perfect sense. And yet, as Charlotte rose in response to the boiling kettle, she couldn't shake off a niggling feeling that reason might be overpowered by other forces.

His face grey with fatigue, Henning ran a hand over his unshaven jaw and blew out a harried breath, then paused in the doorway to stomp the mud off his boots before entering the room.

"Bless you, Lady Charlotte," he rasped as she handed him a steaming cup of tea, well fortified with brandy.

Hosack flashed a grateful smile as he, too, watched her splash some spirits into his cup. "Thank you." In response to her gesture, he took a seat on the sofa. "Once again, allow me to express my sincere regrets for having turned your evening plans topsy-turvy."

"Please don't give it a thought, sir," replied Charlotte. "You've far more important things on your mind than whether I sat down to a fancy supper."

Tyler smiled. "I told you there was no need to fret."

"Indeed, let us put aside politeness," said Wrexford, "and get down to brass tacks, as it were." Henning's face had been easy enough to read. "I take it that the examination has confirmed that Becton was murdered?"

"Aye, laddie, I've no doubt about it," said the surgeon. "Hosack soaked up a spill of the champagne with his handkerchief. The three of us examined the crystals from the cloth, as well as those from the glass, under my microscope and concur that the concentration was lethal."

"The question," mused Wrexford, "now becomes how you will identify the culprit and prove the crime." He looked to Charlotte, who nodded for him to go on. "We can offer one small clue, yet I can't say whether it will be ultimately of any use." He hesitated, choosing his words carefully. "A witness saw the gentleman who tossed the glass into the greenery of a gallery near the scene of the crime—"

Hosack put down his cup with a clatter.

"But alas, it was dark and the person only caught a momentary glance. It was impossible to make out any distinguishing details, save for the fact that he was about my height."

"Who was the witness?" demanded the doctor. "Perhaps if we press the fellow, he'll recall more—"

"I'm quite satisfied that he won't," cut in Wrexford.

"His Lordship was involved in military intelligence during the Peninsular War," explained Tyler to Hosack. "He's very skilled at extracting information, so I think we can take his word on that."

Hosack's face fell, but he nodded in understanding. "Still, it tells us something . . ."

Us. Wrexford intended to nip *that* thought in the bud. But he decided to allow the American to finish.

"Logic dictates that the murderer was one of the invited guests," continued the doctor. "After all, he and Becton were in the conservatory, drinking champagne together."

"It's an assumption, which we can't yet prove," Wrexford pointed out.

"But I believe we eventually will," insisted Hosack. "Because I think I know the motive for the crime."

For several long moments, silence seemed to have hold of all their tongues. Henning pursed his lips and rubbed his fingers down his bristly jaw, while Tyler frowned in thought. As for Charlotte, she sat still as a statue and watched the doctor intently.

What does she see? wondered Wrexford, finding it impossible to read her eyes through the flitting shadows.

"Yes, you hinted that Becton possessed some momentous secret earlier this evening," he finally said. "Now that we have more time and privacy, can you explain more fully what you meant by that, and why someone would wish to stop him?"

"What I fear is . . ." Hosack pressed a palm to his brows, taking a moment to compose his thoughts. "But first, I think I had better explain what set all of this in motion."

A curt nod indicated for him to continue.

"A little over a year ago, Becton had sent several members of the Royal Society's governing council a brief overview on his research and several preliminary results," recounted the doctor. "They were very excited about its significance. They asked him to be one of the main speakers at this symposium so that the revelation would be made here at the Royal Botanic Gardens—the world's most respected venue of botanical knowledge and innovation," explained Hosack. "Becton was delighted to comply—"

"Forgive me, Doctor, having had little sleep in the last two days, I've no patience for flowery habble-gabble," grumbled Henning. "Might you cut wind and simply tell us what the devil the discovery is?"

"In a nutshell, it's a miracle potion that will save countless lives," replied Hosack.

"What ingredients, and what illness?" shot back Henning.

The queries drew a wry grimace from the doctor. "Alas, there's no simple answer to your questions. It requires a very long-winded tale of international diplomacy, exotic travel, dangerous hardships—and fortuitous luck."

"Fair enough." Henning reached for the whisky bottle and filled his empty teacup. "I shall endeavor to listen. But just ignore me if I fall asleep."

"I'm not trying to play coy," said the doctor. "Becton was a very reclusive fellow, and tended to be closemouthed about his work. However, he had become even more secretive during his last weeks in America. He confided to me that he feared someone was trying to steal his research papers and specimens. So he thought it best not to tell me—or anyone—the details of his discovery, lest they be put in danger."

Wrexford held back a sarcastic comment. He was of the belief that neither histrionics nor an overwrought imagination had any place in science.

"Yes, yes. I know it sounds like something out of an Ann Radcliffe novel," said Hosack, correctly interpreting the earl's expression. "Skulking villains, clanking chains, and dark dungeons full of torture instruments—"

A gusty snore from Henning suddenly rattled the saucers.

"Do go on," urged Wrexford. The small paned window overlooking the backyard showed that mist was silvering the blackness of night, a harbinger that dawn was not far off. "As succinctly as possible, if you please."

"I will try. But first, allow me to indulge in a bit of history, which I promise has some relevance."

Charlotte signaled her agreement with a quick nod. "The motivation for murder can rarely be summed up in a simple sentence. If we are to understand the crime, we need to hear what the doctor has to say."

Wrexford wasn't convinced that was a good idea, but for the moment, he kept his reservations to himself.

Hearing no objections, Hosack picked up the thread of his story. "Are you all familiar with cinchona bark, from the Spanish colonies in South America?"

"It's a genus of flowering trees and shrubs, and the bark of several species is highly effective in treating the disease we call malaria—which comes from the Italian *mal aria*, or bad air," said Tyler.

Hosack's grave expression gave way to a momentary glimmer of humor. "Perhaps I'll tempt you to abandon chemistry and concentrate on botany. You clearly have an expertise in the subject."

"A jack-of-all-trades and master of none," replied the valet. "I fear my curiosity prevents me from committing to serious study in any one subject."

Wrexford chuffed a laugh. "I could phrase that a little less elegantly."

"If you wish your boots to maintain their impressive shine, you will leave it at that," murmured Tyler.

Ignoring the retort, the earl let out an impatient growl. A

glance at Charlotte showed that the night had taken its toll on her. Her face appeared ashen, accentuating the bruise-dark shadows pooled beneath her eyes.

"On second thought, Hosack, fascinating as your long-winded tale may be, might you save it for later and cut to the heart of why we're all here? Surely, there has to be a simple answer as to why Becton was murdered."

A fraught sigh. "In a word, it's money."

CHAPTER 4

The word seemed to come alive, its grim echo growing louder and louder as it reverberated against the wall.

"Money," mused Tyler. "I suppose that should come as no surprise. It's the root of most evil in this world."

"Aye," repeated Hosack. He looked as exhausted as Charlotte. "I can explain, if you wish."

"Please do," urged the valet.

"Getting back to malaria, it's a pernicious illness that strikes all over the globe—the New World, your Indian colonies, the African continent, and even here in Britain." The doctor grimaced. "Indeed, we scientific scholars suspect that Shakespeare's mention of the ague refers to malaria."

"Hosack, as I said, let us please leave history for later," growled Wrexford.

"Sorry, sorry." The American paused for a sip of his now-cold tea. "The discovery of cinchona bark, and its curative properties, was brought back to Europe from the Spanish colonies in the New World by Jesuit missionaries. And while the Spanish tried to prevent others from getting hold of the plant, in order to have a monopoly on the medicine, it grew too widely to keep it to themselves."

"I see what you mean," interjected Tyler. "Imagine what a unique medicine would be worth. It would likely have generated more riches than their silver trade."

"Precisely," agreed the doctor.

"A pox on all those whose selfish greed makes them value money over human lives," muttered Henning, who had been roused from sleep by the mention of money. "Discoveries like that should be shared, not kept secret in order to make an obscene profit."

"Yes, it's morally wrong," whispered Charlotte.

Wrexford didn't bother pointing out that lofty principles rarely triumphed over the baser urges of human nature. Instead, he pressed, "As you've just pointed out, cinchona is readily accessible, though it doesn't come cheap. So I'm still waiting for your revelation."

"I think," replied Hosack, "that Becton discovered a way to make cinchona even more effective by combining it with a certain other botanical. And that he was going to speak here at the symposium about his research and reveal his new formula."

He hesitated. "More than that, I believe he was going to gift specimens of the unknown plant to the Royal Botanic Gardens so that they could propagate them, and share seeds with other important botanical gardens around the world."

"Making the miracle medicine available to all physicians and apothecaries," said Wrexford.

"Correct, milord," answered the doctor. "Which is why I suspect that Becton was murdered for his formula and the plant specimens. A person possessing them would then have the ability to sell the potion"—his expression tightened—"and at whatever price he wishes to name."

It made perfect sense in theory. But Wrexford preferred to

base his conclusions on fact, not conjecture. "Have you any evidence to support such a claim?"

Henning muttered an unflattering word.

"That's unfair—His Lordship is right to ask," chided Charlotte. "We ought not to let our imaginations run wild without some clue, however small, to support such suspicions."

"I agree wholeheartedly," said Hosack. "I'll tell you what I know, and leave it to you to decide whether I'm merely whistling into the wind."

Wrexford began drumming his fingertips together.

The doctor took the tapping as permission to continue. "Becton was a member of our most learned scientific society in New York and was happy to talk about his discovery at our meetings, but only in general terms. Out of courtesy to the Royal Society, he had pledged not to reveal the actual formula or ingredients until this symposium. Most of the members respected his decision. But not all."

Hosack appeared to be considering his words before going on. "In particular, there's a very wealthy merchant by the name of Tobias Quincy, one of the pillars of New York Society, who handles all the sales and shipping for his cousin's vast cotton plantations in South Carolina. He kept pressing Becton to renege on his commitment to the Royal Society, and instead to create a highly profitable venture within Quincy's business consortium."

The tapping stopped. "You mean the merchant asked Becton to make a fortune with his miracle medicine, rather than giving it away."

"Precisely, milord."

"But Becton was too ethical to even consider the proposal," guessed Charlotte.

"Yes," confirmed Hosack.

"To be fair to Mr. Quincy, he's in business to make a profit," said Wrexford, deciding to play devil's advocate. "Hearing of an opportunity that could potentially produce untold riches, he can't be blamed for trying to convince Becton to transform his brilliance into gold."

"Modern alchemy?" murmured Tyler.

"These days, new concepts, new innovations are bubbling up with increasing frequency in every field of endeavor," Wrexford pointed out. "Commerce is no exception."

"There's nothing wrong with exercising a bit of persuasion," responded Hosack. "As long as words don't give way to outright treachery."

Wrexford heard a slither of silk as Charlotte sat up a little straighter.

"And did they, sir?" she demanded.

"Tired of the merchant's constant badgering, Becton finally asked in no uncertain terms that Quincy drop the matter," answered the doctor. "Two days later, my friend returned to his home after an evening engagement with friends, only to find the place had been ransacked."

"It's hard to imagine it was a mere coincidence," said Tyler.

"Thank heaven Becton had set the specimens on the window ledge outside his bedchamber that afternoon to soak in a passing rain shower, and had not yet retrieved them," Hosack went on. "As for his formula, by sheer good fortune, he had taken his document case with him, in order to show some of his other papers to his friends."

"Are you suggesting Quincy arranged for your friend's murder from across the ocean—"

"He didn't have to, milord," interrupted Hosack. "He's here in London, and attending the symposium."

That, conceded Wrexford, put some flesh on the bones of Hosack's fears.

"Quincy crossed the Atlantic with a group of other scientifically-minded Americans who are also taking part in the lectures and discussions," stated the doctor. "Including a former army officer by the name of Adderley, who has an expertise in botany—and an unsavory reputation for intrigue. Rumor has it, he tried to steal some botanical specimens from the viceroy of New Granada's conservatory while in South America as part of an official United States naval diplomatic mission a number of years ago." Turning to Charlotte, he added, "The Spanish are known for guarding any commercially valuable plants within their territories. It's strictly forbidden for anyone other than government officials to possess valuable botanicals."

Charlotte nodded. "I see."

"As for Adderley," said Hosack, resuming his narrative, "a short while after the naval delegation returned to the United States, he resigned his military commission." A pause. "I find it unsettling that he's now employed by Quincy to work on ways to improve the yield of the cotton plant."

Wrexford heard Charlotte draw in a harsh breath. A bad sign, as it meant her sense of moral outrage was sharpening.

"I understand your alarm," he said. "Have you any idea where Becton's specimens and formula are now?"

"Alas, no. Though he told me he had taken pains to ensure their safety until he announced his discovery and turned them over to the Royal Society."

Rising from his chair, Wrexford moved to the hearth and stirred the dying flames. Much as he regretted the murder, he and Charlotte couldn't right all the sordid wrongs in the world.

Though he feared she would disagree about trying.

"I can put you in contact with a Bow Street Runner who is extremely skilled in solving complicated crimes," he said. "Mr. Griffin doesn't come cheap when he takes on private commissions . . ." Seeing Hosack's face fall, he quickly added, "But I will, of course, cover the costs of seeing that justice is done."

"That is more than generous of you, milord." The doctor rose and gave a jerky bow. "I would never have reached out to you, had I known of your impending nuptials." He looked to Charlotte. "Forgive me, milady."

"Come, sir." Seeing the doctor was a little unsteady on his feet, Tyler took his arm. "I'll see you back to your hotel. In the morning, I'll return and we'll arrange to meet with Mr. Griffin."

Charlotte awoke with a throbbing head and a sour taste in the back of her throat. Wincing, she tried to sit up, only to find that her limbs were tangled in the bedsheets.

"Lud, what a nightmare." Bad dreams had plagued her sleep, but as the memory of the previous night came flooding back, she pressed her fingertips to her temples and forced a few deep breaths, trying to loosen the clench in her chest.

Murder. Like a fanged serpent slithering through the darkness, it was a threat to poison everyone around it. Granted, her nerves were on edge for other reasons. And Wrexford had assured her that there was no earthly reason for them to be drawn into the investigation.

Still, Charlotte had a bad feeling about the crime. Call it intuition . . .

A sudden blade of sunlight speared through her gloomy thoughts. She glanced at the window and realized it must be nearly noon.

"Ye heavens, I'm never such a slugabed," she muttered, pushing a tangle of hair back from her brow. From downstairs came the sounds of McClellan moving around the kitchen. Tidying up, no doubt. The boys would have had their breakfast long ago. Were they now at their lessons with their tutor?

Charlotte squeezed her eyes shut. Lud, she couldn't remember what day it was—

Metal rattled, followed by several loud thumps.

Packing, realized Charlotte. Her maid was packing up the various household items in the pantries that would be moving along with them to the earl's townhouse on Berkeley Square.

The clench in her chest slid down and turned into a knot in her gut.

It wasn't that she was having second thoughts about marriage. Wrexford was . . . Wrexford. An impossibly complex man who had found a home in her heart in ways she couldn't begin to explain.

A smile touched her lips. He had recently drawn up an elaborate scientific equation, showing a bewildering array of chemical symbols and notations to explain the natural phenomenon of Love.

Thank heaven a sense of humor softened his steel-edged sense of logic.

And yet . . .

Refusing to wallow in self-pity, Charlotte flung off the covers and began her morning ablutions. A splash of cold water helped clear her head. Fear was a natural reaction to change, she told herself.

"Wrexford will likely have a formula to explain that as well," she murmured, finding the thought lifted her spirits. Yes, there were concerns about giving up her hard-won independence. The act of marriage stripped a woman of so many rights. In the eyes of the law, she became her husband's chattel, with no more rights than a hound or a horse. One would have to be a ninny-hammer not to worry over such a momentous loss of freedom.

It all came down to trust.

Charlotte shucked off her night rail and dressed quickly in one of her ink-stained work gowns. Wrexford had pledged that he would never rattle the legal leg shackle that bound her to his whim. Indeed, he had insisted the marriage articles include the settlement of money—quite a generous amount of it—in an account under her control. It would, he had pointed out, give her the freedom to live very comfortably on her own should she ever decide that their life together didn't suit her.

Freedom. He had taken pains to hand it to her on a platter.

She sighed. Her inner fears had never been about his actions, but rather her own. She knew in her heart he would never ask her to give up the things that mattered most to her. Her passions . . .

Her pen.

Her breath caught in her throat. What if marriage made her shy away from certain issues? In the past, nothing was safe from her sense of justice and fair play. *Be damned with the consequences*—fear played no part in her decisions.

And now?

Ah, that was the crux of the conundrum. Becton's murder had raised the unsettling question of moral choices. It was exactly the type of crime that cried out for A. J. Quill's attention. The Royal Society was a well-respected organization, with a reputation for doing good. But if there was also a dark side to it, someone needed to shine a light on it.

"So, why am I hesitating?" Charlotte whispered, even though she knew the answer. Wrexford was a member of the Royal Society. He respected their mission, seeing them as one of the bright lights of scientific progress, and had friends among their leaders. Poking her pen into their symposium would do damage, even if the crime had nothing to do with the organization.

Choices, choices. What is the right thing to do?

It was a question she always asked herself. But now, she couldn't deny that how her actions affected Wrexford had crept into her considerations . . .

She took a seat at her dressing table, taking a long, hard stare at herself in the looking glass.

Ha—as if she didn't know that only one answer would allow her to face that reflection every day.

Dropping her gaze, she quickly took up her brush and made short work of pinning up her hair.

McClellan—who served as both lady's maid and housekeeper-cum-drillmaster for their eccentric little household—looked up from the wooden box she was packing as Charlotte entered the kitchen.

"Awake from the dead, are we?"

"That's not overly humorous, Mac." She had no doubt that over breakfast Hawk had explained about the murder.

"That bad?" The maid was already up and pouring a mug of coffee from the pot set on the hob.

"Actually, as murders go, the victim wasn't nearly as gruesome as some of the other bodies we've tripped over," responded Charlotte. "Bless you," she added after taking a swallow of the steaming-hot brew that had been thrust into her hands. "That's ambrosial."

"When was the last time you ate?"

"I . . . I don't remember."

McClellan gave a crucial squint. "No wonder you look like hell. Sit. I'll fix you something to fill your breadbox."

The thought of poor Becton laid out on Henning's mortuary slab made Charlotte sure she had no appetite. But the delicious aroma of frying gammon, perfumed by the scent of bread fresh from the oven, quickly made her realize that she was ravenous.

"That will put some color back in your cheeks," said the maid, watching with approval as Charlotte dug into her meal.

"Where are the Weasels?" she asked through a mouthful of shirred eggs.

"I put them to work in the garden," answered McClellan, "so that they won't pester you with ghoulish questions about what happened at Henning's surgery until you've finished your breakfast."

A clatter at the rear door, followed by the thump of steps in the pantry passageway, signaled that plan had died an early death. Sure enough, Raven rushed into the kitchen, with Hawk right on his heels.

McClellan winced, watching their filthy boots leave a trail of muck across the just-swept floor. "Your orders were to stay outside so milady could dine in peace."

"Oiy, but a note just came from Aunt Alison." Raven held

up the pristine piece of paper clutched in his grubby hand. "We assumed you would wish to read it right away."

"Right—because in another few minutes, it wouldn't be legible," said McClellan. Her eyes narrowed. "What *is* that disgusting substance on your fingers?"

The slime, noted Charlotte, was the exact color of horse piss.

"I swear," grumbled the maid, "if Tyler has given you two another set of noxious chemicals—"

"Aren't you going to open it?" interrupted Hawk, fixing Charlotte with an expectant look.

The boys were very fond of Alison, who had insisted they call her their aunt, even though they were unrelated by blood.

But then, love was the true bond that tied all of her odd little family together.

Putting down her fork, Charlotte cracked the wax seal and read over the short message. As she expected, Alison was all afire to hear what had kept her and Wrexford from appearing at the gala supper.

The dowager was one of the few people who knew about Charlotte's secret identity, and how her passion for justice occasionally drew her into danger. Indeed, Alison had been involved in their last murder investigation—and had shown a frightening enthusiasm for puzzling out mysteries.

"Would you like for us to run a message back to her?" pressed Hawk. The dowager's cook was very generous with sweets.

Charlotte was fairly certain that the death—much less the suspicion that it might be murder—had not yet been made public. Alison would have far too many questions to be satisfied with a mere note.

"I had better go myself." On hearing a chuff of disappointment, she added, "But I'd be grateful if you would hare along to her townhouse and tell her I'll come by for tea at four."

The boys spun around in a flash. But McClellan was just as

quick. She reached out and snagged Raven's collar. "Wash your hands first. A young gentleman doesn't appear in polite company stinking of . . ."

Hawk began to giggle, only to find his own collar caught in the maid's clutches. "That goes for you, too."

"We ain't gentlemen," retorted Raven. "We're Weasels. Which, like ferrets and polecats, are part of the genus *Mustela.*"

Their tutor had recently been teaching them the classification system for animals and plants created by the legendary Carl Linnaeus.

"*Ergo,*" he added, "we don't have to wash our *damn* paws."

McClellan gave him a shake. "I don't care whether you're a bloody lion from the wilds of Africa, use bad language in this house again and you'll have soapsuds bubbling over your tongue, as well as your hands."

Charlotte cleared her throat with a cough, unsure whether to be amused or appalled by the deliberate transgression. Raven was well aware of the rule against swearing within the walls of their home. But he was reaching a difficult age—not quite a child, not quite an adolescent—and she feared there would be a great many similar challenges to authority in the days ahead.

"But *ergo* is Latin!" chirped Hawk, looking a little confused. "It means *therefore,* so—"

"Mac meant *damn,*" explained his older brother with a grin.

"Oh." Hawk made a face. "Right."

Charlotte watched the boys hurry to the washbasin. Abandoned at a tender age, they had learned to survive in London's toughest slum. Clever and resilient, they had been living as homeless urchins when Charlotte had first met them and taken them under her wing. Patience and love—along with schooling and lessons in manners—had polished their rough edges. They now could speak with a plummy accent and charm their way through a Mayfair drawing room. But a streak of hardscrabble independence would always set them apart from the pampered scions of the aristocracy.

And thank heaven for that, she reflected. She was of the opinion that adversity sculpted character. It made an individual strong, and it was to be hoped that it also made an individual compassionate for those who struggled against the odds. But as she well knew, strength of character was rarely admired in the beau monde.

Raven and Hawk wouldn't easily fit in . . .

She shook off such worries. All that lay far in the future. As for the present—

"Excellent," intoned McClellan as she inspected Raven's scrubbed hands, ignoring his scowl. "*Now* you may go." As they scampered off, she called, "And there just might be some ginger biscuits when you return!"

The prospect of Alison's inquisition did nothing to lighten Charlotte's mood. Sliding back onto her stool, she looked down at her half-eaten breakfast, suddenly finding her appetite had vanished.

"It's normal to be nervous when making a change in life," observed the maid, after she had refilled Charlotte's mug. "Yes, I know it's a platitude, which I detest as much as you do. But there's often a truth to such sayings.

"You're right, of course," Charlotte replied, forcing a wry smile. "If it were merely family matters—entering into marriage, facing my estranged brother, worrying about how the Weasels will adapt to a new world—I would not be batting an eyelash. But the prospect of a murder investigation . . ."

"There's no reason you should be drawn into one," replied McClellan. "From what Hawk explained of the events, the man's demise had no connection to you and Wrexford. And as for the boy, he saw nothing other than a momentary glimpse of a tall shadowy figure moving through the gloom."

"Alas, murder's tentacles rarely respect reason. I fear . . ."

Charlotte couldn't quite articulate what it was that she feared. And yet, that didn't make it any less real.

For a long moment, the only sounds in the kitchen were the hissing and crackling of coal within the belly of the stove.

"How did Tyler come to know Dr. Hosack?" Charlotte asked. McClellan was Tyler's cousin, and like him, she had been part of the earl's household until a previous murder investigation had led to her taking up residence with Charlotte. "The American appears a good deal older."

"Aye, he is," answered the maid. "They met six years ago, when the doctor visited Scotland to give a series of lectures at the University of Edinburgh, where he had studied in the early 1790s. Tyler attended them, and was impressed with his intellect and passion for working with plants to develop medicines for curing the diseases that cut short so many lives."

"Hosack sounds like a very admirable man," mused Charlotte. She had been struck by the doctor's kindly face and his fierce determination to have justice for his murdered friend.

"A compassionate one as well. He lost his first wife and two children to yellow fever, so understands the pain of losing a loved one to illness," said McClellan. "He's devoted his life to championing the creations of botanic gardens in America so that medical men have a resource for research. Tyler says that Hosack's Elgin Garden, just outside the city of New York, have garnered great praise here in Europe."

The maid paused. "Indeed, that was how the two of them met. After giving his lectures in Edinburgh, Hosack wished to journey north and collect specimen plants from some of the remote areas in the Highlands. As Tyler was familiar with the area, he offered to serve as a guide. They worked several weeks together, and formed a close friendship. Tyler has kept up a regular correspondence since then, and he was very much looking forward to spending time with the doctor here in London."

"As your beloved Scottish poet Bobby Burns said, *The best*

laid schemes o' Mice an' Men . . ." Charlotte pushed back her plate. "That explains how Hosack came to know of Wrexford." A sigh. "Though I can't pretend not to wish that Tyler had been a little less loquacious about the earl."

McClellan nodded, her eyes pooling with concern.

But there is no use in fretting over spilled milk, she thought as McClellan rose and began to clear the table. The task now was to keep the damage from spreading.

CHAPTER 5

"Words can't express how sorry I am, milord." Tyler brushed a nonexistent mote of dust from the coat draped over his arm before holding it up for the earl to slip on. "I know that I'm responsible for ruining Lady Charlotte's first appearance as the future Lady Wrexford. I don't expect her—or you—to ever forgive me. But be assured that—"

"Oh, do stop sniveling. It doesn't become you," snapped Wrexford. "If I wanted an obsequious valet to fawn over me, I would have given you the boot long ago."

As he had hoped, the rebuke drew a grudging snort.

"You know damn well that Lady Charlotte is profoundly grateful to you for the excuse to be absent from the frivolities of the gala supper," he added. "As am I."

Tyler was no longer looking quite so green around the gills. "Be that as it may, milord, I've put the two of you in a very awkward position. Not to speak of inadvertently involving Hawk in a bloody murder."

"Actually, there wasn't a drop of blood involved." Wrexford moved to his dressing table and picked up a small glass vial set by the looking glass. "If you wish to make amends for your abandoning the boy for hours in the conservatory, set up the microscope in the workroom and prepare all the implements and chemicals we'll need in order to determine the exact composition of this substance."

"Ah." Curiosity replaced the lingering look of remorse from the valet's face. "I was hoping you had convinced Henning to give you a sample from the wineglass. His magnifying lenses and testing methods are far more primitive than ours."

"Precisely." Wrexford took up the freshly ironed cravat from the back of the chair and began looping it around his upturned shirt points.

Tyler winced. "You may consider me thoroughly punished for my verbal transgressions, milord. To go out in public looking like that is deeply humiliating for a man of my professional sensibilities. My reputation as a valet will be ruined."

"I don't employ you for your sartorial expertise." Wrexford finished yanking a careless knot into place. "By the by, make sure to have plenty of vitriolic acid on hand. We will need it."

"Hmmm—that must mean you suspect . . ." Tyler tapped a finger to his chin. "A very interesting surmise, milord. I'll have everything ready by the time you return, and we'll see whether you are right."

Even if his guess was correct and the experiments proved that Becton had been killed by a poison more potent than foxglove, that didn't change the fact that he had been murdered. And it likely wouldn't offer any clue as to the identity of the scoundrel who had committed the foul act.

Not as of yet, amended Wrexford as he smoothed the tails of his cravat into place.

And then he gave a guilty grimace at his reflection in the looking glass. Griffin and his fellow Runners at Bow Street would have to catch the killer on their own, he reminded himself.

"I've sent word to Griffin that you and Hosack will meet him tonight at his favorite tavern. Though given the political ramifications of the case, I daresay he will have to discuss things with his superiors before he begins his inquiries."

"Very good, sir."

"I've left a hefty purse on my desk. He will expect to be fed a very generous supper while he listens to the facts of the case."

Tyler nodded. The glass vial carefully cupped in his hands, he headed off to the workroom and its adjoining laboratory.

Wrexford quelled the urge to follow. He had a more important obligation to attend to.

"There isn't a snowflake's chance in Hell that I'm going to allow a stranger's death to delay our nuptials," he muttered, descending the stairs two at a time and hurrying out the front door of his townhouse to the waiting carriage. The coming week still held a number of social obligations, and for once, he was loath to stir any gossip by failing to appear.

He didn't give a fig for his own reputation, but he wished to protect Charlotte from the tattle-mongers of the ton, whose silky smiles hid sharklike teeth. At the slightest scent of blood, they would swarm in a vicious frenzy, looking to tear their victim to shreds.

Charlotte wouldn't care. But he did. She had suffered enough indignities from her own family, cast out for refusing to live her life as a pasteboard cutout, devoid of any color or individuality.

Her courage, her strength, her passions, her sense of right and wrong—all the myriad things that made Charlotte who she was—took his breath away.

"Damnation—I *won't* let her be hurt. Not by anyone."

Though uttered in naught but a whisper, the fierceness of his pledge took him a little by surprise. Wrexford leaned back against the soft leather squabs and took a moment to settle his jumpy nerves. There *was* no threat, and no reason to imagine that one would rear its ugly head.

With that in mind, he called for the coachman to crack his whip and set the carriage wheels in motion.

"Dear heaven, another dead body?" Alison's eyes widened as she looked up from her book.

Charlotte didn't like the speculative gleam that flashed to life behind the lenses of the dowager's reading glasses. Taking a seat in the facing armchair, she quickly gave a bare-bones account of the previous evening's events, careful to omit certain details that might encourage her elderly great aunt's curiosity to run amok.

"Murder, eh?" With a fluttery *thump*, the pages snapped shut. "What are we going to do about it?"

"*We* are going to do *nothing*," she replied. "Wrexford is arranging for Griffin to handle the investigation, and will pass on what little we know of the crime."

"Griffin is very skilled at what he does," conceded the dowager. "However—"

"Speaking of skillful friends," interrupted Charlotte. "Which of the new gowns from Madame Françoise's shop do you think I should wear to the scientific soiree at Kensington Palace tomorrow evening—the slate-blue or the sea-green one? The Royal Duke of Sussex is hosting the party, so I imagine the crème de la crème of society will be in attendance."

Appearing momentarily at a loss for words, Alison fixed her with an owlish stare. "I confess, I'm not sure which shocks me more," she said, once she had regained her voice. "Your concern with fashion or your concern with the guest list."

"You know very well that I couldn't care less about either. But Wrexford seems as skittish as a cat on a hot griddle about whether some of the high sticklers will whisper unkind gossip about my past. He's been acting oddly protective of late, so I'd rather not give him cause for . . ."

"Explosion?" suggested Alison. "Oh, pish, the duke's parties are usually dreadfully boring. A bit of pyrotechnics would liven up the evening. The earl is delightfully amusing when he loses his temper."

"Heaven forfend," murmured Charlotte. "However, it's not just Wrexford. I confess that I'm also worried about meeting my brother and his family after all these years. So I would prefer not to stir any memories of past scandals." She sighed. "Or create any new ones. I have enough to explain as it is."

It was doubtful that her brother knew anything about her late husband's family tree. But even though Wrexford had created a very official-looking trail of paper, she would rather not have him—or anyone—look too closely at her claim that Raven and Hawk were orphans from Anthony's side of the family.

The laughter in Alison's eyes quickly died. "Never fear, my dear. Nothing will upset the upcoming reconciliation. Your brother is as eager as you are to resume cordial relations."

However, any further talk of family affairs was cut short by the boys, who burst through the drawing-room door in a helter-pelter of good-natured pushing and shoving.

"Aunt Alison's cook just baked a batch of jam tarts!" exclaimed Hawk. "She let us sample one."

The sticky raspberry-red smear on his chin made the announcement superfluous.

"One?" The dowager raised a brow.

"Or maybe two." Unlike his older brother, Hawk had not yet mastered the art of guile. "They're very good."

"Well, then, I hope there's one remaining for *my* supper."

Hawk swallowed hard and slanted a guilty look at Raven.

"Oiy." Raven grinned. "We left a crust."

Alison laughed, which drew a sigh of relief from Hawk.

"Do you need us to run any more errands?" he went on, turning to Charlotte.

"No, I think you locusts have devoured enough sweets for

one day," she replied dryly. "In any case, I imagine you have lessons to finish for tomorrow's meeting with Mr. Linsley."

"Hawk wishes to return home and work on his botanical drawings. But my lessons are finished, so I plan to pass by Grosvenor Square and visit with Lady Cordelia," responded Raven. "There is a very intriguing mathematical problem in the latest issue of the *Ladies' Diary*."

Charlotte knew that despite its name, the magazine featured a very sophisticated section on mathematics that was read by all the top scholars in the field. Each issue challenged readers to solve a problem, and the competition was quite fierce to be the winner.

Her lips quirked. Submissions were accepted from anyone, and the winner was frequently a woman. Which, of course, drove the professors from Oxford and Cambridge to distraction.

"I have an idea on how to solve it, but I wish to ask her advice," finished Raven.

Lady Cordelia was a good friend and a brilliant mathematician. Some months ago, she had been drawn into a highly dangerous enterprise to save her brother from ruin at the hands of a ruthless financial consortium. Charlotte felt her throat seize as she recalled just how close to disaster they all had come.

If not for . . .

"Actually, I think I shall stop at Lord Wrexford's townhouse before heading home," piped up Hawk. He flashed a grin, but his eyes didn't quite meet hers. "And ask Mr. Tyler when Harper can come back for a visit to London. I've grown since he was here last, and I'm sure that I'm now tall enough to take him for walks in Hyde Park by myself."

Charlotte hesitated. Harper was a *very* big hound, and Hawk, despite his assertion, was still as slight and skinny as a weasel, despite all the pastries he consumed. "Have you discussed this with Wrexford?"

The boy bit at his lower lip. "Not precisely. But I'm sure he would say yes. Harper and I won't get into any trouble. He's very well-trained."

"Trained in filching slabs of roast beef from the meat larder." Raven snickered. "And sleeping for hours in front of the hearth. Other than that, the beast is—"

Hawk nudged him none too gently in the ribs.

"The trouble lies with others, sweeting," explained Charlotte. "People tend to find Harper a trifle terrifying." The hound was the size of a small pony, and with his wire-grey fur and massive jaws, he bore an unfortunate resemblance to a wolf. "And alas, it will only exacerbate their fears if they see his only handler is a . . . a very young person."

Alison shot her a look of sympathy.

"So for the time being, I think it best that you wait until we all pay another visit to Wrexford's country estate. There you may take him out for as many walks as you please."

The boy nodded, but disappointment was writ plain on his face. Raven had recently shot up several inches, and she sensed Hawk was feeling a little small amid all the momentous changes going on around him.

She reached out and ruffled his hair. "How about after supper we sit down together and choose one of your sketches from the Royal Botanic Gardens to try as a watercolor?" Hawk had just started to experiment with the art of painting and was already showing an aptitude for it.

The offer coaxed a glimmer of a smile.

Impatient to be off, Raven sketched a very gentlemanly bow to Alison, though the effect was slightly marred by his raggle-taggle clothing.

The dowager, however, was aware that appearing as naught but guttersnipes helped keep the boys from drawing unwanted attention as they flitted about the city. Ignoring the malodorous streaks on their jackets—not to speak of the grease on their cuffs—she merely smiled and gestured for both boys to come get a hug before they raced off.

"You won't escape that easily," she murmured before planting a peck on each of their cheeks. "Especially as you've eaten all my tarts."

The mention of art had reminded Charlotte that she had yet to fully resolve the wrestling with her conscience over the subject of her next drawing for Mr. Fores's printshop. The Royal Society would, of course, prefer that Becton's death remain unknown to the public.

But murder among the high and mighty was not a crime that ever went quietly to the grave.

Nor should it. It wasn't a question of whether she would draw attention to the death, but how she would frame it and the accompanying commentary. Already an idea was taking shape . . .

"If you'll forgive me, Alison, I must be going as well. I must have a finished drawing ready by tomorrow."

Grumbling under his breath, Wrexford returned to his carriage after being informed by McClellan that Charlotte was paying a visit to her great-aunt. Happy to cede her the task of parrying the dowager's all-too-active curiosity, he called out the order to return home. By now, Tyler should have the laboratory ready for analyzing the poisonous substance . . .

And then, as the wheels began to clatter over the cobblestones, another idea suddenly popped to mind.

Don't. A warning whisper rose up, intent on batting it away. He ignored it.

Raising his walking stick, Wrexford rapped on the trap and gave his driver a new destination. Granted, he had assured Charlotte that the investigation would be handed over to Griffin. But no harm could come of gathering a few morsels of information to drop on the Runner's plate.

The quicker Griffin solved the case, the fewer expensive suppers it would cost him.

The carriage headed east and threaded its way down through the narrowing streets toward the river. Mist rose from the slate-grey water, bringing with it the pungent odors of the ebbing tide. From Earl Street, a sharp turn brought Wrexford to a row of brick buildings overlooking White Lion Wharf.

He climbed down and made his way through a dark-painted door with a discreet brass sign affixed above the dolphin-headed knocker.

From his perch behind a reception desk guarding the entrance foyer, a clerk looked up from his accounting book.

"Milord." Smiling, he rose and hastily opened the door, giving access to the inner offices.

"Is he in, Jenkins?" asked Wrexford, handing over his hat and coat. He didn't need to elaborate. The other three owners of the trading company were women.

"Yes, sir. This way—he's in the chart room with Miss Howe." The clerk led the way down a short corridor to a large, light-filled room overlooking the docks.

"I hope I'm not interrupting." Wrexford glanced at the various nautical maps hung on the near wall, all festooned with a colorful array of string and pins marking certain routes. "I take it business is good," he added, giving a friendly nod to the woman chatting with Christopher Sheffield.

"It is, milord." Octavia Howe shifted the stack of folders in her arms. "And likely to get better in the coming months, as one of our main competitors' ships has just been reported as lost at sea." She expelled a mournful sigh. "They scrimped and hired a captain who was inexperienced in transatlantic crossings, and alas, the hurricane season started early this year. It's not only a foolish business practice, but it's also morally shameful. A goodly number of men lost their lives because of such penny-pinching."

"Indeed." As principal investor in his friend's company, Wrexford happened to know that Nereid & Neptune was scrupulously careful when it came to the safety of its employees. Not only that, but they paid handsomely, and so attracted the most competent captains and crews for their merchant ships.

"Well, I shall leave you and Mr. Sheffield to chat." Octavia added several books from the table to the top of her pile. "I need to check on the expected arrival of cloth from the mills in Yorkshire and map out the logistics for our next transatlantic voyages."

Stepping aside, Wrexford held the door open and watched her sail through it. "A force of nature," he murmured, once the flutter of her skirts had disappeared around a turn.

"She makes a few waves," answered Sheffield. It was no secret within the company that Miss Howe had very high standards and sometimes allowed her temper to get the better of her when they weren't met. "However, Lady Cordelia usually manages to calm the waters."

He gestured to a side door that connected to the adjoining room. "Come, my office is a tad less spartan. The chairs have cushions." A corner of his mouth lifted in a wry smile. "As you see, we don't piss away the money of our investors on creature comforts."

The earl made a pained face as he took a seat in the straight-backed chair facing his friend's desk. "I'm sure there are some old armchairs in my attic. I shall have Tyler arrange to have them delivered here."

"No, please don't!" Sheffield gave a look of mock horror. "I might start sleeping through the working hours, and cause my partners to give me the boot." He shuffled several piles of paper and swatches of fabric off his blotter.

The desk, noted Wrexford, had a very well-used look, with

ledgers and other samples stacked in an orderly arrangement. And the sideboard and shelves held only books and boxes. Not a bottle of spirits was in sight.

"I'm still not sure why they tolerate my presence," added Sheffield. "The three of them are far smarter than I am."

Tapping his fingertips together, he fixed his friend with a critical squint. The two of them had been close friends since their days at Oxford, a fact that had puzzled most people. The earl was known for his razor-sharp intellect, while Sheffield . . .

Sheffield had earned the reputation for being a charming but frivolous rogue. The younger son of an imperious aristocrat was often trapped in a damnably difficult position. The heir and firstborn usually had a generous stipend. But those who trailed behind were dependent on parental purse strings. Sheffield's father, however, was a notorious nipcheese, who kept him on a very puny allowance. In retaliation, Sheffield had made a point of acting badly since his university days, a vicious cycle that did no one any good.

But that was no longer the case. Sheffield had finally been allowed to let his true colors cut through the hazy fugue of drinking and gambling to excess.

"Bollocks," retorted Wrexford. "You've a brain, and thank God you've finally decided to use it. Your partners—especially Lady Cordelia—owe their success to your cleverness." A pause. "Not to speak of your sense of loyalty."

Sheffield's gaze betrayed a flicker of surprise. The earl was not known for doling out praise. Nonetheless, it was true. Despite all the evidence to the contrary, Sheffield had refused to believe Lady Cordelia could be guilty of using her genius at mathematics to create a nefarious financial swindle. He had convinced Wrexford and Charlotte to help in unraveling the truth. And in the process, he had made some very sharp, spur-of-the-moment business decisions.

"A few lucky guesses," murmured Sheffield.

"Ha!" Wrexford let out a low snort. "Madame Luck is the one lady who's *never* succumbed to your charms." Sheffield was notorious for his losses at the gaming tables. But his charm made him a great favorite with the fairer sex.

One in particular . . .

"However, Lady Cordelia seems to be of the opinion that you don't need luck. She's mentioned on several occasions that you possess a remarkable talent for the import-export trade."

A faint flush rose to his friend's cheeks. Looking down, he began to shuffle through the items on his desk. "I merely help choose the knickknacks we buy and sell. Without her financial acumen and management skills, the firm of Nereid and Neptune would have a hard time staying afloat."

During their last investigation, the romantic attraction between Sheffield and Lady Cordelia had become clear to all around them. But he sensed that the relationship was fraught with complications.

He, of all people, knew that love—if it be love that was plaguing his friend—rarely twirled along as smoothly and sweetly as a waltz. Cupid's dance had no set steps and spun to a dizzying variety of tunes.

It was damnably easy to trip at every turn.

Sheffield snapped the lid of a lacquered box shut and cleared his throat. "Is there a reason you stopped by to see me?" A pause. "Other than to discuss my personal peccadilloes?"

"As a matter of fact, there is. There's been a murder . . ." Wrexford gave a quick account of what had occurred at the Royal Botanic Gardens.

Sheffield let out a low hiss. "But—"

"I'm wondering whether you or your partners might know anything about a wealthy New York merchant," continued the earl before his friend could interrupt. "A fellow by the name of Tobias Quincy, who owns—"

"Quincy Enterprises," intoned Sheffield. "Yes, I'm familiar with him and his consortium. They are our biggest competitor in the trade between Europe and the New World." He frowned. "From what I heard, he's a rather unsavory fellow. Aggressive—perhaps to a fault."

"Anything illegal?"

Sheffield lifted his shoulders. "Not that I know of. We have, however, heard rumors that he may be making shady deals to undercut us and other reputable merchants in certain markets." His frown deepened. "But surely you're not implying that Quincy has any connection to the murder."

"It's possible," answered Wrexford. "Apparently, Quincy and Becton were fellow members of a botanical society in New York, and the merchant was pressing Becton hard to partner in a venture to sell his new medicinal discovery. According to Tyler's friend Dr. Hosack, the formula would be worth a fortune."

"Profit." Sheffield let out an unhappy sigh, his gaze drifting to the bank of windows and the wind-rippled river below them, where a merchant ship was slipping its hawsers and loosening its sails in readiness to depart on the ebbing tide. "As we know all too well, profit is a powerful motive for murder."

"Greed is an elemental part of human nature. As is the urge to abandon all moral scruples in pursuit of self-interest," observed the earl. "Or so it seems to me."

"I wish I could argue with you on that." The air between them was stirred by another sigh. "Lady Cordelia remained at home today in order to advise her brother on some financial matters concerning the family estate. But I shall send word asking her to see what she can learn about Quincy. I have a few ideas as well on where to make some inquiries."

"You should probably hear the full story—or at least as much of it as I know—so that you'll have a better idea of what might be relevant." He proceeded to sum up all that Hosack had revealed the previous evening.

"With your permission, I'll pass all that on to Lady Cordelia." Seeing Wrexford confirm it with a nod, his friend added, "We've both been invited to attend the reception at Kensington Palace tomorrow evening, so I shall endeavor to have some information by then."

"I'm grateful, Kit."

His friend's expression turned troubled as his gaze returned from the window. "Far be it for me to pretend that I have any idea of how the feminine mind works. However . . ."

The silence expanded and quickly felt as if it had squeezed all else from the room.

"However," repeated Sheffield, "I can't help but wonder if it's a wise idea to become embroiled in a murder investigation at this moment. Lady Charlotte is facing some daunting, and perhaps difficult, transitions in her life—"

"The worst of which is becoming leg-shackled to me?" said the earl dryly.

The statement drew a twitch of amusement. "That doesn't worry me. Though only the devil knows why she seems to have no reservations about subjecting herself to your snaps and snarls. However, the upcoming meeting with her estranged brother and the surrender of her own independent little household may be . . ."

Sheffield made a helpless little hand gesture. "I dunno—it all may be stirring mixed emotions."

"Pigheaded though I may seem at times, I'm aware of that," answered Wrexford. "As I've said to her, I see no reason for us to become involved in the investigation. My intention is simply to give any information we can gather to Griffin. Indeed, Tyler is meeting with him this evening to discuss the terms of taking on the case."

Sheffield's face relaxed. "Excellent, excellent. I confess, that relieves my reservations. Griffin is very good at what he does, so if ever there was a time to leave a crime to the proper authorities . . ."

"The same thought occurred to me." He rose. "Be assured that the last thing I desire is to put my new family in any danger before I've even uttered my marriage vows."

CHAPTER 6

McClellan finished threading a silk ribbon through Charlotte's upswept topknot and flicked a few ringlets into place before stepping back to assess the effect.

"You look like . . . a countess," she murmured, giving a gruff nod at the reflection in the looking glass.

"Ha, ha." Charlotte forced a smile. "Thank you for the reminder." *Black sheep of her imperious family. Gadfly to the rich and powerful. Secretive widow. Occasional sleuth of crimes.* "I slip in and out of so many second skins that at times I fear I'm losing track of just who I really am."

The maid raised a brow. "Sounds like a very interesting life to me. Or would you rather dress yourself every day in conventional boredom?"

Charlotte smoothed at the tiny ruffles that trimmed her bodice. "Thank you, Mac. You have a knack of putting problems into the proper perspective."

That drew a rare chuckle. "In my experience, a positive outlook is both practical and pragmatic."

"A very wise observation." Charlotte took up a bottle of

scent and dabbed a bit on the pulse point on her throat. "Let us hope Wrexford will be of the same opinion tonight."

"You're a vision of loveliness," said McClellan. "That should dispel any foul mood lingering from the murder."

"That," replied Charlotte, "will depend on whether or not he has seen A. J. Quill's latest drawing."

She had been relieved when the earl had sent a note yesterday apologizing that due to the complexity of the chemical experiment he wished to perform on the poison, he would be unable to stop by for a visit. A cowardly reaction, she conceded. But her drawing for the printshop and the accompanying wording had taken a great deal of soul-searching. She believed she had been scrupulously fair—Becton deserved that justice be done, and the Royal Society deserved not to have its good name blackened unfairly. However, she was grateful that she didn't have to explain herself to him at that moment.

The maid moved to the armoire to fetch a Kashmir shawl. "Wrexford may not always agree with your choices, but he always respects them."

"Yes, but that doesn't mean he won't express his opinion." A sigh. "In no uncertain terms."

"And you will respond by telling him—tactfully, of course—to go to the devil."

"A rather eccentric arrangement on which to base a marriage," she murmured.

"*One person's heaven is another person's hell,*" observed McClellan, draping the feather-soft wool over Charlotte's bare shoulders. "All that matters is it works for the two of you."

So it does.

"Try to put aside thoughts of death and enjoy the festivities," counseled the maid.

Repressing a shiver on recalling that Kensington Palace had been the site of a previous murder, Charlotte rose and took up her reticule. *The past is the past,* she told herself. *Evil must never be allowed to overshadow Good.*

"Yes, of course. It promises to be a very engaging evening. I'm looking forward to mingling with such an interesting group of scholars."

The earl's carriage arrived at the appointed time, and since Wrexford had fetched the dowager as well, the three of them passed the ride discussing the upcoming trip to his country estate, and the arrangements for hosting her brother's visit.

Alison was quick to remind her that he was expected to arrive sometime during the next few days for the long-awaited family reconciliation. Which did nothing to settle Charlotte's already-jumpy nerves.

"Perhaps we should ask the head gardener at the Royal Botanic Gardens to create the flower arrangements for the chapel and the wedding breakfast," suggested Alison. "Something exotic—"

"Something simple," corrected Charlotte, before the dowager got any grand ideas. "Keep in mind that Wrexford is notorious for his eccentricities. If we were to allow it to turn into a vulgar spectacle, I'd have to do a parody of my own nuptials."

A gleam of unholy amusement flickered beneath the earl's lashes. "I'm sure you would render a very imaginative ball and chain. One that would likely send all the demure Diamonds of the First Water fleeing in terror from the altar of Bliss."

"Hmmph. As if I would suggest anything *vulgar.*" Alison looked a little disappointed at being deprived of a chance to let her imagination run wild. "I never had a chance to attend the first ceremony, so I thought we might make up for it with something special . . ."

Charlotte felt a twinge of guilt. *Choices, choices.* The ramifications had a way of rippling out with unintended consequences. Her youthful elopement had saved her own sanity. But it had hurt people she loved dearly.

"Wrexford's estate has a hothouse, and Hawk has come to

have a keen eye for the whimsical beauty in everyday flowers," she mused. With all the distractions of late, she had been worrying that the boy might feel lost in the shadows. But perhaps . . . "Come to think of it, perhaps the two of you could create something special out of those simple treasures."

A speculative smile brightened the dowager's expression. "The idea holds possibilities."

One challenge solved. As to the others that lay ahead . . .

As the receiving line snaked its way slowly up Kensington Palace's opulent King's Staircase, Wrexford felt the tension thrumming through Charlotte. A sidelong gaze showed a polite smile pasted on her lips, but her eyes had a faraway look, which signaled her thoughts were anywhere but here.

A surmise accentuated by the fact that she had taken no notice of the surrounding art.

"What do you think of the murals?" he murmured, seeking to draw her back to the moment. Alison had paired off with her friend Sir Robert, leaving the two of them to proceed on their own. "They are quite renowned, you know. William Kent was commissioned to create them for George the First in the 1720s. The faces of the figures are said to be courtiers of the day—and include a portrait of himself."

She looked up and studied the walls and ceiling for a long moment. "Kent was an excellent draftsman and colorist."

"I fear the poor fellow has just been damned with faint praise."

"It's lavish decoration, meant to impress, and it suits its purpose quite well," said Charlotte, lowering her voice to a near whisper. "As you know all too well, I prefer art that has some higher purpose."

Something in her tone warned him that he had touched on a raw nerve. But with others close by, he merely raised a brow in question.

Her hand tightened on his arm, a signal he would get no answer right now.

However, a comment from the two gentlemen behind them gave him an inkling of the problem.

"Have you seen the latest commentary from A. J. Quill?" asked one of them. "I swear, that dratted scribbler seems to know everything that goes on within the world of the beau monde. How the devil does he do it?"

"Bribery and blackmail—there's no other explanation," muttered his companion. "I suppose we should consider ourselves lucky. He merely announced that our gala evening at the Royal Botanic Gardens was marred by death, and added a sarcastic speculation at how many exotic poisonous plants poor Becton might have rubbed up against. Let us pray he's not tempted to imply it was deliberate."

"Murder? Oh, surely he wouldn't have the nerve to imply it was murder! Such a charge, no matter how scurrilous, has a way of tainting those who have the misfortune to be touched by it," exclaimed the other man. He cleared his throat and addressed the earl. "Isn't that so, Wrexford?"

The earl turned. "I beg your pardon?"

"A. J. Quill," said the man's companion, "has announced to the world that Mr. Becton shuffled off his mortal coil during the symposium's gala evening at the Royal Botanic Gardens, and made some sly references to poisonous plants. What if his next drawing says it's murder?"

"Well, if A. J. Quill says it," drawled Wrexford, "then it must be true."

Both men uttered embarrassed little laughs.

"Quite right, milord. Quite right," said the man who had drawn him into the conversation. "The idea is, of course, absurd that someone would murder a scholar. But I suppose these gadfly scribblers must seize on any excuse to stir up trouble and sell their wares."

His companion added an apologetic nod to Charlotte. "Forgive us for raising a topic unfit for a lady's ears."

"Think nothing of it," she replied graciously as they reached the top of the landing.

Quickening his steps, Wrexford drew her through the requisite greetings with the president of the Royal Society and on into the King's Gallery.

"So," he murmured, pausing in the shadows of one of the display pedestals, "I take it your current drawing is why you appear a little tense. Were you worried that I would take issue with it?"

"We haven't always agreed in the past—"

"An understatement if ever there was one," he cut in. "And likely we won't in the future." He shifted a little closer to her, feeling the silken skirts of her gown flutter against his trousers. "I may snap and growl, but surely you know I would never seek to silence your pen."

Charlotte lifted her chin. Her expression was coolly composed, but her eyes betrayed a tiny flicker of uncertainty. "I will have new responsibilities to consider."

"None that will ever ask you to crush your conscience."

Her hand was still resting lightly on his sleeve. Holding his gaze, she tightened her fingers in a quick caress. "I wish I was as sure as you are. Worries—unreasonable ones, I know—seem to be clouding my thoughts."

"Understandably so," he responded. "As you so sagely point out to the public, change is frightening, and you are facing a number of changes in your life. But never fear. As I've said before, we shall deal with whatever worries arise."

He looked around. "However, this evening we have more pressing concerns. Come, let us make our way to the King's Drawing Room. Kit and Lady Cordelia are among the invited guests and they may have found some important information for me to pass on to Griffin." As they moved through the gallery, he quickly explained about his meeting with Sheffield.

"You've been far busier than I have in gathering clues," she said. "Some of my contacts around the dockyards may also know . . ." She fell silent as one of the scholars in a group by the refreshment table detached himself from the others and approached her.

"*Ciao, bella* Charlotta!" He bowed in greeting and looked up with a mischievous grin. "Ah, and this must be Mr. Wrexford."

"*Lord* Wrexford," corrected Sheffield, who entered the drawing room just in time to overhear the exchange.

By his expression, noted Wrexford, his friend was also of the opinion that the man's manners left a good deal to be desired.

"A *lord*?" The man widened his eyes and then flashed a wink at Charlotte. "*Santi numi*—Anthony enjoyed calling you milady. To think that you will soon be a *real* one."

Wrexford took an instant dislike to the fellow. Clenching his teeth, he fought to keep his temper in check.

She gave a tight smile. "Marco, allow me to introduce my fiancé, the Earl of Wrexford. And our friend, Mr. Christopher Sheffield." To the two of them, she added, "This is Marco Moretti, an old friend from my time in Rome."

Wrexford gave a gruff nod, not trusting himself to speak.

Sheffield, however, showed no such restraint. "Actually, Lady Charlotte has always been a lady, in every sense of the word, Signore Moretti," he said in a low voice. "It would be wise for you to have a care with what you say here in London, lest you give people the wrong impression about her past."

It seemed to Wrexford that a speculative gleam lit for just an instant in Moretti's eyes.

"Ah, yes, yes," murmured Charlotte's friend with a knowing nod. "Gossip is the same in any country. Innocent comments can be turned into nasty rumors, which can damage a reputation, no matter how spotless. Of course you wish to ensure that doesn't happen."

"Kit, Lady Charlotte looks in need of some champagne," said Wrexford. "Would you kindly escort her to the refreshment table. Signore Moretti and I will join you in a moment."

The Italian smiled as Charlotte followed Sheffield's lead—stirring further temptation to knock several of those pearly teeth down his gullet.

Wrexford took a step closer. "Allow me to correct your misconception. Gossip would be a nuisance for a short while, and then it would give way to some new rumor and be quickly forgotten. You see, not only do I have influence and connections within the highest circles of Society, but it seems I've also earned an unpleasant reputation as a man who doesn't suffer fools gladly. So people go out of their way not to make an enemy of me."

Moretti's expression had turned a little tentative.

"Here in London, an acquaintance reunited with an old friend refrains from acting overly familiar in public. I'm sure you don't wish to cause offense, so I expect you'll keep all further exchanges with my future wife respectful, as is befitting of a gentleman and a scholar. As for any mention of her personal life in Rome, that would be out of place, I think. Especially at a gathering such as this."

The earl bared his own teeth in what only an idiot would take for a smile. "I trust I've made myself clear?"

To his credit, Moretti stiffened to attention and raised his chin. "I comprehend English quite well, sir. So you may be sure there is no misunderstanding between us."

"Excellent."

"I am sorry if my exuberance offended you," continued the Italian. "Charl—that is, Lady Charlotte is a good friend, and I wouldn't ever knowingly do anything that might hurt her."

Perhaps he had misjudged Moretti. Still, there was something he didn't like about the fellow, though Wrexford couldn't put his finger on exactly what it was.

"Well, then, I've no need to keep you any longer from your colleagues." It was a rude dismissal, and Charlotte's friend was well aware of the snub.

He colored slightly, but matched the earl's polite nod and made a dignified retreat.

"Good heavens, what did you say to poor Marco?" murmured Charlotte, once the earl had rejoined her and Sheffield in a secluded spot in the far corner of the room. "He looks as though you just threatened to carve out his liver with a dull penknife."

"Wrex was right to chase him away. There is an air of oiliness to his effusive show of friendship," muttered Sheffield. "He strikes me as a slippery fellow."

"That's unfair." She made a little huff of exasperation. "And unreasonable to form such an instant dislike. Italians are more . . . expressive than we English." Her chin rose a notch. "He was a good and loyal friend to me and Anthony, so I hope you will reserve judgment until you are better acquainted with him."

"Fair enough," growled Wrexford. "But let us put aside Moretti for the moment and hear if Kit has uncovered anything useful about our primary concern."

"I've learned a few things, though I'm unsure of how helpful they will prove," replied Sheffield. "One of my friends in the shipping business, whose trade is based in the West Indies, has heard rumors that Quincy has recently purchased controlling interest in a small Spanish trading company that runs routes between New Granada and Guyana in Spanish America and the French island of Martinique."

Wrexford frowned. "I can't see how that has any relevance to Becton's murder."

"Nor can I," said Sheffield. "I'm simply passing on what I've been told about Quincy—"

"Wait." Charlotte's eyes widened. "Hosack mentioned something about a botanist now working with Quincy on improving yield of American cotton plantations. I believe he said the fellow was a former army officer named Adderley, who tried to steal some specimens from the New Granada viceroy in Spanish America."

"You're right," agreed the earl. "It's a possible connection." He pursed his lips. "And as Adderley is here in London attending the symposium, along with Quincy, Griffin may be able to find out more about him."

"Adderley will be under no obligation to meet with Bow Street," pointed out Charlotte.

"As we all know, there are other ways of getting information about people than to make a polite request," he replied grimly.

Neither of them responded.

"Anything else?" he asked Sheffield.

"One other tidbit, though it's not directly related to Quincy," came the answer. "Another American was a passenger on the same ship that brought Quincy here from New York. A naval captain, granted permission to visit London despite the tensions between our two countries as a concession to the Royal Society and its cordial relations with American scientific societies."

"He is part of the New York scientific delegation to the symposium?" asked Charlotte.

"Actually, he's attending as the representative of the Philadelphia Botanical Society. And curiously enough, it seems that Samuel Daggett is a distant cousin of the country's former president, Thomas Jefferson, and served for some time as his naval adjutant."

"I believe Mr. Jefferson is a man known for his interest in science, as well as the arts and literature," said Charlotte.

"He also showed a taste for fine wine and witty women during his time as American envoy to Paris," remarked the earl dryly. "He's now a private citizen. Are you implying he arranged for Becton's murder in order to steal the formula for himself?"

Put that way, it sounded absurd. By all accounts, Jefferson was an honorable and much-admired man.

"It's unlikely, but still, it's a connection that can't be ignored," said Charlotte, though she knew she was grasping at straws.

"Perhaps Lady Cordelia will have learned something more substantial." A note of apology shaded Sheffield's voice. "I'll keep making inquiries. Ships arrive every day from the other side of the Atlantic, so there's always fresh news."

Wrexford nodded, but on spotting Lord Bethany, the secretary of the Royal Society, making his entrance into the drawing room, he let out a reluctant sigh. "I had better go speak with Bethany and discuss how the Society intends to handle Becton's death."

Charlotte gave a wry grimace.

"I will counsel him to hold off on any mention of murder," he went on. "Let the villain who committed it think his cleverness has fooled everyone. Hubris leads to making mistakes."

"Let us hope that is so," murmured Charlotte as the earl walked away. She couldn't help but wonder whether she had committed an error in judgment by making the death known to the public. She had done so to make sure the authorities could not decide to turn a blind eye on the crime. The Royal Society would be happy to see the matter quietly buried, whether or not the killer was ever caught. But . . .

Looking up from her brooding, she caught Sheffield watching her in concern. But before he could speak, they were interrupted by Sir Robert, the dowager's good-natured friend from the gala evening at the Royal Botanic Gardens.

"Ah, Lady Charlotte—there you are! Might I steal Her Ladyship away from you, sir?" he said to Sheffield, and then flashed a reproachful smile at her. "You must make amends for abandoning me at last night's supper by coming and meeting a few of our visiting scholars from afar."

"I would be delighted to do so," she said.

Sheffield stepped aside, an inscrutable look flickering in his gaze. "Indeed, it's an evening for convivial conversations, and mingling with friends, both old and new."

Was that an oblique urging to step away from any further investigation of the murder? She understood his worries. Ye gods, she had them, too . . .

Sir Robert offered his arm, and together they rounded the table holding the punch bowl and joined a group of scholars engaged in what looked to be an animated discussion, German and English mixing with a smattering of Latin.

"Now, now—mind your language, gentlemen," counseled Sir Robert. "There is a lady present."

A reed-thin man, with a shock of dark hair greying at the temples and a pair of steel-rimmed spectacles perched on his beaky nose, turned and clicked his heels together as he bowed. "*Dankeschön*, madam, for compelling us to be civilized in our disagreement over certain details of Linnaeus's classification system."

"Herr von Stockhausen believes he has created a more precise method," murmured one of the Royal Society scholars, after the formal introductions were made. His voice held a note of thinly veiled skepticism.

"I've been told that discussing different points of view regarding scientific matters is how advances come to be made," responded Charlotte.

"A *very* wise observation, madam!" responded von Stockhausen. "Have you an interest in botany?"

"I draw the occasional flower, but have no claim to any expertise on the subject," she replied, which earned a round of polite chuckles.

"I would very much like to see some of your artwork, Lady

Charlotte," said one of the other Royal Society scholars with a gallant smile.

Be careful what you wish for, thought Charlotte as she inclined a gracious nod. "Actually, it is my young ward who has quite a talent for botany and botanical illustration. I have brought him to the gardens at Kew on several occasions to sketch . . ."

The talk quickly turned to plants, and the gentlemen all offered suggestions concerning what species might interest a curious boy. Von Stockhausen, in particular, made some interesting recommendations. He seemed very knowledgeable on flowering plants, and seemed to have a good eye for color and detail.

"Thank you for the advice," she said, once everyone had finished. "I know you have serious scholarly subjects to discuss, so I should allow you to get back to your work."

Spotting a footman circulating through the crowd with a tray of sparkling wine, Sir Robert quickly said, "Allow me to offer you some refreshments, Lady Charlotte. The Society always serves a very fine champagne."

She accepted his arm. Wrexford was nowhere to be seen among the sea of strangers . . .

"I've heard the Americans are represented very well at the symposium," Charlotte observed, once they had their drinks in hand, "despite the long ocean voyage and the troubles between our countries."

"Indeed! We are all friendly allies in the world of science," he responded. "It's a pity the politicians and military men aren't as collegial as we are. Our government takes pains to paint the Americans as an uncouth, belligerent people. However, I find them very interesting and erudite."

Charlotte took a sip of her wine. "Yes, generalities are rarely accurate. I had the pleasure of meeting Dr. Hosack at the Royal Botanic Gardens, and he strikes me as a very admirable gentleman. So it's always best to judge for yourself, isn't it?"

"Indeed," repeated Sir Robert, lifting his glass in salute. "Would you care to meet the rest of his countrymen? I believe they are in the adjoining room, admiring one of the palace's grand treasures—the eighteenth-century musical clock known as the 'Temple of the Four Great Monarchies of the World.'"

"I would very much like that." She added a coy smile. "As well as to see the grand clock."

"This way." Looking pleased by her interest, Sir Robert led her through the archway and into the adjoining Cupola Room, another magnificent chamber designed in the Italianate style and decorated with murals by William Kent.

"Ah, there is Captain Daggett standing with Dr. Hosack at the far side of the pedestal," pointed out Sir Robert.

Charlotte would have had no trouble picking out the naval officer, even if he hadn't been in uniform. His well-weathered face, scoured by wind and salt into austere angles, stood out in a sea of pale, soft-featured scholars. Sun had bronzed his skin and gilded his auburn hair with golden highlights.

In response to something Hosack said, he shifted slightly, setting off a rippling of lithe muscle beneath his coat.

A tiger among toothless tabbies, thought Charlotte.

Did that make him dangerous? She was quick to remind herself that appearances could be deceiving. There was likely a murderer among the guests tonight, but it would be foolish to leap to conclusions.

As Sir Robert led her closer, Daggett turned and she caught a flash of his ocean-blue eyes. Her flesh began to tingle, as if touched by the cold steel of a naval saber.

"Lady Charlotte, how lovely to see you again." Hosack, to his credit, schooled his expression to hide any hint that their acquaintance was more than superficial. "May I present my fellow American—and scholar—Captain Samuel Daggett."

"So for the duration of this symposium, the pen shall be mightier than the sword, eh?" quipped Sir Robert. "Ha, ha, ha."

"A sword should only be unsheathed as a last resort,"

replied Daggett. He acknowledged Charlotte with a small bow. "Milady."

"Quite right," agreed Hosack. "May our two countries settle their differences with words, not steel."

"You must have a very keen interest in botany, sir, to have managed to arrange all the official permissions to be here," said Charlotte.

"A sailor has much time for solitary study," responded Daggett. "As it happens, my presence here has a very practical purpose. Like Dr. Hosack, I'm interested in the medicinal use of plants. Men at sea can fall prey to a vast array of illnesses. You have only to look at scurvy and how we've learned to conquer it—with lemons, limes, and oranges—to understand the importance of botany. So attending symposiums like this one, as well as being part of a scientific society when I am ashore, allows me to further my knowledge and perhaps prevent needless deaths."

"A very admirable sentiment," said Sir Robert. "And I'm sure it's one appreciated by your government."

"An officer's duty is to serve his country."

Charlotte couldn't argue with the captain's sentiments. But he struck her as a bit of a prig, and someone with a ruthless dedication to rules and regulations. And in her experience, freedom of imagination was what helped to spark creativity. She would be greatly surprised if Daggett made any momentous scientific discovery.

As the group began to discuss the schedule of lectures for the following day, Charlotte found her attention wandering. Spotting Moretti across the room, she gave an inward cringe on recalling Wrexford's rudeness. Marco had been a loyal friend to her, and without his stalwart support during her husband's black moods, life in Rome would have been a good deal harder.

She owed him an apology—

A courtly greeting suddenly cut through the hum of conversation, the mellifluous voice coiling and coiling like a cobra around her rib cage.

Her heart squeezed to a stop.

Breathe, she told herself. *Just breathe.*

By sheer strength of will, Charlotte regained control of her emotions and forced air into her lungs. She wouldn't—she couldn't—betray any hint of weakness.

Not to this monster.

Slowly, slowly, she pivoted to face Justinian DeVere.

CHAPTER 7

"DeVere!" Sir Robert sounded surprised. "I wasn't aware that you had returned to England."

"I only just arrived."

From his sleek, silver-threaded hair and patrician profile to his perfectly tied cravat and well-tailored evening clothes, De-Vere was the very picture of a faultless English gentleman. Charlotte, however, knew better.

"Thank heaven the wind and weather were in our favor," continued DeVere. "The symposium promises to be a memorable event, what with the impressive array of international scholars gathered for the occasion. I simply felt I couldn't miss it."

DeVere's companion, a tall, handsome man with an oily smile, looked to Hosack and quickly assumed a mournful expression. "What a shock about Becton. I knew his heart was weak, but . . ." He shook his head. "A cruel twist of fate that it should happen now. My condolences—I know the two of you were good friends."

"Thank you, Quincy," replied the doctor.

"We, too, were close," replied Quincy, and then heaved a

sigh. "Indeed, we were on the verge of entering into a partnership. But alas, now that is not to be."

A tiny frown pinched between Hosack's brows, but it was gone in an instant. "Let us turn the talk to more pleasant things. Allow me to introduce Lady Charlotte—"

"Mr. DeVere and I are acquainted with each other," she said.

"Indeed, we are." DeVere inclined a well-mannered bow. "Congratulations on your upcoming nuptials."

She acknowledged his words with a cold smile.

"And tell me, how is your dear cousin Nicholas?"

Her face froze for an instant. How *dare* DeVere have the gall to ask such a question!

His role in the horrific Bloody Butcher murders of the previous year—the spree had left one of her cousins dead and his twin brother unfairly accused of the crime—had never been made public. The authorities had deemed that revealing the truth would result in a scandal that might do irreparable harm to the highest circles of Society. Granted, DeVere hadn't actually wielded a weapon. His crime had been one of omission, as he had not lifted a finger to prevent his ward from carrying out her mad scientific experiments.

But to Charlotte, who had nearly lost her own life in stopping the madness, he was guilty as sin.

"Nicholas is settling into his duties as Baron Chittenden," she replied. "But he misses his brother terribly."

"Understandably so, after such an unfortunate tragedy," he replied calmly. "But time eventually dulls the pain of such loss."

"Does it?" Charlotte held his gaze, refusing to flinch.

It was DeVere who looked away. "Dr. Hosack, do I guess right in assuming the officer with whom you were just chatting is Captain Daggett?" he asked.

It was as if she had ceased to exist.

"Quincy and I have heard excellent things about his scientific expertise," continued DeVere. "Might I ask you to introduce us?"

Hosack complied, and in the ensuing exchange of pleasantries, Charlotte learned that DeVere had spent the last year in the Unites States, including a lengthy stay in the city of New York, where he had become a member of the same scientific society as Hosack and Becton. A chill snaked down her spine at the discovery that he had a connection, however slight, to Becton's murder. The cloak of Evil fit him even more perfectly than his elegant evening clothes, and she couldn't help but speculate . . .

"If you'll excuse me, gentlemen," she murmured. "While you discuss your scientific matters, I really ought to return to the King's Gallery and see if my friends have arrived."

The polite responses fuzzed by the ringing in her ears, Charlotte withdrew into one of the side corridors that led in a roundabout way back to the main entrance. To her relief, the shadowed passageway was deserted. Slowing her steps to a halt, she drew in several quick gulps of air, willing her heart to stop thumping against her ribs.

"Lady Charlotte."

The devil-damned voice was hardly more than a whisper and yet it sounded loud as cannon fire to her ears.

She turned.

In the low light, the silvery threads in DeVere's hair seemed to pulse with an unnatural glow.

"Since we shall be finding ourselves moving within the same circles of Polite Society, I suggest we put the past behind us. What is done is done. There's no reason we can't both be civilized about this."

Charlotte stared at him in disbelief. "*Civilized?*"

"A few unfortunate mishaps—"

"How *dare* you speak as if a toy soldier was broken or a child's ball punctured." Fury, bitter and burning as acid, rose in

Charlotte's gorge. "My cousin was foully murdered because of your obsession with . . ." She hitched in a breath. "With fame, with immortality, but most of all with your overweening hubris."

DeVere's smile was coolly mocking in its utter lack of emotion. "It seems you are a female of hopelessly overwrought sensibilities, Lady Charlotte. Wrexford is a pragmatic man, who doesn't allow emotions to cloud his judgment. Perhaps he'll shake some sense into you, once you're under his thumb."

Most people assumed Wrexford's heart was carved out of granite and ice. They were much mistaken.

"Your delusions have only grown more pronounced," replied Charlotte.

He took a step closer, his eyes narrowing, turning the irises black as onyx. "You seem to forget that I, too, lost a loved one. I don't know exactly what happened in the laboratory, but any rational man would assume that you were responsible."

Charlotte maintained a steely silence.

"My ward was very dear to me, and yet I'm willing to let bygones be bygones. I suggest that for the good of everyone, you do the same."

"Is that a threat, Mr. DeVere?"

"Good heavens, no." His well-shaped mouth curled upward. "I'm not the type of man who makes threats."

No, your malevolence is far more subtle.

DeVere waited for a moment, but Charlotte decided not to give him the satisfaction of provoking a reaction.

"Speaking of wards, how is that delightful little boy for whom you serve as guardian?"

The floor suddenly felt as if it had tilted beneath her feet. Somehow she managed to maintain her equilibrium as he continued.

"Such a bright fellow, so full of curiosity and imagination," continued DeVere. "You ought to send him to me for lessons in botany. He deserves to be tutored by someone with expertise in the subject so that his talents are properly nurtured."

Over my dead body.

"Be assured," she said, "that Wrexford and I have the boy's education well in hand."

"If you change your mind, you have only to ask." He inclined a nod. "As I said, I don't carry grudges." A pause, and then he turned and walked back through the archway of the Cupola Room.

Charlotte waited until the shadows ceased fluttering before slumping back against the wainscoting, her rigid self-control crumbling. Every muscle in her body was quivering, and a sob welled up in her throat.

No, no, no. She couldn't—she wouldn't—allow DeVere to know he had found a chink in her armor. Predators pounced on a weakness. Sucking in a ragged breath, she swallowed hard—

"Charlotte?" Wrexford came around the corner and stopped. Then, in a heartbeat, he was holding her upright.

His palms felt blessedly warm against her flesh.

"You're cold as ice. What's wrong?"

"DeVere," she said through chattering teeth.

"DeVere?"

"He's here," Charlotte explained, Wrexford's presence allowing her to shake off the last lingering bit of panic. "He sailed over from New York with Quincy. Apparently, he headed to America when he left England." She repressed a shiver on recalling his words. "He told Sir Robert that he had been drawn to the country by its reputation as a land of opportunity."

The earl muttered a low oath. "I wondered where he was. I assumed he had returned to India."

"Would that he was half a world away," she whispered.

Wrexford caressed her cheek and let his fingertips linger. "He can't hurt us, my love. The authorities know his dirty little secret, and that in itself will keep him on his best behavior. I doubt he wants to reopen Pandora's box, given that all the evils shoved into its darkest crevasses are tied to him."

Perhaps not, but I think he's willing to risk it.

Charlotte looked up. "He threatened Hawk."

The warmth of Wrexford's touch disappeared when for an instant his hand clenched into a fist. He forced it to relax, but the look in his eye would have spooked the Devil himself.

"Not in so many words," she added. "He's far more insidious than that. He suggested that we put the past behind us, acting, of course, like a perfectly reasonable gentleman. But we both know he's not."

The earl's expression hardened. "Two can play at cat and mouse, my love. There are ways of exerting pressure that will cause him to think twice about attempting to hurt our family."

She wished she could believe that. But . . .

"Wrexford, he's mad. Not in a way that is obvious to others. Which makes him all the more dangerous. It's a question of obsession. He wants to go down in history among the great minds of science. And he'll do anything—*anything*—to achieve his goal."

She paused as he drew in a measured breath, then hurried on before he could respond. "To him, murder is no obstacle to obtaining what he wants. Given his friendship with Quincy, it seems he's found a new idea of how to grab the fame and glory for which he so desperately yearns."

"That's a logical assumption," replied Wrexford. "But actual evidence often proves it's dangerous to leap to conclusions. Griffin will be thorough in investigating Becton's murder. We must trust him—"

"Of course I trust him," interrupted Charlotte. "But you can't think that I can turn away from this now, and leave it to others to solve the murder."

He looked away for a moment, the muddled gloom making it impossible to read his expression.

"I can't turn away," she said simply. "This is no longer a crime that doesn't touch us. DeVere has made it personal."

"We don't know that for sure yet. But regardless, I promise you that he won't harm those we love." He twined his hand with hers. "We need to return to the soiree. Given our absence from the festivities at the Royal Botanic Gardens, it's best not to stir further speculation."

Stirring speculation was not to be wished for. But its threat paled in comparison to having a poisonous serpent once again slithering through their world.

CHAPTER 8

"Hell's bells." Sheffield took a gulp of wine after Charlotte finished giving an account of her encounter with DeVere, and then blew out his breath.

Wrexford had found his friend with Cordelia, and together with Charlotte, the four of them had moved to a secluded spot in the small portrait gallery off the King's Drawing Room. Under the guise of admiring the paintings, they were able to have a private conversation.

"That's bloody awful news," added Sheffield, after another quick swallow of his drink.

Cordelia nodded in grim agreement, her face creasing in concern as she looked at Charlotte. "I can't believe he's returned to London out of sentimental yearning. He's here for only one reason—to gain something he wants very badly."

Revenge. That was Wrexford's immediate thought. Like Charlotte, he had no illusions as to DeVere's true character. The so-called gentleman's polished veneer—courtly manners, elegant parties, immense wealth, and taste, which he used as a generous patron of the arts and sciences—hid a dark rot that had eaten away at his soul.

There was a certain irony to the evening, decided Wrexford, as he took in the stately surroundings. The graceful melody of the string quartet . . . the sparkle of the bubbling champagne . . . the sonorous tones of conversation . . . the sumptuous art . . . the distinguished guests . . .

And among them was a cunning killer.

However, he wasn't as quick as Charlotte was to conclude that DeVere was the guilty party. Granted his expertise in exotic plants and his utter disregard for human life were marks against him. However, Wrexford was familiar enough with the world of science to be aware of the jealousies, the fierce ambitions, and the fight for accolades and acclaim that swirled within all the high-minded scientific societies. There were likely a number of possible suspects.

Which made their task all the more difficult.

He released a terse sigh. Charlotte had taken up the challenge. And like a mastiff with a bone clamped between its jaws, she wouldn't surrender it until justice was done. She was so damnably stubborn, so damnably principled.

He loved her for her passions. But they scared him half to death.

Charlotte fisted her hands in her silken skirts and moved closer to the mullioned window, drawing the earl's attention back to the moment.

"I think we have a good idea of what he wants," she murmured, finally responding to Cordelia's comment.

Charlotte's revelation had come first, but Wrexford sensed that Cordelia was also anxious to share some news.

"I think we can all *guess*," said Sheffield. "But no doubt Wrex will warn us—"

"*Not* to jump to conclusions," intoned Cordelia.

"I don't disagree with him," said Charlotte. "I'm merely saying, *Where there is smoke, there is likely fire.*"

"But let us be alert to the fact that several different blazes may be contributing to the haze," cautioned Cordelia.

Charlotte's expression sharpened. "You've found some other clue?"

"Perhaps." Cordelia looked around to make sure they were still alone before continuing. "I had one of our clerks cozy up to a sailor from the American naval frigate. It seems Captain Daggett's last assignment was conveying several government envoys to Martinique for talks on trade between the French islands and America."

Sheffield frowned in thought. "You think the Americans—Daggett, Quincy, and Adderley—may be working together, and that DeVere is merely a chance acquaintance?"

"I'm merely pointing it out as a possibility," answered Cordelia.

"There are," mused Wrexford, "a number of dangling threads . . ."

The rustle of silk at the entrance to the portrait gallery warned that their council of war was about to be over.

"But whether any of them tie together remains to be seen."

Threads. Was there one that she might grasp and turn into a drawing without giving too much away?

Splashing water on her face, Charlotte contemplated the question as she began her ablutions the next morning. In many ways, she was caught between a rock and a stone. DeVere's perfidy had been kept a strict secret on orders from the highest echelons of the government, as they had feared the scandal would taint both the aristocracy and the august scientific institutions of the country. As a result, the Royal Society and the Royal Institution had no idea that DeVere's decision to leave England for an extended period of foreign travel was for any reason other than curiosity.

Or perhaps mourning. The scientific world had all been

greatly saddened by the news of his ward's accidental death during an experiment with electricity in her laboratory. Much admired for her beauty, grace, and intellect, Lady Julianna Aldrich had been seen as an extraordinarily gifted student of science . . . rather than a murderous monster.

Charlotte expelled a sigh, knowing there would be hell to pay if A. J. Quill ever hinted at the truth. The government would be furious, and the repercussions would fall on Griffin and Wrexford . . . not to speak of herself, who had been seen as another of Lady Julianna's victims.

She couldn't afford to stir such scrutiny.

"Damnation, if I want to hint that he's evil, it must be over something in the present," she muttered. Which was all the more reason to learn the truth about Becton's murder.

After stabbing the last hairpins into her coiled topknot, she rose and headed down to the kitchen.

The aromas of breakfast—strong coffee, frying gammon, fresh-baked bread—wafted out from the half-open door, along with the clatter of pans and the cheerful banter between McClellan and the boys.

Her heart gave a lurch at the thought of DeVere's veiled threat to her family.

"How was the palace?" asked Hawk through a mouthful of shirred eggs. "Mr. Linsley says it's filled with magnificent paintings."

"Don't speak with your mouth full," chided McClellan as she handed Charlotte a steaming mug of coffee.

"The paintings are splendid," she replied, taking a seat at the worktable. "It's a very impressive place."

"I wouldn't want to live in a palace," said Raven, after slathering strawberry jam on a piece of toast and cramming it into his mouth.

The maid winced. "Just as well, as your table manners are more suited to a barn. And that's maligning the horses, who make far less of a mess chewing their oats."

The boys both chortled and helped themselves to the sultana muffins she had just brought to the table.

"Hmmph." The warning sound, however, was softened by a smile.

Charlotte took a swallow of the scalding brew, willing its warmth to loosen the knot in the pit of her stomach.

McClellan, who missed very little, set a fist on her hip. "Is something wrong?"

Both Raven and Hawk stopped chewing.

She had already decided that they all had to be apprised of the danger. Having grown up in the slums, the boys were no strangers to evil. They wouldn't be frightened.

Though she wished they would be. DeVere was more cunning than most miscreants in that his charm hid the depths of his depravity.

"Yes," she replied simply. "I discovered a very unsettling thing last night. Mr. DeVere has returned to London."

The maid let out a sharp hiss.

Placing his elbows on the table, Raven leaned forward and looked up expectantly, waiting for her to go on. Neither of the boys knew exactly what had taken place in the secret laboratory within the DeVere mansion. But they knew that Lady Julianna had not survived.

"He blames Wrexford and me for the death of his ward," continued Charlotte, making no effort to turn a sow's ear into a silk purse. "And I have reason to believe he may seek revenge by harming one of you two."

"*An eye for an eye,*" murmured McClellan.

"Yes," said Charlotte. "And so I want you both to be extra vigilant whenever you leave this house." The boys, she knew, were savvy beyond their years, and had eluded all sorts of mortal perils. But all it took was one lightning-quick strike that they didn't see coming . . .

"I don't know if he's aware of this residence. But he certainly knows the location of Wrexford's townhouse, and we'll soon be living there. I don't wish to alarm you, but there's a chance he may decide to have people watch your comings and goings."

Raven made a rude sound. "We've already mapped out a way to slip in and out of His Lordship's back gardens with nobody seeing us. And as for surveillance, our street friends will have any spies spotted in a trice."

Charlotte couldn't help but respond with a look of concern. Their closest friends were no longer in London . . .

As if reading her thoughts, Raven quickly explained, "Our network is as strong as ever. Billy Bones and his gang are now sweeping the streets where Skinny and Pudge worked. And Ghillie has taken over Alice the Eel Girl's work."

"Oiy—there's always plenty of urchins to fill in any holes," piped up Hawk.

The matter-of-fact way he said it tugged at Charlotte's heart. She and Wrexford had made life better for some of the homeless children roaming the streets. But there were so many more.

She took another swallow of coffee, using the moment to surreptitiously study the boys over the rim of her mug. When she had first met them, their whole world revolved around two basic needs—staying safe from predators and finding enough scraps of food to survive. They were now safe, they were loved, they were nurtured. More than that, they had discovered passions—mathematics and science for Raven, art and botany for Hawk—that gave them entrée into a whole new realm of possibilities.

Their lives certainly seemed to be better. But were they happy? Truly happy? Raven was fiercely independent and chafed against the strictures of rules. Perhaps he regretted the loss of his unfettered freedom.

"Are you sorry to be moving into Wrexford's townhouse?" she asked abruptly. "It will likely mean a more regimented life. Being part of a family brings responsibilities and duties."

Both boys looked thoughtful. And though she saw Hawk

dart a sidelong glance at his older brother, she had recently noted that he was beginning to voice his own opinions.

"Like what responsibilities and duties?" asked Raven.

A very logical question. "Like escorting Aunt Alison to an exhibit at the British Museum this afternoon after your lessons," answered Charlotte. "She doesn't wish to go alone, and as I am meeting with Wrexford and can't accompany her, I would feel more comfortable if a family member goes with her, rather than one of her dowager friends, in case she becomes fatigued and needs a shoulder to lean on."

"That's not a duty, that's a treat." Raven grinned. "She'll take us to Gunter's after the visit and ply us with sweets."

"Yes, well, not everything that is asked of you will be sugar and spice."

"S'all right," said Hawk softly. "We . . . we like being part of a family."

Raven's grin stretched a touch wider. "Oiy, it's better than a kick in the arse."

McClellan gave a warning rap with a cooking spoon to the top of Raven's head. "Bad language from you Weasels won't be tolerated within the earl's residence."

A snicker. "Wrexford says a *lot* worse words than *arse.*"

Hawk brushed the crumbs from his chin and slipped down from his stool. "We had better go, or we'll be late to our lessons with Mr. Linsley."

"You'll need to return here and dress in your best clothes before going to meet Aunt Alison."

Raven rolled his eyes, but didn't utter a protest. "I was thinking . . ." He, too, rose from his seat. "After we finish doing our duty with Aunt Alison, we could pay a visit to the docklands this evening and ask around for any gossip about the American ships and their passengers."

Charlotte drew in a troubled breath. The last thing she wanted was to draw the boys further into an investigation in-

volving DeVere. "Why would you think I need any information about the Americans?"

He angled his brows in a frightfully accurate imitation of the
earl's skeptical scowl. "I'm rather good at mathematics, m'lady.
I can put two and two together."

His brother tried to stifle a chortle.

"It was an American who was murdered," explained Raven,
"and his colleague, Dr. Hosack, is friends with Mr. Tyler. *Ergo*
it seems likely that you and Lord Wrexford are going to help
solve the crime."

"You're being impertinent," said McClellan.

"No, I ain't," he retorted. "I'm being truthful."

Charlotte put down her mug and crouched down to bring
herself eye level with the boy. She knew it was pointless to forbid them. Like her, they were impossibly stubborn when it
came to loyalty. But she could demand a compromise. "You
must take extreme care to dress as ragged urchins. DeVere has
met Hawk, and I don't doubt he'll find a way to meet you. He's
clever and observant, and if he connects street urchins poking
around in places they shouldn't be with this household, he may
look a lot closer at all of us."

Understanding flickered in Raven's eyes.

"As I said, being part of a family has responsibilities and
ramifications," she said softly.

"What does *ramifications* mean?" asked Hawk.

"It's like when you throw a stone into the water," answered
Raven, though his eyes remained on Charlotte. "The ripples
fan out and may do damage in places you weren't aiming to hit."

She nodded.

"We'll be very careful," he added. "I promise."

Alas, promises, however solemn, weren't always enough to
ward off harm. But Charlotte put aside such dark thoughts for
now, not wishing to appear too grim. *Iuventuti nil arduum. To
the young, nothing is difficult.* The boys had proved their met-

tle in other dangerous situations. She would have to trust their innate gift for staying a half step ahead of the Devil's pitchfork.

"You had better be off," she replied. "It would be rude to keep Mr. Linsley waiting."

As the front door slammed shut behind them, McClellan began to tidy up the kitchen. "So, what's your next move?"

Charlotte had been asking herself that since waking. "I'm not sure. But I've arranged to meet Wrexford at Hatchards bookstore later this morning to discuss what steps we intend to take."

"Which, don't forget, include walking down a church aisle in the near future."

Charlotte blinked, feeling a tiny clench of guilt on realizing that thoughts of murder and DeVere's unwelcome reappearance had nudged marriage from her mind. "As if I could possibly forget that," she murmured.

The clang of pot against pot muffled the maid's snort.

Indeed, the thought of Wrexford becoming elementally entwined in her life was a source of joy that defied words. *Which is just as well,* she mused wryly. While they were extremely eloquent on any number of subjects, expressions of love still didn't come easily to their tongues. *We are both careful. Guarded. Wary of allowing anyone to touch our hearts.*

Perhaps the intimacy of marriage would change that.

A sudden flush of heat stirred an odd, prickling sensation, as if tiny dagger points were dancing down her spine. Charlotte pressed her palms to her cheeks, sure they were aflame.

Desire. A gossamer-soft flutter tickled against her rib cage, like butterflies coming alive in the first rays of dawn.

"If you are heading to Hatchards, I had better go change into more suitable attire for a lady's maid and come along, too." McClellan's gruff Scottish burr stilled such private thoughts as she wiped her hands on her apron.

In response, Charlotte muttered an unladylike word. Lud, how she resented all the silly strictures that hobbled her freedom.

The maid shrugged. "You're a mysterious widow engaged to the most notorious bachelor in London. Polite Society is abuzz with curiosity. People will be watching you."

"And hoping I do something outrageously awful." She grimaced. "I'm tempted to oblige."

"Wait until the vows are made. As a married lady—and one with a high-ranking title—you'll merely be considered eccentric when you break the rules, not scandalous. Think of the Duchess of York."

"How very reassuring," said Charlotte dryly. The duchess was known for her menagerie of pets—including a number of exotic animals—which lived in sumptuous splendor at her country estate, as she much preferred them to people. "However, I shall do my best to stay out of the public's eye."

"You have an advantage there," pointed out McClellan, "as you're the one telling them what to see."

"Mr. Gillray is just as influential as I am," replied Charlotte. James Gillray was another of London's sharp-eyed satirical artists, and his commentary was often more cutting than hers. "And his network of informants is very good. So let us have a care about spitting in the face of Luck."

McClellan took up a pinch of salt from the dish on the stove and tossed it over her shoulder. "An old Scottish superstition for warding off evil."

"I wouldn't have expected you, of all people, to believe in such fiddle-faddle."

"I may be pragmatic, milady, but I'm not stupid." The maid wiped her hands on the front of her apron again, then untied the strings. "There is much we don't understand about the workings of the universe, so it's best to keep an open mind."

It was very sage advice. For any number of reasons.

"Well, then, much as the rules of the beau monde make no

sense to me, we had better go dress to play our roles of perfect propriety."

An hour later, the two of them entered Hatchards, McClellan dutifully trailing a discreet distance behind Charlotte. They were early, and as Wrexford was nowhere to be seen, Charlotte wandered into the section devoted to books on flora and fauna, intent on looking for an illustrated volume that might interest Hawk.

Perhaps an edition of Maria Sibylla Merian's art—

"Charlotta?" The voice floated out from one of the small nooks created by the shelves.

Marco. She sidestepped a pile of books on the floor and joined him within the secluded space.

"If Lord Wrexford is with you, let us move to a more public place," he said, darting a quick look over her shoulder. "I'd rather not attend the rest of the symposium sporting a blackened eye."

"He'll be arriving shortly, but I promise you there will be no threat of bodily harm," replied Charlotte. "I owe you an apology. Wrexford is . . . reserved. However, I've explained to him that he misunderstood your enthusiasm."

"Hmmph." Moretti's expression betrayed a momentary flicker of injured pride.

Men. In many respects, they were far more sensitive than women.

"The earl strikes me as a fellow who doesn't like to have his judgment questioned," added her friend. His brows drew together. "Forgive me, but as an old friend, I feel beholden to say . . ." He cleared his throat. "To say that I hope you are not making a mistake. You were never a . . . how do you English say it . . . a wilting violet, so—"

"I assure you, there's no cause for concern," she cut in. "Wrexford and I are well matched. Yes, we butt heads on occasion, but I think it does both of us good."

That drew a ghost of a smile. "Anthony was a trifle too delicate for butting heads. You were always very gentle with him."

Their eyes met and a flash of understanding passed between them.

"As were you." Charlotte shifted her stance. "But let us talk about the present, not the past. Are you enjoying the symposium?"

"Very much so. It's a great privilege to meet members of the Royal Society, who are the leaders in botanical knowledge." His face came alight. "Last night at Kensington Palace, I was introduced to Sir Joseph Banks!"

Sir Joseph was one of the luminaries of the scientific world.

"And as I mentioned," he continued, "there is a possibility of a patron for my current work."

"That's wonderful," she replied.

Moretti had always possessed a very sharp mind, as well as the ambition to make a name for himself. A frustrating combination, when one was poor as a church mouse. But unlike her late husband, Moretti had possessed the grit and resilience to pursue his passion, despite all the obstacles.

"Might I inquire—"

"No, no." Exaggerating a grimace, her friend held up his hands and waved off any further words. "It's bad luck to say anything more until the agreement is finalized."

"Very well. But allow me to wish you good luck—and good fortune."

"*Sì,* that is acceptable."

Hearing Wrexford's voice resonate in one of the outer rooms, Charlotte placed a hand on Moretti's sleeve. "The earl has arrived. Let us go greet him."

"If you don't mind, I prefer to remain here and continue my search for a certain book," he replied.

She had forgotten that a prickly pride had been a volatile part of Moretti's temperament. It had always rubbed him a little raw that the students who possessed wealth and social status, rather than talent, waltzed through doors that were closed to him.

"As you wish." Perhaps she could convince Wrexford to go out of his way to be pleasant at the next symposium gathering . . .

The sound of footsteps was coming closer.

"*Ciao*, Marco," she murmured, and then slipped out of the alcove.

CHAPTER 9

"Ah, there you are." Wrexford glanced at the shadowed opening between the shelves, a tiny frown tugging at the corners of his mouth. "McClellan said you were looking for a certain book. Have you found it?"

"I believe I have." Charlotte had spotted a portfolio of botanical illustrations by Merian just before Moretti's greeting had distracted her. Backing up a few steps, she turned and plucked it from the shelf, then hurried to join him.

The earl offered his arm.

Smiling, Charlotte set her hand on his sleeve, only to find it was rigid as steel. But as she looked up in question, his lashes flicked in a warning to hold her tongue.

"It's a pleasant day," he remarked. "If you've finished your shopping, I thought we might take a stroll in Green Park."

"Of course."

They made their way out to Piccadilly Street, McClellan trailing along behind them to maintain the rules of propriety.

"Was that Moretti with whom you were speaking?" he asked as they turned into the park and started down one of the side footpaths.

"It was," she answered, a little nettled by his tone. "Why do you ask?"

Gravel crunched underfoot as Wrexford walked on in silence, the brim of his hat casting just enough shadow to muddle the top half of his profile.

Crunch, crunch. His pace slowed as the path led through a small copse of trees. "Because he worries me," he finally answered.

Marco? It seemed so absurd that she almost laughed. However, his expression stilled her mirth. "Good Lord, surely you're not jealous."

"I have many faults," he replied. "That is not one of them." Catching her frown, he added, "Both Kit and I sense something self-serving about him. Which makes us question whether he can be trusted."

"You judge him on a fleeting few minutes? That's terribly unfair—and unlike you, Wrexford."

"Nonetheless, that's my impression," he responded. "You've been urging me to trust my intuition."

"Marco has an inner strength—an ambition to excel, if you will—that perhaps strikes you as aggressive. But to me . . ."

How to explain?

"Within our group of artistic friends in Rome, he and I seemed to be the only ones who possessed a certain pragmatism—and resilience," she said, choosing her words with care. "There were times when Anthony was bedeviled by inner demons . . . I would have felt very alone without Marco's quiet support and sense of humor."

She released a tight sigh. "We were friends, nothing more. But that friendship was important."

"Perhaps I am wrong about him." Wrexford's gaze was on the nearby trees, whose leaves were darkening to shades of autumn and growing brittle around their edges. "But given the stakes, I would rather err on caution."

"What—"

"Allow me to explain," he interrupted, and then paused, taking a long moment to compose his thoughts. "Your cousin was foully murdered—and then, right around the same time, you reappeared in Society. Those two mysteries stirred a number of murmurs and questions, but they quickly died away, as you infrequently appeared in Society."

He turned to face her. "A quiet, retiring widow makes for little sport—the tabbies prefer to chase after bigger game. But our upcoming nuptials have reignited interest in you."

Jealousy. Shakespeare was right about it being a green-eyed monster, reflected Charlotte. Wrexford's wealth and title made him one of the most eligible bachelors in all of Britain. Money and privilege had a way of blunting the sharp edges of his eccentricities and rapier-like tongue, and many highborn ladies with daughters to marry off did not like seeing him snatched up by a stranger to London Society.

"I'm of the opinion that we should do all we can to give them no grist for the gossip mill. Especially with Becton's murder reminding people of old scandals," continued the earl. "That's why your friend Moretti's presence is of great concern to me. His loose-lipped talk of knowing you in Rome raises questions about your past—ones that might turn awfully uncomfortable."

He let his words sink in before pressing on. "You, of all people, know how gossip finds its way into every nook and cranny of the city. Imagine if Gillray gets wind of such titillating rumors. He might very well become curious about a mysterious countess-to-be and seek to uncover the secrets of her past."

Charlotte wished she could deny it. But hadn't the same thought just occurred to her and McClellan this past morning?

"Damnation," she whispered. "I suppose I've turned a blind eye on both those dangers because I didn't wish to see them."

Wrexford remained silent, and that echoed louder than any reproach.

"Gillray has an even more caustic wit than I do," admitted Charlotte, her throat suddenly feeling dry as old bones. "And he's awfully good at sniffing out secrets. I . . . I shall take your warnings to heart."

His face relaxed ever so slightly.

"But still," she couldn't help but add, "Marco is not the sort of fellow who would ever betray a friend."

"Not knowingly perhaps," replied Wrexford. "But a friendly stranger who remarks on his acquaintance with the future Countess of Wrexford would likely elicit any number of details about your life in Rome. Like the fact that your husband was an artist, and you, too, had talent. And that it was the offer of lucrative commissions that brought you back to London."

She felt herself go pale. The thought was a terrifying one— and he was right to frighten her with it. *A few strokes of Gillray's pen, a splash of color, a cutting caption revealing A. J. Quill's identity* . . . her professional life would be over the moment the satirical drawing was hung in the window of Humphrey's Print Shop.

"You often say that no secret is safe in London," said the earl. "So it's imperative to take every precaution. Once we're married, the interest in us will die down again. But until then, I think it best to keep your distance from Moretti."

She nodded, not trusting her voice.

A gust shivered through the trees, rattling the branches.

Drawing her shawl tighter around her shoulders, Charlotte waited for him to offer his arm and resume their walk. But a small shuffling of his boots stirred a niggling suspicion.

When still he didn't take a step, she looked up. "I take it Moretti isn't the only subject you wish to discuss."

"Correct." The earl made a face. "There's been more trouble."

Charlotte waited for him to go on.

"Dr. Hosack's rooms at the Albany Hotel were ransacked

last night, along with the ones occupied by Becton," explained Wrexford. "The doctor was out for the evening, and the porters claim they neither saw nor heard anything suspicious."

"Which likely means—" she began.

"That the culprit was a fellow guest?" finished Wrexford. "Perhaps. But a clever fellow would have no difficulty finding his way into the premises. It's hardly a fortress, and as many of the foreign scholars attending the symposium are staying there, I'm sure there is much coming and going through the main lobby."

"I suppose we can guess what the intruder was after." A tiny furrow creased her brow. "I take it he didn't find what he was looking for?"

Charlotte being Charlotte, she had immediately focused upon the key question.

"Hosack, of course, is adamant that Becton's secret wasn't in his possession," he answered. "After all, he's told us from the beginning that he doesn't know where Becton put his precious discovery for safekeeping once he arrived in England." A pause. It wasn't that he doubted the doctor, but the essence of scientific analysis demanded that one put aside emotion and consider all possible permutations. "However, we have to ask ourselves whether we think the doctor is telling the truth."

"You think he ransacked his own quarters to make it look like he, too, was a victim?"

"It would be a wise move."

She didn't answer right away.

"It turns out that his financial motive for murder is compelling," he continued. "I had a long talk with Tyler. And though he insists that Hosack is an honorable man with a reputation for strong moral principles, he admitted that the doctor had paid all the costs of creating his magnificent Elgin Botanic Garden out of his own pocket, and was forced to sell it to the state of New York as he could no longer afford to fund it."

"Passions make people do desperate things," said Charlotte. "But the fact that he summoned you to investigate, when all signs pointed to a natural death, seems a mark in his favor." She thought for another moment. "And Hosack was with you, so he couldn't have been the man Hawk saw throw the glass into the plantings."

"He could have been an accomplice," suggested Wrexford.

Charlotte shook her head. "It doesn't make sense. Why go through such an elaborate charade when the poisoning would likely have gone unnoticed?"

He acknowledged that the scenario seemed far-fetched.

"I have to agree with Tyler about Hosack's character," she went on. "He strikes me as utterly lacking in guile and ruthlessness . . ."

She hesitated. "There is only one scenario that seems plausible to me—Becton entrusted the formula and specimens to him. And when his friend was murdered, Hosack then decided to keep them for himself, with the plan of claiming the momentous discovery as his own, once he returns to America."

Charlotte took another long moment to consider what she had just sketched out. "The fact is, nobody really knows the exact ingredients Becton used in creating his momentous discovery. There may be nasty speculation if Hosack announces he's created a miracle botanic formula. But he's a respected man of medicine, and America's leading expert on botanicals. So without any solid proof of perfidy, I don't see how he could be stopped from reaping the money and fame from the discovery."

The glade momentarily darkened as a cloud scudded over the sun.

Wrexford chuffed a grunt. "You have a *very* devious mind."

"Oh, come, we both do." A hint of humor shaded her voice. "How else would we be so good at solving crimes?"

"I prefer to call our minds imaginative." Deciding that they ought not linger any longer within the trees, he took her arm and resumed walking. "We are willing to think outside the usual constraints."

"Griffin should be grateful that each of us has a conscience, as well as a brain," she quipped.

"I think it's my purse for which he is most grateful," replied Wrexford. "He can't eat abstract ideals."

A chuckle twined with the flapping of her bonnet's ribbons. "Let us put aside the Runner and his prodigious appetite for now and get back to Becton's murder."

He loved the look of fierce concentration that took hold of her features when she was contemplating a conundrum.

"Can we agree that for now we'll assume Hosack is innocent of any wrongdoing?" continued Charlotte.

"Yes. I agree it's a reasonable conjecture."

"And given the search of Hosack's rooms, can we also agree that it means the murderer hasn't yet acquired the formula and specimens?"

"Yes." Logic certainly pointed to that conclusion.

"Well, then . . ." Charlotte came to an abrupt halt and fixed him with a searching stare. "Where the devil are they?"

Where, indeed? It wasn't as if he hadn't been asking himself the same question.

"My imagination," answered Wrexford, "hasn't quite caught up to that question. However, I have an idea that I want to pursue." He nudged her into motion. "Let us keep moving, so the drawing rooms don't flood with gossip about us having a quarrel in the middle of Green Park."

As the footpath had brought them back to one of the main walkways, the earl spotted a pair of gentlemen coming toward them, walking in the direction of St. James's Palace.

"Lady Charlotte, Lord Wrexford—a lovely day for a stroll in the park, is it not?" Sir Robert paused to incline a friendly bow. "Forgive us if we're interrupting your discussion of wedding details."

Sir Robert's companion, one of Wrexford's fellow members of the Royal Institution, flashed a smile and added, "My advice is to leave all decisions to Her Ladyship." A mischievous twinkle lit his eyes. "Trust me, Wrex, our opinions don't matter."

"On the contrary, I'm always happy to hear Wrexford's advice," replied Charlotte. "That doesn't mean I always follow it."

The gentlemen laughed appreciatively, and after another quick salute, they continued on their way.

"Dear heaven," muttered Charlotte, once they were out of earshot. "I think I've forgotten to speak with your cook about the wedding breakfast. She—"

"She will have it well in hand," he cut in. "Indeed, I wouldn't have the nerve to question her choices. Tyler informs me that she's sworn the kitchen maids to secrecy over the menu."

"She's quite welcome to keep firm hold of the cooking spoon." Charlotte let out a sigh of relief. "I've enough other things on my mind."

They had skirted around the milking sheds and arrived back at Piccadilly Street, where the carriage was waiting.

"I'll leave you and McClellan here." Wrexford seemed equally relieved to drop the matter of wedding details. "I want to head on to Albemarle Street and make some inquiries at the Royal Institution. And then this evening, I'm attending one of the symposium lectures with Dr. Hosack. So perhaps by tomorrow, I'll have some facts, rather than mere speculation to pass on."

"Hmmph." Pursing her lips, McClellan leaned back against the squabs after Charlotte finished recounting her conversation with Wrexford. "So much for the two of you having an interlude of peace and quiet in which to settle into connubial bliss."

"From the very beginning, our relationship has hardly been a traditional one," observed Charlotte. "I suppose there's no reason to start now."

"Actually, I can think of a number of them," replied the maid. "However, I shall remain tactfully silent."

That was probably for the best. Once they started to make a list . . .

The carriage wheels hit a rut in the cobblestones, and all at once, the scenery outside the windowpanes began to blur. Squeezing her eyes shut, Charlotte sought to steady her nerves. It was only now, after repeating it to McClellan, that she realized the conversation with Wrexford had left her badly shaken.

Had she really misjudged Hosack's character, as well as the threat from fellow satirical artist James Gillray? Was it because of overweening hubris?

Or am I simply losing my edge?

The question seemed to unleash all her pent-up fears. Unable to stop them from tangling her thoughts, Charlotte couldn't seem to muster any answers. *Focus, focus.* She stared down at her lap, only to realize she was twisting the fringe of her shawl into knots.

The seat leather creaked as McClellan leaned forward, her thick, work-roughened fingers gently taking hold of Charlotte's clenched hand and easing it open. The simple gesture—a touch that told her she wasn't alone—was enough to bring the steel back to her spine.

"Diabolical challenges are nothing new for us," murmured the maid, releasing Charlotte's hand in order to unravel the silky strands of the fringe and smooth them back into place. "We shall solve them." A gruff chuckle. "We always do."

"Thank you, Mac." Charlotte gave a wry grimace. "Forgive my momentary show of weakness. My doubts are only about myself, not any of you."

"Doubts aren't a sign of weakness. Only a bloody fool doesn't worry over the pitfalls of a dangerous task."

"I confess, my fears about this one . . ."

"Are no worse than the ones that have come before," counseled McClellan. "They just seem so at this moment."

Strangely enough, the nugget of practical wisdom made her feel better. Or perhaps it was simply that the act of sharing fears took some of the weight off her shoulders.

The maid shifted again, and reached up to rap a signal to the coachman. "Let us leave off thinking about the murder—it can wait until this evening. In the meantime, I suggest we go meet Lady Peake and the boys at the museum, and join them for ices at Gunter's."

Charlotte couldn't help but smile. "I'm sure Raven and Hawk would assure us that fear and danger are much easier to stomach when one is stuffed with sweets."

"Sometimes *out of the mouths of babes*—"

"Good heavens, don't voice *that* sentiment in their presence," she replied. "They are . . ." She swallowed a lump in her throat. "They are growing up so very fast."

McClellan gave a sympathetic nod. "Aye. But not as fast as they think. There are still some years to go before they are fully-fledged. And they'll never fly too far from the nest."

The maid's words further loosened the grip of uncertainty. Even the clatter of the iron-shod hooves striking the cobblestones took on a more cheerful ring. The murderer was clever and cunning. Which made him, and any henchmen, a formidable opponent.

But so are we.

In short order, the carriage rolled to a stop in front of Montagu House. "They will be in either the exhibit of the South Seas specimens and artifacts brought back by Captain Cook's expedition"—Charlotte spoke as they climbed down and started up the broad walkway leading to the museum's entrance—"or the galleries holding the collection of Greek antiquities donated by Sir William Hamilton. Alison is fond of classical sculpture, and I believe some of Lord Elgin's marbles are currently on display there, too."

Following the porter's directions, they made their way to the South Seas galleries, where the items on display included specimens of brightly-colored stuffed birds, pressed flowers, and exotic shells.

"Hawk will be clamoring to return here with his sketchbook," said Charlotte, gazing around to make sure the boy wasn't lingering in one of the corners, entranced by the wondrous objects within the cases.

"Indeed." McClellan cleared her throat with a cough at the sight of a spotted sea snake coiled in a large glass cylinder filled with preserving fluid. "Thank heaven these, er, rare and valuable things must remain in a museum."

"The classical antiquities have more aesthetic appeal," said Charlotte. Up ahead was a well-lit corridor. "This way."

Several turns took them to the display alcove of the famous Rosetta Stone, which the king had donated to the museum. Charlotte paused for a moment, intrigued by its intellectual puzzle.

"Raven will likely be anxious to come again and try his hand at deciphering the Stone. Lady Cordelia has told him that solving codes is based on mathematical principles." Wrexford, too, found the challenge fascinating . . .

A cough from the maid drew her back from such musings.

"According to the porter, we need to turn left here, and then right . . ."

The corridor brought them to an arched entranceway flanked by fluted marble columns, their creamy white contours accentuated by the sherry-colored hue of the paneled wood doors. One was standing half open, and Charlotte led the way through it.

A massive classical statue of Hercules at battle with a lion was positioned at the head of the long and narrow gallery space. As Charlotte moved closer, she found herself cloaked by the long shadow cast by the sconces set high on the walls. From close by, the murmur of voices rose above the whisper of the dancing flames.

Pausing by the stone rump of the snarling beast, she set a hand on the marble and ventured a look into the room.

"What a pleasant surprise to encounter you here, Lady Peake."

Charlotte froze.

"Are you and your escorts aficionados of antiquities?" continued the sinuous-as-a-snake voice.

What in the name of Hades is DeVere doing here? she wondered. She didn't imagine he indulged in idle sightseeing.

"My two nephews are explaining all the lessons they are learning from their tutor about Greek mythology," replied Alison. "And how the gods punish mere mortals for becoming too puffed up with hubris."

"There are many ways to interpret the Greek myths," answered DeVere. "That's what makes them so interesting."

"And yet," said Alison, her voice clear as ice, "I've always found the difference between Good and Evil to need no interpretation."

Ignoring the comment, DeVere turned his gaze to Hawk. "I see you're accompanied by your great-niece's charming ward." To the boy, he added, "I do hope you are keeping up with your drawing, Master Sloane. With the right guidance, you have the potential to be a very fine artist. I'm well connected with the art world here in London, and would be happy to offer my counsel on how to develop your skills."

Afraid that Raven might retort with an impudent comment, Charlotte quickly stepped out from behind the statue.

"A generous offer, but it won't be necessary, sir," she said. "As I told you, Wrexford is overseeing the education of the boys."

DeVere's smile held a hint of mockery. "Then they will, of course, acquire all the necessary poise and polish to fit in with Polite Society."

"I think they will learn a great many more important lessons from Wrexford than how to assume a superficial glitter in Society," replied Charlotte. "After all, one can cut delicate facets into a piece of glass, buff it to a radiant sparkle, and try to pass it off as a diamond. But it's still just a piece of glass."

Is that a flicker of annoyance beneath his well-schooled features? If so, it was gone in an instant.

Flicking a speck of dust from his cuff, DeVere turned to Raven. "Are you interested in botany, too?"

"Come along, boys," cut in Charlotte before Raven could answer. "Kindly finish telling Aunt Alison about the Greek myths without further dawdling. I'm very much looking forward to our visit to Gunter's Tea Shop."

Hawk dutifully offered Alison his hand. "Shall we go see Lord Elgin's marbles? Mr. Linsley says they depict the mythical battle between the Lapiths and the centaurs . . ."

Raven, however, hesitated for a moment, fixing DeVere with an unblinking stare before turning to follow his brother and the dowager.

McClellan, who had been standing between two pedestals holding busts of Homer and Sophocles, trailed after him. No doubt intent on making sure he didn't have any second thoughts about staying out of trouble.

"I do hope you're encouraging your younger ward to pursue his art," murmured DeVere as the others made their way to the far end of the gallery. "It would be a pity to see such prodigious talent nipped in the bud."

Is that another veiled threat?

Charlotte told herself not to read evil intent into his every word. "As I said, you needn't worry about his education. Wrexford and I are aware of his gift for art and have engaged a very well-regarded drawing master."

"Excellent," replied DeVere. "All advanced knowledge, no matter in what subject, is vitally important, as it contributes to the higher good."

No matter the cost? Tempting as it was to ask the question, she held her tongue. Needling him might bring a childish satisfaction for a moment or two, but taunting a devil could ignite dangerous consequences.

She acknowledged the statement with a small nod. "And now if you'll excuse me, Mr. DeVere . . ."

"Of course." His flawless manners fitting him like a second skin, he executed a graceful bow. "By the by, I highly recommend the strawberry ices at Gunter's."

Gathering her skirts, Charlotte started to turn away, only to have a dark-on-dark flutter within the shadow of Hercules catch her eye. A gentleman's silhouette—and while she couldn't make out his face, she knew him instantly by the way he moved.

Damnation.

It seemed that yet another sticky strand was weaving its ugly way into the web of intrigue.

CHAPTER 10

"That's a very thought-provoking question, Wrexford." Lord Bingham, a fellow member of the Royal Institution, and a noted expert in plant chemistry, looked up from his work counter. Steam rising from a glass beaker set over a spirit lamp swirled around his face, misting his forehead and leaving a droplet of water hanging from the tip of his beaky nose. "Thank heaven that I can always count on you to raise an interesting scientific challenge."

A sniff, which caused the drop to splash onto his cravat. "Indeed, it's a welcome distraction. Craven asked me to help him test one of his theories. I told him from the first that it was all wrong, and this particular experiment—a very boring one, I might add—is proving me right."

"I'm always happy to provide a diversion," replied the earl. "But as to the question, have you any ideas?"

Bingham didn't answer right away. Lips pursed in thought, he extracted a pair of spectacles from his coat pocket, then pulled a well-worn leather-bound book from the pile on the counter and cracked it open.

Pages rustled as he thumbed through it, setting off the musty scent of old ink and damp paper.

"Hmmm." Bingham turned back to a previous section and read through it before skipping to the back of the book.

Wrexford waited, knowing that creative thinking rarely moved in a straight line.

The liquid boiling in the beaker continued its low gurgling.

"Hmmm." The chemist finally snapped the book shut. "We've known for several centuries that cinchona bark has a re-markable effect on fevers, but as to why . . ." He made a face. "We know that the ground bark won't dissolve properly in water—it needs to be placed in distilled wine in order to dissolve properly. But as to its other chemical properties—most of them still remain a mystery. We simply don't yet understand why it's so effective."

Bingham sighed. "I wanted to refresh my memory, to see if any new thoughts would leap to mind. But alas, at present, I haven't a clue of what other botanicals might strengthen its effects."

The earl hadn't really expected any miraculous revelations, but he had thought it worth a try. "My thanks."

"Might I inquire why you asked?" Bingham was aware of Becton's death, but like the rest of the scientific community, save for a few members of the Royal Society's governing committee, he had no idea of what momentous discovery the American scholar was going to reveal in his presentation.

"It was just an idea that came to mind." Wrexford knew the chemist to be a solid, sensible fellow. "However, I would be grateful if you kept our meeting confidential."

"But of course." Bingham blew out the flame on his spirit lamp. "If you like, I can do some additional reading on the bark and see if I come up with any other ideas."

"I would appreciate that."

"Excellent. As I said, a scientific challenge is always stimulating." The chemist was already reaching for the stack of books. "And I'm grateful for you giving me the excuse to turn my thoughts to something more interesting than Craven's experiment."

"Then I shall leave you to it."

Wrexford was soon back out on Albemarle Street, but instead of heading for home, he clicked open his pocket watch to check the time and then turned his steps toward White's.

"Lady Charlotte! What a delightful surprise!"

"Mr. Moretti." Charlotte forced a smile in response to his greeting. It should come as no surprise that he would pay a visit to one of London's most famous cultural attractions. And yet, his presence couldn't help but stir a niggling sense of unease.

Coincidences did happen. But Moretti's next words only deepened her suspicions.

"Forgive me for being a few minutes late, Mr. DeVere. The corridors here are like a maze, and I fear I became a trifle confused in finding my way to this gallery."

Charlotte, too, was feeling a little disoriented.

"The two of you are acquainted?" asked DeVere, his gaze darting from her to Moretti.

Lies would only come back to bite her, she decided. But there was no reason to volunteer any information.

"We had a very pleasant chat during the gala celebration at the Royal Botanic Gardens," she replied.

If Moretti was taken aback by her response, he hid it well. "Indeed, we did," he said, his face maintaining a blandly polite expression. He said nothing more.

"And you, sir? I imagine you, too, met at the gala, given your mutual interest in botany. Do you share a specific field of study?" Charlotte spoke to DeVere, curious as to how the two of them had come to know each other.

"Oh, I've been following Mr. Moretti's work for some time,"

responded DeVere. "His scholarship shows a great deal of promise. I have no doubt that we can expect great things from him."

For a moment, her breath seemed to stick in her lungs.

The praise brought a faint flush of color to her friend's cheeks. "You are exceedingly kind, sir. I—I shall do my very best to live up to such lofty expectations."

"I'm sure that you will." DeVere gave a friendly pat to Moretti's shoulder. "Come, allow me to show you the highlights of the museum, and as we admire the timeless beauty of man's creative efforts, we can discuss the details of my offer, and see if it is acceptable to you."

"I . . . I . . ." Moretti appeared a little overwhelmed. "I am quite sure it will be *more* than acceptable, sir." He turned to Charlotte, a beatific glow lighting his hazel eyes. "Mr. DeVere wishes to offer me a stipend and a place to work here in England for the next year, in order to continue my research."

Charlotte managed to mask her shock though the announcement shook her to the core. "How very generous," she murmured, avoiding DeVere's gaze.

"*Sì, sì,*" said Moretti. "I am . . . how do you English say it . . . in alt at my good fortune."

Be careful what you wish for, my friend, she thought. But perhaps Moretti already knew he was making a deal with the devil.

"I wish you the best," replied Charlotte, hoping against hope that she was wrong.

"We ought not keep you any longer from your ices at Gunter's, Lady Charlotte." DeVere gave a genteel wave to the dowager and the boys, who were waiting at the far end of the room.

Was that a twitch of malice in his smile as he turned back to face her?

"Enjoy your outing," he added.

"*Ciao, bella* Lady Charlotte," murmured Moretti as DeVere gestured toward Lord Elgin's marbles.

She walked away, careful to maintain a straight spine and a measured pace. It felt as if DeVere was taking every opportunity to poke and prod her, looking for a chink in her defenses. A way to strike at her most vulnerable weakness.

And one of Greek mythology's most elemental lessons was that every mortal being had an Achilles' heel.

As he had hoped, Wrexford found Sheffield in the main reading room at White's. But in his hands was a sheaf of papers, rather than a glass of the club's port or brandy. Indeed, on the side table by his armchair sat a pot of coffee.

"I swear," grumbled his friend as Wrexford settled into the chair beside him, "there are times when numbers give me a bigger headache than cheap Blue Ruin."

"Yes, but with numbers you actually profit from the pain."

Sheffield pinched at the bridge of his nose. "Only if I can find a way to lessen the transportation costs from Bruges to Dover, now that our lace supplier has raised the cost of his wares."

"Speaking of shipping . . ." Wrexford glanced around to check that there was no one within earshot. "Have you had a chance to ask around about Quincy's business?"

"As a matter of fact, I have." His friend shuffled through his documents and fished out a dozen sheets. "One of our dock-yard foremen is well acquainted with the fellow who supervises the unloading of all goods that come into the West India docks. Two of Quincy's ships have delivered cargos during the past three months. Here's the manifests for both of them."

Wrexford skimmed the sheets that Sheffield passed over. "Cotton, tobacco . . . it seems like nothing out of the ordinary." He looked up. "Or am I missing something?"

"No, it's as expected. The only thing suspect is the price he charges. Lady Cordelia has done a number of sophisticated mathematical calculations based on our knowledge of the markets, both here and in America," explained Sheffield. "She's convinced that Quincy Enterprises has to be losing money on its cotton exports. Our guess is, he's trying to force us out of the market, and then he'll recoup his losses."

"A risky strategy," observed the earl. "Assuming you have the funds to force him into a prolonged price war."

A smile played on Sheffield's lips. "My partners dislike it intensely when men try to use ham-fisted tactics to best the competition. They are of the opinion that if one can't triumph through wits rather than skulduggery, then one doesn't deserve a victory."

"I take it Mr. Quincy is going to continue losing money," said Wrexford.

"Yes. More than he might imagine." Sheffield glanced at the papers still in his hands. "But never mind that for now. I've something more interesting to show you."

The earl straightened in his chair.

"Looking into cargos and deliveries got me thinking. So I took it on myself to have our foreman ask some additional questions of the cargo supervisor—ones that pertained to the ship that brought Quincy and DeVere to London. It was one of the company's smaller, faster vessels, a type that is usually employed to transport valuable goods rather than bulk cargo."

"And was it?" he asked.

Sheffield made a pained face. "Allow me to finish, Wrex. It's not quite as simple as yes or no."

Wrexford signaled for his friend to continue.

"A number of plant specimens in specially designed crates were off-loaded and delivered to the Royal Botanic Gardens. I have the list here." Sheffield passed it over. "As you see, there are nut-bearing trees from the southern states of America— hickory, pecan, black walnut—as well as conifers from the New

England region. All given as a gift from Quincy to fill out the gaps in the Royal Society's collections of North American trees."

"Very generous of him," murmured Wrexford. "One can't help but speculate as to why he wishes to curry favor with the Society's heads. But in truth, it's not uncommon for would-be members to give extravagant gifts in hopes of obtaining a coveted invitation to join."

Sheffield shifted impatiently, setting off a muted crackling of the papers still in his hands. "Yes, well, here's where it gets more interesting—another set of plant specimen crates was also off-loaded into the wagons going to the Royal Botanic Gardens. But these were clearly labeled as the property of a private collector, to be held there for a later delivery."

"I'm waiting with bated breath," murmured the earl.

"As well you should," shot back his friend. "They're destined for DeVere's mansion in Marylebone Park. Which could mean that he and Quincy are more than mere casual acquaintances."

"Or simply that DeVere paid very well to bring back an assortment of American plants," pointed out the earl. Sheffield was anxious to help, but jumping to conclusions could lead them on a wild goose chase. "We know he has one of the finest private conservatories in all of Britain."

"I'm well aware of that." A shadow passed over Sheffield's face. He had been present at DeVere's mansion on that terrible night when Charlotte had been within a hair's breadth of death. Lady Cordelia had been in danger as well . . .

They had all been extraordinarily fortunate that Luck had been on their side, reflected Wrexford. *But Luck is fickle. It would be foolish to assume otherwise.*

"I know what you're thinking. But before you dismiss what I've said, please listen to the last bit of information," said Sheffield. "And then you may make of it what you will."

"I've always respected your judgment, Kit," he answered. "Even when you yourself doubted it. So be assured that I'm paying attention—and keeping an open mind."

Their eyes met, the years of friendship making any further words unnecessary.

A fluttery whisper stirred the air as Sheffield raised the single document left in his hand. "There was one last consignment of cargo unloaded from Quincy's ship. The regular stevedores weren't allowed to touch it—the crew handled moving a half-dozen heavy iron-banded chests—each fastened with pad-locks—down to a waiting carriage."

Sheffield glanced down at the paper. "But the supervisor considers the dockyard his bailiwick, and doesn't like it when ships try to circumvent the proper procedures. So he made a point of hefting one of the chests while the carriage awaited his permission to depart."

A pause—his friend had a penchant for drawing out a dramatic moment.

"And made sure to learn the name of the recipient, and the address to which the goods were being delivered."

Wrexford's lips twitched. "Perhaps you should take up writing horrid novels, Kit. You've quite a knack for creating suspense. I'm assuming you're about to tell me to whom the chests were sent." He, too, paused. "And why it's important."

"Show a little more appreciation for my cleverness," grumbled Sheffield. "It *is* important—or at least intriguing enough to merit some further thought."

With a flourish, he dropped the document in the earl's lap. "The chests contained gold coins—any dockyard supervisor worth his salt can open even the most complicated padlocks—and the amount was a very large sum. As for the recipient, they were delivered to a man by the name of Reginald Lyman."

"Lyman . . ." Wrexford frowned. The name didn't strike a chord.

"I daresay, Lady Charlotte might remember who he is." All trace of bantering humor had disappeared from Sheffield's face. "Several years ago, A. J. Quill penned a drawing concerning his activities. He's a ship captain for hire, with a very fast Baltimore Clipper and a reputation for taking on jobs that others find too dangerous. The voyage that drew A. J. Quill's attention concerned rumors of delivering a shipment of gold to French forces during the Peninsular War."

Wrexford stiffened. His younger brother, a decorated British cavalry officer, had lost his life fighting in the mountains of Portugal. "Bloody hell, was that the bastard who was—"

"Suspected of carrying the payroll for General Soult's troops just before the battle at Badajoz?" interjected Sheffield. "Yes, that's Lyman. As you know, the war for the Spanish Peninsula was draining Napoleon's coffers. As our forces began to take the offensive, he desperately needed to get funds to his armies, but much of his resources were already heading east."

"As I recall the rumors," said the earl, "the gold came from Prussia."

"So it was said," agreed Sheffield. "Having forced the Prussian king into an alliance with France at the Treaty of Tilsit, Napoleon demanded that he contribute to the war effort. However, the emperor worried about the delays and other perils of sending it west by wagon, and time was of the essence. So Napoleon decided to take a chance sending the shipment from Hamburg by sea, betting that a very fast and cunning captain could slip through the British patrols."

"And Lyman accepted the job, even though it would leave his hands covered in his fellow countrymen's blood," muttered Wrexford.

"Even within the shark-eat-barracuda world of smugglers and pirates, Lyman has a filthy reputation," replied Sheffield. "He's said to be a man without a shred of conscience."

The details of the incident were slowly drifting back to him.

"A British naval frigate spotted him sailing out of a Spanish harbor, but couldn't catch up with him, and eventually lost him in the fog. When the accusation was made against Lyman—informants in Spain corroborated that the gold had been off-loaded from his schooner—he claimed that he'd been blown off course from making a routine run along the Cornish coast after delivering documents and ore samples to a mining company in Falmouth."

Sheffield nodded. "The company confirmed the delivery, and as there was no evidence or eyewitness to any wrongdoing, no charges were brought."

"But the scuttlebutt in both Britain and the Continent was that Lyman was guilty as sin."

"Indeed."

It was just the sort of self-serving treachery that would spark Charlotte's outrage. He must ask her if she had a copy of the published print.

"Lyman sailed for the West Indies soon after that, likely to allow things to cool down on this side of the Atlantic. He returned around eight months ago, and has done nothing to attract attention. As far as I can gather, his only activity is to do occasional runs to the north and the Baltic states."

Wrexford was still trying to grasp the thread that tied the three deliveries from Quincy's ship together—and how they connected to Becton's murder. He slowly sorted through the papers his friend had given him, but the manifests didn't offer any answers.

"You've done an excellent job of sleuthing, Kit." He squared the papers in his lap into a neat pile and sat back. "I'm all agog to hear how all the information ties into Becton."

Sheffield's expression pinched to a wry grimace. "Actually, I haven't got a clue."

"Then why the devil—"

"My point is, there are three very disreputable and dangerous men who have recently crossed paths—however obliquely—with the victim," interjected his friend. "DeVere, Quincy, and Lyman have all shown they're willing to do whatever it takes to get what they want—even if it requires others to die."

Wrexford couldn't argue the point.

"You and Lady Charlotte are stepping into a nest of vipers, Wrex," continued Sheffield. "I just want both of you to be damnably careful as to how you tread through the tangle of forked tongues and fangs."

CHAPTER 11

Charlotte watched Raven and Hawk race down the stairs and fly out the front door, their gentlemanly clothing replaced by the far more familiar—and filthy—rags of a street urchin.

"Weasels." Soft as a sigh, the word slipped from her lips. Not that she would wish them to change. Yes, the slums taught brutally hard lessons, and one learned to be smart and strong in order to survive. But in addition, they also could teach other important life lessons—that friendship and loyalty, along with kindness and compassion, were often more important than toughness in overcoming adversity.

Still, the demands of living in both worlds weren't easy—

"Of course you worry about them." McClellan, her hands dusted with flour, had quietly come out of the kitchen to stand beside her. "It is an elemental irony, isn't it, that the more we love, the more we fear. However, we must keep fear from clouding the joy from our hearts."

"Thank you, Mac." Charlotte smiled. "For always knowing what words I need to hear to buck up my courage."

"Your courage needs no help from me. If anything, your

heart is *too* big. It needs an occasional reminder that you can't try to take on every injustice that you see."

There was great wisdom in the maid's words. But Becton's murder *was* personal. DeVere had gotten away with too many unspeakable evils. If he was guilty of this one, she was determined to see that he would not escape justice.

"However, in this case, I understand your feelings," added McClellan. "If that scoundrel DeVere was involved in the poisoning of Dr. Hosack's friend, we'll see that he answers for the crime."

Before Charlotte could reply, a brusque knock on the front door indicated that they had a visitor.

"Are we expecting company?" asked the maid, quickly coming to full alert.

She shook her head.

"I'll answer it." McClellan wiped her hands on her apron and ducked into the kitchen for a brief moment. "Please wait in the parlor."

Charlotte didn't look too closely at the bulge in the maid's pocket. *Cavendum est optima parte errare. It is best to err on the side of caution.* One man already lay dead.

The door clicked open a moment after she slipped into the parlor, the metallic *snick* followed by the sound of voices.

Releasing her pent-up breath, Charlotte stepped away from the bookcase, where a mahogany tea chest on one of the shelves concealed a loaded pistol.

"Forgive me for dropping by unannounced, as I know how busy you are," said Cordelia, untying her bonnet and then setting it on the sideboard. "But Octavia just received a letter from her American cousin, who works with our business agent in New York, and I felt it important that you be aware of some of its contents."

Charlotte had become acquainted with Octavia Howe at Lady Thirkell's salon for intellectually-minded ladies. She was impressed with her air of highly-organized efficiency and razor-sharp logic. Indeed, the wife of a high-placed general had quipped at a recent meeting that if the military men at Horse Guards appointed Miss Howe as quartermaster for Wellington's army, the war would be over in a fortnight.

"I'll make tea," said McClellan. "Shall I also bring ginger biscuits?"

"Bless you, Mac." Cordelia sank into one of the armchairs and blew out a harried sigh. "I confess, I'm famished. It's been a hellish day, and I've not eaten since breakfast."

"I hope you've not had any bad news about your ships and crew," said Charlotte.

"Thank goodness, no," replied Cordelia. "Just some problems with a few regular clients." She made a face. "Quincy Enterprises is undercutting our prices in several American markets, and it's hard to convince people that saving a few pennies now will come back to bite their bank accounts."

Her mouth thinned for a moment. "I happen to know Quincy is scrimping on sail canvas to save money, as well as deferring maintenance on caulking and fastenings for the hulls of their ships. In my opinion, they ought to be strung up from the nearest yardarm for negligence. For mark my words, a disaster will happen—it's merely a question of when." A pause. "And hurricane season is coming to life in the Atlantic."

"That they are deliberately putting their crews in danger ought to be a criminal offense," mused Charlotte.

"And yet it's not."

An idea suddenly occurred to her. She had sworn a solemn oath to herself never to use A. J. Quill's pen for personal reasons. But regardless of her own feelings for the man, if Quincy was a threat to innocent lives, then pointing a finger at this particular evil was in the public's interest.

And if stirring a stick in that dark cesspool brought other wrongdoings to the surface . . .

The clink of cups and plates interrupted her musings.

"I took the liberty of bringing more substantial sustenance than mere biscuits," said McClellan as she placed a large tray on the tea table. A basket of bread, still warm from the oven, sat beside a platter of sliced cheddar and ham. Next to it was a wedge of apple pie.

Cordelia closed her eyes and inhaled the earthy fragrance of the fresh-brewed Oolong tea. "That smells positively ambrosial."

"Eat," ordered the maid, handing over a plate heaped with food.

After a few quick bites, Cordelia put down her fork. "I'm very grateful, but I didn't come here to impose on your hospitality—"

"Among close friends, there's no such thing as imposing," said Charlotte. "Just as there's no need to conform to polite manners." A smile. "You can eat and talk at the same time."

That drew an answering grin. "Very well—as you know, I take great delight in breaking Society's rules." Cordelia broke off a bit of bread and swallowed it before continuing. "Getting back to my earlier announcement, Octavia received some news from her cousin. I'm not sure if it means anything, but as it relates to possible suspects in Mr. Becton's murder, I thought you ought to hear it right away."

"As of yet, none of the fragments of information we've uncovered are fitting together into any discernable picture," Charlotte replied. "So any additional piece is most welcome."

"Then here is what Henry Chauncey passed on to Octavia's cousin," replied her friend. "Chauncey is our American agent, and he's based in New York. He was born and raised there, so is intimately familiar with the city, and has friends in every strata of society."

"A useful thing for a man of business."

"Very useful," agreed Cordelia. "He was drinking with an

acquaintance in one of the rougher taverns in the vicinity of the city's harbor when a conversation concerning Quincy Enterprises caught his ear. The two men involved were in a secluded booth, but Chauncey and his companion were in a shadowed nook close by and must have gone unnoticed."

Cordelia paused for a bite of cheese topped with a sliver of ham. "In any case, he could hear the two men clear as a bell. One of them was Captain Samuel Daggett of the United States Navy. And the other was Reginald Lyman, who is someone my partners and I consider to be no better than a blackguard mercenary for hire."

"How do you mean?" asked Charlotte.

"He's a devilishly good sailor with a very fast ship, and he makes his living doing very dangerous—and usually very dirty—jobs for people willing to pay him a king's ransom because of his reputation for being slippery as an eel—and for keeping his mouth shut."

"I see," she murmured.

"Thankfully, what we know of him is hearsay, as our business has never crossed paths with his. However, what Chauncey overheard has us very concerned," explained Cordelia. "Daggett was clearly angry and threatened Lyman with dire consequences if Lyman betrayed their agreement and did the shipping deal with Quincy on his own."

"Shipping what?" queried Charlotte.

A chuffed sigh sounded in answer. "Would that I could tell you. No details were mentioned, only the fact that it was a very lucrative job."

Damnation. This bit of information was like all the other clues, thought Charlotte. A quicksilver gleam that caught the eye, but turned into vapor when one tried to grab hold of it.

"Chauncey did his best to uncover more about the plan," went on Cordelia. "However, people were either too frightened to talk, or the conspirators have guarded their secret very well. He couldn't discover anything, but said he would keep trying to learn more. However, it could be months before we hear anything from him. In the meantime, he said that our office here should be on guard for any attempt by Quincy to tamper with our trading routes or partners."

She poured herself some more tea. "Sheffield has some friends among the dockyard administrators and is doing some further digging into Quincy's business. However, I've not yet heard from him on whether he's found anything new."

After taking a sip of tea, her friend looked up. "I realize that this is all damnably vague, like ghostly specters flitting through the night. But I thought you should be aware of it."

The note of frustration in Cordelia's voice was echoed in her own thoughts. Intuition told her that there had to be a connection between the three men and Becton's murder—that DeVere would somehow also be part of it.

But feeling it was one thing. Proving it was quite another.

And at the moment, that possibility seemed as far away as the Man in the Moon.

Wrexford joined in the polite applause as the Dutch scholar gathered up his notes and stepped down from the stage. It had been an interesting lecture on Linnaeus and his classification for plants, but his mind had been wandering for most of it. Murder, not *monadria,* was foremost in his thoughts.

Hosack, too, had seemed distracted, his gaze occasionally slipping away from the speaker to the audience. However, as the gentlemen around them rose and began to file out to the main salon, the doctor muttered something under his breath and turned in his chair.

"I've suddenly remembered something that may be of help to us. Let us hurry to join the others."

They followed the crowd to the postlecture reception, where

already the *pop-pop* of champagne bottles was adding a festive note to the buzz of conversation.

"The lecturer's mention of Alexander von Humboldt reminded me of an expedition to Spanish America that took place around the turn of the century," said Hosack, looking around the room after accepting a glass of wine from one of the passing footmen.

A famous explorer and man of science, von Humboldt was renowned throughout Europe and America for his scientific expeditions and writings on the natural world.

Wrexford, who was growing impatient with diversions that led nowhere, was about to respond that history, however interesting, wasn't proving to be much help when the doctor added, "Come, we need to find Markell von Stockhausen, who is part of the Prussian delegation."

Swallowing his misgivings, along with a gulp of champagne, the earl fell in step beside Hosack.

As if sensing Wrexford's reluctance, the doctor paused behind one of the floral displays in order to explain.

"Becton traveled for an interlude with von Humboldt's first expedition to Spanish America, and I seem to recall having heard that von Stockhausen, who, like von Humboldt, is from a very prominent Prussian noble family, was also part of the group. Perhaps if the two of them kept up a correspondence, he'll have some idea of who might have had any ill feelings for Becton."

"Possibly," said Wrexford, though it seemed grasping at a very fragile thread. "However, we must be very discreet with our questions. I'm aware that there are already some rumors being whispered among our colleagues that Becton's death might not be from natural causes . . ." Charlotte's drawing, alas, had done nothing to quell them. "And we don't wish to encourage them."

Hosack nodded. "Quite right, sir." He finished his wine in

one long swallow and set the empty glass on the pedestal. "I confess, I don't have your expertise in this sort of investigation, so I will endeavor to let you do most of the talking."

"Lead on," said Wrexford.

Hosack soon spotted von Stockhausen conversing with several botanists from Sweden. Halting a short distance away, he and the earl waited for the group to drift apart before approaching him.

"Herr von Stockhausen, I've been looking forward to making your acquaintance!" said Hosack. "I've read your papers, and I must say, you have some very interesting ideas on how to improve Linnaeus's classification system of plants."

"Ha! The Swedes do not agree with you, sir. But I appreciate your sentiments," replied the Prussian wryly. "You are Dr. Hosack, are you not? I, too, have been anxious to meet you. Word of your marvelous Elgin Garden in America has spread throughout Europe."

"I am, sir, though the Garden now belongs to the state of New York," replied the doctor. "And please allow me to introduce my friend, Lord Wrexford, who is a member of both the Royal Society and Royal Institution . . ."

The three of them went through the ritual of formal introductions, and requisite exchange of pleasantries, and then it was von Stockhausen who solved the earl's dilemma on how to bring up Becton by broaching the subject himself.

"Dr. Hosack, please accept my condolences on Mr. Becton," said the Prussian, inclining a stiff bow. "He mentioned you often in his letters as an esteemed man of science and a dear friend."

"Thank you. I feel his loss deeply," replied Hosack. "He was a brilliant botanist and a very fine fellow—always cheerful and exceedingly generous about sharing his knowledge with others." A pause. "But then, I believe you already know that. Didn't the two of you spend some time together traveling with von Humboldt and Bonpland on their epic expedition through the wilds of Spanish America?"

"Indeed, we did." A faraway look seemed to soften von Stockhausen's gaze for a moment. "Though Becton left us after several months to travel on his own through Guyana, and then to Cuba and the West Indies, while I remained with the main expedition for another six months."

"It must have been quite an experience to work with von Humboldt," observed Wrexford. "The breadth of his knowledge and his discoveries—minerals, insects, and animal specimens, as well as the wealth of new plant species—are legendary."

"Yes, he's a man of extraordinary accomplishments," agreed von Stockhausen. "I learned a great deal from him." He stared meditatively at the tiny bubbles fizzing in his wine. "But it's important not to dwell on what one has experienced and accomplished in the past. I believe that to keep making progress in science, one should focus on the present and the future."

"I'm sure Becton shared your sentiments," murmured Hosack. "He never basked in the glory of his past achievements, but kept looking for new ways to make life better for everyone."

Von Stockhausen's brow furrowed slightly. He appeared to hesitate, as if trying to decide whether to speak or not. Wrexford held his tongue, hoping silence would encourage the Prussian to speak his mind.

"As to that . . ." Clearing his throat with a brusque cough, von Stockhausen shifted his stance before going on. "In his last few letters, Becton hinted that he was working on a very important project, one that he felt held great potential. I do hope his papers and research have been passed to the Royal Society, so that despite his death, his ideas will live on."

The truth, decided Wrexford, was the best answer. "I'm not aware of what happened to his papers."

His response deepened the Prussian's frown. "I . . ." Von Stockhausen took a moment to glance around. "I had supper with Becton before the start of the symposium, and I had the impression he was nervous about something. However, when I mentioned it, he made light of the matter. But then . . ."

His mouth thinned for a moment. "But then, at the end of the meal, a man came over to our table and began pressing Becton to reconsider the deal he had been offered."

"A deal?" asked Wrexford, feigning surprise. "Did Becton elaborate on what that was?"

Another hesitation. "Actually, he did. He told me the man was a fellow member of his scientific society in America. A merchant by the name of Tobias Quincy."

It appears Quincy hadn't been willing to take Becton's refusals in New York for a final answer, thought Wrexford.

Von Stockhausen looked to Hosack. "Are you acquainted with him, sir?"

The doctor glanced at Wrexford, who took care not to react. The Prussian's English might be a little rough around the edges, but his eyes held a sharp intelligence.

"Yes," answered Hosack. "Quincy is a founding member of the New York Botanical Society, and has been a generous benefactor of many of its projects."

A look of distaste quivered at the corners of von Stockhausen's mouth. "He struck me as a very havey-cavey sort of fellow. And I don't think Becton thought highly of him, either." The Prussian frowned. "Are you saying that Quincy possesses any botanical expertise? He didn't strike me as a man of science."

"Yes, he does," confirmed Hosack. "In fact, he's working with his cousin, who owns vast cotton plantations in South Carolina, on ways to improve the plant's yield. To that end, he hired another American botanist—a man named Jeremiah Adderley—to assist in the research."

The information appeared to further unsettle von Stock-hausen. "Adderley?" He sucked in his breath. "But . . ."

"But what?" said Wrexford softly.

The Prussian's expression pinched in uncertainty for a mo-ment, but then he decided to speak. "It's just that, well, having traveled in Spanish America, I have kept up a correspondence with acquaintances there, and hear news from time to time. Several years ago, there was an incident concerning a man named Adderley, who was part of an American naval visit to the Spanish viceroy in New Granada."

After a quick look around, he continued. "It was said he tried to smuggle some rare plant specimens that were forbidden to be exported onto his ship."

"I see," responded the earl, keeping his voice neutral.

After waiting for a trio of scholars to pass by them and enter one of the display rooms, von Stockhausen ventured to ask, "This man Quincy—you mentioned that he is a generous bene-factor of the New York Botanical Society. Does that mean he's very wealthy?"

Hosack looked a little surprised at the question, but nodded. "Yes, he's a very wealthy man."

Von Stockhausen pondered the answer for a moment. "Bec-ton didn't mention Quincy's money. Nor did he explain the de-tails of the deal for which the merchant was pressing."

He shifted abruptly and drew back into the shadows of the decorative colonnade, gesturing for them to join him.

Wrexford was a little wary of the direction the conversation was taking. As he had noted, von Stockhausen appeared very observant—no surprise, of course, for a man who studied the nuances of flora, but an unwelcome complication to a very del-icate subject.

"I have heard my colleagues discussing the latest drawing by one of London's popular artists," said the Prussian once they had moved closer. "Apparently, it hinted at the possibility that Becton was the victim of foul play."

Lowering his voice to a whisper, he added, "You don't think . . ."

Wrexford gave a dismissive laugh, intent on nipping the Prussian's suspicion in the bud. "Good heavens, sir—if you were more familiar with the scurrilous scribblers of this city, you would understand that it's their bread and butter to indulge in lurid speculations and stir up titillating gossip." Another curt chuckle. "Pray, don't allow your imagination to run wild. My understanding is that Becton had been suffering from a weak heart for some time."

"That's true," murmured Hosack. "His health appeared strong enough for him to make the journey, but . . ." The doctor lifted his shoulders in dismay. "But alas, Nature takes its own course."

Von Stockhausen made a wry grimace. "*Ja,* come to think of it, he demurred from drinking any wine or brandy at supper, saying his physician had warned him against having any strong spirits." A mournful sigh sounded. "Forgive me for indulging in childish fantasies. It's just that it seems like . . . like such a cruel twist of fate for the Grim Reaper to strike at this, of all moments."

"Life is often unfair," said Wrexford. "We men of science like to think that we live in an orderly, clockwork universe, where immutable laws govern the workings of the forces of nature. But there are many mysteries of life that defy rational rules. Death is one of them."

The Prussian responded with a solemn nod.

"And besides," added Hosack abruptly, "who would wish Becton harm? He was a gentle soul, and though a trifle eccentric, he was admired and respected by his peers. I can't think of anyone—can you?"

"*Nein.*" Von Stockhausen looked abashed. "As I said, I reacted foolishly, wishing to find a reason other than bad luck."

"Understandably so," said Wrexford. The Prussian had given them some useful answers, and he didn't wish to encourage further speculation. Nor did he wish for their tête-à-tête to draw attention . . .

Sensing scrutiny, he shifted slightly and caught the hawklike gaze of Captain Daggett, who was watching them, before the American quickly turned away.

"Come, let us go mingle with the other guests, and talk of happier subjects than death."

CHAPTER 12

The much-anticipated day was finally here. The previous evening, a note had arrived from the dowager informing Charlotte that her brother would be arriving in London by early afternoon. As her family had long ago sold their townhouse in London—both her father and grandfather were country gentlemen who disliked the crowds and filth of the city—Alison had insisted that Wolcott stay with her, rather than take up residence at his club, in order to have a private place for the first meeting.

An intimate family supper for just the four of them was planned . . .

Charlotte wasn't sure whether to feel elated or terrified.

No wonder her stomach had been roiling like a bubbling cauldron. She had managed to down no more than a few crusts of bread throughout the day, despite several tart rebukes from McClellan.

"Sit still," commanded the maid, after expelling an exasperated oath. "Unless you wish to greet your brother with hairpins rather than sapphire earbobs hooked through your lobes."

She forced herself to stop fidgeting. Somehow the hours had slid by and it was now time to ready herself for the occasion. "Are you sure I shouldn't wear the garnet-colored gown rather than the slate blue?" A glance in the looking glass showed that her face was pale as bleached muslin. "It might help reflect a touch of color to my cheeks."

Before McClellan could answer, Charlotte huffed a sigh. "No, no—the color red, however muted, might bring to mind a fallen woman." She bit her lip. "And I suppose a pastel hue would be far too virginal. He's all too aware that I'm no innocent schoolgirl."

McClellan slapped down the hairbrush and set a fist on her hip. "You are wearing the blue. If your face is white as a ghost, you have only yourself to blame. Flesh and blood requires hearty nourishment—"

"Before riding into battle," finished Charlotte. "Forget food. Perhaps I'll have a wee nip of brandy."

"Aye, that will bring some color to your face—as you fall flat on your arse."

Charlotte couldn't conjure up a clever quip. Her sense of humor was fast giving way to dread. Afraid to look at her own reflection, she averted her eyes and forced herself to breathe.

"Don't fret. I'll not send you to meet your brother looking like death warmed over," assured McClellan, her tone softening in sympathy. A few deft twists and hidden pins created a graceful topknot. After loosening a few curls to frame Charlotte's face, the maid threaded a slender silk ribbon through the upswept tresses.

"Now turn here and let me smudge a bit of kohl on your lids. A hint of shadow adds an air of mystery."

She submitted to the maid's ministrations, then ventured a peek. To her surprise, the glass didn't crack into a thousand shards.

"You look lovely," murmured McClellan. "Not that your brother will be looking for glitter or glamour. From what Lady Peake says, he's as anxious as you are to repair the rift in the family."

"Yes, but . . ." Charlotte's heart gave a tiny lurch. "What if he's disappointed? Or takes a dislike to me?"

"If he says an unkind word, Wrexford will plant him a facer."

"Is that supposed to reassure me?"

"No, it's supposed to make you laugh." A pause. "Though I daresay, the earl wouldn't hesitate to darken your brother's deadlights if he dares be rude to you."

"I shall pray that fisticuffs won't be necessary." Charlotte watched the candlelight flicker over the delicate trim of her bodice. The gown was exquisitely tasteful—its cut revealing just enough flesh to be stylishly au courant, and yet not too racy.

The necklace must be equally understated and elegant. "I think the pearls would look good, don't you?"

To Charlotte's surprise, McClellan shook her head. "No. You ought not gild the lily, as it were."

"You're suggesting I wear no jewelry?" Charlotte touched a hand to her throat. "It seems . . . odd."

"Trust me," replied the maid. "I've discussed this with Franny." Madame Françoise—née Franzenelli—was a clever Italian who had established herself as London's most exclusive modiste. She was also one of Charlotte's informants on all the spicy gossip being whispered in Polite Society, and had become a good friend over the years.

"Well, if Franny says to wear nothing . . ." She cast a doubtful glance at the looking glass. "Then I had better trust her judgment over mine." Though this was one of the rare times when she thought her fashionable friend was wrong.

McClellan handed her a feather-light Kashmir shawl woven in muted tones of indigo. "We had better go down. I hear the Weasels making a ruckus, so I assume Wrexford has arrived."

Wrexford. That he would be with her made all her fears seem less daunting. Charlotte managed a smile—the first real one of the day—and took up her reticule.

"We better hurry. I overheard the boys talking earlier, and apparently Tyler has given Raven a new formula for making stinkbombs."

"He wouldn't dare," muttered McClellan. Nonetheless, she hurried for the stairs.

The Weasels, however, were the very picture of perfect little gentlemen when they entered the parlor, save for their none-too-pristine clothing. Raven had fetched a bottle of Scottish malt from the side cabinet and was offering to pour the earl a glass—hoping, no doubt, to be offered a sip.

"No, thank you," demurred Wrexford. "A word of advice to you for the future. It's best not to reek of whisky when going to meet your future bride's family for the first—" The rest of the words seemed to catch in his throat as he looked around.

Charlotte fumbled for her sash, fearing that she had somehow caused it to come undone.

"You look . . ." An odd sort of light seemed to flicker beneath his lashes. "Exceedingly lovely."

"Is that good?" whispered Hawk to his brother.

"It's more than good," answered the earl, his eyes never leaving her.

She felt a touch of color blossom on her cheekbones. "Is everything in order? I haven't got a corset string dangling down my back or my shift showing beneath my hem?"

"Turn slowly in a circle," murmured Wrexford.

The room was silent, save for a gossamer-soft rustling of silk.

"Hmmm, something seems to be missing," he said, once she

was done. "Ah—I know. That bare expanse of flesh above your bodice looks a little . . . naked."

"*Naked,*" repeated Charlotte. She turned to McClellan. "You see! Far be it for me to disagree with you and Franny, but—"

The maid began to chuckle softly, and her mirth was quickly echoed by the boys.

Confused, Charlotte looked back to Wrexford.

He was holding a slim leather box. It was open, and nestled on a bed of black velvet was a necklace.

"Oh . . ." For a moment, she was utterly bereft of speech. The double strands of finely-wrought gold links were highlighted by delicate smoke-tinged sapphires, their polished facets glimmering in the muted light of the candles. And hanging from its center was a teardrop pendant of filigree gold set with tiny seed pearls framing a diamond-cut sapphire. Its hue was an exact match of her gown's shimmering silk.

Her breath was barely able to form a whisper. "Oh, Wrexford."

"D-Do you like it?" That the earl—a man feared throughout the beau monde for his fierce temper and cutting tongue—could sound so sweetly vulnerable made her heart flutter.

Charlotte looked up through the tears pearled on her lashes. "M-More than words can possibly express."

A smile touched his lips. "I'm so glad. It belonged to my mother, and my grandmother, and great-grandmother before her. The family has come to call it the Wrexford Sapphires. It gives me great joy that they are a perfect match for the next countess."

"Franny combed through the East India warehouses for just the right shade of silk to complement the gems," said McClellan.

"You knew?" exclaimed Charlotte, and then looked around at the boys as she recalled their laughter. "As did you two!"

"O'course," drawled Raven. "Wrexford had several loose gemstones, and he sent us along with them to accompany

Madame Françoise so that she could test them against the different fabrics in a variety of lights."

"Both Mac and the Weasels were sworn to secrecy," said Wrexford. "I wanted it to be a surprise."

"And yet," she replied, "you claim to be a man who doesn't have a sentimental bone in his body."

A gleam of unholy amusement lit his eyes. "I don't. I merely like surprises."

Charlotte leaned in to feather a kiss to his cheek. "You," she whispered, "are a source of constant surprises."

"In a good way, I hope."

"Always—even in prickly moments. The fact that we sometimes challenge each other keeps us both from becoming too complacent."

"We face a good many dangers in our daily lives," said Wrexford dryly. "Complacency is not one of them." He traced a quick caress along the line of her jaw and then stepped back. "Now turn around so that I may have the honor of bestowing the family heirloom on my countess-to-be."

A tiny flutter danced down her spine as his hands brushed against the nape of her neck. Charlotte bowed her head, the coolness of the precious metal and gemstones accentuating the warmth of his touch as he fastened the clasp.

And somehow all her fears seemed to melt away.

"Ooooo!" Raven and Hawk let out appreciative gasps as she straightened and turned back to face them.

McClellan nodded in satisfaction. "It's perfect. Absolutely perfect."

Wrexford remained silent. All that needed to be said was swirling in the depths of his gaze.

"Now it's time to be on your way." McClellan made shooing gestures toward the door. "You mustn't be late."

The earl offered his arm. "Shall we?"

"Yes," answered Charlotte. "I'm ready."

*   *   *

The dowager's drawing room was ablaze in a cheery light. The polished candelabras glowed like liquid silver as the flames danced over the graceful curves. Floating above the mellow crackling of the coals in the fireplace was the sound of two voices. Alison's distinctive drawl was one of them. And as for the other . . .

Charlotte hesitated, pausing in the corridor several steps short of the open doorway as the butler went in to announce them.

"*Fortes fortuna juvat,*" whispered Wrexford, giving her arm an encouraging squeeze.

Fortune favors the bold—the Latin aphorism made her smile. "Boldness has never been a failing of mine. If anything, it's been a flaw." But she had promised herself not to dwell on the past. What mattered was the present. She had changed a great deal— and so, she imagined, had her brother.

Alison's delighted exclamation cut short her reflections. "Don't dawdle in the shadows, gel—come in, come in!"

Squaring her shoulders, Charlotte gave Wrexford a nod and together they crossed the threshold.

Her brother—now the Earl of Wolcott—was standing by the sofa, hands clasped behind his back. He was a little stouter, and a touch of grey silvered his temples, but his face was un-changed. *Broad brow and blue eyes, just a shade lighter than her own . . . slanted cheekbones and a long, patrician nose . . .*

And the same crooked smile that had always made him the most approachable of her straitlaced family.

"Charlie!" Wolcott, too, seemed to be studying her counte-nance. "By Jove . . ." After an awkward hesitation, he stepped forward. "How . . . How very wonderful to see you."

Charlotte extended her hand for the perfunctory bow and polite kiss to her gloved knuckles—only to be drawn into a fierce hug.

Thump, thump.

Through the layers of well-tailored wool, she could feel the racing of his heart. Perhaps, she realized, he was as nervous as she was. In an instant, she was holding him just as tightly, her eyes squeezed shut to keep the tears from spilling down her cheeks.

The dowager began making odd little noises in her throat.

Wolcott slowly released his hold and gave a brusque cough. "Forgive my informality—I must call you Charlotte now, mustn't I?" His gaze held hers. "You're no longer my hellion baby sister who dared to defy convention by riding roughshod over the rules of Polite Society."

He drew in a ragged breath. "You've grown into a . . . a very beautiful and polished lady."

"Oh, trust me, I haven't changed very much." Charlotte gave a watery sniff. "J-Just ask Wrexford. Alas, I'm sure he can tell you some stories that will make your hair stand on end."

The earl cleared his throat with a cough. Or maybe it was a laugh.

"Allow me to introduce—"

"Lord Wrexford." Wolcott quickly inclined an embarrassed bow. "My apologies for allowing emotion to overrule manners." He smoothed the tails of his cravat and then tentatively offered his hand. "I'm Wolcott."

"Like your sister, I'm of the opinion that formal manners are vastly overrated," replied Wrexford. "It's a pleasure to make your acquaintance."

"The pleasure is mutual." Wolcott chuckled. "Is what my sister says true? Have you some harrowing tales to share?"

A dangerous glint flashed in Wrexford's eye, but with a flick of his lashes, it was gone. "If I did, it would be very ungentlemanly of me to say so, sir."

"Very wise of you, Wrexford," said the dowager. "Now

please go pour us all some champagne from the sideboard so that we may toast to family and the future."

The glasses were dutifully passed around, and the wine, along with the exchange of lighthearted pleasantries, added to the convivial mood.

"Aunt Alison is being very coy about how the two of you came to meet each other," said Wolcott, once the dowager had made everyone settle into the sofa and facing armchairs. "I look forward to hearing the story."

"We won't bore you with that," said Charlotte quickly. "You know how these things happen." In truth, she was quite sure that he couldn't begin to imagine the scenario.

And thank heaven for that. Her brother appeared extremely tolerant, but the details of the encounter were best left unsaid.

"Tell me about your family," she added quickly. As a younger son, Hartley had been under no pressure to marry and provide an heir, so he had taken his time in marrying. "I-I've never met your wife."

"Elizabeth wanted very much to come, and to bring our children to meet you—our two daughters are ten and seven, and our son is five. But I felt this first encounter might become too overwhelming were my entire family to descend upon you," he explained. "We shall all—I hope—have plenty of time to become acquainted in the days ahead."

"Nothing would please me more," answered Charlotte.

"Alison tells me you have two young wards from Mr. Sloane's side of the family," continued Wolcott.

"Yes." The boys had no idea how old they were, but Henning had estimated their ages. "Thomas is twelve, and Alexander is nine." A smile. "Alison spoils them dreadfully with sweets at Gunter's."

"A prerogative of old age," said the dowager tartly. "They are *such* charming and well-mannered lads," she added with a straight face. "Just the other day, they escorted me to the

British Museum and explained all about classical Greek civilization as we viewed Lord Elgin's marbles."

"They sound like very bookish lads," responded Wolcott.

Charlotte bit her lip to keep from laughing.

"Thomas shows a remarkable aptitude for mathematics," said Alison. "While young Alexander takes after Charlotte and is a budding artist."

"Ah, you still sketch, Charlotte?" asked her brother.

"A bit," she replied.

"I recall you were very, very good at it." He chuckled. "Especially the wicked little satires you drew about the local gentry." To Wrexford, he added, "If you aren't aware of it, I give you fair warning. She has a sharp eye—and even sharper pen."

"You don't say?" murmured Wrexford.

"Oh, come." Charlotte regarded Wolcott over the rim of her champagne glass. "Surely, you aren't suggesting that I'd lampoon my own fiancé."

"No, no—not at all! Good heavens, what a thought!"

What a thought, indeed.

On that note, supper was announced, and Alison gestured for Wolcott to lead Charlotte into the dining salon. More candles, their flames flickering off the crystal and warming the table with a rosy glow. The dowager had created an intimate seating arrangement at one end of the long mahogany table, with her and Wolcott facing Charlotte and Wrexford.

Charlotte felt her breath catch in her throat as she looked over the heirloom epergne and caught her brother's smile. *Memories, memories.* Painful ones, rubbing raw against the good times. But family was family. She hadn't dared admit until just now what a void the long-ago estrangement had left in her heart.

"So, Charlotte," said Wolcott, once the soup was served, "tell me about . . . egad, I suppose what I want to ask is about your life since—"

"Since I flew in the face of all sanity?"

He gave a self-deprecating grimace. "An absurd request, I know, but there is so much that I don't know." An uncomfortable pause. "Father and Wynton refused to tell me anything other than the fact that you had eloped with Anthony Sloane. I wished to write to you, but they claimed they had no idea where you were, save to say that it was somewhere in Italy."

"We were in Rome," answered Charlotte. "A marvelous place for anyone interested in art . . ."

Somehow the account came out far easier than she ever imagined. Wolcott listened intently, and asked thoughtful questions about the details she mentioned, while tactfully avoiding any queries into things left unsaid. The explanation of Anthony's delicate health leading to an early demise was the truth—just not the whole truth, and her brother accepted it with naught but a murmured condolence on her loss.

As the meal continued, Charlotte, in turn, pressed him for more details on his marriage, and his time spent running a lesser estate, well to the north of the family's ancestral lands. From his answers, she sensed that he, unlike her father and elder brother, accepted that an aristocratic title brought with it both privileges and responsibilities . . .

The dowager, however, interrupted to suggest that they all retire to the parlor, where the gentlemen could enjoy their postprandial brandy or port in the company of the ladies.

"An excellent suggestion," said Wolcott, her words sparking a mischievous twinkle lighting his eyes. "As I recall, you always insisted on having a glass—or two—of spirits with the gentlemen before withdrawing, much to Father's irritation."

"Your father was a pompous prig." Alison settled on the sofa and smoothed her skirts. "He needed an occasional challenge to his authority to take the wind out of his sails."

"You took delight in needling his friends as well," replied Wolcott, taking a seat next to her. "There was the time that you lit up one of Sir Albert Endicott's expensive cigars one night after supper, which had the baronet blowing smoke out of his ears." A chuckle. "Didn't Father accuse you of being foxed?"

"My wits weren't in the least fuzzed—I knew exactly what I was doing." The dowager eyed him through her quizzing glass. "Can you claim the same thing regarding the incident involving the garden fountain and Lord Ashleigh's hat?"

Charlotte laughed. "Oh, Lud, I remember that. Didn't you remove your trousers in order to—"

Her brother cleared his throat with a loud cough. "Let us not bore Lord Wrexford with puerile pranks from our family's past." He quickly shifted his gaze to the earl, who had moved to the tray of decanters on the sideboard. "I seem to recall having read that you are a patron of the Royal Institution, sir, and have written a number of papers on chemistry."

"I have," answered Wrexford, handing a brandy to Alison and Charlotte, then fetched one for himself and Wolcott. "*Slàinte.*"

"A fascinating area of study," said Wolcott, after he returned the earl's salute. "What do you think of Sir Humphry Davy's experiments with magnesium . . ."

As the two of them fell into a conversation on the famous chemist and his work, Charlotte leaned back, taking a moment to simply bask in the joy of her brother's presence. *His face, his voice, his touch*—he was all no longer just a hazy recollection, conjured from the recesses of memory, each time a bit more blurred by the passing years.

She closed her eyes for an instant, and on opening them again, she found Alison watching her intently, a glimmer of wetness sparkling on her lashes.

Their smiles met and the room seemed to shimmer with an unworldly light.

"You appear to have quite an interest in science, Lord Wolcott," observed Wrexford.

His words brought her thoughts back to earth. Anxious to learn all about her brother's current interests, Charlotte turned her attention to the exchange.

"Oh, I'm a mere neophyte. Your field of chemistry is quite interesting, as is geology and the new advances in electricity. I enjoy reading about them, but I can't claim to have any real knowledge on the subjects."

Wolcott's mouth quirked. "Now, ask me something about botany, and I'm on less slippery footing."

CHAPTER 13

Charlotte sat up straighter. "B-Botany?"

"Yes, I know, it's not the most exciting of the scientific disciplines." He made a wry face. "But I've always had more of an interest in the land than Father or Wynton, for whom the estates were merely ways to squeeze out guineas for their personal pleasures. I enjoy learning about plants, soils, and yields. And I find the gardens a relaxing place in which to cultivate flowers and fruit. It's endlessly interesting to experiment with what does well in what environment."

There was, reflected Charlotte, so much they didn't know about each other.

"You remember the old abandoned conservatory attached to the east wing of the manor house?" he asked.

Repressing a shiver, she nodded. It had been a cold, dreary place in her youth, with cracked windows, dank stone, and creatures that slithered through cracked terra-cotta pots and rusted gardening tools.

"I've restored it," he said. "I occasionally attend the meetings of a scientific society in Leeds, and a number of us have been sharing specimens from different areas in the north of England and Scotland. I've become particularly interested in evergreens . . ."

As if the current conundrum needed to sprout yet another curling vine! thought Charlotte. That her brother had an interest in botany seemed an awfully odd coincidence. Whether it was one that possessed hidden thorns remained to be seen.

"Indeed, through one of my fellow club members, I've been corresponding for the last few years with Professor Murray, a botanist at the University of St Andrews. He was kind enough to send some *Pinus sylvestris* specimens from the Highlands, which I'm testing on the upper slopes of one of my lesser estates near the Scottish border. And through him, I was put in contact with a botanist in the American city of New York, who—"

Her brother must have caught the sudden change in her expression, for he gave an embarrassed cough. "But enough about all my scrabbling in the soil. I'm boring you to perdition."

"O-On the contrary," assured Charlotte.

"Please continue," urged Wrexford. "Your sister is extremely tolerant of my fascination with anything scientific. I'm quite sure that she'll humor us."

Wolcott waited for Charlotte's confirming nod before allowing an uncertain smile. "If you're sure . . ."

"Do go on, Hartley," murmured Alison.

"Well, then, I admit it was quite an honor to exchange letters with such a notable expert in the field—though, of course, my area of interest must have struck him as awfully mundane. Nonetheless, he was generous-minded enough to arrange for specimens of *Quercus velutina, Quercus rubra,* and *Quercus macrocarpa* from New England to be sent to me."

"*Quercus?*" questioned Charlotte.

"Oak trees—three hardy species of American oak trees," he explained. "I'm hoping such stock will thrive in our northern climate, too, and perhaps provide a stock of excellent timber for shipbuilding. Something that would be both patriotic and profitable."

"A very excellent and admirable idea, Wolcott," said Wrexford. "If more of us aristocrats used our heads as more than just perches for our fancy hats, Britain would be much the better for it."

"That same thought has occurred to me." He sighed. "The strictures that limit what a highborn gentleman can do with his talents make no sense to me. Most of us are packed off to the finest universities in the land, and then find ourselves forbidden to apply our knowledge in any meaningful endeavor. It's a terrible waste."

"Your ideas sound almost as radical as those of your sister," murmured the dowager.

"I understood your frustrations, Charlotte," he said. "And applauded your courage in refusing to let your wings be clipped."

"Courage is woven into every fiber of your sister's being," said Wrexford. A hint of humor touched his lips. "After all, she agreed to marry me."

The dowager smiled through a mouthful of brandy. "Which shows Charlotte's intelligence is just as strong a thread. Your bark is far worse than your bite."

As soon as Wolcott's chuckle died away, the earl said, "But getting back to botany, I, too, have a botanist friend in New York. Dr. Hosack—"

"Ah, Dr. Hosack!" exclaimed her brother. "My correspondent speaks very highly of him. He studied in Scotland as a young man, and I've been told that it was our botanic gardens in the north that inspired him to create the very first one in America. Apparently, it's quite magnificent."

"Yes, he's recognized as a leading expert in plant medicine," replied Wrexford.

Wolcott's eyes lit with enthusiasm. "Indeed, indeed! That's

what my correspondent tells me." A pause. "He, too, has quite a reputation for medicinal expertise, though he's far too modest to have mentioned it to me."

"Would your correspondent perchance be Josiah Becton?" asked Wrexford.

Charlotte held her breath.

"Why, yes! How did you guess?"

"There is currently an international symposium on botanical medicine taking place at the Royal Botanic Gardens at Kew—" began Wrexford.

"Merciful heavens—what a cork-brained idiot I am!" exclaimed Wolcott. "I had heard of it months ago from Professor Murray, but somehow the fact that it was taking place now managed to slip my mind." He made a self-deprecating face. "Do you think it might be possible to arrange a meeting with him so that I may express my thanks for all his help?"

"I'm afraid that won't be possible," said Wrexford. "His heart had been weak for some time, and alas, he suffered a fatal spasm last week."

"Oh, I'm so sorry to hear that. What a distressing loss," responded Wolcott in a voice tightened by shock. "Professor Murray will be greatly saddened by the news." He fell silent for a moment, his brow furrowing in thought. "Now that you mention the symposium, I recall a mention in his last letter of being very excited about the discovery Becton was going to reveal in his lecture."

Charlotte had gone pale, but refrained from joining the conversation. A wise move, decided Wrexford. Her relationship with her brother was fraught with enough complication without having him wonder why she had any knowledge about the death of a stranger.

"Did he say what it was?" Wrexford asked.

Wolcott shook his head. "No, but that's hardly surprising, as I'm a mere neophyte." He rolled his glass between his palms, watching the amber spirits slowly spin. "At least Becton will live on through his work."

"Indeed." However meaningful Wolcott's unexpected revelations might prove, Wrexford decided this was neither the time nor the place to parse through them. "It's a pity that you'll not have the opportunity to make his acquaintance. But I imagine you'll still find a visit to the Royal Botanic Gardens fascinating. Charlotte is familiar with the grounds, and I'm sure she would be delighted to give you a grand tour."

"Yes, it would be a great pleasure," she confirmed. "Death should not overshadow the celebration of Life, in all its glorious profusion of shapes and textures and colors." A glance at the dowager. "Might we convince you to join us?"

"What a splendid idea!" replied Alison. "And we must bring the Weasels."

"Weasels?" Wolcott raised his brows in confusion. "But surely such destructive creatures would cause great damage to the delicate flora."

Charlotte let out a burble of laughter. "These Weasels are capable of causing a great deal of mayhem, but I assure you, the plantings are quite safe from them. You see, it's a term of, er, endearment that we use for my two wards, who—for the most part—don't behave like wild beasts."

Her lips twitched. "However, I'll make no promises about the cleanliness of their paws or clothing. Like a magnet drawing iron filings, they seem to exert a powerful force for attracting all sorts of muck."

Wolcott chuckled. "Boys will be boys."

And Weasels will be Weasels, thought the earl. *Confuse the two at your own peril, Lord Wolcott.* But that was a lesson his soon-to-be brother-in-law would need to learn for himself.

"Shall we make it for the day after tomorrow?" suggested the dowager. "Hartley and I must make some morning calls tomorrow after nuncheon."

"And then I've an engagement to dine with some old friends at my club," added her brother.

"That's perfect," Charlotte assured them. "I'll have my maid pack a picnic and we can make a day of it."

Any lingering shadows from the mention of death gave way to a lighter mood as the plans were quickly finalized and a time set for the dowager's barouche to fetch Charlotte and the boys. The talk then moved on to other London landmarks that might interest Wolcott.

"Ye heavens, I'm exhausted just listening to such peregrinations," quipped the dowager as she patted back a yawn.

Charlotte quickly rose. "Much as I don't want the evening to end, we ought not keep you up any longer."

"There will be many more of them," said Wolcott as he shot to his feet and drew her into a parting hug. "I can't begin to express how happy I am that we've reconnected."

As Wolcott drew back and cleared his throat, Wrexford saw both of them were blinking back tears.

"Dash it all, I've missed you, Charlie."

"And I you, Hartley."

Ebb and flow, mused the earl. Life was in a state of constant motion, of constant flux—the elemental forces of the universe inexorably pushing and pulling at each other. Light giving way to dark, and then reasserting itself . . .

Watching Charlotte and her brother, he vowed to himself that her future would not be as shadowed as her past.

"You're up awfully late." Wrexford shrugged out of his overcoat and eyed the jumble of open books spread out over the counter of the workroom after letting it drop to the floor. "Dare I ask why?"

Tyler looked up from the leather-bound codex he was reading and pinched at the bridge of his nose. He was sitting in one of the armchairs by the fireplace, but the coals had burned down to ashes. "So far, there's nothing worth mentioning." An uncharacteristic note of defeat shaded the valet's voice. "I've done naught but fritter away the hours in looking for . . ." He blew out his breath. "In looking for something that likely doesn't exist."

The earl poured out two measures of whisky and carried them over to the chairs. "By its very nature, science involves many wild goose chases. Failure is often just as important as success for what it tells us."

"This isn't about science." Tyler waved away the glass. "It's about making amends."

Wrexford frowned, the show of uncertainty taking him by surprise. Whatever his inner emotions, the valet usually hid them beneath a show of sarcastic self-confidence.

"Here, drink this." He forced a glass into Tyler's hand. "Then stop sniveling and tell me what pitchfork the devil is jabbing in your arse."

The valet took a morose sip and remained silent.

Not a good sign. Needling usually roused Tyler from any brooding. After coaxing the fire back to life, he took a seat and waited for the flames to warm the chill from the air.

"Brooding only begets brooding," he murmured. "I should know."

That, at least, elicited a glimmer of a smile.

After another moment of silence slid by, the earl rose and went to examine the books on the counter. *Compendiums of plant engravings, von Humboldt's accounts of his travel through Spanish America, medical texts on malaria . . .*

"Hmmph." Wrexford quaffed a swallow of whisky and set his glass on the sideboard before returning to his chair. "You're a logical fellow, Tyler. So I don't need to tell you that looking for the proverbial needle in a haystack is an exceedingly difficult task under the best of circumstances." He tapped his fingertips together. "And when you have no idea what the needle is, it becomes an impossible one."

The valet's nostrils flared as he drew in a ragged breath.

"This investigation seems to have turned very personal for you. I understand that Hosack is an old friend—"

"It's not Hosack. It's . . ." The fire-gold glow of the flames accentuated the deep hollows beneath Tyler's eyes. "It's you. It's Lady Charlotte. It's Hawk." His gaze angled away from the flames. "Due to my blabbering, I've drawn all of you into a murder, and put you in danger—especially Hawk."

"You think Lady Charlotte would have kept her distance, once she got wind of DeVere's possible involvement?"

"We can't say for sure what she would have done," countered Tyler. "However, there's no question that the boy wouldn't have been involved, save for my negligence. If I hadn't left him alone in the conservatory, he wouldn't have been the only one to see the murderer."

"The murderer doesn't know about Hawk."

"We don't know that!" The valet's voice took on a brittle edge. "You're breaking your own damnable rules by making an assumption we can't prove."

"I'm not merely spitting into the wind," he replied. "I'm basing the statement on rational deductions. The killer has shown himself to be both cunning and clever. If he knows about the boy and what threat he might pose—which seems highly unlikely, given Hawk's account of the incident—he would have made a move by now."

Tyler couldn't muster a retort to that.

"The investigation is already a diabolically difficult one. Let us not make it more so."

The air slowly leaked out from the valet's lungs. "I know what you say is sensible. And yet I can't help feeling to blame for this bumblebroth."

"Then let us resolve it quickly," replied the earl. "By finding tangible clues and then piecing the puzzle together."

"Any ideas on where to look next?" Tyler glanced at the books on the counter. "I feel as if I'm simply turning in circles."

"As a matter of fact," answered Wrexford, "something I heard this evening has given me pause for thought. Put together with some information I received from Kit, it might lead us somewhere . . ."

Charlotte looked down at her finished drawing, feeling gratified that she had satisfied both Wrexford's request to avoid stirring further rumors about Becton's demise and the demands of her own conscience.

A storm-tossed ship with torn sails and leaking hull . . . a grim-faced North Wind about to engulf the foundering vessel in a maelstrom of rain clouds and thunderbolts . . . Cordelia's information on Quincy's shoddy practices was just the sort of topic that suited A. J. Quill's pen. The public would be roused enough to demand answers, forcing the government to take a closer look at the American's shipping business.

If Quincy was involved in murder and theft, the scrutiny might well pressure him into making a slip as he tried to cover up his crimes.

After adding highlights of color to the pen and ink lines, Charlotte rolled up the paper in a protective covering of oilcloth. The boys would be happy to run it down to Fores's printshop after they returned home from the tutor.

Her work done, she headed downstairs to brew a cup of tea.

"There's a kettle on the hob, and a pan of fresh shortbread about to come out of the oven," called McClellan from the pantry.

Charlotte looked at the worktable, where several tins were already filled with sweet and savory delicacies. "There will be just six of us at the picnic tomorrow, not a regiment of the King's Hussars."

"The boys eat more than a troop of cavalry officers *and* their horses," quipped the maid. "And besides, good food makes for good cheer."

She caught a glimpse of the large herb-dusted chicken McClellan was about to put into the oven and smiled. "Then we shall all be happy as kittens who've knocked over a creampot."

"Cream," muttered McClellan. "Where's the cream for the custard and apple tart?"

As the maid went to search the larder, Charlotte made tea and set out two cups and saucers. As the fragrant steam filled her lungs, she tried to make herself relax. The meeting with her brother had been more heartening than she had dared imagine. And yet, she hadn't been able to shake a niggling worry regarding his botanical interests.

"Why the long face?" McClellan settled onto one of the stools. "I thought you said the reconciliation with Lord Wolcott couldn't have gone any better."

McClellan and the boys had, of course, demanded a full recounting of the evening over breakfast, and the announcement that they would all soon be meeting her brother was met with great enthusiasm.

"Is there, perchance, something you haven't yet mentioned?"

Charlotte sighed. There was no sense in prevaricating with McClellan. She had a sixth sense for Trouble.

"There is." A pause. "Though I'm not certain it's any cause for concern." She quickly explained about Wolcott's interest in botany, and his connection to Becton through Professor Murray of St. Andrews.

"Another Scottish connection," mused the maid, a pensive grimace deepening the lines at the corners of her mouth. "Hmmph. One can't help but wonder . . ."

"It's not as unsettling as you might think," she pointed out. "The Scottish universities are among the best in the world for the study of medicine, and they created the concept of botanical gardens for healing purposes. Men come from near and far to study in St. Andrews or Edinburgh. And the professors who teach there correspond with scholars in all corners of the globe."

So, why don't such rational words put my own fears to rest?

"A fair point," murmured McClellan. "What does Wrexford think?"

The earl hadn't appeared to find the coincidence as disturbing as she had. During the carriage ride home, he had seemed far more concerned about the information she had passed on from Cordelia concerning Captain Daggett.

"My sense is, he's more worried about the American naval captain than my brother."

"But you don't agree." It was more of a statement than a question.

"I'm not quite sure what to think," replied Charlotte. "However, my intuition tells me there's one thing for certain—when we finally identify the snakes slithering through the leaves, Justinian DeVere will be one of them."

CHAPTER 14

Hawk darted away from the parlor window. "They're here, they're here!" he called, skidding into the corridor, where Raven was helping McClellan with the hampers of food.

Charlotte gathered her shawl, and eyed both boys, checking that no noxious substances had managed to rub off on their best clothing in the short time since dressing.

"Straighten your collar, Raven," she murmured after fishing out a small satchel from behind the boot box. "And, Hawk, don't forget your sketchbook and pencils."

Hawk rushed over to take the bag.

"Just a moment." Smiling, Charlotte wet her finger and rubbed away a small smudge from his cheek. How dirt managed to adhere to the boys within moments of their being scrubbed was a sorcery no rational law of science could explain.

A knock rapped on the door. One of the dowager's footmen had accompanied the coachman in order to assist with the picnic things. As McClellan began barking orders to bustle everything out to the boot of the barouche, Hawk hesitated, fixing Charlotte with a look of uncertainty.

Crouching down, she asked, "What's wrong, sweeting?"

"W-What if your bruvver doesn't like us?" he asked in a small voice.

Her heart gave a little lurch. Hawk only mangled his speech when he was very, very nervous. Drawing him into a hug, she held him tightly, achingly aware of all the bony juts and angles of his body.

"My bruvver," she whispered, "will adore you. He's very happy that our family has reunited."

Hawk didn't appear entirely sure. "B-But when he finds out that we're really just guttersnipes—"

"As I've told you before, sweeting, family isn't defined solely by blood. An even more elemental bond is love." She smiled as she smoothed a hand over his unruly curls. "And Aunt Alison will crack him over the head with her cane if he dares to say otherwise."

His quivering lips slowly curled upward. "Wrexford says she's an unholy battle-axe when her blood is roused." He blinked. "But I would never repeat that to her in case it hurt her feelings."

"Actually, it would probably make her laugh, but it's a very gentlemanly sentiment." She gave him another quick squeeze. "Now, come, let us not keep everyone waiting."

"Are you busy?" Wrexford poked his head into Sheffield's office. "Or do you have a moment for a few questions?"

"Thank heaven!" His friend dropped a thick sheaf of shipping manifests onto his blotter, and heaved a theatrical sigh. "Fire away—and feel free to ask more than a few. I've been drowning in the minutia of Kashmir wool and calico bolts—and to which mill each needs to be shipped. So you've just thrown me a lifeline."

"Miss Whitney won't thank me for providing *too* much of a distraction," responded Wrexford. After clearing a set of ledgers from a chair, he took a seat. "Do you, perchance, still have the manifests from the unloading of Quincy's merchant ship?"

In answer, Sheffield opened one of his desk drawers and pulled out a folder.

"I'm impressed, Kit."

"A tidy mind is necessary for tidy profits." His friend sorted through the papers. "Have you something specific in mind?"

"I've been thinking . . ." Wrexford moved to the windows and gazed out over the wharves, where the spiderweb of masts and rigging seemed to mirror the tangled threads of the damnable conundrum. "You said the plant specimens being gifted to the Royal Society had a manifest detailing what was in the crates," he answered. "I'm wondering whether the delivery marked for DeVere did as well."

Papers rustled as Sheffield skimmed through them. "As a matter of fact, yes." More rustling, then he passed over a handful of sheets.

Wrexford paged through them and let out a grunt of satisfaction. "Might I keep these for a bit?"

"On one condition."

He lifted a brow in question.

"You include me in whatever you have planned."

"As I said, I'm merely thinking," answered Wrexford. Yes, an idea had come to mind. But there were dangers involved that might have ramifications that rippled out—

"Granted, I'm not as skilled in clandestine forays as you—or the Weasels," added his friend. "But you have to admit, I'm getting better at it."

He sat back and tapped his fingertips together. "Besides, if you're going to break into DeVere's conservatory, you could use a sentry to keep watch while you're fiddle-faddling among the plants. As we both have reason to know, that godforsaken place is a jungle of greenery, making it easy for an adversary to sneak up on you."

"Who says I'm planning on breaking into DeVere's conservatory?"

Sheffield responded with a very rude word.

The earl folded the papers and tucked them into his coat pocket.

Maintaining a stoic silence, his friend waited.

Choices, choices.

"Wear soft-soled shoes, and bring a black toque to hide that flaming-gold hair," Wrexford finally muttered. "We'll meet in the mews behind my townhouse a half hour before midnight."

"For what are you looking?"

"I'm not precisely sure." A pause. "But I'm hoping that Hosack—who's the leading expert in American botanical specimens—might be able to spot something that's out of place."

"By Jove." Wolcott let out a low whistle as he descended from the barouche and looked around at the sprawling gardens, whose endless array of colors, shapes, and textures seemed to stretch out in all directions as far as the eye could see. "It's absolutely magnificent."

"There is a grove of evergreen specimens just past the Temple of Aeolus, Lord Wolcott," said Hawk. "Would you like for us to take you there?"

"That would be splendid, Master Alexander," replied Charlotte's brother. "I should very much like to see it."

Raven offered the dowager his arm. "The grass is still a little slippery with dew, Aunt Alison."

"That's very gentlemanly of you, Master Thomas," murmured Wolcott—which caused an odd little sound to rumble in Raven's throat.

Charlotte recognized it as a swallowed snigger. "Actually, Hartley, the boys prefer being called by their avian nicknames."

"*Avian?*" He shot her a quizzical look. "I thought you called them Weasels. Which are in the same phylum as birds, but a different class."

Raven and Hawk started to chortle.

She eyed them sternly. "Don't be impertinent. Please explain yourselves to Lord Wolcott."

"On all the fancy official papers, my name is given as Thomas Ravenwood Sloane," said Raven. "But I've always been called Raven."

"And mine is given as Alexander Hawksley," chirped his younger brother. "But—"

"But let me guess," said Wolcott. "You are called Hawk."

The boy grinned. "Yes, sir."

"Well, that's a very fine pair of names." A smile rippled through his eyes as he set Charlotte's hand on his sleeve. "Shall we all flap our wings and head to the evergreens?"

Flanked by both boys, the dowager set off at a brisk walk, while Charlotte and her brother followed at a more leisurely pace, with McClellan and the footman bringing up the rear with the picnic hampers.

"They are very fine lads," remarked Hartley. "I look forward to them meeting their cousins." A smile curled the corner of his mouth. "It will be nice for Geoffrey to have such well-behaved older boys setting a good example of gentlemanly deportment."

"You may revise your thinking," drawled Charlotte, "when they show him how to make stinkbombs."

A peal of laughter. "I'm glad to hear they aren't too perfect." Hartley made a wry face. "Come, come—the smell can't be so bad. It's not as if they have access to—"

"Oh, trust me—the stink is far worse than you can imagine," she interjected. "Remember, Wrexford is a chemist." A pause. "And he has a very peculiar sense of humor."

Another chuckle. "Ah. Thank you for the warning." A pause. "I take it Wrexford and the boys rub along well together?"

"Exceedingly well," answered Charlotte. "The bonds may not be forged by blood, but they are no less elemental."

"Alison clearly dotes on them as well," he observed.

"And they adore her."

"With good reason. She's always understood that individuals have different temperaments and different dreams. And that no amount of raging or punishment will change that." Hartley tucked her hand a little more firmly into the crook of his arm. "It makes me so profoundly happy that we have all managed to reunite as a family."

Family.

Charlotte watched a lone hawk circling high overhead, a solitary black speck against the vast expanse of the cloud-dotted sky.

The reckless flight to Rome . . . the death of my husband . . . the daunting challenge of finding a way to survive on my own . . .

Never in her wildest dreams had she allowed herself to think the terrible rift with those she had left behind could ever be repaired.

"I am fortunate beyond words." Halting abruptly, she turned and wrapped him in a quick, impulsive hug. "You are the very best of brothers, Hart. I love you dearly."

"Well, er . . ." A flush colored his face as he stuttered for words, tongue-tied between delight and embarrassment. "By Jove, Charlie, I love you dearly, too." A cough. "Always have."

Charlotte took his arm once again, and they resumed walking, a companionable silence settling over them as Wolcott allowed his gaze to wander admiringly over the surrounding plantings. A hail from Hawk soon drew them off the main walkway and into the glade of evergreen specimens.

"Would you like for me to show you the *Pinus armandii* from Cathay, Lord Wolcott?" he added as he darted around a thickly needled bush.

"I should like that very much." Relinquishing his hold on Charlotte, he gave a cheery wave. "Lead the way!"

Charlotte found Alison settled on a bench in the shade of a fragrant Norway spruce and took a seat beside her as Raven flew off to join Wolcott and Hawk. "Thank you for ignoring my sniveling fears and pressing me to do this," she murmured. "I should know by now in my life that cowardice is always the wrong choice."

"Oh, pffft. You're not one to shy away from a challenge. You would have taken the bull by the horns—I simply encouraged you to do it sooner than later."

A pause. "Not that Hartley bears any resemblance to a bull. The two of you were always kindred souls. While Wynton . . ." The dowager shrugged. "Hmmph, I shall refrain from speaking ill of the dead."

Instead, Alison quickly turned the talk to the more agreeable topic of the upcoming wedding, and all the many little details that still required attention. They passed a pleasant interlude parsing logistical arrangements—the ceremony was to take place at the local church by Wrexford's country estate, with a celebratory nuncheon at the ancestral home after the ceremony—until the boys returned and began making thinly-veiled hints about the perils of starvation in the wilds.

"Take the blankets, Weasels, and ferret out a nice flat, sunny spot for the picnic," called McClellan from the pile of provisions.

Raven feigned a stagger toward the hampers. "I think we may need a ginger biscuit to stave off fainting from hunger."

"Touch that bag at your own peril," warned the maid. But after another threatening wag of her finger, she fished out a bundle wrapped in oilcloth. "You may have *just one,* and then be off with you."

Wolcott reappeared a few minutes later, his eyes wide with wonder. "What a marvelous place. Master Hawk tells me there is a room in the main conservatory that showcases the original specimens brought back by Sir Joseph Banks from the South Seas."

"Would you like to see them after our meal?"

"Oh, very much so!"

With both the boys and her brother anxious to continue their explorations, there was no leisurely lingering over the meal, especially as McClellan spotted Tyler heading from one of the outer hothouses to the lecture room adjoining the Orangery and she waved him over.

"Do join us," said Charlotte, after introducing him to Wolcott. "We've plenty of food—the pigeon pie and apple tart are delicious."

"Thank you." The valet accepted a wedge of the pie. "Alas, I can't stay long. I've promised to set the microscope for the afternoon program so that the attendees may have a look at some rare treasures of the Royal Society's seed collection."

"May I come help?" volunteered Raven.

"Of course, lad." Tyler looked to her. "Assuming Lady Charlotte approves."

"By all means," she agreed.

"Come to think of it, the storeroom in the Orangery has a shipment of exotic specimens waiting to be shipped north to the University of St. Andrews—a gift from the Royal Society to spread rare botanicals to other teaching gardens in Britain. Hawk might enjoy sketching them while Raven and I work."

Hawk looked up with a pleading look. "May I, m'lady?"

Tyler's gaze met hers. "I'll keep a close watch on both lads so they don't wander into any mischief."

"Yes, of course you may. But do have a care not to distract Mr. Tyler from his duties," said Charlotte. "And as my brother wishes to see Sir Joseph's famous South Seas collection, I'll escort him and Alison—"

The dowager, who was comfortably settled beneath a lap robe on a bench in the sun, waved off the suggestion. "You two go on. I shall remain here with McClellan." She patted back a yawn. "And polish off what remains of the ginger biscuits."

The boys surreptitiously stuffed their pockets with sweets—

still leaving plenty for Alison—and then their little group split up and headed off to their separate destinations.

Charlotte led the way to one of the side entrances to the main conservatory and took her brother through a meandering tour of the various galleries, pleased to hear his frequent expressions of delight as he stopped to admire one new treasure after another.

The way to the South Seas specimens led through one of the reception areas, and as they circled around a group of scholars studying a display of botanical engravings laid out on the worktables, a hail from Sir Robert drew them to a halt.

"Lady Charlotte!" The dowager's friend stepped away from his colleagues and approached with a friendly smile. "How nice to see you here again. It appears we shall make a botanist of you yet!"

"I fear you shall be disappointed on that," replied Charlotte dryly. "However, my brother, who is visiting from the north, more than makes up for my sad lack of knowledge."

Her introduction of Wolcott elicited an enthusiastic response from the baronet. "Why, what a pleasure it is to meet you, Lord Wolcott! One of our Scottish members, Professor Murray from St. Andrews, has made mention of you as a leading member of the botanical society of Leeds."

"I'm a mere dilettante, but the professor has been very kind in helping me expand my knowledge in the subject. Indeed, he connected me with his good friend and frequent correspondent in New York . . ."

Charlotte caught a sudden tiny movement out of the corner of her eye. One of the scholars had shifted his position, angling himself just a little closer. His face was still hidden, but she immediately recognized the sun-bleached gleam of his auburn hair.

Captain Samuel Daggett.

"Though I've just learned the very sad news that Mr. Becton

passed away from a heart ailment just after he arrived here in London for the symposium," replied her brother.

Daggett seemed to excuse himself abruptly and drifted another step away from the gentleman who was speaking to him—Charlotte recognized von Stockhausen, and didn't blame the Prussian for looking a trifle offended by the American's rudeness.

"Horribly sad," agreed Sir Robert. "Especially as he was planning to present a very important research report on his latest discovery."

Was it merely her imagination, or was Daggett intent on eavesdropping? Something about his eyes—their ice-sharp intensity—had unsettled her from the moment she had met him. He appeared to be interested in an orchid on one of the display tables, but Charlotte sensed his attention was really elsewhere.

As if intent on annoying the American, von Stockhausen moved to examine a cluster of bougainvillea, forcing the captain to give ground.

"Then Professor Murray will be doubly affected by the news, since Mr. Becton was both a friend and a fellow scholar," replied her brother. "They frequently exchanged papers and specimens."

Her suspicions stirred by Daggett's sly behavior, Charlotte was anxious to prevent any further talk about Becton. "If you'll forgive us, Sir Robert, my brother wishes to see the famous South Seas collection, and I fear Aunt Alison has grown a bit fatigued from our outside walks." She flashed an apologetic smile. "She's resting right now, but we ought not dally too much longer."

"Oh, don't let me keep you!" The baronet made shooing gestures. "Sir Joseph's treasures are not to be missed!" To Wolcott, he added, "Though I do hope to see you here again before you leave London."

"Alas, I will be departing soon," replied her brother. "However, I shall be returning south in a fortnight for my sister's nuptials, and will be making a more extended stay in Town with my wife and children."

"Excellent! You must allow me to give you an extensive tour of all our treasures here at the Royal Botanic Gardens, as well as attend one of our meetings at the Royal Society headquarters in Somerset House."

"I shall look forward to it, sir," responded Wolcott with great enthusiasm, and after a last exchange of well wishes, Charlotte managed to lead her brother into the adjoining corridor.

"What a splendid idea it was to come here," murmured Wolcott as she quickened her steps. Charlotte knew she was letting her imagination run away with her, but she couldn't help straining to hear any sound of following footsteps through the gentle whispering of the surrounding leaves.

"The sights, the scents . . ." Her brother drew in a deep, appreciative breath. "It's a place—one could even call it a paradise—that celebrates the constant blossoming of Life." A sigh followed. "Which," he added, "helps soften the pain of loss."

The light fluttered as they passed through a set of brass-framed glass doors. The air was suddenly warmer and heavy with moisture.

Yes, but even in paradise, deadly evils lurked within the shadows. Waiting to strike.

She clicked the latch shut behind her.

Let them try.

They would find themselves in for a rude awakening.

CHAPTER 15

"I say, milord . . ." Hosack took a nervous look around and then made a turtle-like withdrawal into the upturned collar of his overcoat. It was well past midnight and the air was taking on a knife-edge chill. "Is this, er, legal?"

"Not in the least," answered Wrexford, shifting a little to his left to allow the moonlight to flitter over the door's lock. After studying the keyhole for a moment, he drew a steel probe from the hidden sleeve in his boot.

"But doesn't that mean—"

"Sssssshhhhh," warned Sheffield. "Hold your questions for later—that is, unless you wish to spend the foreseeable future as His Majesty's guest in Newgate Prison."

The hide-and-seek glow showed the doctor's face had gone unnaturally pale.

"I did make it clear that this foray was bending the letter of the law," murmured the earl.

"Don't worry," added Sheffield. "Wrex has never yet been caught at this."

"Ye gods—bite your tongue." Silent as a stalking panther,

Tyler materialized from the swirls of mist. "One never voices such hubris in the middle of a mission." To Wrexford, he added, "There are no lights lit in the adjoining section of the house. The only signs of life are in the east wing."

The lock released with a soft *snick.* "So far, so good," said Wrexford. "Let us hope our luck holds."

Easing open the door, he motioned for the others to enter Justinian DeVere's grand conservatory.

Tyler went first, in order to move ahead and reconnoiter the darkened specimen galleries. Sheffield followed, taking care to tread lightly over the flagged walkway. Hosack, however, stumbled in the gloom and hit up against a cart of terra-cotta pots, setting off a brittle *chink.*

"Try to relax." Wrexford placed a steadying hand on the doctor's shoulder. "As I told you, we're merely here to look around."

Earlier in the day, the earl had sought out Hosack to explain his suspicions, and how the doctor's expertise was critical in confirming whether or not there was any incriminating evidence to link DeVere to Becton's murder. He had, of course, warned of the risks if they were caught. However, to his credit, Hosack hadn't hesitated in agreeing to be part of the covert excursion.

But theory was one thing, and reality quite another when push came to shove.

"Sorry. I-I've never done anything criminal before." Hosack drew a deep breath, which seemed to calm his nerves, and managed a brave smile. "But my friend deserves justice, so I'm ready to do whatever I have to."

"I don't expect any trouble," assured Wrexford. That DeVere had tried to kill him the last time he had entered the sprawling mansion was a fact he refrained from mentioning. The circumstances had been different.

"Come, the sooner we find the crates from the Quincy's merchant ship and have a look at them, the sooner we can be on our way. As you seem quite certain that Becton's miracle plant was from the tropical forests of Spanish America, you need only look at the specimens and confirm that they are only ones native to the United States."

"I can do that, milord. If DeVere and Quincy have stolen my friend's specimen and hidden it among North American species, I shall spot it."

"Excellent. Now let's keep moving."

The glass-paneled walls and roof of the conservatory admitted enough light from the cloudless night sky to allow them to navigate the winding paths through the raised beds of specimens planting. Dotting the way were groupings of potted trees and bushes, their foliage swaying gently as they brushed past the shadowy branches.

Tyler and Sheffield were waiting at the entrance to another section of the building. "The rooms ahead look to be storage areas and study rooms," said the valet. "Which seems the likely place to begin searching for the recent shipment from Quincy's ship."

Wrexford nodded his agreement. Though he truly didn't expect trouble, he eased his pistol out of his coat pocket before signaling Tyler to continue on.

Once they passed through the doorway, the air turned chillier, and the floral scents less pronounced. In fact, as the earl ventured deeper into the space, passing stacks of folded canvas and shelves of glass bottles, an oddly metallic tang tickled at his nostrils.

Tyler must have noticed it as well, for he, too, stopped short and drew his weapon.

Turning, Wrexford motioned for Sheffield to stop. "You and Hosack take cover behind those burlap sacks of earth," he whispered, indicating the amorphous shapes half hidden in the gloom. "Do it quickly, Kit, and stay with him until I signal that it's safe to come out," he added before his friend could argue.

Up ahead, the valet had inched forward and positioned himself to one side of an archway leading into another room. Wrexford hurried to join him.

"There looks to be a candle lit at the far end," said Tyler.

The earl ventured a peek into the space. But the fitful light from above was playing tricks with the eye, turning the shadows into a helter-pelter tangle of shifting shapes.

The silence was deafening.

"I'll go first," said Wrexford. "Stay behind me and several paces to the right." Tyler possessed a cool head and steady hand.

"Do be careful. Lady Charlotte will have my head on a platter if you have to march down the aisle with a bloody bandage around your brow."

He checked his priming. "Yes, but think what a juicy drawing she could make of the event." Clouds were beginning to scud in. As one drifted over the moon, he darted forward.

On reaching a barrow filled with tools, he ducked low and cocked an ear.

Nothing.

Another quick traverse brought him closer to the candlelight. Just a few more steps would bring him to the corner of the stacked crates and give the right angle to see what lay within the alcove.

"Hell and damnation." The oath slipped through his gritted teeth as he ventured a look.

Tyler was at his shoulder in a flash. His eyes widened in shock. "Lord Almighty."

Charlotte added a bit of cross-hatching and then leaned back to assess the effect. It was a strong drawing, she decided, and sharp enough to raise more queries about the questionable shipping practices of Quincy Enterprises.

After opening her box of watercolors, she picked up a brush and began mixing a range of hues. It had been awfully tempting to add names to the text of her satire—oh, how she longed to strip away DeVere's cloak of respectability with a few razored words! But even though poking a stick into the nest of vipers would make them writhe, and perhaps commit a fatal mistake, it was still too early to risk putting them on guard.

Wrexford had urged caution. And he had given his word to Griffin that past crimes would remain secret.

Charlotte released an unhappy sigh. "And so I must tread a damnably fine line." Adding a last splash of water to her palette, she wet her brush and set to work.

"It's late." The patter of bare feet paused in the corridor right outside her doorway. "You're supposed to be sleeping."

Charlotte didn't look up. "So are you."

"We woke up . . ." *Crunch-crunch.* "And went to fetch a glass of milk from the kitchen," said Hawk through a mouthful of crumbs.

"To go with all the biscuits you purloined from the picnic?" she asked with a smile.

"Technically, we didn't purloin them," shot back Raven. "McClellan made them, and as she's part of our family, they would have come back here. And as we're welcome to help ourselves from the jar in the kitchen, putting them in our pockets was merely a . . . convenience, not a theft."

At that, Charlotte set down her pen. "Perhaps you should consider becoming a barrister."

"What's a *barrister*?" asked Hawk.

"A man who makes his living talking round and round in circles until everyone listening is tied into knots," quipped Charlotte.

Hawk nodded sagely. "Raven would make a very good barrister."

His brother made a rude sound. "A barrister is someone who argues cases in a court of law." A pause. "The law is boring."

"It's not the least boring when you break it," she replied.

"That's assuming you get caught."

The casual comment stirred a frisson of alarm. The fact that they were wearing their nightclothes was somewhat reassuring, but still . . .

Narrowing her eyes, Charlotte demanded, "Just what are you Weasels planning?"

"*Nothing!*" responded Hawk.

She relaxed slightly, as he hadn't mangled his consonants.

Raven held up a mug of milk to emphasize their innocence. After handing it to his brother, he came around to study her drawing. "We ought to do a little more looking around the West India docks, where Quincy's ship is docked. I figure there's a lot more scuttlebutt to be learned if we ask around."

The thought of icy-looking Captain Daggett and the ruthless men with whom he was consorting made her blood run cold. "This is a very complicated investigation. We mustn't run off half-cocked. If Wrexford wishes our help, he will ask for it."

Eyes still glued on her drawing, Raven considered her words. "Very well," he finally conceded. "Unless we're asked, we won't hare off on our own."

"Thank you." Repressing a yawn, Charlotte flexed her tight shoulders and rinsed out her brush. "And now, I think it's time for all of us to seek our beds."

Careful to avoid the puddles of blood on the stone flagging, Wrexford approached the nearest of the two bodies sprawled on the floor. The corpse—for no man could possibly be alive with a large chunk of his skull blown to Kingdom Come—was lying facedown. Aside from the bullet wound to the head, there was no sign of violence to the well-tailored clothing. The victim didn't appear to have fought for his life.

Tyler cleared his throat. "Is it . . ."

"Yes," said the earl as he crouched down for a look at the lifeless profile. "It's definitely Justinian DeVere."

"So the devil has finally gotten his due," muttered the valet.

He, too, could summon no real sympathy for the fellow, who, in his judgment, was utterly lacking in basic humanity.

But does anyone deserve to die in such a horrible way?

"Let us leave morality aside for the moment." Wrexford moved to examine the second body. There was even more blood—Tobias Quincy's throat had been slashed. And by the cuts on his fingers, it appeared he had tried to ward off his attacker.

"Hmmph." He rose and absently wiped his hands on the lapels of his coat, earning a pained wince from his valet. "It would appear that the two men were taken by surprise. I would guess that DeVere was killed first with a shot, and then Quincy was attacked."

"There may have been two assailants," said Tyler, already moving slowly around the room, looking for any clues.

Wrexford, however, remained standing where he was, trying to make sense of these grisly murders. And yet, they seemed to defy all logic.

Damnation—what am I missing? Had hubris led him to force the pieces of the puzzle together in order to fit the pattern he wished to see?

A grunt from Tyler drew him back to the moment. "There's a drop of blood here—it's still damp." He looked around. "And there's another."

Following the trail brought him to an archway leading to a different section of the conservatory.

"Redraw your pistol," murmured Wrexford as he joined the valet, "and let's see where it leads. The murderer may still be here."

Easing into the murky darkness, he moved over the flagging as silently as he could. He was back in a specimen gallery, this one filled with potted palms in a variety of shapes and sizes.

The fluttery, knifelike greenery was thick and drooping . . .

Covering a multitude of sins?

Holding his breath, Wrexford stopped to listen.

A small rustling caught his ear, just a little louder than the whispers stirred by the drafts snaking in through the mullioned glass.

He crept closer to the alcove, where a half-dozen squat date palms were arranged in a circle, the lush, fan-shaped fronds curtaining the interior space. For a long moment, all was still.

Then the rustling came again.

Kicking over one of the trees—it toppled with a crackling thud—the earl lunged into the tangle of branches. A scream shattered the silence. A fist smacked flesh. Another tree went flying.

Tyler raced closer, pistol ready as he danced around the thrashing greenery, trying to discern friend from foe.

The sound of running steps pounded over the walkway as Sheffield shot through the archway, Hosack right at his heels.

The struggling suddenly ceased as Wrexford landed a hard right cross that stunned his adversary. The man went limp, allowing the earl to haul him free of the trees and slam him up against one of the interior walls. A bruise was purpling the blackguard's cheek and blood was trickling from his nose.

Wrexford shook him again, like a mastiff toying with a bone. "You bloody, two-faced monster!" Rage bubbled up inside him, hot as acid, on recalling the man's charming little flirtations with Charlotte. His murderous hands had dared to touch her—

"Wrex!" Sheffield grabbed his arm before he could slam his fist into his captive's bleeding nose. "Enough, Wrex! Enough."

The blackguard's eyelids flew open, fear dilating his pupils.

His friend's words cleared the haze of fury from the earl's head. Lowering his clenched hand, he drew a measured breath. "Count yourself lucky. Unlike your victims, you're still alive. But I shall take great pleasure in watching you dance the hangman's jig, once we turn you over to the authorities for the murder of Josiah Becton, as well as the two just now . . ."

Wrexford couldn't refrain from giving the man another teeth-rattling shake.

"So, tell me, how did you learn about Becton's discovery, and when did you begin plotting this diabolical crime, Mr. Moretti?"

CHAPTER 16

"Oh, *Dio del cielo!*" Beneath his bruises, Moretti had turned white as a ghost. "I—I—I haven't killed anyone—I swear it, milord!" He was trembling so badly that his knees would have collapsed if the earl hadn't kept him pinned to the wall.

"Then what the devil are you doing here?" demanded Wrexford, giving him another shake.

"I was asked to come!" replied Moretti in a strangled voice.

"Why?" asked Sheffield. "And, Wrex, do take your hand off his throat so that he might give us a coherent answer."

It was, decided Wrexford, a reasonable request. He released his hold, but balled his hand into a fist. "Go on, Moretti. However, you had better tell the truth or I'll knock your lovely pearly teeth down your gullet."

Hosack looked a little rattled. "Would His Lordship really do such a thing?" he whispered to Tyler.

"Not usually. But he's in a rather foul temper at the moment."

Moretti swallowed hard. "I will tell you all I know, though I fear it won't shed any light on . . . on w-what h-happened here tonight."

"Nonetheless, go on," encouraged Sheffield.

"I—I met Signore DeVere at the beginning of the Royal Society's symposium. He was very friendly and complimented me on my research papers, which was, of course, very flattering, as I'm a mere nobody in the world of science. He invited me to dine on several occasions, and showed me some of the famous sites of the city—"

"Get to the point, Moretti," growled the earl.

"Patience, Wrex. I believe he's trying," said Sheffield.

"Yes, I am!" The Italian's face was sheened in sweat. "The point is, he said he was impressed with my scholarship and offered me a very generous stipend and a laboratory to stay on in England after the symposium and spend a year pursuing my research."

"What is your specialty?" asked Wrexford.

"B-Botanical medicine," replied Moretti. "I work on a sickness called malaria."

The admission should have been yet another black mark against the man. And yet, now that his initial fury had died down, Wrexford found that logic had reasserted itself. He had already noted that Moretti had no blood on his hands or clothing—an impossibility if he had wielded the knife that had slit Quincy's throat.

Even more telling, the Italian simply didn't have the demeanor of a murderer. His shock and terror were, alas, all too genuine.

A mean-spirited thought, he conceded. Murderer or not, he didn't much like Moretti. However, he wouldn't let that cloud his judgment.

"And DeVere wished for you to continue research on that subject?" he pressed.

"Yes," answered the Italian. "As I said, he told me he thought my work had . . . exciting potential."

Wrexford shot a look at Hosack. "Are you familiar with Mr. Moretti's research?"

The doctor shook his head. "I'm not, but my concentration has been on other medical challenges."

The earl thought for a moment. "I suggest you recall my earlier comment about truth before answering my next question. We think DeVere and Quincy murdered Becton and stole papers and specimens—"

"M-Murder." Sheffield had lit a lantern, and the light filtering through the palm fronds had turned Moretti's face a ghastly shade of green. He looked truly bewildered. "This is the second time you've mentioned Becton's murder. I—I thought he had succumbed to natural causes."

"A botanical poison made it look that way," said Wrexford. "You see, Becton was on the verge of revealing a new cure for malaria at the end of the symposium, and making the formula and ingredients public knowledge, without asking for any remuneration."

"*Dio mio.*" The Italian looked like he might faint. "I swear, I knew *nothing* about that. I—I thought Signore DeVere admired my work . . ." Closing his eyes, he let out a shaky sigh. "But I now see . . ."

"See what?" asked Wrexford, hoping for more than histrionics.

"I think I see why DeVere asked me to come here tonight." He grimaced. "In truth, it was more of an order than a request, but despite the odd hour, I was, of course, happy to oblige."

"How did you get in?" queried Sheffield, before Moretti could go on. "Did he have you come to the main house, or did he let you in through the conservatory?"

It was a good question, acknowledged the earl. His friend was acquiring a knack for investigating.

"I was told the north door of the conservatory would be open, and I was to come meet them in the study room," answered the Italian. "I had been here once before, so I knew the way."

A pause. "I arrived at the appointed hour and started down the walkway when I heard a muffled bang. I—I assumed a shovel or rake had fallen from its rack, or that a crate had tipped over. So I thought nothing of it."

He swallowed hard before continuing. "When I arrived at the room, I saw Mr. Quincy lying on the floor. At first, I thought he may have been struck by apoplexy and that Mr. De-Vere had run for help and to send for a physician. It was only when I got closer that I saw the blood."

A spasm passed over Moretti's face. "My first instinct was to check whether he was still alive, but as I started to crouch down, I saw Mr. DeVere's body. A-And then I heard voices and I . . . I panicked, thinking it might be the murderer returning. So I ran and hid."

"That's very understandable," said Sheffield. "It must have been quite a shock."

The Italian stared down at his boots, which were speckled with clots of dried blood. "*Sì,*" he whispered.

Moretti had explained his actions, thought Wrexford, which all seemed to fit into place. However, it seemed to him that the key piece of the puzzle was still missing.

"What I'm wondering is, *why* did he summon you here, and at such a late hour," he said. "There must have been a compelling reason, but as of yet, you've not told us what it is."

"He wanted to see the drawing—and it's now clear as to why," answered Moretti in a rush.

For an instant, the air went completely still. Even the leaves seemed to be holding their collective breath.

"Don't keep us in suspense, Moretti," growled the earl. "*What* bloody drawing?"

In response came the rustle of wool and a whispery crackle as the Italian shoved his hand into his pocket and pulled out a folded sheet of paper. "The one Mr. B-Becton gave me."

Wrexford took it from Moretti's outstretched hand and carefully smoothed open the creases as the halting explanation continued.

"I met him in one of the study rooms at the Royal Botanic Gardens the day before the symposium officially opened. We were both looking at specimen drawings from the Royal Society's vast collection. Mr. Becton was very friendly—he had been pointed out to me as a very distinguished scholar, and not many of them deign to converse with young nobodies."

Moretti took a moment to steady his voice. "He asked me about my work, and when I told him of my interest in treating malaria, and the experiments I was working on back in Rome, he was very encouraging. We had a fascinating exchange on the concept of experimenting with medicinal botanicals from the same genus to see if those types of combinations would create more potent medicines."

"Did he mention his own work?" interrupted Hosack.

Moretti shook his head. "No. He merely smiled politely when I inquired. He then passed me this drawing from his own portfolio of papers and said that I should consider it an invitation to attend his keynote lecture at the end of the symposium." The Italian took a moment to compose himself. "And added that I might find the topic very interesting in light of our discussion."

Wrexford wordlessly passed the drawing to Hosack, who studied it carefully before lifting his shoulders to indicate it meant nothing to him. "Sorry," he murmured, and handed it back.

"I was saddened to hear of Mr. Becton's collapse, but I confess, as I was unaware of his field of interest, I didn't give it much thought," continued Moretti. "It was only a passing reference to him during a conversation this afternoon with Mr. DeVere that prompted me to mention the drawing to him."

Moretti's brow furrowed. "He gave no indication of any interest at the time. But then, early this evening, I received an urgent summons, requesting that I come here for a meeting with an associate of his who wished to see the drawing without delay."

That answered a number of questions, reflected Wrexford as he folded the drawing and tucked it into his pocket. But it raised even more ominous ones.

As in—who the devil murdered DeVere and Quincy?

As to the reason why, that seemed obvious. But he was beginning to think that nothing about this conundrum was as it seemed.

Moretti slumped back against the wall. The effort of telling his story, along with having to relive the grisly discovery of the bodies, seemed to have sapped the last of his strength.

"Kit, I'd like for you and Hosack to take Moretti into the main house and find him a measure of brandy, while Tyler and I have a quick look around the entrance that was left unlocked. It seems likely that the murderer also came in by that way."

"You think there may be a clue?" asked Sheffield.

"It's worth checking."

As his friend and the doctor went to assist Moretti, Wrexford and Tyler moved stealthily into the gloom. "You search through the side galleries and see if you find any sign of disturbance," he whispered, "while I check whether the doorway and outside path yield anything of use."

The valet veered off down one of the narrow walkways, taking care not to rustle the greenery.

Another winding turn through a cluster of trees—some deciduous specimens that looked to be varieties of the hardwood genus *Betula*—brought him within sight of the brass-framed double doors. Wrexford slowed his steps as he approached, scanning the stone flagging for any sign of footprints. A bit of mud streaked the tiles, but closer inspection showed no other details.

The latch was, as Moretti had indicated, unlocked. He stepped outside, but the footpath was graveled and all he found was the indentation of a barrow wheel that had recently rolled over the stones.

The earl returned to the moist warmth of the conservatory, and after a moment's pause, he began to make his way along the outer glass walls, heading toward the opposite end of the structure, and the door through which he and his friends had entered.

He wasn't sure why. Charlotte would call it intuition.

But as Wrexford paused in the shadows of a soft-needled alpine larch tree and stared out into the night, he wasn't feeling anything other than a frustrated confusion.

A state that prickled uncomfortably against his penchant for order and precision.

He stood for a little longer, watching the moonlight wax and wane over the nearby grove of oaks. The clouds were beginning to clear. Dawn would soon be dappling the horizon.

Then, just as he started to turn and begin retracing his steps, a tiny creak caught his ear. He froze, and waited. The *snick* of a latch followed, and Wrexford suddenly realized that there must be another exit door close to him. He started to move, only to spot movement within the long shadows cutting across the lawn.

A shape—a man moving stealthily—disappeared into a glade of elms. A moment later, he suddenly broke free of the trees. For a heartbeat, he was visible in the muted light before darting through the opening in the walled gardens that sloped down to the main road.

Pursuit was pointless. The runner would be long gone before Wrexford reached the door.

And yet, for the brief instant the man had been visible, the moonlight had shone a little brighter. And although he had a muffler hiding half his face, his head had been bare . . .

Allowing a telltale flicker of sun-bleached mahogany-colored hair.

"Well, well, Captain Daggett," muttered Wrexford. "What mischief is America up to on British soil?"

CHAPTER 17

After breakfast, Charlotte had rolled her latest drawing in a protective covering and sent the boys off to deliver it to Mr. Fores. Now she was determined to set aside all thoughts of murder and deal with the normal little everyday tasks of ordering their household.

"As if," she huffed while gathering up a pair of Raven's mud-encrusted boots from the entrance foyer, "my life bears any resemblance to normal."

A chuckle rumbled behind her. "You would be bored to flinders by a normal life," said McClellan. She was carrying a jar of beeswax and a polishing cloth into the parlor. "As would I."

"True," Charlotte conceded. "But if only we could stop tripping over dead bodies."

"Alas . . ." The boys had left the front door ajar, and Wrexford poked his head in through the gap. "Then you're not going to like hearing what I've come to tell you."

She felt her blood turn to ice. *"Who?"*

"Should I pour a glass of brandy for m'lady?" asked the maid.

His hesitation stirred another frisson of fear.

"Perhaps you ought to make it whisky, Mac."

"*Hartley*—"

Wrexford caught her sleeve and drew her close. "No, no—it's no one dear to us."

The scent of his shaving soap and the steady beat of his heart calmed her nerves.

"Quite the opposite, in fact," he added.

Charlotte let him lead her into the parlor, and dutifully obeyed his command to sit on the sofa, before demanding, "Explain yourself, Wrexford."

"As soon as Mac arrives with the spirits," he replied grimly.

The maid quickly reappeared, carrying a tray with two mugs of tea—and the bottle of malt. The earl added a healthy splash of it to Charlotte's brew before passing it over.

The warmth of it made her realize that her hands had gone cold.

"Go on," she said after a quick sip.

"I decided to follow a hunch I had, based on several things Kit had discovered. So he and I—along with Tyler and Hosack—decided to have a look around DeVere's conservatory last night."

The mention of that terrible place, where she had very nearly lost her life, sent a shiver down her spine.

Wrexford's eyes clouded with concern, but after a tiny hesitation, he continued. "We were looking for Becton's specimen. But instead, what we found was an unexpected shock."

She listened in stunned silence as he recounted the gruesome discovery and the presence of Moretti.

"Dear heavens—Marco isn't a murderer!" she exclaimed. "I would wager my life on it."

"I've come to the same conclusion," admitted the earl. "Reluctantly, I admit, as I don't like the fellow."

"He's been nothing but a good and loyal friend to me when I needed one," replied Charlotte.

His mouth twitched. "Perhaps that's what bothers me."

She made a face.

"Still, I did take pity on the fellow. It must have been quite a shock to stumble upon the bodies." A note of grudging sympathy had crept into his voice. "Even I, who am no stranger to violence, admit that the murder scene was not for the faint of heart," continued the earl. "Kit and Hosack took him back to his rooms at the Albany Hotel. The doctor promised to stay with him through the night, and first thing this morning, I made arrangements for both of them to stay for the time being with an acquaintance from my military days whose estate is not far from the Royal Botanic Gardens."

"Thank you, Wrexford." That her old friend was alone in a strange country and likely terrified tugged at her heart. "I must go see him."

"For now, I think it best that you don't," said the earl. "There's a chance that the killer saw Moretti enter the conservatory, which might put his life in danger. The man behind all this is both clever and ruthless, and as he was present at the Royal Society's gala supper on the night of Becton's murder, he might have observed that you and Moretti know each other."

Charlotte paled. "Was there no clue as to who might have killed DeVere and Quincy?"

"I haven't quite finished my account of the evening." Wrexford's expression darkened. "Tyler and I took a look around, in case there were any clues near the door that was left unlocked," he said, and went on to explain about spotting the American slipping out of the conservatory.

"Captain Daggett?" She immediately grasped the ramifications. "One has to wonder whether he has betrayed his oath to his country by becoming involved in some sordid scheme for personal profit. Or whether he's carrying out some clandestine plan for his government. Though what that might be..." Frowning in thought, she let her words trail off.

"Some reasonable speculations come to mind," said the earl. "Illness is always a very pressing worry for the military. It can be a ruthless enemy, incapacitating an army far more quickly and efficiently than any force of opposing soldiers. So a country that possesses a miracle cure for a dangerous illness has a great advantage on the battlefield."

That made great sense, she realized. "Have you informed Griffin yet about Daggett's presence at the murder scene? Surely, he—"

"He can likely do nothing," replied Wrexford. "Our government is in a devilishly difficult position. Daggett is here under a special invitation. To arrest him without irrefutable evidence of wrongdoing would provoke an international scandal. One doesn't break the code of honor between nations lightly."

"But you saw him—" began Charlotte.

He cut her off with a curt laugh. "Ha—a momentary glimpse in the dead of night? That won't fadge with the authorities. Perhaps if we had caught him bloody-handed, with four of us as witnesses. But the truth is, he still might get away with murder if the Foreign Office deems it in the country's self-interest to turn a blind eye on the crime." He made a face. "At least officially."

"But..." *But Wrexford is right.*

"My guess is that the newspapers will announce it as an unfortunate robbery. After all, DeVere's wealth is well known," he continued. "Then it all depends on whether the government can be convinced that Daggett might have stolen an important medical discovery. And I'm not terribly sanguine about that—

too few of our officials understand that science is not merely a hobby for rich dilettantes."

Again, Charlotte knew he was right.

"That doesn't mean I can't confront the miscreant and have a private word with him," said Wrexford. "I happen to know he's staying at the Sun and Sextant Club, a place favored by mariners from around the world."

The statement punched the breath from her lungs. "No— that's too dangerous!" Much as she loathed DeVere, the news of his violent demise, and the horrific stabbing of Quincy, had shaken her to the core. "If Daggett is a cold-blooded murderer, he won't hesitate to strike again."

"Forewarned is forearmed." The earl's gaze hardened. "He won't find me quite so easy a victim."

"Is that supposed to quell my fears?" she snapped. "The fact that he won't find it *easy* to kill you?"

Wrexford took her hand and pressed her palm to his cheek. "I promise you, sweeting, there's not a chance in the world that I will miss my wedding night."

Tears prickled against her lids. "Don't jest about the risk. I don't find it remotely funny."

His expression turned very serious. "Then let me make another promise—I shall take precautions and won't do anything rash. Though he has no authority to arrest the captain, I'll have Griffin accompany me, and I shall take care to confront Daggett within the club, where he won't be expecting any trouble."

It didn't allay all her fears, but it was at least something, and Charlotte sensed that she would wring no further concessions from him. Leaning closer, she brushed a kiss to his lips. "Be careful. If you allow anything to happen to yourself, not even Lucifer will keep me from finding you in the netherworld and ringing a peal over your head."

"That, my love, would almost be worth witnessing."

"Trust me, you wouldn't find it amusing."

He shifted slightly, setting off a faint crackle of paper. "Oh, by the by, here is the sketch that Moretti gave me. Hosack didn't recognize it, but perhaps your brother will."

"If the doctor wasn't able to identify it, I doubt Hartley will do any better. He cheerfully admits that he's not a botanical expert," she answered, giving it a cursory look. "Nor am I."

"Still, it can't hurt to ask him before he departs for the north." Wrexford rose and drew her into his arms. "I must be off and find Griffin. He's likely just learning about the murders, so the quicker I can explain to him the circumstances, the better."

She traced a fingertip along the line of his jaw. "Be careful," she repeated. A lame expression, but no words could possibly capture the depth and breadth of her emotions.

"Don't fret, my love. I won't come to any grief."

Charlotte watched him go, doing her best to suppress the sense of dread creeping into her consciousness. He was right— a gentlemen's club in London gave Daggett little room to arrange some vile attack.

And yet, she was finding it hard to breathe. The fast-approaching wedding had made her all the more aware of how she couldn't imagine her world without Wrexford. That they would soon be sharing a life together . . . that she would wake up every morning to find him close . . .

The idea that he might . . .

"No." Charlotte forced herself to quell the sudden flutter of panic.

DeVere. DeVere was dead. Perhaps that was why her emotions were so tangled in knots.

A part of her rejoiced that a man utterly lacking in morality had suffered the same fate as his own victims. *Vives in gladio, in gladio mori. Live by the sword, die by the sword.* Five people were dead because of his obsession with fame and glory. And yet, her conscience rebelled against taking pleasure in any violent death. All men and women, no matter how evil, deserved a fair trial to determine how they must answer for their sins.

She fisted her hands in her lap. Still, it was a relief to know that DeVere couldn't threaten the boys. If that was wrong, so be it.

I have never claimed to be a saint.

"Might I ask you to come help me shift the side table in the foyer?" asked McClellan, passing by the doorway with a bucket and broom in hand. "I swear, there's more mud beneath it than in a barnyard. How two skinny little Weasels manage to track in more than their weight in muck is a mystery."

"Yes, of course." Charlotte shook off her brooding and hurried to offer assistance. "Good Lord," she murmured on approaching the table. "You're right. We could start a garden under there."

"I shudder to think what might grow."

The maid was already on her hands and knees, scooping up the unknown substances and dumping them in the bucket. Charlotte took up a rag and began cleaning the wooden top. They worked in companionable silence, scraping and scrubbing.

Slowly the tightness in her chest subsided. "Thank you, Mac," she murmured.

"For what?" McClellan gave a grunt as she hefted the bucket. "Getting your gown spattered with dirty soapsuds?"

"Idle hands make for idle thoughts," she replied. "And mine were heading in a very depressing direction."

"Don't worry about His Lordship," counseled the maid. "He has a very good reason—indeed, several good reasons—to tread lightly and stack the odds in his favor."

Yes, but even the best of gamblers lose an occasional hand.

Shoving the dark whisper out of her head, Charlotte forced a smile. "Quite right. Luck wouldn't dare spit in his eye."

McClellan gathered up the cleaning supplies, and then set a hand on her hip as the latch rattled and the front door flung open. "A word of warning. The Weasels had better not dare spit—or track in unmentionable substances—onto my pristine floor."

Hawk paused in midstep and crinkled his nose. "Fawwgh, what's that unpleasant odor?"

"Strong soap and vinegar. They may be foreign fragrances to you little beasts. But add the stench of rotten cabbage to them, and there will be no ginger biscuits for a month."

Eyes widening in horror, he bent down and promptly slipped off his muck-encrusted boots.

"Where's your brother?" asked Charlotte. Concern for Wrexford still hung heavy over her thoughts.

"He stopped off at Wrexford's townhouse to see if Mr. Tyler needed any assistance with his chemical experiments," answered Hawk.

That the boys were up to no mischief was one less worry weighing on her mind. She hadn't yet told them about DeVere's murder, and decided to hold off until suppertime, when Raven would also be present.

"Give me those, and I'll brush them off in the garden," she replied, holding out her hands for the boots.

Deciding that more mundane tasks would help keep her demons at bay, she added, "Then perhaps Mac will give you some milk and biscuits while I make a trip to Mr. Mattison's art emporium. I need to purchase several new sable watercolor brushes."

"Biscuits will be forthcoming if a certain Weasel washes his hands and combs his hair," announced McClellan. "Oh, and by the by, m'lady, if you're going out, might you make another stop . . ."

As she and McClellan compiled a list of items to purchase for the pantry, Hawk hurried for the stairs.

It wasn't until a little later, after Charlotte had left on her errands and the biscuits had been served, that Hawk went into the parlor to fetch his sketchbook.

And spotted the sketch that Moretti had received from Becton lying on the tea table.

CHAPTER 18

"Must you keep serving up such damnably complicated murders, milord?" said Griffin as Wrexford entered his tiny office.

"Unpalatable as they may be, the government can't ignore the ramifications. And as you're the best of the Bow Street Runners, I feel I must put them on your plate."

"Don't try to sweeten me up," groused Griffin. A sigh. "I never thought I would say such a thing, but the sight of you is beginning to rob me of my appetite."

Wrexford chuckled. "My purse will be happy to hear that."

Griffin didn't smile. He rose and shut the door. "All jesting aside, milord, I must ask you a very serious question, and I hope you'll give me an honest answer. I wouldn't blame you, given your relationship with Lady Charlotte and what happened to her in that devil-cursed place. But if—"

"No," answered Wrexford, before the Runner could go on. "I would never put you on the horns of such an impossible choice." He brushed a mote of dust from his cuff. "If I had any-thing to do with DeVere's death, I would have made sure that the bodies were discovered by another constabulary—one far less skilled than yours."

A look of relief softened Griffin's scowl. "Thank you. I trust you understand it was a question I had no choice but to ask."

"Of course," replied the earl. "However, kindly hold your thanks, for you're not going to find what I have to say next very pleasing. I think I know who killed both DeVere and Quincy. And the government isn't going to like it."

Muttering an oath, the Runner sat down heavily in his chair. "They are already unhappy that I've begun asking the symposium committee some uncomfortable questions about Becton's death."

"This will make them even more unhappy," said the eail. "I happened to spot Captain Samuel Daggett racing away from the scene of the crime."

"The naval officer who is part of the American scientific delegation?"

"Yes," answered Wrexford.

"Why the devil would he want to murder those two men?" A glimmer of hope lit in Griffin's eyes. "Unless, of course, it was some personal quarrel involving Quincy, his fellow American, and DeVere, who spent the last year in that country."

"I'm afraid it's not going to prove that easy," said the earl. "You see, I have reason to believe that DeVere's insatiable hunger for fame and glory had not slacked . . ."

The Runner's expression turned grimmer and grimmer as Wrexford explained about the dead men's connection to Becton and the information Sheffield had passed on about their sending money to the notorious rogue ship captain Reginald Lyman.

"Bloody hell," muttered Griffin, once the earl finished. "I need to take this to the head magistrate." He grimaced. "I'm glad I'm not the one who will have to inform the Foreign Office and the Admiralty—"

"Before you do so, I have an idea . . ."

The head porter of the Sun and Sextant Club bowed a polite greeting to Wrexford. "If you are looking for Sir Darius, milord, I'm afraid he left last week for a visit to the Levant."

"Actually, I'm seeking another guest—Samuel Daggett, a visitor from America."

"Ah, yes, the captain." The porter pursed his lips. "Alas, he went out a short while ago."

"Did he say when he might return?" asked the earl.

"No, milord."

Holding back a huff of frustration, Wrexford thought for a moment. "It's rather pressing. Perhaps I should check his rooms, just in case he returned when you were otherwise engaged."

"Yes, of course." A gesture directed them to the imposing center staircase at the far end of the entrance hall. "His quarters are one flight up and located at the end of the corridor, just past the chess room."

"A word of caution, milord," murmured Griffin, quickening his pace to keep up with the earl. "Cornering a desperate predator is a dangerous strategy." The Runner had brought along several men, who had been discreetly stationed around the building to prevent their quarry's escape. "If he is in, don't enter his rooms. Wait for him to emerge before confronting him. That way, he'll have fewer options for attack."

"I'm touched by your concern," replied Wrexford. "But if you're worried about your future suppers, don't be. I've made provisions for you with my man of affairs . . ."

He started up the stairs two at a time. "In the event of my demise, a generous stipend will keep your belly full."

"I'm not concerned about the state of my stomach." As they reached the top of the landing, Griffin caught the earl's arm and looked around. "I'll station myself in that alcove to watch your back," he whispered, indicating the entrance foyer to one of the card rooms. "I still say you should allow me to accompany you."

Wrexford shook his head. "I've more options for negotiating if I confront him alone."

The Runner released an unhappy sigh as he turned to take up his position. "Don't make me regret this. Lady Charlotte will have my guts for garters if anything goes wrong."

Regrets, however, proved unnecessary. Pressing an ear to the door, Wrexford held himself still and waited. But after hearing naught but silence for several long minutes, he had to concede that Daggett wasn't inside.

His hand slid over the dark oak and found the door latch. It was tempting to have a look around . . .

A warning hiss from Griffin reached his ears just a heartbeat before he heard the scuff of steps on the landing. Straightening, he turned away, and quickly moved over to the doorway of the game room.

"Ah, Wrexford." A fellow member of the Royal Institution nodded a friendly greeting as he and three other men paused at the entrance to the card room. "If you're looking for a game of chess, Cathcart is in the reading room downstairs and I'm sure he'll oblige you."

"Thank you, but no," replied the earl. "I thought I had an engagement with Sir Darius, but I just realized that I muddled the dates, and he's already departed for a trip to the East."

"Like a leaf on the wind, Sir Darius seems to blow hither and yon," mused his acquaintance. "What a strange life." A puzzled frown. "How does he manage to survive on all that deucedly odd foreign food?"

"Perhaps he is of the opinion that man does not live on beefsteak alone," Wrexford murmured, then resumed walking, leaving the four men to chew over his parting words.

Griffin slipped free of the shadows and fell in step with him. The earl paused as they reached the front entrance. "Do me a favor and don't mention to Captain Daggett that I was looking for him," he said to the porter, and passed over several guineas to emphasize the request. "I have a surprise for him and I don't wish to ruin the moment."

The Runner refrained from comment until they had turned the corner and the club was out of sight. "Now what, milord?" he asked after signaling to one of his men to round up the others.

"I need to think about that," he replied. An idea had come to mind, but it wasn't one that he intended to reveal to Griffin. "In the meantime, I suggest you stay mum about all this for now. If you go to the head magistrate now, you'll be asked some very uncomfortable questions about how you learned all this. And it could put you in a very awkward position."

Griffin's expression altered just enough to show he comprehended how fraught with complications the situation was. Their unofficial partnership had ensured that justice was done in several past crimes, and the authorities had been happy to welcome the results without looking too closely at how they had come about. However, if things went awry, the Runner could very well become the scapegoat.

"And yet, by guarding my own neck, I may allow Daggett to elude justice. I take my duty to heart, milord. Now that I know the facts, it would be wrong—indeed, it would be cowardly— to withhold them—"

"You know damn well that the government isn't going to make any sort of decision today," interrupted Wrexford. "So let us take the night to consider all the ramifications."

"Do you swear that you're not contemplating something dangerous on your own?"

"I do," avowed the earl with a clear conscience. He wasn't intending on pursuing Daggett on his own. Seeing the Runner's resolve wavering, he quickly added, "Come by my townhouse in the morning. We'll assess our options over breakfast."

Griffin narrowed his eyes. "I could arrest you for bribery, milord."

"And forgo Cook's fried gammon and shirred eggs? I think not." The earl stepped into the street and waved down a passing hackney. "I promise you—and your breadbox—that we'll uncover the truth and not let Daggett get away with murder."

Releasing a satisfied sigh, Charlotte set down her marketing basket on the newly-cleaned table and began unknotting the strings of her bonnet. Oddly enough, an afternoon of bustling through the ordinary, everyday demands of life had brightened her mood.

Murder's grim shadow, she reminded herself, could smother every spark of light if one wasn't careful. Evil must not be allowed to extinguish all that was good in the world—

"M'lady, m'lady!"

The smile died on her lips. Gathering her skirts, Charlotte raced for the parlor, sending her bonnet skittering down the corridor.

Hawk was standing by the sofa, sketchbook clutched in his hands.

Skidding to a stop, she looked around.

No blood, no intruder.

"Good heavens, you scared me half to death," Charlotte gulped in a breath, willing her heart to stop hammering against her ribs. "I thought—"

Something in the boy's expression caused her to pause.

"You need to look at this!" he said, holding up the book. "It's wery, wery important."

"Of course I will, sweeting." She crouched down, feeling a stab of guilt. More so than in the past, this current murder investigation had touched the lives of all her family. No wonder Hawk's emotions appeared unsettled. She hadn't been as attentive to his blossoming talents as she should have been.

He flipped the pages open to a detailed drawing and then shoved it into her hands.

Charlotte recognized the plant immediately. The boy's sketch wasn't an exact copy of Becton's drawing, but the distinctive shape and color of the specimen's leaves were the same.

"You've done a very nice interpretation of the plant," she said, "but I need to keep the original sketch from which you drew this in a safe place—"

"But that's just it, m'lady—I *didn't* copy this plant from the sketch!" interrupted Hawk. "I drew this yesterday from a plant I saw at the Royal Botanic Gardens."

The book slipped through her fingers and fell to the carpet. "Yesterday? Good Lord—*where?*"

"In the storeroom," he answered. "It was among a number of specimens awaiting shipment to the University of St. Andrews." A look of trepidation shadowed his features. "I didn't sneak into some place I shouldn't have been. Mr. Tyler gave me permission."

Charlotte smoothed a tangle of hair back from his brow. "Yes, I know that. I was merely surprised, not angry." She took a moment to steady her own nerves. "Indeed, you may have made a terribly important discovery."

"Aye, I wondered about that." McClellan, her hands dusted with flour from the bread she had been kneading, was standing in the doorway, looking very serious. "I wasn't sure whether to send Hawk straight to His Lordship's townhouse with the news, or to wait until you returned. I hope I made the right decision."

Charlotte rose and retrieved Becton's drawing from the tea table. "I doubt Wrexford was at home earlier. He left here intending to meet Griffin..." *And then confront a cold-blooded killer.* "I believe they were going to pay a visit to the Sun and Sextant Club. But Lord only knows where the two of them are now."

"What do you think we should do?" asked the maid.

Drawing a deep breath, she considered the question... The web of intrigue seemed to spin more and more malicious threads, which threatened to tangle their every step.

"The mystery of who murdered Becton is a devilishly difficult one," she said slowly, "and has us all chasing helter-pelter after shadowy specters." A pause. "However, there's one element to it that seems clear as crystal to me..."

She met McClellan's gaze. "Becton's plant specimen is key to the conundrum. We mustn't let the villains get their hands on it."

"You aren't thinking of going after it on your own, are you?" demanded the maid.

"No," answered Charlotte. "Though I confess, for a moment, I was tempted." She stared down at the drawing. Such a sweet, innocent-looking plant. And yet three men lay dead because of it. "However, I know all too well what dangers can arise when we act without knowing what the others are doing."

After a moment, she added, "Damnation, where is Wrexford?" and then lapsed into another pensive silence.

Out on the street, a carriage rattled by, drawing a sharp bark from a stray dog.

"M-maybe your bruvver can help," suggested Hawk after the sounds had died away. "He mentioned that he's attending a lecture at the Royal Botanic Gardens this evening. One of the symposium's Swedish guests is speaking about Linnaeus."

Out of the mouths of babes.

"How very clever of you to remember about that, sweeting!" exclaimed Charlotte. Wrexford's attention had been focused on unraveling the mystery of Becton's murder, and he hadn't felt compelled to attend all of the symposium's presentations, especially as botany was not one of his specialties. But given her brother's interest, Alison had made sure that Hartley had received invitations to all the remaining events. Which likely meant . . .

"If Wrexford hasn't returned to his townhouse in an hour or two," she mused, "I shall join Aunt Alison—"

"I think that I should come with you," said Hawk, trying very manfully to imitate Wrexford's drawl. "So I can show you exactly where it is."

Charlotte ruffled the boy's curls. "I don't think that would be—"

She stopped abruptly as an idea suddenly came to mind. "On second thought, fly up to your aerie and change into your fancy clothes while I dress for the evening."

Seeing McClellan's questioning frown as Hawk darted for the stairs, she explained, "Both Tyler and I have taken Hawk to sketch in the Royal Botanic Gardens recently, so the attendants know the boy and won't find a visit out of the ordinary. If the two of us go out there now, we can keep an eye on the storeroom—"

She saw the maid was about to speak and quickly added, "Before you begin to protest, be assured that I've no intention of taking any chances. I mean to stop at Wrexford's townhouse, and if he's not yet returned, I shall ask Tyler to accompany us."

McClellan gave a grudging nod. "That seems safe enough. Tyler can be counted on not to take any silly risk."

"And as Raven should be there as well, helping in the workroom, I'll dispatch him with a note to Aunt Alison, asking her to accompany Hartley to the evening lecture, and to be sure that they arrive early," went on Charlotte. "She'll understand that some intrigue is afoot and will follow my instructions to tell Hartley that they are needed to assist Wrexford with a delicate situation. I'll explain things more fully when I see them."

"But Hawk can hardly stay for the evening's event," pointed out the maid.

"No, of course not. I plan to send him home with Tyler—we'll travel out there in one of the earl's carriages. If for some reason, Tyler needs to stay with us, Hawk can return to Town with Alison's coachman, who'll bring him here."

McClellan picked at a bit of dough that was clinging to her cuff. "What will you do if Wrexford doesn't return home and never gets your message? I'm assuming you're counting on him to convince the secretary of the Royal Society to put Becton's specimen under lock and key until the killer is unmasked and brought to justice."

"I've thought of that," replied Charlotte. "It's the reason I'm making sure Aunt Alison attends the event. She wields a good deal of influence in Society—"

"Not to speak of a very sharp stick," murmured McClellan.

"And I shall ask her to use her cane, if need be," responded Charlotte. "But I don't expect violence to be necessary. That Hartley is an earl should provide enough gravitas to our request to keep the specimen under guard until Wrexford has a chance to explain matters. After all, Lord Bethany owes him a rather large favor."

Pursing her lips, the maid considered the plan.

Charlotte waited. She trusted McClellan's judgment. "If you see any flaws, please point them out."

"No, no," responded the maid. "It's an excellent strategy, one that is both prudent and pragmatic." She tucked a loose strand of hair behind her ear. "It seems that we are finally about to bring this pernicious investigation to an end. Wrexford has learned the identity of the killer, and thanks to Hawk, the specimen has been found and shall soon be safe . . ."

"Yes, but Daggett is still free to foment evil," whispered Charlotte.

"As Wrexford said, it is now up to the authorities to apprehend him and see that he's punished for his misdeeds," replied McClellan. "Our part in this unholy mess will soon be over."

Charlotte forced a smile, but a niggling sense of unease robbed it of any warmth. "I had better hurry and change so that Hawk and I can be on our way."

CHAPTER 19

"Damnation," muttered Sheffield as he and Wrexford entered the earl's workroom. "I will shed no tears over the deaths of DeVere and Quincy, but no matter how unsavory, one deserves a fair trial in which to answer for one's sins."

"So says the law of the land. And for the concept of justice to hold any meaning, it must apply equally to everyone." Wrexford took a seat at his desk, feeling frustrated and discouraged. After failing to find Daggett at the Sun and Sextant Club, he had paid a visit to an old friend, who held a senior position in military intelligence at the Horse Guards, to discuss the political ramifications of arresting an American naval officer. Only to be told that principle would likely give way to pragmatism.

"However . . ." The earl picked up his letter opener and ran a finger along the blade. "Norris informed me that private negotiations have just begun to end the war between our two countries, so he is of the opinion that—"

"That the dastard is going to get away with murder," interrupted Sheffield. He grimaced. "Lady Charlotte isn't going to be happy."

His friend's words sent a spike of fear through Wrexford's gut. "Do you think I don't know that?" His hand tightened on the hilt of the letter opener. "I'm aware that she'll not turn a blind eye on it, and will use her pen to provoke the public into asking more questions about the crime."

"What can we do to protect her?" asked Sheffield.

"I need to find Daggett. Our government may be loath to confront him, but I'm not," growled Wrexford. "Griffin has two men keeping the Sun and Sextant Club under surveillance, so I'll be alerted as soon as he returns there. I've some ideas of where else to look—"

A slight rustling in the storage alcove caused him to stop in midsentence. "Weasel?" he called sharply.

Silence. And then a whisper of movement as Raven slipped out of the shadows, a glass beaker and polishing cloth in his hands.

The earl swore under his breath. "I ought to birch your bum for eavesdropping."

"I wasn't eavesdropping, sir," replied the boy. "I was working . . ." A pause. "At the task that Mr. Tyler assigned to me."

Sheffield cleared his throat to mask a chuckle.

"Is Mr. DeVere dead?" added Raven, before the earl could respond.

Wrexford hesitated, but only for an instant. "Yes. He was murdered last night in his conservatory. Quite violently, as a bullet blew away half his skull."

A flickering of his lashes was the boy's only visible reaction. As to what he was thinking . . .

Out of the corner of his eye, the earl saw Tyler had come to stand in the archway connecting the main workroom to the laboratory. "I didn't tell him because I didn't feel it was my revelation to make, milord."

"I'm glad he's dead," announced Raven. "M'lady wouldn't

tell us what happened that night she was trapped there." His eyes narrowed in accusation. "And neither would you."

"Nor will I ever," said Wrexford. "Some things simply aren't meant to be shared. Not even with you and your brother."

"Whatever it was, it must have been bad." Raven tried to sound tough, but his voice betrayed a note of vulnerability.

"It left no lasting scars, lad." Wrexford met the boy's gaze. "That is all you really need to know."

Raven looked away, but not before the earl saw the look of relief in his eyes.

Further discussion was forestalled by the sound of hurried steps in the corridor.

"Wrexford!" Charlotte rushed through the doorway in a swirl of emerald-colored silk.

He shot up from his chair. The sight of Hawk at her heels stilled the first jolt of alarm. As did the fact that she was stylishly dressed in formal finery. But there were others who might be in danger.

"What is it?" he began, only to have the air squeezed from his lungs as she flung herself forward and wrapped him in a very un-Charlotte-like hug.

"Oh, Wrexford!" Her voice was fuzzy with emotion. "Thank heaven you're unharmed."

"Not a scratch," he murmured, savoring her closeness and the beguiling scent of her perfume. "Though I daresay, I'll soon have some bruises darkening my ribs."

She leaned back, flattening her palms on his chest. "Never mind your ribs. You must hurry and change into your evening clothes."

"Alas, much as I would enjoy waltzing with you, I've more pressing matters—"

"We've found Becton's missing specimen!" exclaimed Charlotte. "That is, Hawk did." She sucked in a quick breath. "Or rather, we know where it is, but we must hurry."

"*How?*" cried Raven.

"*Where?*" demanded Tyler.

"*Who?*" asked Sheffield.

"*Silence!*" ordered Wrexford.

The room fell still.

"Now, please explain yourself, my dear."

In answer, Charlotte gestured at Hawk. "Open your sketch-book, sweeting." She took Becton's original drawing—the one handed over by Moretti the previous evening—out of her reticule and unfolded it. "Now let us place both of them on the desk so everyone can have a look."

"I drew mine at the Royal Botanic Gardens just yesterday," explained Hawk as the others all gathered around to study the two sketches.

"Holy hell." Tyler let out a low whistle. "In the storage room?"

"I think I've pieced together what happened," said Charlotte. "Becton was becoming more and more fearful that someone was going to steal his precious papers and specimen. Because of the previous break-in, he didn't trust that they would be safe in his rooms, and he wasn't sure whether he dared confide his fears to the secretary of the Royal Society. After all, he wasn't acquainted with Lord Bethany."

"And for all he knew, Bethany might have been in league with an unknown villain," interjected Wrexford. "After all, the prospect of fame and fortune can seduce even the most noble of men."

"Yes," agreed Charlotte. "But on recalling something Hartley mentioned, it suddenly occurred to me that there is, in fact, one person here in Britain that Becton *did* trust—Professor Murray, who is in charge of the botanic gardens at the University of St Andrews."

"How so?" asked Wrexford.

"Hartley has come to be friends with the professor, and the other day, when the topic of Becton's death came up, he mentioned that Murray would be very saddened, because the two of them had been close friends for years. Apparently, they corresponded frequently, and often exchanged specimens. Indeed, Murray was particularly excited about all medicinal plants from Spanish America that Becton propagated in his own gardens and shared with him."

"I see where your thoughts are taking you," said Wrexford. "The Royal Botanic Gardens receive exotic specimens from all over the world, and the gardeners there propagate them and share them with other study gardens, both here and abroad. And it so happens that the Royal Society sends a regular monthly shipment north to St. Andrews."

"Yes, I learned that yesterday," she murmured.

"So you believe that Becton hid his specimen among the routine shipment going to the university there, knowing that his friend Murray would be the one to receive it. But how would the professor know . . ."

Wrexford paused for a moment. "Ah, if you're right about the specimen being sent north, then it stands to reason that Becton also decided to mail his notes and formula to Murray, along with a warning to keep both the papers and the plant safe."

Charlotte allowed a ghost of a smile. "It all seems a very logical assumption."

"So it does." He loved the artful agility of her mind, and how easily she could see a problem from so many angles and then choose the proper perspective. However, admiration quickly yielded to the pressing need for action. "Tyler, have Riche send for the carriage."

"And you'll need to dress for the evening. I'll lay out your clothes," said the valet. He took a step and then paused. "I think I should come with you, milord. Hawk and I have been in and out of the storage room together this past week. Our doing so today won't draw attention, while your sudden interest might provoke the enemy to wonder why."

The earl considered the suggestion.

"While Hawk leads me to the plant and I secure the crate, you can be hunting down Lord Bethany and explaining the need for putting it under lock and key and then sending a trusted courier to St. Andrews to retrieve Becton's missing note and formula."

"You have a point," conceded Wrexford.

"I was going to send Alison a message alerting her that I might need her help this evening," said Charlotte. "But I don't think that's necessary, now that you're here. The fewer people who know where Becton's discovery is hidden, the better."

He saw the shadow of worry in her eyes. A vicious killer was still free, and wouldn't hesitate to strike again if he thought his misdeeds were under investigation.

"I agree," answered Wrexford. Turning to Raven, he added, "Not a word to anyone about all this, lad. Especially the dowager and Lord Wolcott."

"Yes, sir." The boy's reply came without argument.

"Actually, we need to inform one person about our plans," said Charlotte. "I want you to fly back to our residence and inform Mac that I've found His Lordship and that we're headed with Tyler and Hawk to the gardens."

That command didn't sit quite as well with Raven. "But I could be of help in keeping watch—"

"No." It was said softly, but her tone brooked no argument. "First of all, she needs to be informed of what we're doing. And secondly, I would feel more at ease if she wasn't left alone tonight." Charlotte hesitated. "Daggett is diabolically clever. If he senses we're on his trail, he might seek to strike where we are vulnerable. So I want you to bring her back here, and *both* of you are to remain inside these walls until we've returned from our mission."

"You heard m'lady," intoned the earl as he caught a flicker of frustration pass over Raven's face. "Keeping our family and friends safe is a critical part of any dangerous undertaking."

Raven's shoulders slumped in resignation. "Of course, sir. I just wish I could do something to help you bring the miscreant to justice."

"I'm sure you'll get your chance to help," replied Wrexford. "Now, off with you."

"The carriage will be ready shortly, milord," called Tyler from the corridor as Raven darted past him. "I've laid out your evening clothes. You had better hurry and change."

Sheffield followed the earl out to the stairs. "Speaking of helping, I, too, wish to aid in catching the villain."

"I appreciate it, Kit, but it's best that I speak to Bethany alone," replied Wrexford. "He's very worried that a scandal involving murder and skulduggery will blacken the good name of the Royal Society, so he'll be more apt to follow my suggestions on how to handle things if he trusts that what has happened is being kept a well-guarded secret."

"Right," answered his friend. "But another idea occurred to me. I've kept up occasional appearances at a number of disreputable gambling hells . . ." Before becoming involved with Lady Cordelia and discovering his talents for business, boredom and frustration had driven Sheffield to drink and gamble more than was good for him.

"I thought you had given up such destructive behavior," he replied.

"I still keep my hand in the game, and take care to lose, though my mathematical skills are greatly improved. But it's all for a good reason," explained Sheffield. "I visit places that cater to the dockyards and merchant ships. A night of play allows me to pick up all the scuttlebutt of the maritime world, which often proves quite useful for our company."

"Clever," said Wrexford as he entered his dressing room and shrugged out of his coat. "But why—"

"If Daggett is holed up somewhere along the river, someone may know about it."

It was a savvy suggestion. But it was also dangerous. Charlotte's worries had put his own nerves on edge. "I appreciate the suggestion. But be very careful in how you do your probing. You've seen that Daggett is not a man with whom to trifle."

"Don't worry, Wrex. I've no desire to have my liver sliced into mincemeat." Sheffield smiled. "I've actually learned a modicum of discretion since my wastrel days."

"Be sure to use it." The earl turned to the looking glass and began knotting his cravat. "If anything happens to you, Lady Cordelia will cut out *my* liver."

Sheffield let out a low laugh, which struck Wrexford as strangely at odds with the spasm of emotion that suddenly passed over his friend's face. "No, no, you're quite safe." A careless shrug. "I don't think she would even notice if I went missing."

The earl heaved an inward sigh. "Given my own muddlings, I'm hardly one to offer advice—"

A warning flashed in Sheffield's eyes that any counsel on vagaries of the heart wouldn't be welcomed.

"But be that as it may . . ." Wrexford donned his evening coat and smoothed a wrinkle from his sleeve. He and Charlotte had assumed the relationship between Sheffield and Lady Cordelia was deepening. However, he knew from experience that love rarely chose to travel along a smooth and straight road. It seemed to take a malicious delight in twists and turns that led up steep peaks and dipped into plunging valleys.

"But be that as it may," he repeated, "I'll advise you again to be careful. I would rather you didn't stick your spoon in the wall."

"Let us both try to stay in the land of the living," said Sheffield as the two of them turned and hurried for the stairs. "After all, we have an important wedding to attend in the near future."

Charlotte tried to loosen the knot of dread in her chest. There was, she told herself, no cause to be worried. Her fears were unreasonable. Tyler and Hawk would make quick work of identifying and retrieving the specimen, while all she and Wrexford had to do was mingle with the other scholars who had come to attend the evening lecture and wait for the valet's signal to approach Lord Bethany.

Hardly a scenario that should strike fear into her heart. She had faced far more dangerous situations without a qualm . . .

Wrexford curled his fingers around her hand and leaned closer. "Rest easy, my dear," he murmured, the words just loud enough for her to hear. "If Daggett had any inkling of where Becton had hidden his precious plant, it would have disappeared long ago."

"That makes perfect sense," she replied.

"And yet?"

A *thump* rattled the carriage as the wheels hit a rut in the road.

How to articulate the nameless sharp-as-needles prickling at the nape of her neck? Charlotte sighed. "And yet, it seems that I can't help acting like a flighty peagoose."

"You are the least featherbrained lady I've ever known," responded Wrexford. "If your intuition is telling you something, be assured I am listening as well." He gave her hand a squeeze. "We will all exercise caution, and be on the alert for any trouble."

Tyler must have heard the last exchange because he looked up quickly from Hawk's sketchbook. "We've just been going over the location of the specimen. Hawk has drawn a diagram of exactly where it is, milady. Once we reach the Orangery, we'll be in and out of the storage room in a flash. Add another few minutes for us to get it into Wrexford's hands, and the danger will be over."

"He's right, my dear," added the earl. "The fact that Becton's plant and papers had gone missing was, as you know, kept a secret. But I will convince Bethany to make an immediate statement explaining that given the unexpected nature of Becton's death, there was some question as to where his work had been kept. He'll then announce that the Royal Society is delighted to report that the research and the special formula that Becton intended to reveal in his presentation have been found and locked away in a safe place—along with the plant specimen that is the key ingredient to the formula."

Wrexford shifted, the fluttery lamplight threading sparks of gold through his dark hair. "That will put an end to any further threat of violence. Daggett and any co-conspirators will have no reason to continue their hunt. Indeed, their concern ought to be arranging their flight from Britain before they can be arrested for murder."

Charlotte saw that Hawk was watching her intently. Softening her own misgivings with a smile—he had lapsed into an unnatural silence for the last few miles—she was about to say something, when yet another jolt of the wheels suddenly roused him.

Scooting closer to the window, Hawk angled a look out into the fast-fading light. "We're here!" he exclaimed.

"An hour," intoned Tyler. "Things will all be settled and we shall be back on the road within an hour, milady."

"Unless, of course, you wish to stay for supper and champagne," said the earl dryly.

CHAPTER 20

"Let us circle around the main conservatory," suggested Tyler as they moved out of earshot of the reception area. "Then we can split up. Hawk and I will head to the Orangery, while the two of you go stroll through the special exhibits set up in the display rooms." He slanted a look at the earl. "Make your way to the area that opens onto the connecting corridor. As soon as I have the specimen, Hawk and I will pass through it, and that will be the signal that you should go ahead and find Lord Bethany and put the final part of the plan in motion. We'll wait for you in the print study room."

Charlotte refrained from asking how they should proceed if things didn't go as expected. Her own misgivings had cast enough of a shadow over the mission. However vaporous, she could feel its bone-deep chill dogging their steps.

Wrexford gave a gruff assent as they passed through the opening in the yew hedge. Taking Charlotte's arm, he slowed his steps, allowing their companions to forge ahead as they crossed through a garden of late-blooming *Helleborus orientalis.*

"Good day, Mr. Tyler," called one of the gardeners. "And to you, Master Sloane. How nice to see such enthusiasm for plants in a young man of your age."

The valet returned the greeting with a cheery wave. "Indeed, it's never too early to start learning about the world around us."

"Aye. But even here in the gardens, where light and beauty abound, there are lessons about life that are perhaps best left until the lad is older," came the reply.

"A sage observation, Mr. Gage," replied Tyler. "I shall keep it in mind."

The well-tended footpath curled around the main section of the conservatory and then forked as it came to a majestic sessile oak.

"Good luck," murmured Charlotte, once she and the earl reached the spot where Tyler and Hawk were waiting.

"It won't be long now," assured Tyler. After snapping a jaunty salute, he and the boy set off.

Wrexford hesitated a moment, scanning the surroundings before heading in the other direction. They walked in silence, the rippling of the long grasses and a few faint birdsongs the only sounds fluttering around them.

Such a peaceful setting . . . and so at odds with the emotions roiling inside her.

"I'm sorry, Wrexford," said Charlotte, turning abruptly as the wing housing the lecture hall and study room came into view. "I don't know what's come over me. I'm not usually so pessimistic." The cloudless sky and golden light of the setting sun made her feel even more ridiculous. "Thank you for ignoring my mood and pressing on with such resolve." She forced a self-mocking smile. "You may tease me unmercifully about it on the way home."

"It's tempting, as you are so rarely wrong," he answered. "But I shall refrain from lording it over you. In truth, I think all of us shall feel nothing but relief when this sordid business is behind us."

"You truly think Daggett will cut his losses and abandon his plan to steal Becton's discovery?"

"I do, my love," answered the earl. "He's vicious and un-principled—but he's also clever and pragmatic. Once the plant is in the hands of the Royal Society, his chances of stealing it are virtually nil, and I don't think he would dare risk it. The government has turned a blind eye on the murder of two unsavory gentlemen, but an assault on the most august scientific institution in Britain would force them to act."

Charlotte suddenly felt as if a leaden weight had been lifted from her shoulders. "Thank you. I don't always fully appreciate your clear-eyed logic, but in this case, I'm exceedingly grateful for it."

Wrexford chuckled. "You see what a perfect pair we make. Given our often opposing ways of solving a problem, one of us is bound to be right."

She tightened her hold on his arm. His sense of humor was yet another thing she loved about him. Without laughter to counter the injustices and absurdities of the world, life could so easily crush one's spirit.

They resumed walking, and after winding through a small stand of beech trees, they entered the building.

A series of connected display galleries featured an impressive array of plants, rare manuscripts, and colorful botanical paintings, chosen to complement the upcoming lectures. There were only a few other scholars perusing the collections, as the lecture wasn't scheduled to start until six o'clock. Charlotte found that the artwork, with its meticulous details and luminous colors, helped distract her from counting every second that ticked by.

The earl was greeted by several fellow members and traded the requisite pleasantries before escorting her into the adjoining gallery.

She quelled the urge to sneak a peek toward the next one. *Let us keep moving!* Surely, more than ten minutes had passed . . .

Finally Wrexford drew her through the archway leading into the last of the gallery spaces, and sure enough, there was the corridor connecting it to the Orangery. The earl paused at a glass case near the opening and pretended to be reading the set of manuscript pages on display.

Forcing her gaze downward, Charlotte tried to make herself focus on the spidery script. But the words were naught but a blur.

Another moment ticked by . . .

Then another.

"What do you think is keeping him?" she whispered. A ridiculous question, she knew, and yet she couldn't keep from voicing it.

The earl didn't answer right away. Shifting his stance, he stared into the shadows within shadows of corridor, watching for any sign of movement.

The stillness seemed to amplify the thrum of tension in the air.

"Tyler knows to err on the side of caution." Wrexford turned his attention back to the manuscript pages. "There were likely people around the storage room and he decided to delay his entrance." A pause. "Let us give him a little more time."

She nodded, not trusting her voice. *That Hawk would be caught in the chaos if anything went wrong . . .*

Tick, tick.

Closing her eyes, Charlotte tried not to count off every dratted second.

"Wait here," said the earl, after an achingly long wait. Moving with unhurried nonchalance, he strolled into the corridor and disappeared around the corner.

She forced herself to match his air of calm and went to admire a series of watercolors hung on the nearby wall. They were lilies, by the renowned French botanical artist Pierre-Joseph Redouté, who late in the last century had spent a year at the Royal Botanic Gardens studying its plants. The brushwork was breathtakingly beautiful.

It deserved more than distracted glances—

Catching at the corner of her eye, a sudden dark flutter—the tails of a gentleman's coat—nearly made her jump. She was no longer alone in the gallery.

"Charlo—Lady Charlotte?"

She spun around. "Marco?" The presence of her old comrade stirred a rush of both relief and guilt. Thank heaven he had survived the dreadful night at DeVere's conservatory.

Though not because of any help from me—I should have been a better friend. But there was no time for explanations, and superficial apologies would only ring hollow.

Keeping her voice low, Charlotte added, "I'm so glad to see you. But is it wise for you to be here? I thought . . . I thought it had been decided that you and Dr. Hosack were to remain in seclusion for the time being."

"*Sì.*" He looked around before going on. "Lord Wrexford told me that it is for my own protection. But apparently the Royal Society asked my host if I might be permitted to give my scheduled lecture, so as not to add any more speculation as to what intrigue is going on at this symposium. And he agreed to the request."

Moretti lifted his shoulders. "So here I am." The corners of his mouth quivered in a weak attempt at a smile. "*Dio del cielo,* forgive me for saying so, but your fiancé can be a very frightening fellow. Does he make a regular habit of involving himself in murder and—"

"*Shhhh!*" she warned. "We mustn't speak of that here. But be glad that it was he who found you, and not the killer."

Moretti paled, but maintained his composure. "It is my understanding that the fiend is still at liberty."

"Yes." Charlotte glanced at the corridor.

Still, no sign of Wrexford.

"I'm so sorry you were drawn into such a diabolical web of deception," she continued. "I hope—indeed, I pray—that it will soon be over. But in the meantime . . ." Charlotte darted another look into the gloom. The doleful tick of time now seemed to echo loud as cannon fire inside her head. "In the meantime, you mustn't let down your guard."

His eyes narrowed in question.

"Did Captain Daggett, who is part of the American delegation, ever show interest in your research, or ask about the drawing that Becton gave to you?"

Moretti shook his head.

"What about any of the other attendees?"

"Again, no," answered Moretti. "W-Why do you ask?"

Charlotte didn't wish to frighten him. But better safe than sorry. "I can't explain that now. Please just trust me that you need to be very careful tonight. If anyone tries to probe for more detailed information on your research and methods, be sure to deflect the questions. And if anyone makes a reference to Becton's sketch, you must feign bewilderment . . ."

Mention of the sketch caused a tiny muscle in his jaw to clench.

"Not only that," she quickly added, "you must send word to Lord Wrexford immediately and let him know who asked. Your host will know how to reach him."

"Am I . . ." Moretti squared his shoulders. "Am I in danger?"

"I don't believe so," replied Charlotte, feeling her old comrade deserved an honest answer. "But I would rather not take any chances."

"As always, you don't try to make a silk purse out of a sow's ear." This time, his smile was a genuine one. "I'm so glad you haven't changed."

She, too, was happy to see he hadn't lost the qualities that had forged their youthful friendship. Her words had alarmed him, but she sensed resolve rather than fear.

"Be assured that I will do as you say," he said softly. "And, Charlotta, you must take care as well. I don't pretend to understand how you are involved in all this, but it stands to reason that you may be at risk as well."

"I—"

"Moretti!" A call from the adjoining gallery interrupted their tête-à-tête. "Come, I wish to introduce you to Professor Dixwell, who has journeyed down from Oxford for several days to attend our symposium."

"I had better go," he murmured.

Charlotte watched him return to the group of scholars. She hoped her words had done some good. Too many people close to her were in danger . . . and Daggett was still lurking in the shadows, free to strike at will.

Fisting her hands in her skirts, she crossed over to a display of various tree barks used for reducing fever, hoping the ornate marble pedestal would hide her growing agitation.

If only there were a botanical antidote for fear. Her heart was beginning to hit up against her ribs.

Distracted by its thumping, Charlotte didn't hear Wrexford's approach. His touch nearly made her jump out of her skin.

"Come with me," he murmured, placing her hand on his sleeve. The look in his eyes turned her innards to ice.

She let herself be led back through the adjoining galleries and out to the gardens. The earl didn't pause and took the pathway leading back to the carriage yard. Drawing in several deep gulps of fresh air, Charlotte remained silent, dread warring with impatience.

Lantern light glimmered through the leaves. The guests were starting to arrive for the evening lecture. Gravel crunched under iron-shod wheels as several carriages maneuvered up to the reception area.

Keeping to the shadows, Wrexford skirted around the dark bulk of two parked barouches. His own carriage was up ahead, the horses already turned for the journey back to Town.

"Hell's bells." Charlotte couldn't hold back any longer. "Don't keep me in suspense, Wrexford. If—"

He quickened his pace. The iron step was already down and the door cracked open. A hand—Tyler's—reached down and helped her scramble inside. Her wrap slipped from her shoulders, tangling in the earl's legs as he climbed in right behind her.

A bit breathless, she slid across the seat—and hit up against Hawk. "Oh, thank heaven," she gasped, gathering him in a fierce hug and burying her face in his tangled curls.

"Oiy, oiy!" came his muffled protest. Charlotte didn't care. She tightened her hold.

The crack of a whip set the horses in motion, the sudden lurch allowing the boy to wriggle free.

Regaining her equilibrium, she looked around, the silvery moonlight allowing just enough illumination for her to see both Hawk and Tyler were empty-handed.

"Where the devil is the specimen?" she demanded.

It was the boy who chirped an answer.

"It was gone!"

CHAPTER 21

"*Gone?*"

Wrexford met Charlotte's incredulous stare with a grim smile. "Yes. *Gone.*"

"Allow me to explain, milady," interjected Tyler.

"Please do." She slumped back against the squabs. "How is it that Daggett keeps finding a way to stay one step ahead of us?"

"He hasn't," replied the valet. "We can take a measure of solace in the fact that the specimen isn't in his hands. Alas, it's merely a matter of bad luck, not cunning malice, that it slipped through our fingers."

"The collection of plants bound for the University of St. Andrews was taken to the docklands this morning," explained Wrexford as he took a seat beside her. "The ship taking it to Scotland sailed on the afternoon tide."

Charlotte muttered an oath, her look of frustration mirroring his own.

"A special courier, traveling by royal mail coach, will almost certainly arrive in St Andrews before the ship," he continued. "As soon as we return to my townhouse, I shall write an explanation to Professor Murray, with the request that he entrust both the plant and the documents to the courier in order for them to be returned to the Royal Society."

"I'll go," volunteered Tyler.

"Actually, I think Edwards is the right man for the job," replied Wrexford. The head groom was the earl's former bat-man from his military days and a battle-tested veteran of the Peninsular War. "I'll have Seth accompany him."

A spasm of disappointment passed over Tyler's face, but he didn't protest.

As for Charlotte, her expression had turned pensive, but Wrexford didn't like the shadowed look that lingered beneath her lashes.

Damnation. He had an inkling of what she was thinking. "Don't let your imagination get the better of you, Charlotte. Even if DeVere had mentioned Becton's sketch to Daggett, we know that he never saw it. In that regard, luck and timing worked in our favor. Had Moretti arrived a half hour earlier, it would have been a different story. But even so, it's too far-fetched to think the captain would have ever worked out where Becton had hidden the specimen."

He paused briefly, letting her consider what he had just said before adding, "It was only because of your brother that we pieced together the connection to Professor Murray. And then it took Hawk, who has developed a trained eye for the nuances of plants, to spot it among all the other plants."

Charlotte took her time in replying. "That makes perfect sense." Her voice resonated with the same precise control as her pen strokes. "There's just one thing that bothers me . . ."

Wrexford waited. He wasn't sure what to expect. But Charlotte being Charlotte, he knew it wouldn't be something easily dismissed.

The moonlight gave way to sudden gloom. A few fat drops of rain spattered against the window glass.

"Nothing about this mystery," she said, "has gone according to reason."

It was his turn to take his time in answering. "I beg to differ," he finally said. "Logic didn't let us down. We made earlier assumptions based on incomplete information. In my scientific experience, that leads to errors, causing one to reassess and revise. Now that we know more of the variables, I believe we've created a more accurate hypothesis."

With only flickers of watery light breaking through the clouds, it was difficult to read her face. In moments like these, when decisions threatened other lives, Charlotte often retreated into herself.

"You think we have it right this time?" she asked.

"The gods punish mere mortals who have the hubris to claim such omniscience," he responded. "But yes, I think we have it right enough. I don't think Daggett is a danger to any of us."

"Even to Moretti?" challenged Charlotte. "I saw him just now. He's one of the speakers on tonight's program." She went on to tell him about the Royal Society's request, and her own warning to her old friend.

"You were right to caution him, but I truly believe Moretti is in no danger. As I've said before, Daggett is ruthless, but he's also pragmatic. He would be a fool to pursue his original plan, now that it's gone awry. And my sense is, he's no fool."

She looked away. Only one question now lay between them, and to him it was the most important one. Again, he waited, knowing she must come to the answer herself.

The carriage picked up speed as it turned onto the main road leading into Town. The shower had passed and the swirls of vapor were dissolving into the darkness.

"I confess that my judgment in this affair hasn't been as sharp as usual," said Charlotte softly. "I'm grateful for your patience with my uncertainties"—her smile was fleeting, but it warmed his heart—"and will trust your wisdom in this."

"I won't let you regret it," he replied.

Hawk stirred and made a small sound as he curled closer to Charlotte. He had fallen asleep, his head pillowed against her shoulder. She shifted and gently slipped her arm around him.

"Right. Let us look ahead rather than behind us."

"Indeed."

The earlier tension in the air gave way to the comfortable rhythms of the road—the muted creaks and jangling of the harnesses, the steady *clip-clop* of hooves.

Wrexford leaned back and closed his eyes. And yet his thoughts couldn't quite settle into silence. Nor could his heart—it ached for Charlotte. She was dealing with more worries than anyone should have to bear. Hawk and Raven were growing older, and mothering them was taking on new and more complex challenges . . . He also sensed that the new reconnections with her family, while a source of great happiness, had stirred some uncomfortable self-examination.

And then there was their impending marriage.

Any intelligent, independent woman would likely be wrestling with the ramifications of such a momentous decision. After all, it was, in effect, a surrender of self. Under the law, a woman became the property of a man when she married, with no more rights than his horse or his hound. She had no recourse if it turned out that he had an iron fist hidden beneath the velvet glove of his courtship.

So even the most sincere promises from a fiancé must carry an undertone of uncertainty.

Shifting against the squabs, Wrexford conceded the utter unfairness of it. However, he quickly reminded himself that he had already made sure that would never be an issue. Charlotte knew that the marriage articles settled enough money on her to provide financial independence. She would always have the freedom to live an independent life if she so chose.

Though I shall do my best to see it never comes to that.

Aside from marriage worries, Wrexford also sensed that she was struggling with her identity as A. J. Quill, and how to stay true to her principles while balancing all the responsibilities for family and loved ones . . .

He must have made some sort of sound, for Charlotte came alert, and reached over to twine her fingers with his.

"Bad dreams?" she murmured.

"Dreams would imply that I've been napping rather than pondering the current situation," he said lightly. A glance at the facing seat showed Tyler had nodded off.

Be damned if he hasn't, thought the earl as he lifted her hand and brushed a kiss to her knuckles. "I hope you know—I hope you believe—that you're safe with me in every way that matters."

"Wrexford." Charlotte touched his cheek. "I confess that I am unsettled about a great many things. But you are not one of them."

"And yet—"

She stilled his lips with hers. Her trust in him took his breath away.

"Whatever lies ahead," murmured Charlotte, her whisper tickling against his skin, "we shall face it together."

The rest of the journey seemed to pass quickly and the carriage soon rumbled onto Piccadilly Street.

Wrexford rapped on the trap and called for the driver to head on to Charlotte's residence. "I shall drop the two of you first, before setting plans in motion for a courier to head to Scotland. Raven and Mac are no doubt anxious to hear about the evening."

"I wish we had better news," replied Charlotte as she roused a sleepy Hawk.

"Let us be patient," he counseled. "Our pieces are positioned well on the chess board. Another few moves, and I expect that the game will be won."

*   *   *

Charlotte gave a horrified huff as she opened one eye and saw the bright blade of morning light cutting across her bed-covers. It was later than she wished, given all the tasks on her list. Idling the morning away in sleep was for the indolent rich.

"While I have far too much to do."

Though it wasn't as if she hadn't been working half the night. After Wrexford had dropped her and Hawk at their door, and explanations had been made to Raven and McClellan, she had slipped into her workroom. An idea had come to mind for a drawing. The lines had been inked in and the text had been lettered.

All that remained was to paint in the final washes of color.

The government wouldn't be happy with questions raised about whether DeVere's time in America had anything to do with his death, given that Quincy had been a victim as well. But the great unwashed public would lap it up. They loved any hint that their so-called betters were just as flawed and filthy as they were.

As she dressed, Charlotte turned her attention to more personal matters. She was determined to take Wrexford's advice to heart and trust that the investigation no longer posed a threat to family and friends. What with Becton's murder, she had given short shrift to the wedding plans, much to the dowager's disappointment. A morning spent allowing Alison a more active role in planning the festivities would make her great-aunt exceedingly happy.

"And perhaps me as well." Charlotte made a wry face in the looking glass. Though in truth, the fuss had always struck her as excessive. "I suppose it's one of the reasons I chose to elope."

After sliding the last hairpin into place, she hurried downstairs and followed the sweetly spiced aroma of fresh-brewed coffee into the kitchen. Raven had a book on mathematics open on the worktable and was writing in his notebook.

"Damnation," he muttered under his breath.

"Language," she chided as she poured herself a cup from the pot on the hob.

"Wrexford swears when he's puzzled."

"Wrexford does a great many things that aren't permitted to someone of your years."

"I hate being a child," groused Raven.

As far as Charlotte was concerned, he was growing up far too fast.

"Oiy," agreed Hawk as he chewed on a forkful of shirred eggs and gammon.

"And you—don't speak with your mouth full." She took a sip of the blissfully hot brew. "What has happened to your manners? They seem to have wandered off this morning."

"Perhaps they went to Gunter's for ice cream," Raven quipped, then turned to his brother. "Wouldn't it be a treat to have sweets for breakfast?"

"Are you two complaining about my cooking?" McClellan appeared from the depths of the pantry and tapped a cooking spoon to her meaty palm.

Hawk fixed Raven with a look of wide-eyed warning. "No, no. He was just jesting, ha, ha, ha."

McClellan raised her brows.

"Ha, ha, ha," added Raven.

"Hmmph. It's a good thing you Weasels know on which side your bread is buttered." The maid moved to the oven and pulled a pan of pastries from the oven. A yeasty fragrance, perfumed with the scent of cinnamon and melted sugar, filled the air. "As well as your muffins."

"Oh, that smells ambrosial," murmured Charlotte.

McClellan plucked a half dozen of the hot pastries from the pan and arranged them on a serving plate. "Help yourself, m'lady," she said, placing them in the center of the worktable and giving Charlotte a mischievous wink. "There should be plenty for us, seeing as some people seem to prefer frozen treats at this hour in the morning."

"It wasn't *me*," said Hawk with a grin. "It was my manners that went astray."

"Assuming you—and your brother—ask in a gentlemanly fashion," drawled McClellan, "I daresay, there are enough for all of us."

Once the chuckles had subsided, Charlotte broke off a bite of her pastry and let the spiced sweetness melt on her tongue. A pleasant warmth spread through her limbs. She hadn't felt this relaxed in days.

Seeing Raven pick up his pencil after gobbling down his muffin, she asked, "What are you working on?"

"A mathematical problem in one of the books that Lady Cordelia lent to me." He frowned. "But it's proving damn—er, deucedly difficult."

Raven had a special talent for numbers. If he was puzzled, it must be a diabolically complex one. "I'm sure she would be happy to help you work it out."

His expression turned a little mulish. "I haven't given up yet."

Charlotte repressed a smile. Like herself, he had a stubborn streak, and was loath to ask for assistance. "I, too, need to return to my work." She finished the last of her pastry and rose. "I have a drawing to finish for Mr. Fores."

Hawk carefully swallowed before asking," Do you need for us to deliver it?"

"I should be very grateful if you would. It should be done within the hour," she replied.

Adding the colored washes turned out to be a quicker task than expected. She had already decided what hues would be best, and after mixing the paints on her palette, the final touches were soon done. After rolling up the finished work, Charlotte returned to the kitchen.

Raven hadn't budged from his stool.

"There's no need to accompany Hawk if you don't wish to interrupt your work," she said, looking around for his brother.

He made a face and slapped down his pencil. "No, I'll go with him." A sigh seemed to concede that the equation had defeated him. "And perhaps after that, I will pay a visit to Lady Cordelia's office."

The docklands. Charlotte hesitated, but quickly quelled the frisson of alarm, determined to heed Wrexford's assurance that the American naval captain posed no threat to any of them. "I'm sure she'll be delighted to see you."

Another sigh as Raven snapped his notebook shut. "The answer is likely obvious. I just can't see it."

She couldn't help but smile. *A truism if ever there was one.* "Where's your brother?"

"In the garden." Raven gave a shrill whistle to summon him. "Dissecting a cornflower and drawing the details with the aid of a magnifying glass."

"Don't make light of his interests," she counseled. "Passions give us purpose. He sees things we don't, and that's a special gift."

Raven allowed a small smile. "He's good at it, isn't he?"

"Very," she answered.

The back door opened and slammed shut, followed by the *squish* of steps. Charlotte winced at the sight of Hawk's muddy boots and stained fingers. "Wash your hands, please."

Grumbling, he did as he was told.

"And go out the way you came, so as not to track dirt through Mac's freshly-swept corridor." Charlotte handed her drawing to Raven. "Do try to hand this over to Mr. Fores without any additional colors being added to the paper."

The boys raced off, their laughter lingering for a moment before the house settled into a peaceful stillness. McClellan had gone out to the Covent Garden markets, leaving Charlotte to wait for Alison's arrival. She had sent word to the dowager late last night, asking her to stop by for tea and a discussion of the wedding plans.

Given the subject of the invitation, she rather expected . . .

A knock on the front door announced that Alison had indeed decided to arrive early.

"Where is everyone?" asked the dowager as Charlotte clicked open the latch. Only the plumes of her bonnet were visible above the jumble of fabric swatches, menus, and paper samples clasped in her arms.

"Out running errands," answered Charlotte, quickly taking charge of all the items. "Come, let us spread all this out in the parlor and then I will make us a pot of tea."

"You had better bring a platter of Mac's ginger biscuits," came the cheerful reply. "This may take some time . . ."

"Slipped through your fingers?" Wrexford put down his pen. "I thought you had two of your best men keeping watch on the Sun and Sextant Club."

"I did, milord," answered Griffin. "Unfortunately, there was a robbery at the Earl of Audley's townhouse last night, and I needed their help until reinforcements arrived to take over the case."

"Bloody hell," muttered the earl.

"It was only for an hour," responded Griffin, "but it seems that Daggett chose his moment well."

Yes, the dastard seems to have the devil's own luck.

"You're sure he's gone for good?" demanded the earl.

"Yes. One of my men had a word with the porter—who, thanks to the purse you left with us, was very willing to talk. Apparently, the captain paid his bill and left with his bag just before dawn."

Wrexford rose and began to pace back and forth in front of the hearth. That the American had absconded was no surprise.

But it stuck in his craw that he hadn't had the chance to confront the damned fellow and shake some answers out of him.

"I suppose," murmured the Runner, "that this means you're not going to offer me breakfast."

"If I did," snapped the earl, "it would be naught but bread and water."

Griffin hung his head and let out a mournful sigh.

The coals emitted a whispery hiss as Wrexford pivoted—and stopped short. "I suppose you're now going to tell me that you toiled all night without rest or a morsel of sustenance."

The Runner pursed his lips and said nothing.

Wrexford resumed his pacing, but directed his steps to the sideboard, where he poured a measure of brandy into a glass.

"Tyler," he called to the closed laboratory door as he handed the spirits to Griffin.

No answer.

"Thank you, milord," murmured the Runner.

"*Tyler!*"

Still, no response.

"Hmmph." Puzzled, he picked up the handbell from the work counter and rang for his butler.

As if summoned by some invisible force, Riche appeared an instant later. "Yes, milord?"

"Where the devil is Tyler?"

A spasm of surprise passed over the butler's normally impassive face. "He left a half hour ago. I assumed he informed you . . ."

"Clearly not," growled the earl.

Riche's expression betrayed his misgivings. "He was accompanied by the younger Master Sloane." He cleared his throat. "Who, I must say, looked rather agitated."

That made no sense. If Charlotte had dispatched Hawk with a message for him, the boy wouldn't have hared off without delivering it.

"Was Raven with them?"

"No, milord. It was just the two of them."

Even more puzzling. Wrexford took a moment to mull it over.

"Thank you, Riche. Kindly have Cook fix a hearty meal for Mr. Griffin."

The Runner let out a blissful sigh.

"Which he may enjoy at his leisure in the breakfast room." Wrexford took up his coat from a chair. "I need to go out."

Griffin came instantly alert, his smile giving way to a more serious mien. "I'll come with you, milord. If there's trouble brewing—"

"No, no. There's no need to forgo filling your breadbox. I'm merely paying a visit to Lady Charlotte's residence."

CHAPTER 22

"Excuse me, Lady Cordelia, but Master Sloane wondered if you have time for a question." The clerk paused as he peered into the room. "Oh, forgive me, I didn't realize that Mr. Sheffield was meeting with you."

"No, no—show him in," replied Cordelia. "We were just finishing our work."

"Thank heaven," murmured Sheffield, grimacing as he began to straighten up the array of papers spread out over the worktable. "All these dratted numbers were beginning to make my head ache."

"But they tell such interesting stories, sir." Raven took a moment to study the weekly report on the transportation costs of bringing calico fabric from the mills in the north to the docks for export to the West Indies before looking up. "Imagine when rails can be laid from London to Yorkshire, allowing the goods to be moved by a steam-powered locomotive."

"That, lad, is still some years off, though the test tracks at the coal mines are proving very successful." Sheffield had been an early investor in William Hedley's "Puffing Billy," a mechanical prototype that was generating a good deal of excitement within the world of engineering. "But yes . . . what a grand improvement they will be, saving both time and money."

"You made an excellent gamble on Hedley's invention," remarked Cordelia. "For once."

Sheffield laughed. His reputation for losing at card games was legendary among his friends. "I am getting much better at playing vingt-et-un, now that you and Raven have explained the mathematics to me." He made a wry face. "What a pity that honest work is taking up so much of my time. I rarely have a chance to indulge in such idle pleasures anymore."

"*No rest for the wicked,*" replied Cordelia, allowing a hint of a smile. She held out her hands for the stack Sheffield had gathered. "I had better get to work analyzing our shipping schedules . . ." She glanced at Sheffield. "We may be getting more business in the near future."

Raven's gaze came alight with curiosity. "Is that because of Mr. Quincy's murder?"

"Yes," answered Sheffield. "Lady Charlotte's drawings had already raised questions about his company's shoddy maintenance of their ships. I daresay, they won't be in business much longer."

"What about the murderer?" asked the boy. "Is there any word around the dockyards—"

"Did you have a question, Raven?" interrupted Cordelia. "Or would the two of you rather gossip about blood and mayhem?" She glanced at the clock on the side cabinet. "I have a few minutes before I have to meet with a representative of the Wedgwood Company."

"Oiy, I do," answered the boy. "It won't take long. It's about a certain equation . . ."

"Oh, by the by, do stop by my office before you leave," called Sheffield as he turned for the door, "and let me show you the knife I just purchased from a lascar seaman. I think you might find it very interesting."

*   *   *

"Consider yourself lucky that you didn't arrive a quarter hour earlier," announced Charlotte as she escorted Wrexford into the parlor. "Alison is a more intimidating force of nature than an Atlantic hurricane."

She tucked a loosened lock of hair behind her ear as she cleared a pile of fabric swatches from the sofa. "Must we really make up special napkins and tablecloths to match the floral—" Looking up, she stopped short on seeing his expression and felt her heart lurch.

"Is something amiss?"

He took a seat before answering. "Is Raven here?"

The question stirred another frisson of alarm. "No, the boys left this morning to deliver my drawing to Mr. Fores, and then—" Charlotte sat down beside him. "Ye gods, Wrexford, is something amiss?"

"Not that I know of," he answered. 'It's just that Riche saw Tyler and Hawk leave my townhouse together, and I find it odd that they said nothing to me about it. Since he said that Raven wasn't with them, I simply wanted to ask the boy whether he knew anything about it."

"Raven hasn't yet returned home. He was planning on paying a visit to Lady Cordelia at her office."

Was it merely a shadow thrown by the shifting sunlight, or did the earl's gaze suddenly darken with concern?

"The dockyards!" she exclaimed, realizing the import of what she had just said. "Are you worried—"

"I'm not worried about anything yet," he answered. Her huff caused him to hastily add, "I'm merely concerned. However unreasonable, I suspect Tyler feels some measure of guilt at having let the specimen elude us. So I simply wish to talk with Raven and assure myself that Tyler and Hawk aren't poking around in places that are best left undisturbed."

"Raven would never let his brother venture into danger," protested Charlotte.

Unless . . .

"Hell's bells." She slumped back against the pillows. "You think the three of them might be up to some unholy mischief together?"

"I would like to believe that Tyler wouldn't allow emotion to overpower reason," answered the earl.

Oh, but I know all too well what a powerful force emotion is.

"However, I think it wise for me to pay a visit to the office of Nereid and Neptune, just to be sure," he finished.

"I'm coming with you." Charlotte shot up before he could react. "Dressed as Magpie, of course. If there's trouble, we'll need to act quickly."

"If I thought I had a ghost of a chance of convincing you—"

"Save your breath." She held his gaze, daring him to challenge her.

He looked away. "Hurry and change."

Sheffield waited for Raven to have a seat facing his desk before nudging a knife across to him. "Have a look. The hilt is made of silver, and the carnelian stones are an unusual shade—more a rich cinnabar red than orange."

Raven picked it up, and after a cursory look at the decorative elements, he ran a thumb lightly along the blade. "Oiy, it's pretty enough. M'lady would like the color. But the steel is inferior—it can't hold a sharp edge."

He slid the weapon back across the polished wood and looked up. "No point in having a knife that might let you down in a pinch."

"Seeing as I'm not planning on slicing through anything other than envelopes and sealing wax with it, I daresay it will do the job without any trouble," replied Sheffield as he tucked it into his desk drawer. "Be that as it may, I—"

"Why don't you stop fiddle-faddling, Mr. Sheffield," interjected Raven, "and tell me the real reason that you asked me to come back here and see you."

"Er, I was just about to do so, lad." The chair scraped over the floor as Sheffield shifted in his seat and darted a look at the door to make sure it was firmly shut. "But do keep your voice down. I'd prefer to keep this just between us."

"Of course." Raven propped his elbows on the table and leaned in a little closer. "What do you need me to do?"

"*Us,*" corrected Sheffield. "We need to do a little sleuthing around the docks."

"Looking for what?"

Sheffield gave another glance at the door. "The man who murdered DeVere and Quincy. I dislike involving you in such sordid doings, lad, but I need your help on something. I would never ask you to do anything dangerous. However, Wrex won't like my request. And neither will Lady Charlotte. So think hard on it before saying yes."

For a moment, Raven stared down at his boots, the battered brim of his cap hiding his face. And then he looked up.

"Does it have to do with DeVere's murder?" A pause. "I'm bloody glad the miscreant is dead."

Sheffield hesitated, and then gave a gruff nod. "So am I, lad. But his death clearly ties into Becton's demise, and that is a crime for which all of us wish to see justice done."

"And Wrexford saw Daggett, one of the American scholars, sneaking away from the scene," interjected the boy.

"Yes, he's a scholar," replied Sheffield, "but he's also an officer in the American Navy, and sailed here from New York with DeVere and Quincy. Apparently, the three of them were thick as thieves for a while, and one can't help but wonder—"

"Whether they quarreled over whatever dark mischief they've been plotting," finished Raven.

"Logic says yes," answered Sheffield. "And we know how fond Wrex is of logic."

Raven grinned. "Now we just have to prove it."

"Precisely." Sheffield rose and began to pace. "It occurred to me that one reason Daggett may have betrayed DeVere and

Quincy is because he's made a better deal for himself with new partners in crime."

"You're getting very good at devious thinking, sir."

"Thank you," replied Sheffield absently. "So I thought we might ask around among your friends about whether Daggett has been spending time here in the dockyards and with whom he is consorting."

"Strings, Mary Mussels, Chips, Smoke . . ." Raven rattled off a few additional names. "Oiy, they all keep their peepers open. A flea can't scratch its arse down here without one of the gang noticing."

"Excellent! Shall we—"

"Just two things, sir." The boy eyed Sheffield's coat and trousers with a critical squint. "You can't come with me. You stick out like a rose in a dung heap. Within minutes, every wharf from here to Billingsgate will be abuzz with the news that some toff is making inquiries."

"But the workers around here are used to seeing me," protested Sheffield. "I often visit the harborside tavern and mingle with people."

"Not the people I need to meet."

To his credit, Sheffield surrendered without further argument. "And the second thing?"

"What does Daggett look like?"

"Oh, er—right. Let me think on how to describe him . . ." A gust of wind rattled the windowpanes. Clouds were scudding in, and a greasy grey mist was beginning to drift in from the river.

"He's about my height, with sun-bleached auburn hair, worn long—nearly to his shoulders—and often tied back in a queue. In the right light, the color is distinctive—a rich, reddish brown."

Sheffield spoke slowly, appearing to choose his words with care. "His eyes are slate-blue, and his gaze scrapes like flint over your skin. He has broad cheekbones—they're sharp as well—and his face tapers to a pointed chin with a cleft. There's a small, but noticeable, scar cutting across it."

Raven gave an approving nod. "You're learning to notice the little things, just like one of us urchins."

"High praise, indeed," responded Sheffield dryly. "Oh—and one last thing. Daggett moves with a catlike grace, and yet his gait has a tiny hitch. He seems to favor his left knee."

"You've painted a very good picture, sir." Raven tugged at his cap and turned for the door.

"Just a moment." Sheffield stepped into a small storage alcove. He reappeared a few moments later wearing a shabby coat, well-worn boots, and battered hat.

"Give me a little credit," he murmured in response to Raven's raised brows. "I'm trying to establish my own friendships in the area, and I'm not so beef-witted as to think I can do that if I'm prancing around in my Mayfair finery."

He joined Raven by the door. "Er, we need to move very stealthily. I would prefer that Lady Cordelia doesn't see us leave."

"I wasn't planning on going out through the main corridor," answered Raven. "We'll use the side door next to the storage room at the back of the building. The stairwell leads down to the cellar warehouse, and from there, we can slip out into the alleyway leading to the chandlery yard."

"We can?" Sheffield looked perplexed. "How the devil do you know that?"

"You still have a lot to learn about skulduggery," responded the boy patiently. "It's important to be familiar with your surroundings, and have several options of how to slip away if trouble suddenly strikes."

"Point taken."

Raven cracked open the door, and after a glance around, he gestured for Sheffield to follow.

It wasn't until they had reached the cellar and made their

way out to the alleyway that Sheffield ventured to ask, "Do you think we have a chance of learning anything about Daggett?"

"Oiy, if the dastard is up to mischief around here, one of my friends will know it."

Lady Cordelia looked up in surprise as the clerk announced that there were visitors wishing to have a word with her.

"Wrexford! Yes, yes, do come in." She waited until the clerk withdrew and shut the door behind him before addressing Charlotte in a taut whisper. "If you're dressed like that, I take it there's trouble."

"That remains unclear," answered Wrexford, before Charlotte could answer her. "We're hoping you might help rectify that."

"H-How so?"

"Did Raven come here earlier to ask you a mathematical question?" responded Charlotte.

"Yes, he did," answered Cordelia.

The answer appeared to soften the tension in Charlotte's face. "Perhaps we're seeing specters when there's naught but thin air."

"Then Sheffield wished to speak with him," continued Cordelia.

Wrexford felt a tickling of foreboding.

"I'll go ask him why."

Cordelia returned a few moments later. "That's odd—he's not there." She quickly checked the adjoining storage room, then turned to them with a mystified shrug. "He must be here somewhere. The door to my office has been open and I didn't see him leave the building."

Charlotte closed her eyes for an instant.

Wrexford, too, was now sure that mischief was afoot. "Is there another way out of the building?" he asked.

"I—I confess, I don't really know." She hurried to the doorway and called for the clerk in the copy room to join them. "Mr. Mulligan, is the front entrance the only exit from the premises?"

"No, milady," he answered without hesitation. "There's a back stairwell leading down to the cellar storerooms."

"There is?" Cordelia's brow furrowed. "Then why do we always take a roundabout route to go there?"

"Because . . ." The clerk's face turned a trifle red. "Because the smell isn't fit for a lady."

The word that Cordelia muttered under her breath wasn't fit for a lady, either.

Mulligan's ears were now a vivid shade of crimson.

"Show us the stairwell," murmured Wrexford.

"Perhaps I should come with you," suggested Cordelia. "I know my way around—"

"That won't be necessary." He hesitated. "Is there any place around here where Sheffield might be headed?"

"He sometimes has a pint of ale at the Golden Galleon," volunteered Mulligan.

"Thank you." To Cordelia, Wrexford added, "If he returns, please ask him to wait for us."

"What—" she began.

But the earl and Charlotte had already disappeared around the corner of the corridor.

After resettling his hat a little lower on his brow, Sheffield took a swig of ale and slanted a look around. Smoke shrouded the taproom, the flickering oil lamps doing little to penetrate the haze. Given the less-than-pristine state of the tabletops and pewter mugs, that was perhaps by design. It appeared that the Golden Galleon had lost its shine several centuries ago.

Sheffield winced as he watched a barmaid hurry by with a tray heaped with bowls of fishy-smelling stew—the only identifiable signs of its contents were several eel tails sticking from the soupy broth. He had not yet given himself the pleasure of dining at the tavern.

"Anudder drink, ducky?" asked the barmaid, pausing on her return to the kitchen. "Or a platter of mussels?"

"Thank you, but no." However, Sheffield did slide several coins across the sticky wood. "If an urchin comes looking for 'Sheff,' bring him to me." He had chosen a table tucked in a shadowed corner, allowing him to survey the room without drawing notice.

"My pleasure." She leaned low and tucked the coins down her bodice. "Anything else I can offer you?"

"Not at the moment."

His reply earned a throaty laugh. "What a pity." She gave a flounce of her skirts. "Just wave if ye change yer mind."

As he waited for Raven, he kept an ear cocked to the jabbering voices around him. A group of sailors—one sounded vaguely American—was playing darts in the alcove behind him. The rhythmic *thump* of steel against the painted board punctuated the curses uttered in several different languages.

He was so caught up in his surroundings that he wasn't aware of Raven's arrival until the boy jabbed a fist rather sharply against his shoulder. "Never woolgather in a public place, sir," whispered the boy. "You've got to stay alert. Trouble can sneak up on you when you least expect it."

"I'll remember that," muttered Sheffield as he slapped the boy's hand away from his mug. "Any luck?"

The question drew a smug smile. "Swill the rest of your ale and come with me."

CHAPTER 23

Hawk climbed down from the hackney. "Mr. Tyler, are you sure we shouldn't send for Lord Wrexford? If you think the ship carrying the specimen might have been delayed—"

"I've merely said it's a possibility, and an unlikely one, so I'd rather not disturb His Lordship until we know for sure," replied the valet. They had stopped several streets away from the dockyards in order to make their way into the area via one of the many cart paths leading into the loading areas. "There are any number of reasons for a sailing to be put off for a day or two. Shrouds can snap, spars can break . . ."

He led the way into a narrow alleyway. "If perchance the ship is still here, I need for you to corroborate the identity of Becton's specimen, so we can demand that the shipment be held until word is sent to Wrexford and he is able to arrange for the proper authorities to take official charge of the plant."

"But—"

Tyler stopped and turned. "Look, you need not come along if it goes against your conscience. However, I feel responsible for all of you being mired in yet another murder, and at a time when Wrexford and Lady Charlotte ought to be free from worries." A pause. "If I can find the specimen and ensure its safety, then perhaps the two of them will agree we've done our part in bringing justice for Becton, and we'll leave the capture of Daggett to the Bow Street Runners."

Beneath the brim of his hat, his expression turned even more shadowed. "The sketch will be good enough for me to work from. And I feel that I must at least try."

Hawk made a rude sound. "If that's how you feel, then, of course, I'm coming. Friends don't leave friends in the lurch."

Charlotte squinted through a hazy fugue of smoke and stale ale. *No luck.* Sheffield wasn't among the men eating and drinking in the wharfside tavern. Wasting no time, she retraced her steps through the fishmonger's alley and turned into a passageway behind the ship chandlery yard, where Wrexford was waiting.

Her first impulse on catching sight of a ragged stevedore standing in the shadows was to draw the pocket pistol hidden in her jacket. Her second was to choke back a laugh.

"Wherever did you get those disgusting clothes?"

"I traded mine with a fellow who was more than happy to make the exchange," answered Wrexford.

"No doubt, as he got far the better of the bargain." She covered her nose. "You stink of mackerel."

"Lords can't be choosy when in the territory of beggars." He readjusted his hat. "I take it you had no luck."

"No," she answered, "but if Raven and Sheffield are involved in some intrigue, one of Raven's urchin friends may have an inkling of what it is. Strings, who picks apart old rope for ship caulking, works not far from here, so let us go ask him."

Charlotte took the lead and soon spotted the ragamuffin sitting in his usual spot on the Great Wapping dock. "Wait here. I won't attract undue attention if I go on my own," she said to the earl. "Oh—and give me a few coins, assuming you didn't hand over your purse, along with your clothes. Strings looks like he needs a decent meal."

Wrexford handed over two shillings.

As she had hoped, the appearance of another grimy urchin turned no heads. Crouching down, she murmured a quick question to the boy.

The reply caused her to grit her teeth.

"Which way did they go?" she replied, carefully slipping the coins into his pile of unraveled hemp.

Strings flicked a glance to the right.

Charlotte rose and circled around a cooper's shop before slipping back to the alleyway where Wrexford was waiting.

"Bloody hell," he muttered on hearing what Strings had told her. He didn't appear to like it any more than she did. "From here on in, I will lead the way."

She wasn't fool enough to argue.

The path that Strings had indicated led to a section of warehouses near the loading docks. Shadows flitted through the fetid air. A prickling of fear spurred her to stay right on Wrexford's heels. Daggett was a hardened military man, skilled in hand-to-hand combat with knife or sword . . .

He was also a cold-blooded killer.

Sheffield wouldn't stand a chance if he was cork-brained enough to confront him. As for Raven . . .

Damn. Damn. Damn.

Hawk wriggled through the gap in the crates and crawled through the trapdoor leading into the storage shed where Tyler had taken cover.

"Smoke says Dusty saw an unfamiliar ship tie up to one of the wharves behind the coal warehouses," he informed the valet. "He noticed on account of it being a fast schooner instead of one of the usual collier scows that makes the runs between here and Newcastle."

Tyler gave a satisfied grunt. "I think we can take that to mean my suspicion was right, and Captain Reginald Lyman is working hand in glove with Daggett. He possesses just such a ship and will do any deed, no matter how sordid, if he's handsomely paid for it."

The valet's initial inquiries regarding the Royal Society's shipment of plants had led them to a small Scottish shipping firm that carried perishable produce from London to the north. The head clerk had confirmed that they were usual agents for sending specimens from the Royal Botanic Gardens to various ports in Britain. However, he had gone on to explain that a man had shown up the previous afternoon with orders that the recently-delivered crates were to be handed over. A change in plans had been made, and the specimens needed to go by a different route.

The paperwork had all been in order, assured the head clerk. And so he hadn't thought twice about off-loading the requested cargo and allowing the crates to be hauled away . . .

"Oiy," agreed Hawk. "It makes sense that a niffy-naffy cove like Lyman would be involved. I heard Lord Wrexford say that he's a dirty dish who betrayed his country."

"A thoroughly dirty dish," agreed Tyler. Further questions around the docks had elicited the welcome information that Lyman's schooner had not yet set sail. "However, we need to get proof that the specimen is aboard his ship before we go rushing back to Wrexford and have him summon the authorities."

The boy looked at him uncertainly. "Are—Are you sure we shouldn't send word to him first? He—"

"As I said, I feel I've put you all in danger because of my carelessness," cut in Tyler. "I wish to be sure before I sound the alarm. If for some reason I'm wrong, and send everyone on a wild goose chase, there's a chance the real culprit may get away with his crimes."

Hawk's narrow face pinched in remorse. "If only I had caught a glimpse of the man's face when he tossed the glass into the greenery, then we would have known the identity of the murderer, and the specimen wouldn't be in danger."

"So we both wish to make amends," replied the valet. "I've an idea. You know these wharves better than I do. Can you get us close to the coal docks without being spotted?"

With nary a hesitation, Hawk nodded. "Follow me."

Quick as an eel, the boy led the way through the serpentine maze of narrow walkways that cut through docklands. Spars, rigging, ironworks, casks—a myriad of nautical supplies were crammed into the spaces between the rows of warehouses. The area was a hub of commerce for merchant ships from all over the world, and the raucous shouts of the stevedores loading and unloading cargo jumbled with the banging from the forges of blacksmiths and workshops of the carpenters. Amid all the jostling and cacophony, it wasn't hard for the two of them to slip by unnoticed.

Things turned a little quieter when they approached the coal warehouses, though the clatter of rock against metal as the cargo carts rumbled up and down the ramps created its own unique din. Several large collier brigs sat high in the water, the last of their dirty, dusty loads being hoisted out of the holds. A few smaller keelboats were being prepared to head upriver with local deliveries . . .

"Look there," said Tyler as he and Hawk took cover behind a large tarp-covered stack of sail canvas. "At the far end, between the collier and coastal packet boat."

"That looks to be a real flier," murmured Hawk, on spotting the sleek ship tied to the stanchions.

"Aye, it's one of those Baltimore Clippers built in America, and they're said to be fast as the wind." The valet slithered out on his belly for a better angle of sight down to the wharf. The area around the ship looked to be deserted.

"If we circle around the sail loft, it looks like we can hide ourselves among the water casks stacked by the pilings."

"Mr. Tyler—" began Hawk. But the valet was already moving toward the stone-and-timber building fronting the cobbled loading area.

The hustle and bustle of the various workers weaving in and out of the crowded quays provided enough cover for their stealthy approach.

"Mr. Tyler," repeated the boy, once the valet had found a hidey-hole among the casks. "H-How do you intend to learn whether the specimen is on board the ship?"

Craning his neck, Tyler studied the wharf for a long moment before answering. "I think that's rather obvious, lad."

"But . . ." A look of misgiving rippled through Hawk's eyes. "But both Wrexford and m'lady said we must be wery, wery careful, and err on the side of caution."

"*Fortes fortuna juvat,*" countered Tyler. "*Fortune favors the bold*—isn't that one of Lady Charlotte's favorite sayings?"

"Oiy, but . . ."

"Come now, we can't allow the scoundrels to get away if they have the plant." The valet allowed a pause. "Can we?"

The boy drew in a troubled breath, but remained silent.

"I'm not going to run off half-cocked," assured Tyler. "I'm going to study the surroundings and choose the right moment when—"

The sudden sound of footsteps on the cobblestones froze him in midsentence. Three men rounded a pile of coiled hawsers and headed for where the Baltimore Clipper sat at its moorings. As they passed the stacked casks, the one closest to Tyler and Hawk caught his boot on an uneven edge of stone and stumbled.

"*Tollpatsch,*" he muttered.

Eyes widening, Hawk sucked in an involuntary breath.

Tyler quickly pressed a hand over the boy's mouth as one of the man's companions—a Cornishman, by the sound of his accent—reacted with a brusque laugh. "Have a care, *mein Herr* One must have steady footing around ships." Another laugh. "Along with steady nerves."

"I think the steadiness of my nerves is not open to question, Captain Lyman," retorted *Mein Herr*.

"Ah, but poison is a gentleman's weapon," said the third man. He was an American. "Unlike me, you've yet to get your hands really dirty."

"And there is a great deal of dirty work left before our plans all come to fruition," Lyman pointed out.

"As an expert in botany," snapped *Mein Herr*, "I have a great deal of experience in getting my hands dirty."

More laughter.

Lyman took a flint and steel from his pocket, along with a thin cheroot, and struck a spark to his tobacco. "Let us hope you're right in your surmise, and that Becton sent his precious specimen to Professor Murray at St. Andrews." He blew out a plume of silvery smoke and watched it dissolve in the breeze. "Otherwise, you'll have wasted a great deal of money in hiring us."

"I'm sure of it. I overheard Lord Wrexford's fiancée and her brother telling Sir Robert about how Becton and Professor Murray were good friends who exchanged both specimens and papers. I'm willing to wager a fortune—"

"You already have," interjected Lyman.

"Yes, and mark my words, it will prove well worth it, for I'm positive Professor Murray has it," continued *Mein Herr*. "He'll be delighted to welcome fellow botanists, especially as we tell him that we took it upon ourselves to personally deliver this current shipment of plants from the Royal Botanic Gardens. Once we gain access to his conservatory, we'll force him to turn over the specimen and formula. And from there, it's clear sailing to Hamburg."

"Making a fortune depends on the fact that no one but us knows the identity of the plant or recipe for the formula," the third man pointed out.

"No one will," replied *Mein Herr*. "It goes without saying that Professor Murray can't be left alive."

"Well, then," said Lyman, after tossing the butt of the cheroot into the water. "Let us get on with sowing the seeds to becoming *very* rich men."

As the scuff of their steps on the brine-dark wooden wharf receded, Tyler released his hold on Hawk.

"That was *him*!" whispered the boy. "The one they called *Mein Herr* said *tollpatsch*!"

Tyler frowned in confusion.

"*Tollpatsch*" repeated Hawk. "That's what the man said—the one who threw the poisoned glass into the plants, where I was hiding on the night of Mr. Becton's murder."

The valet's face went pale as he realized the import of what Hawk had said. "You're absolutely sure, lad?"

Hawk gave a solemn nod. "Yes, sir."

"Then that means . . ." Tyler hesitated. "Then that means we now know the identity of the killer."

"Y-You recognized him?"

"Aye, lad. I caught a good glimpse of his face, as well as recognizing his voice," replied the valet grimly. He darted a look at the Baltimore Clipper. "And you heard what he said. I think there's not a shadow of a doubt that Becton's specimen is currently aboard Lyman's ship." A pause. "Though, thank God, they don't know that."

"Please, sir. We need to let Wrexford know." Hawk tugged on the valet's coat. "*Now!*"

Tyler shot an uncertain look at the river and its eddying currents. "I agree that we need to let him know. The tide has just changed, and will be against them heading out to sea for some hours . . ." He rubbed at his chin as he mulled over what to do. "And yet, there's always the chance that they might decide to move the specimen to some other place . . ."

For the moment, all appeared quiet aboard the Baltimore Clipper. The deck and rigging were clear of any crew.

Tyler's near-silent sigh twined with the swirls of mists blowing in from the river. "I'll stay here and keep watch on the ship. You run to the office of Nereid and Neptune Shipping. Let Sheffield or Lady Cordelia know that we've discovered the identity of the killer." He whispered a name. "And tell them to send word to Wrexford as quickly as possible."

Wrexford slowed his steps as he reached the end of the alley. It opened onto a cobbled carriageway that fronted a cluster of brick warehouses. On the far side, narrow cart paths cut between the building, creating a spiderweb of ins and outs.

Just waiting to entrap an unwary fly.

He hesitated. *Right or left?* A number of small offices were scattered among the storage areas—the sort of places where one could hire a few fellows to move small loads of cargo, row a wherry across the river . . . or perform other tasks for which no questions were asked.

With nothing to go on, Wrexford decided that he and Charlotte had little choice but to start at one end and make a methodical search of the area.

And pray that they found Sheffield and Raven before they met up with Daggett.

The first cart path was deserted, save for a few feral cats scrounging for scraps among a pile of broken crates. As he turned down the second one, Charlotte right at his heels, several shadowy figures standing outside a half-open door quickly disappeared inside. The earl ignored the rusty *snick* of the lock. None of the shapes had matched the silhouettes he sought.

As he hurried through a passageway that connected to the next cart path, the scuff of steps—faint but unmistakable—caught his ear. He waved for Charlotte to halt.

Then, edging forward, Wrexford ventured a peek around the corner. His movements had been carefully controlled, stirring not a whisper of air . . .

Still, one of the two figures standing up ahead spun around and dropped down to a crouch.

"Throw that rock at me, Weasel, and you'll be nursing a sore bum for the next fortnight," warned the earl as he hurried to join Raven and Sheffield.

"Don't ring a peal over the lad's head," responded his friend. "I asked him to—"

"*Shhhh,*" warned Charlotte as she darted out from her hiding place. "Let us find a more private place in which to talk."

Wrexford quickly moved to one of the locked doors of the storage areas and pulled a steel pick from inside his boot. The catch released, and he motioned for the others to step inside. A tug pulled the door shut behind him, leaving them shrouded in darkness.

Which was all for the best, he thought. At the moment, Sheffield and Raven would not wish to see his expression.

"Now, would you care to tell me what in the *bloody* name of Satan, the two of you are doing?"

It was said softly, but Sheffield wasn't fool enough to mistake the depth of the earl's fury. He shifted his stance, unconsciously shielding Raven from the earl's verbal wrath.

"Before you explode, Wrex, please let me explain. During my rounds of the gaming hells last night, I heard some talk that Daggett had been spotted around the docks. It occurred to me that as he had double-crossed DeVere and Quincy, he likely had made a deal with new partners—"

"So you decided to confront him?" demanded Wrexford.

"Well, not precisely. I'm not that stupid," replied his friend.

"I merely wished to follow him and ascertain with whom he was meeting."

"Seeing as you're such a smart fellow, what were you planning to do when Daggett spotted you?" His voice was sharp with sarcasm. "Expect Raven to stick a knife in the captain's leg?"

Sheffield said nothing. Thankfully, Charlotte remained silent as well. He was in no mood for arguments.

"Sir—" began Raven.

"Bite your tongue, Weasel! I don't want to hear another word out of you," cut in the earl. The realization of how close Sheffield and Raven had come to disaster was like a spark, igniting his anger to a fiercer burn. "You ought to have better sense than to lead a lamb to slaughter."

Raven refused to be silenced. "Sir, sir! You can birch me from here to Hades if you wish. But do it later!" He locked eyes with the earl. "We know where Daggett is right now, and if we don't move quickly, we might not have another chance to see what he's up to."

Wrexford hesitated, but only for an instant. "Very well, let us not allow him to slip through our fingers." He cracked open the door and checked up and down the cart path. "But the three of you are to do *exactly* as I order, or there will be hell to pay."

"Understood, Wrex," said Sheffield, pausing for a heartbeat on his way out to touch the earl's arm. "I would never— *never*—have let the boy come to any harm."

Wrexford let out a gruff sigh. "And what about you? Do you think the idea of *you* confronting a vicious killer doesn't make my blood run cold?"

"Ah, but think of all the expensive bottles of brandy and port that you would save with my demise."

"Arse," muttered Wrexford, causing them both to smile.

"Pssst," hissed Raven. "Follow me."

The boy wove his way through the maze of byways, bringing them closer and closer to the far end of the tidal basin. As they approached a chandlery specializing in flour and biscuits for long voyages, Raven crept close to a jumble of barrels. A ragged urchin crawled out from his hiding place, and after exchanging a few words with Raven, he darted off.

"Daggett is still inside," whispered Raven, on returning to where the others had taken cover.

Wrexford surveyed the surroundings. "I've an idea." He pointed to a narrow gap between two of the nearby buildings on the other side of the ship chandlery. "There are only two pathways that will return Daggett to the main part of the dockyards. I'm going to hide in the gap, and when Daggett comes out, I want the three of you to begin an argument here. And do it loudly. My guess is, he'll choose to avoid a scene and come my way."

"And if he doesn't?" asked Sheffield.

"Then let him go," answered the earl. "One of Raven's friends will help us pick up his trail."

Sheffield nodded. "Understood."

"And you, Weasel?"

Raven made a mulish face, but signaled his agreement.

Charlotte nodded without a challenge, though a flicker of fear betrayed how little she liked the idea.

"Then let us take up our positions. And hope that the tide is finally turning in our favor."

CHAPTER 24

A bank of sullen grey clouds was creeping in from the east, dampening the light of the sun. Bracing a shoulder against the wall, Wrexford waited within the sliver of space, trusting that he had made the right move.

In this particular game of cat and mouse, the role of predator and prey could change in the blink of an eye.

Finally, after what seemed like an eternity, the creak of the chandlery door sounded. The earl ventured a peek and saw it was Daggett.

The captain had paused to glance in the direction of Sheffield, Raven, and Charlotte, whose sudden shrill altercation was punctuating the raucous cries of the gulls. Shifting the valise he was holding from one hand to the other, Daggett turned and took the path leading past the earl's hiding place.

Excellent. The rat is about to become a mouse.

Holding his breath, Wrexford drew his pistol and held himself in check until the perfect instant for attack.

It was done in a flash—seizing Daggett's coat collar from behind, he yanked the American into the niche and slammed him up against the unyielding bricks.

"Drop your bag," Wrexford ordered, pressing the snout of his weapon against the captain's forehead. "And do it very carefully. I'm in no mood for games."

Daggett did as he was told.

"You've a great deal of explaining to do," added the earl, after kicking it deeper into the niche.

"Actually, I'd rather not." A pause. "You're a damn nuisance, Lord Wrexford."

"I'm more than a nuisance," he shot back. "I'm the fellow who's going to make sure you don't elude justice for your dastardly crimes. However, depending on how forthcoming you are about your plans and your accomplices, I may be able to help you avoid the hangman's noose."

"I assume you spotted me at DeVere's conservatory." Daggett heaved a martyred sigh. "That was terribly clumsy of me."

The American's mordant sangfroid made Wrexford bristle. "Ruthlessly killing two men in cold blood is no laughing matter. However unsavory they were, they didn't deserve to die in such a brutal way."

"I didn't kill them," said Daggett flatly.

"Oh, come now. I told you that I'm in no mood for games. If you didn't do it, who did? The Man in the Moon?"

"As a matter of fact, I *do* know the killer's identity." Daggett paused, as if considering his options.

Tiring of the American's infuriating drawl, Wrexford gave him another hard shake. "If you're contemplating what bargain you might strike . . ." He slowly centered the cold steel snout of his pistol on the captain's forehead. "Keep in mind that I don't give a rat's arse whether you live or die. If I were you, I wouldn't waste any more time with such ploys, but would simply throw yourself on my mercy."

Two can play at theatrics. He cocked the hammer. "I'm a reasonable fellow, unless I'm goaded into a temper."

To his credit, Daggett didn't flinch. "You're putting me in a damnably difficult position, milord. On one hand, time is of the essence. On the other, I'm sworn to secrecy."

A low growl rumbled in Wrexford's throat.

"Before you twitch your trigger finger, might I show you several documents?"

A ruse?

"They are in an inner breast pocket of my coat," said Daggett. "You'll have no trouble finding them."

"Put your hands on your head," ordered the earl. "One false move and your brains will be spattered over the already-filthy wall."

"Do hurry, milord," replied the captain. "We're wasting precious seconds."

Wrexford quickly fished out a packet bound in a thick red ribbon and then indicated that Daggett could lower his hands. "Open it," he said, thrusting it at his prisoner. "Slowly."

Paper crackled—though in truth the sound was the more refined whisper of official parchment—as Daggett unfolded the top sheet, revealing several ornate wax seals.

The American held it up for Wrexford to read.

Hell's teeth. The earl frowned as he studied the signature. "If this is a ruse, you bloody well don't do things by half measures."

"It's no ruse. As you see, it's signed by Viscount Melville, First Lord of the Admiralty," said Daggett. He unfolded the second document. "This one is from the Foreign Office, and corroborates that I'm here on an official, but secret, joint mission undertaken by both our governments."

Wrexford took a moment to read it.

"And if I don't move quickly, milord . . ."

He hesitated. They both appeared genuine—he had seen enough official documents during his military service on Wellesley's staff to be familiar with them. Still, the American was no doubt cunning . . .

"I would like to believe you, but unless you can give me more details, I'll have to insist that we go to the Admiralty together and have one of Melville's secretaries confirm your story."

"We don't have time for that," growled Daggett. He expelled a harried oath. "The Foreign Office said you would be too distracted by your upcoming nuptials to get involved in a murder mystery. Think of your soon-to-be bride—and leave this sordid case to our two governments."

"My soon-to-be bride has an even more finely honed sense of justice than I do. She wouldn't thank me for dropping the case."

"I suppose she follows that rabble-rousing fellow Quill, who seems so popular in Town, and allows his commentaries to stir her conscience," muttered the American. He swore again. "The Foreign Office seems to think you're trustworthy, so I'll explain why I'm here—but only if you'll promise to keep it in strict confidence."

The earl signaled his agreement by lowering his weapon. "I'm assuming you're going to tell me about the military importance of medical botanicals," he said. "I've already worked out the ramifications of Becton's discovery for myself. What I can't quite piece together is why, given the current conflict between our governments, Britain and America would be working together on it. Unless, of course, it's to keep it out of French hands."

"*Becton?*" Daggett shook his head. "No, my mission has nothing to do with Becton or botany."

Wrexford stared at him in disbelief.

The captain drew a measured breath. "It's all about slavery."

"*Slavery?*" The earl was momentarily nonplussed.

"More specifically, the trafficking of those unfortunate souls captured and sold into bondage in Africa, and then transported as chattel to the West Indies and America."

"But Britain banned that trade five years ago!" exclaimed Wrexford. "And if memory serves me correctly, your country also passed an act prohibiting the importation of enslaved souls."

"That's correct, milord," said Daggett. "Like Britain, America abolished the Atlantic slave trade in 1807. However, the sale of human beings is still permitted within our borders."

"Bloody hell." Wrexford felt a little shaken that he and Charlotte had gotten everything so bungled. "So you're saying that DeVere and Quincy were involved in *that*?"

"Yes, they were up to their elegant necks in it," affirmed Daggett. "Quincy's cousin owns vast plantations and many enslaved souls in South Carolina. And Quincy himself possessed the shipping expertise and logistical skills to plan an illegal voyage that promised to yield a staggering profit. As for DeVere, he had a nose for making money, and provided the funding to put the plan in motion, in return for a share of the ill-gotten gains. Their plot is too complicated to explain at this moment. Suffice it to say, the three ringleaders each possessed an expertise that allowed them to create a devilishly clever smuggling plan whose sophisticated logistics made it infallible."

The captain clenched his jaw for a moment. "All the pieces fell in place for them when Reginald Lyman, a sea captain for hire, agreed to transport the human cargo from Africa. I got wind of the plans over a year ago, and my government has had me posing as a malcontent, looking to become a secret partner with Lyman by offering my position in the United States Navy to his advantage."

"I take it your plan worked," murmured Wrexford.

"Yes. It was then that my government made overtures to

your Foreign Office about catching all of the miscreants in the act. Regardless of our differences, our two countries are united in stopping the terrible trafficking of humans from Africa to America and the West Indies." A pause. "And apparently, your senior officials hold a grudge against Lyman for acts they can't prove."

"A betrayal of our fighting men on the Peninsula," offered Wrexford. "Lyman is suspected of having ferried gold to pay Napoleon's army, no matter that his payment was awash in the blood of his countrymen."

"So you know of him," mused Daggett. "A scoundrel, if ever there was one."

"Indeed," said the earl. "And I'm aware that a chest of money was sent to him from Quincy's ship when it landed here in London."

Daggett raised his brows. "How do you know—"

"I have my sources within the dockyards, among other places," interrupted Wrexford. "And have been using them to try to discover who murdered Josiah Becton."

It was the captain's turn to look shocked. "I was under the impression that he died of natural causes."

"That's the official announcement. However, the truth is, he was poisoned, and his important medical discovery—one that had not yet been revealed—has gone missing, along with the plant specimen involved in his research."

Wrexford let his words sink in, before adding, "Given your knowledge in botany, I imagine you can comprehend how valuable a miracle cure for malaria would be to those who possessed the secret of its formula."

A gust of wind tugged at the documents in Daggett's hands.

"However, Becton was going to announce his discovery, and make it public, rather than create a business consortium to make untold riches selling it."

The captain let out a grunt. "Ye heavens, I knew he was giving the keynote lecture. But I had no idea what he was planning to reveal."

"Quincy and DeVere knew of Becton's discovery—they all belonged to the same scientific society in New York," continued Wrexford. "They tried to get him to join in a business venture to sell his medicine, but he refused. I assumed they murdered him and stole his papers and plants in order to form a consortium of their own. I've been trying to prove it, and the trail led to a connection with Lyman. But after last night . . ." He lifted his shoulders in bafflement. "I confess, nothing is making any sense."

Daggett nodded. "My assumptions are all knocked to flinders as well. I don't know how or why the plans have changed, but I'm quite certain the answers all lie with Lyman." He hesitated. "You see, Quincy and DeVere were murdered by Adderley, who was employed by Quincy. And one of the discoveries I made this morning is that Adderley is Lyman's cousin."

The American shifted his stance and glanced at the half-hidden sun. "Even more important, I also learned that Lyman's ship is readying to sail today. I've been trying to locate where it is berthed . . . that is, assuming he didn't manage to sail out on the earlier ebb tide."

Wrexford shoved his pistol into his pocket and gave a sharp whistle for the others, hoping that Charlotte would have sense enough to keep her head down and stay silent. "If he's still here, we'll find him."

"Don't be so sure of that. It seems that half the world's commerce passes in and out of these dratted docklands—" Daggett stopped short as Sheffield skidded to a halt and raised his pistol.

"You can put your weapon away, Kit," counseled the earl. "It appears Captain Daggett is on our side."

"*What?*"

Ignoring his friend's confusion, Wrexford looked to Raven. "We need to find Lyman's ship—the Baltimore Clipper—as quickly as possible."

Raven grinned. "That's easy, sir. I already know that! Strings heard from Whisky that it's tied up at the wharves behind the coal warehouses at Mill Wall Basin."

Rather than go along with Raven and Sheffield as they rushed to join the earl, Charlotte had slipped away into one of the narrow passageways between the buildings. Daggett possessed a very sharp eye, and now that she was no longer a Nobody, the challenge of keeping her secret—along with her unfettered freedom—was growing more and more perilous.

One small slip . . .

A shiver passed through her, and Charlotte couldn't keep from withdrawing deeper into shadows. Wrexford, she decided, would counsel her to exercise caution.

Or am I simply losing my nerve?

In a fortnight, she would be a countess, expected to do naught but wallow in idleness and indolence. Such strictures would squeeze the life out of her if she let them . . .

A terrifying thought.

The shrill screech of gulls circling overhead roused her from her brooding. Charlotte shifted position to catch a better glimpse of what was happening. The American didn't appear to be a prisoner. Quite the opposite, in fact. The earl and Sheffield were listening intently to whatever he was saying, while Raven kept a watch on the surroundings.

Wrexford suddenly turned to the boy and flashed a signal. Raven scampered ahead as the three men began walking, side by side.

Surely, he hadn't forgotten her—

"Wait over by the barrels, Daggett," said Wrexford, a little louder than was necessary. "I need to speak with one of our other mudlarks, and he's particularly wary of strangers."

A blade of darkness cut across the light as the earl moved into Charlotte's hiding place.

So many queries were on the tip of her tongue. But on seeing the outline of his profile—all the little dips and contours that she knew by heart—the first words to spill out were, "Oh, thank heaven you're safe."

The intensity of her emotion seemed to take him by surprise. A ripple stirred beneath his dark lashes, and then a quicksilver smile flickered for an instant.

"I made a promise to you not to stick my spoon in the wall, remember?" he murmured.

"Yes, but . . ." Charlotte reached up and pressed her palm to his cheek, intimately aware of the faint stubble against her flesh. "But the Fates don't always listen to our mortal promises."

Wrexford pulled her into a quick hug. "The Fates wouldn't dare displease you, my love. They would be far too frightened of being skewered by your pen."

"Never mind my pen," said Charlotte. Much as she longed to linger in his arms, she drew back. "I thought Daggett was the enemy—"

"Yes, we all did," he cut in. "I'll explain, but I must make it quick . . ."

Charlotte listened in stunned silence as he told her about Daggett's secret mission and how it had come to be tangled in the sinister web of their own investigation.

"Ye gods," she whispered once he had finished. "And you're sure that you can believe him?"

"I'd wager my life that the documents are genuine." His short-lived smile held a hint of dark humor. "In fact, I may already have, as I'm about to accompany him to Lyman's ship."

"That's not funny, Wrexford."

"It wasn't meant to be." He placed a hand on her shoulder. "Trust often defies rational explanation."

She sensed what was coming. "I can't believe you're about to throw my words on intuition back in my face."

His gaze softened, but only for an instant. "I know you don't like it, but I need for you to take Sheffield and Raven back to Nereid and Neptune. They'll go if you do."

"That's a low blow," she muttered, hating that he was right.

"No, it's the right strategy for keeping all of us safe, and ensuring the villains don't escape. You and the others can help weave a net around them that will inexorably tighten and sink all their nefarious plans."

"While you put yourself in grave danger?" demanded Charlotte.

"I don't think that I am doing so," replied Wrexford. "But if it's a trap, I'll have a much better chance of escaping it if I don't have to worry about the three of you."

Charlotte slumped forward, pressing her forehead against his chest. "There are times when yielding to logic goes against every fiber of my being."

"If it's any consolation—"

A piercing whistle from Raven cut him off. In a blur of raggle-taggle wool, Wrexford spun around, pistol in hand, and was at the alleyway's entrance.

Heart thudding against her ribs, Charlotte was right behind him, her own weapon at the ready.

"There are times," murmured the earl, "when being part of an exceedingly eccentric household is a cursed nuisance." He uncocked his pistol as Hawk spotted him and broke away from his brother.

"Oiy! Oiy!"

Wrexford's wave silenced the boy, and for a moment, all Charlotte heard was the frantic *slap-slap* of running steps before he burst into the alleyway and fell to his knees, gasping for breath.

Grasping his collar, she pulled him deeper into the shadows as the earl moved to block the entrance from prying eyes.

"C-Come quickly—we've found the p-plant!" wheezed Hawk. "A-And we now know who k-killed B-Becton!"

CHAPTER 25

"Slow down, lad." Wrexford gave him a gentle shake. "Catch your breath and then explain yourself—at a walk, not a gallop."

Hawk gulped down several lungfuls of air and began again. "M-Mr. Tyler and I have found the missing plant. It's on Captain Lyman's Baltimore Clipper."

Charlotte let out a horrified hiss. "How—"

"Let him finish before we pepper him with questions," Wrexford ordered.

"Even more important, we now know that the scholar named von . . . von—"

"Von Stockhausen," finished the earl.

"Yes!" said Hawk. "That's the bloody scoundrel. You see, Mr. Tyler and I had crept close to the ship and overheard . . ."

Wrexford listened to Hawk's agitated explanation, seeing Charlotte's eyes mirror his own shocked disbelief.

"Ye heavens, how could all our carefully reasoned assumptions about the murderer have been so wrong?" he muttered, once the boy finished.

"Because one looks for motive in murder," said Charlotte

softly. "And von Stockhausen was cunning enough to keep that hidden from all of us. Who would have guessed . . ." She caught herself. "But never mind that right now. Recriminations can wait until later. We have to stop him from absconding with the specimen."

"Yes." Wrexford gave a wry grimace. "It's ironic that he has the missing specimen sitting right in his lap, but doesn't know it."

"Thank heaven for that," said Charlotte. "As his ignorance gives us a chance to steal it back."

"And to do that, we must move quickly." And yet, Wrexford hesitated, trying to decide how to marshal his forces to the best advantage.

Charlotte, however, reacted first. "Sheffield needs to return to Nereid and Neptune. Raven should gather several of his friends to serve as messengers, and then join him there, so we have a place from which to coordinate communication. To begin with, Griffin needs to be notified. He and his Runners can wait in Sheffield's office until it's clear where they might be needed."

She lifted her chin, as if daring him to disagree. "Hawk will, of course, need to show you where Tyler is hiding, and Daggett's military prowess may prove useful if trouble arises."

"And you?" he challenged. "Need I point that Daggett's arsenal of weapons also includes a pair of eagle-like eyes?"

"You already warned him that I'm wary of strangers. I'll stay close to you and keep my head down."

"I'm not sure—"

"Wrexford, we can't afford to make the tiniest mistake. These dastards are diabolically clever," she countered. "I may see things about the situation that you don't."

The swirl and slap of the water eddying around the wharves reminded him that every passing moment was critical. Once the tide turned, Lyman's ship could sail for the open sea.

"Pull your hat down," he muttered in surrender. "And stay

back with Hawk while I explain the latest developments to Kit and Daggett."

In response, she crouched down, muddied her fingers, and wiped them on her cheeks.

Hawk started to laugh, but a look from Wrexford speared him to silence. "Wait here for my signal," he growled. "And then we need to move quickly."

"Holy hell," intoned Sheffield as the earl finished his terse report. Daggett said nothing. His face appeared carved out of stone.

"Kit, you're familiar with the rhythms of the river. When, precisely, does the tide turn?"

"The ebb started about ten minutes ago," responded Daggett. "Which means that the flow changes in another six and three quarter hours. Allow another half hour for a ship the size of the Baltimore Clipper to begin moving with the tide, so I calculate that we have a little over seven hours before von Stockhausen and his co-conspirators sail out from under our noses."

A nod from Sheffield confirmed the timing.

"Then we ought not waste our wind in any more jabbering," said the earl. He flashed a signal at the alleyway. "Kit, you and the lad know what I need you to do. Daggett, you'll come with me."

"You seem to have wharf rats crawling out of every muck hole and crevasse of the dockyards," observed the American as he watched Charlotte and Hawk slink out of the gloom. "How do you find all these filthy little vermin?"

"Swallow your insults and just be grateful that I do," snapped Wrexford. "Without their eyes and ears, and their willingness to do the dirty work of ferreting out information, we wouldn't stand a chance at beating the poisonous vipers."

Daggett crinkled his nose. "Who's the new one? He looks even more disreputable than the others."

A laugh rumbled in the earl's throat. "Looks can be deceiving. But leave Magpie to me. He doesn't like to talk around strangers and we can't afford for him to close up tighter than a clam."

Hawk was already standing by one of the passageways threading through the cluster of storage buildings.

"From here on, stay alert. We'll go in single file. I'll follow our guide. Daggett, you'll come after me, and Magpie will bring up the rear."

"You trust an urchin to watch our backs?" murmured the American.

"More than I do you," shot back Wrexford.

To his credit, Daggett allowed a quiver of amusement to touch his lips.

"I've worked with Magpie before," added the earl, "and have never been disappointed."

"Then without further ado, let us spread our wings and fly."

Wrexford's attention was already on the serpentine twists and turns that lay ahead. The back byways were narrow and the light murky—an attack could come in a flash. But stealth was key, so he wished to avoid the main paths that wound through the dockyards. He was counting on the element of surprise—the dastards didn't know their plans had been discovered.

Or so he hoped. Given all the wrong assumptions he had made of late, Wrexford couldn't help but wonder . . .

But he shoved his doubts aside. Hawk kept up a quicksilver pace, a dark shape skittering within the shifting patterns of shade and shadow. After a glance to the rear, the earl quickened his own steps. The tang of brine and the salt-sweet scent of decay were growing more pronounced as the ebbing tide began to expose the river's mud. He could hear the breeze ruffling the water.

They must be getting close . . .

Hawk cut down an even narrower footpath between two massive storage racks for timber, fresh from the Baltic, and then disappeared for an instant as he wiggled under a log that had come to be wedged across the way. Wrexford managed to flatten himself enough to inch his way beneath it.

Daggett, moving with the sinuous speed of a sea snake, was through in a flash. He turned and extended a helping hand to Charlotte.

Wrexford held his breath. One touch—a sea captain's senses were attuned to all the little nuances around him—and the American would know she was no hardscrabble urchin.

But Charlotte hadn't survived life in the stews by making silly mistakes. Quick as an eel, she slithered away from his outstretched fingers and popped to her feet with a casual grace.

"Let's keep moving," prodded the earl.

As he had hoped, the urging distracted Daggett. "Any ideas yet on how to attack the ship?" asked the American, after turning away from Charlotte.

"A diversion seems the logical choice, but Tyler may have some specific ideas, as he's been observing the activities around the wharf."

"Your valet appears to be a man of many talents."

"I'm easily bored. He keeps me amused," answered Wrexford.

Daggett stayed close as they quickened their steps. "Your fiancée must be an unusual lady." A pause. "Or perhaps she's not aware of what an eccentric household she is about to enter."

The earl ignored the comment. "We need to wait here," he said, coming to a halt just short of emerging from between the timber racks. "The lad has gone to fetch Tyler."

Angling his gaze, he began to survey the surroundings. The steep roof of a sail loft and its adjoining storage area blocked his view of wharves, but he could see there were a number of ways to reach the tidal basin where the ship was moored. However, access wasn't the issue. Any attempt to steal the plant from the ship would be a perilous undertaking, and the more he thought about it, the more it seemed a foolhardy risk.

The three ringleaders were murderous cutthroats, and the crew members were likely handpicked for their lack of morals, given the ship's original mission as an illegal slaver. It made far more sense to orchestrate an official impounding of the ship. The question was, did Daggett's documents carry enough clout to make such a thing possible before the tide turned?

A flicker of movement cut short his musing. It was Hawk— Wrexford dropped to a crouch and drew his pistol.

But something was terribly wrong. The boy was flying like a bat out of hell.

Hawk skidded and stumbled as he made a sharp turn around the timbers jutting out from the racks. Wrexford caught the boy as he fell, and pulled him into the shadows.

His face was white with fear.

"What's wrong?" demanded Daggett.

"Hold your tongue," barked Wrexford, thankful that Charlotte had the good sense to remain silent. "Give the lad a chance to catch his breath."

It took only another instant for Hawk to master his emotions enough to speak. "M-Mr. Tyler is gone!" he said. "And so is the ship!"

Gone? Charlotte couldn't believe her ears.

Tyler was very experienced in clandestine activities . . . And how could a ship simply disappear?

She didn't dare look up and try to catch Wrexford's eye. She had come to realize that Daggett was even more dangerous than she had feared. He was like a stalking predator, all razor-sharp eyes and coiled muscles waiting to pounce at the first sign of weakness.

"They may have decided to shift the ship to an even more hidden spot," reasoned the earl. "And Tyler has followed it—"

"No, sir!" exclaimed Hawk. "I asked Smoke, who does odd jobs around the collier's foundry, to keep a watch on him when I left to alert Mr. Sheffield and Lady Cordelia of our discovery. He said two men crept up on Mr. Tyler and dragged him away to the ship. It then cast off its mooring lines and raised its top-sails to scud away to the river."

So the dastards knew their perfidy had been discovered.

That would make them even more dangerous.

Tyler . . . Her heart raced as her blood momentarily turned to ice. Tyler couldn't hope for mercy. His captors had none.

"Even under a full press of sails, the ship can't reach the sea when the tide is against it," said Daggett decisively. "They're hiding somewhere upriver."

His boots squelched in the soft mud as he shifted his stance. "But with all the little inlets and coves—not to speak of the smuggling rings and their well-hidden dens of iniquity—there isn't a chance in hell that we can find them in seven hours."

More like six and a half, thought Charlotte.

"Bloody hell and damnation." To her surprise, the American's steely self-control exploded in a burst of emotion as he hit one of the timbers with a clenched fist. "Two years I've been after Lyman, determined to see that he pays for the evil he's done to so many lives . . ."

This was more than a government assignment to him, guessed Charlotte. It was intensely personal. She found herself liking him better for it.

"And yet once again, the devil-cursed scoundrel is going to slip away unscathed."

"*Oh, ye of little faith,*" responded Wrexford, after a moment of grim silence. "You would be right—save for the fact that we have our band of filthy little wharf rats. Distasteful as you may find them, they will soon have you eating your disparaging comments."

"I will do so happily," said Daggett. "But how—"

"Never mind that now. We need to return to Nereid and Neptune's office as quickly as possible."

The earl crouched down so he was on eye level with Hawk. "I need you to gather up as many of your friends as you can in the next quarter hour and bring them to the cellar beneath the office. Use the fishmonger's alleyway."

"Oiy, sir!" Wrexford's small shove set him into motion, and in the next instant, the boy disappeared into the maze of the wharves.

"Stealth is no longer a priority," announced the earl. "We can take the quickest route back to our destination."

In short order, they were climbing up the steps of the shipping company run by their friends.

"Good day"—Octavia Howe hesitated for just a fraction—"milord." To her credit, she made no comment on Wrexford's shabby clothes, but merely shifted the pile of folders in her arms and pointed to the main meeting room. "If you're looking for—"

The closed door flew open and Raven peered out. "Wrexford! On our way back, Strings told us the ship has left the tidal basin and headed upstream. Is it true?"

"Aye," answered the earl, "and we've discovered some even more disturbing news." Seeing Sheffield and Lady Cordelia had come to stand behind the boy, he added, "Let us join you inside and I shall explain."

Charlotte hesitated. Wrexford entered the room without a glance her way, a tacit sign that he was leaving the decision up to her. Heaving an inward sigh, she turned away and slipped down the back stairs.

Ooooff. The stench of piss and rotting fish was truly foul. "If

I wish to live the life of a lady, perfumed in privilege," she muttered to herself, "the choice is mine."

She rooted around in the darkness and found a lantern. A quick strike of the flint and steel she carried in her urchin-coat pocket lit an oily flame. After checking that the door to the alleyway was unbarred—opening it wouldn't improve the air, as outside was even more odiferous—she sat down on a cask of nails to wait for Hawk and his friends.

The plan to use the urchins was an excellent one. They would act like stones falling on still water, spreading quick-moving ripples throughout the docklands.

A muted jingle of metal drew her gaze to the stairs. Raven hurried down the last few treads and came to join her.

"Wrexford has given me permission to help spread the word," he said, perching himself on the cask next to hers. "I'll take the south side of the river. Strings is bringing a few of his friends to join me."

It was a race against time, and the clock wasn't ticking in their favor. But he knew that. They all did.

The clink of metal on metal sounded again as Raven eased a leather pouch out of his pocket. "His Lordship borrowed all the guineas that Mr. Sheffield and Lady Cordelia had in their safe. Hawk and I are to hand one out to each of our friends, for them to show as proof that the promise of a fifty-guinea reward to whoever discovers the location of the ship is no faradiddle."

The boy undid the strings, allowing a tiny spark of fire-kissed gold to glimmer in the gloom. "He says that unless Satan has opened up a great hole in the Earth, allowing the ship to take refuge in the deepest pit of hell, we'll find it in time."

Charlotte didn't disagree. Fifty guineas was an unimaginable fortune to those who lived around the river. Raven's voice, however, held a note of raw uncertainty.

"Wrexford is right," she said. "They haven't a prayer of eluding us."

He nodded. But by the way he was winding the strings tightly around his thumb, she could tell that something else was troubling him. Reaching out, she gently eased off the loops and twined her fingers with his.

The boy held himself rigid for a moment, and then, in a very un-Raven-like gesture, inched closer and leaned his head against her shoulder.

"Wrexford is angry with Tyler. He says that Tyler was a damn fool for being so reckless."

"He's not angry, sweeting. He's frightened." She drew him into a hug and didn't let go. "We all are. Tyler has become very dear to us."

A tremor—a silent sob?—spasmed through his bony body.

Love. What a change it had wrought in all of them.

When she and the boys had first met, the struggle for survival had been the primary force in their lives. She certainly hadn't been looking for love. She knew its dangers—and yet, it had happened, anyway. That achingly beautiful complexity that took hold of one's heart and wouldn't let go.

Charlotte tightened her hold on Raven. Not for anything would she give up the wondrous joys of love. But it came with a fearful symmetry. That it brought such happiness also meant it could bring terrible pain. The boys had come to think of Wrexford and Tyler as family . . . along with Alison, McClellan, and now Hartley. It made them vulnerable . . .

But it also makes all of us strong.

"Y-You think we will find Mr. Tyler . . . alive?" asked Raven in a small voice.

"I do, my love," she answered without a qualm. "Wrexford would beat the Grim Reaper to a pulp if he dared to swing his scythe at any of us."

That drew a soft laugh. "Mr. Sheffield says even Lucifer himself would run like the devil when Wrexford is in a temper."

"A very wise move. Otherwise, there would be hell to pay."

The rattle of the side door announced that Hawk and the urchins had arrived. Raven wriggled free and swiped his sleeve across his eyes.

"Quite right," he said, blinking away the last of his uncertainties. "The miscreants be damned. We shall find the ship, and then they shall suffer the consequences of their evil."

The next few minutes passed in a helter-pelter of activity. A sharp whistle summoned Wrexford, who gave the motley band of ragamuffins strict orders on how to conduct the search, and what risks to avoid, before passing out the coins.

"Now off you go," he finished.

Charlotte sighed as they scrambled out the door, led by Raven and Hawk.

"*Cry havoc, and let slip the dogs of war,*" murmured Daggett, who, along with Sheffield, had accompanied the earl down to the cellar.

"I'm surprised you read Shakespeare," quipped Sheffield. "That *is* Shakespeare, isn't it?"

"I read a great many things," answered the American. "Between the occasional moments of storms and battles, a naval captain has endless hours for other pursuits."

All of which, guessed Charlotte, he used for sharpening both his intellect and his physical skills. She turned away from the lamplight. No wonder that from the very first, he had struck her as dangerous.

"Wrexford!" called Cordelia from the top of the stairs. "I have found the nautical charts you requested."

"I think we should have a look at the likely hiding places upriver," he said. "Kit, you're familiar with the West India docklands and may know of some hidden nooks among its many docks where a ship would be shielded from prying eyes."

"There are one or two places . . ." Deep in conversation, the two of them headed up together.

Daggett turned to follow, but after a step or two, he stopped.

The back of her neck began to prickle. If he hadn't been between her and the side door, Charlotte would have bolted for the alleyway. Instead, she slipped deeper into the shadows.

He started to move again, his boots scraping lightly over the stone flaggings. She held her breath, waiting—nay, praying— for the sound of his tread on the stairs.

The gloom suddenly seemed to come alive with a crackling tension. With the rush of her pulsing blood filling her ears, Charlotte felt rather than heard him come closer.

"You make a very fetching urchin, Lady Charlotte," whispered Daggett.

"An astute observation, sir." She turned to face him. "And one, I trust, that you will keep to yourself."

"Your secret is safe with me. We Americans may abhor the idea of an aristocracy, but I do consider myself a gentleman when it comes to the personal life of a lady," he answered. "Though it does raise a number of intriguing questions."

"None of which I intend to answer."

A flutter of the lamp's flame caught the twitch of his lips. "A lady's prerogative."

"Speaking of questions, how did you know?"

Daggett hesitated, as if wondering whether to play tit for tat, and then shrugged. "Your eyes are the exact shade of blue as those of my late sister."

He said it in an offhand way, but it didn't fool her. Charlotte now was sure that this mission was a very personal one for him.

"Who, I take it, suffered at the hands of Reginald Lyman."

His jaw tightened. "You have an unnerving ability to read people, Lady Charlotte. I imagine that's a trait that might get you into trouble."

"Indeed," replied Charlotte. "More times than I can count."

His expression turned oddly pensive. "I thought ladies weren't supposed to find trouble alluring."

"It's not a matter of allure, sir. It's a matter of principle. Men aren't the only ones who believe in the concepts of right and wrong, and the notion that nobody is above justice."

"Daggett!" called Wrexford, his voice sharp with worry. In the next instant, Charlotte heard him start down the stairs. It sounded like he was taking them two at a time.

"We're over here," she called, not bothering to disguise her voice as he came into view. "As you warned, the captain has the eye of an eagle."

The earl stopped short. "An unfortunate analogy, as eagles are known as deadly birds of prey."

"I've assured Lady Charlotte that she has nothing to fear from me," replied Daggett. "Even if I were on the hunt, I have a feeling she would be a match for any predator."

"It seems that Captain Daggett has his own secret concerning his pursuit of Lyman," explained Charlotte. "His mission is a personal one, as well as an official assignment from his government."

She fixed the American with a challenging stare. His eyes no longer seemed quite as frightening. "I'm not asking for prurient reasons. However, I think it's imperative that Wrexford and I know exactly what Lyman did to hurt your sister. In the heat of battle—if it comes down to that with our enemies—we must be aware of your weaknesses and how you might react. Our lives may depend on each other."

"It sounds as if you have experience under fire, milady," he responded.

"I served under Wellesley—now Lord Wellington—on Peninsula," interjected the earl, "and am no stranger to the battlefield. If you're questioning my bride-to-be's steadiness in the face of danger, I assure you that she has steelier nerves than most soldiers."

"I'm beginning to understand that," said Daggett. It seemed to Charlotte that a ghost of a smile touched his lips. "Very well, I'll trust the two of you with my personal reason for pursuing

Lyman, even though it is a very painful one that does me no credit. I should have . . ." He shifted. "I should have prevented it."

"You have our promise that we won't share it with others," said Wrexford. "And we don't give our word lightly."

The American seemed to retreat into some deep place within himself. Charlotte recognized the shuttered look in his eyes. She had seen it reflected in her own gaze after the death of her husband—a bleak sadness, shadowed by guilt.

Daggett suddenly appeared human, and she liked him better for being made of flesh and blood, rather than ice and iron.

"My sister and her husband ran a harborside tavern in New York. I had picked up rumors of Lyman's ill doings and so I asked them to keep a watch on him, and pass on to me any information they might overhear. I did warn them to be discreet, but I should have emphasized that."

A costermonger's barrow clattered by in the alleyway, the shrill cry for salted eel rising above the squeaky wheel.

"They did learn certain things, and duly dispatched a letter to me." Daggett looked to Charlotte. "However, like you, my sister and her husband possessed a very strong sense of Right and Wrong, and informed me that in order to prevent one of Lyman's rivals from being murdered, they felt beholden to report it to the local authorities. The next morning, they lay dead, along with the targeted man. All three had had their throats cut."

"I'm so sorry," said Charlotte. "Trite words, I know, but no less heartfelt."

The American acknowledged them with a gruff nod.

"I take it the authorities had been bribed?" asked Wrexford.

"I assume so," said Daggett. "Lyman didn't know of my relationship to the murdered couple, so my investigation wasn't compromised. However, he became more careful, and it took me a while to find a way to get close to him."

"By convincing him that you were like him—a ruthless, un-principled reptile whose cunning and naval connections would make you a perfect partner in crime in the slavery venture."

A grunt of surprise. "H-How do you know—"

"You're not the only one with connections within the nautical world of New York," answered the earl. "But never mind that now. Let us focus on stopping von Stockhausen and Lyman—once and for all."

CHAPTER 26

Sheffield looked up from the chart and pushed back his chair. "So, given the size of Lyman's Baltimore Clipper, I think we've identified the three most likely places for it to be hiding—"

"There's a fourth," interjected Cordelia, tapping a finger to a spot on the south side of the river. "This narrow crevasse of water, just above Mill Stairs, is a perfect refuge. It's a seedy area, catering to small lighters moving goods up and down the river, yet it's wide enough and deep enough for a large ship. And the bend of the river provides an extra measure of privacy."

Wrexford studied it for a moment. "I see your point. I'll send word to our urchins to have a look." He was careful to avoid identifying the boys as Raven and Hawk. Daggett might have observed the boys at the Royal Botanic Gardens, and while he trusted the American, there was no reason for the fellow to know all of the family secrets.

"How the devil do you intend to do that?" Daggett had gone to stand by the window overlooking the river. "They're scattered helter-pelter from here to London Bridge."

"You underestimate the wharf rats," responded the earl

dryly. "One of the ways they survive is to work as sentries for the thieving rings that plague the docklands. They know how to set up a very sophisticated network of communication." He glanced at the door. "There's a boy waiting in the outer office. When I dispatch him with a message, it will make its way very quickly to one of our two leaders."

Daggett pulled a pocket watch from his coat and clicked it open. "We've now less than six hours."

"I will be back momentarily."

When Wrexford returned, the American had his back turned to the room and was staring out over the water, whose lead-dark ripples were frothed with dots of foam from rising breezes.

Charlotte and Cordelia had busied themselves making tea on the coal stove in the corner. Steam rose in a curling plume from the pot as they filled five cups and began to pass them around.

Without a word, Sheffield went through the side door into his office and came back with a bottle of whisky. "I think we all could do with a wee dram to fortify our spirits."

"Are you passing out miracles, as well as malt?" muttered Daggett. He waved off the cup and turned his gaze back to the river. The cutters and wherries of the rivermen were heading upstream, carried along on the swirling currents of the flooding tide.

Wrexford ignored the comment. He was sure the urchins would find the ship. The question of how they were going to free Tyler, once they located it, was a far more daunting challenge.

"Hell's teeth." Daggett suddenly turned around from the mullioned glass. "We've been looking at the problem from the wrong end of the spyglass! We don't have to find Lyman's bloody ship. We just have to stop it from sailing out to sea."

"But—" began Cordelia.

"But how?" he finished for her. "It's quite simple. We commandeer one of the British war frigates docked at the naval yard in Greenwich." Daggett pulled out the official documents and shook them triumphantly. "These give us permission to do so. All we have to do is lie in wait for Lyman's ship. A frigate outguns it, and with no room to maneuver, Lyman will have no choice but to surrender or be blown out of the water." A pause. "And I don't really care which option he chooses."

"But we do," said Wrexford. "Tyler is captive on Lyman's ship."

"You can hire another valet, milord," snapped Daggett.

In a flash, the earl coiled a fist, but Charlotte seized his arm before he could throw a punch.

"Tyler is part of our family, Captain Daggett," she said. "We've a bond that runs far deeper than blood."

"Forgive me—that was badly voiced." The American met Wrexford's scowl without flinching. "But as a military man, milord, you are aware that however difficult, we must be ruthlessly pragmatic in making strategic decisions. If Lyman escapes, he'll continue to wreak havoc on countless lives."

"If you blow the ship to kingdom come, you'll destroy Becton's plant specimen," countered Charlotte, "which will help save far more lives than Lyman will ever harm. So if you wish to go merely by the numbers, they, too, are on our side."

Giving thanks for Charlotte's quick thinking, the earl held his tongue. That they had the drawing of the plant was a detail Daggett didn't need to know. After all, it might take years to locate it in its natural habitat.

"I've a better strategy," continued Charlotte. "You go to the naval yard at Greenwich and organize a blockade of the river. Every frigate carries a detachment of Royal Marines, so using the longboats, it will be easy to deploy a formidable boarding party to row out and seize Lyman's ship. Its crew members are hired mercenaries. Announce that no criminal charges will be brought against them, and they will flee like rats from a sinking ship."

"And while you are handling those logistics," said Wrexford, after catching Charlotte's eye, "we'll take charge of rescuing Tyler and the specimen."

Daggett muttered an oath under his breath. "You know, I could use these documents to have the lot of you arrested so you can't interfere in government business."

"To do that, you would have to pass by me," growled Sheffield.

"And me," added Cordelia, snatching up a heavy brass sextant from one of the shelves.

"I don't think violence will be necessary," said Charlotte. "As you've pointed out, Captain, you're a pragmatic man. So you see that my suggestion allows us to satisfy the demands of both reason and emotion."

A tiny muscle twitched as Daggett clenched and unclenched his jaw. And then he chuffed a laugh. "Much as it galls me to surrender to a British opponent, I know when I've met my match."

"In this, our two countries have a truce, so your honor is saved, Daggett," pointed out Wrexford.

"Then I shall hold my chin up high as I leave—assuming Mr. Sheffield doesn't plant me a facer." He inclined a small bow to Cordelia. "And that Lady Cordelia doesn't crack my skull."

Cordelia set aside her makeshift weapon. "You're quite safe now. Just don't threaten my friends again."

"Loyalty is an admirable trait," he answered.

"It's more than loyalty," she answered. "But we won't quibble over your choice of language."

"Yes, let us not, as that's another fight I won't win," answered Daggett. "I'm not very good with words. I prefer to let my actions speak for me." He turned for the door. "Perhaps if we manage to triumph over the dastards, we'll merit a drawing by that fellow, A. J. Quill—a distinction that I'm told means that you're the talk of London."

"For the most part, being the subject of Quill's pen isn't something one wishes to experience," replied Cordelia. "There have, however, been some exceptions."

Daggett tucked his documents away. "Well, let us hope this is one of them."

"Indeed," murmured Wrexford. "Heaven forfend we draw Quill's ire."

"As time is of the essence, Captain," said Sheffield, after clearing his throat with a cough, "allow me to show you where you may get a hackney for the trip to Greenwich."

Charlotte waited for the sound of the front portal of the building falling shut behind the two men before clicking the latch shut on the meeting-room door. "Please stubble the sly retorts about A. J. Quill. Daggett already knows enough of my secrets—and if given the slightest hint, he's clever enough to guess that one."

"Forgive me." Cordelia flashed an apologetic grimace. "But in truth, a man would need a very lurid imagination, and in my experience, few possess a mind that can stray from the straight and narrow."

"I agree with Charlotte," interjected the earl. "He's not someone with whom to trifle." His brow furrowed in consternation. "Nor is von Stockhausen. It's his unspeakable cleverness that has set all this in motion, and yet for the last little while, we've been focusing on Lyman, his hired henchman, as if he were the puppet master of the plot."

Drawn by some silent force, the three of them sat down around the table. The chart of the river lay open upon the dark-grained oak, a sea-blue snake undulating through the heart of London.

"Any idea of how we spirit both Tyler and the plant off the ship?" asked Cordelia.

Think. Think. Wrexford began to drum his fingers on the tabletop.

The fraught silence was broken by Sheffield's hurried return. "What have I missed?" he demanded.

"A reminder that von Stockhausen has propagated all these heinous crimes," answered the earl. "Along with the question of how we are going to free Tyler and the specimen from his clutches."

"Why the blue-deviled faces?" Sheffield pulled out a chair to join them. "We've beaten devious criminals before." He swiveled the chart and leaned down to study the serpentine curl of the river near the East India docks. "And we shall do so again."

Like love, Charlotte considered optimism to be a very positive, powerful force. But in this case, she feared that it might be just wishful thinking rather than grounded in reality. The humble-jumble curlicues of ink, showing all the myriad juts and bights of the river's north and south banks, defined the enormity of their task.

She closed her eyes for an instant, trying to keep tears from welling up. A world without Tyler . . .

No! Charlotte refused to allow pessimism to crush her spirit.

"I still say that's the most likely spot," muttered Cordelia, pointing out the slivered indentation of water on the south shore opposite the East India Company's main mercantile hub.

"I've dispatched a message to Raven, alerting him of the possibility," said Wrexford. "Much as I hate inaction, we ought not run off helter-pelter until we have word from the lads."

The flesh was drawn tight over the bones of his face. Charlotte's heart ached for him. She knew he would blame himself if anything happened to Tyler. He had been snappish with the valet about involving Hawk, however inadvertently, in Becton's murder.

But ye heavens, Tyler knew the earl's bark held no bite.

"Agreed," said Sheffield. "But that's even more reason for us to come up with a plan."

Wrexford rose abruptly and went to gaze out the bank of windows. The clouds had thickened, mirroring the leaden mood in the room. Charlotte resisted the urge to rise and join him. After several long moments, Sheffield, too, got up and moved to the mullioned glass, though he chose the opposite end of the casement. Mist was beginning to rise up from the swirling currents, blurring the shape of the river.

Charlotte looked back down at the chart. "How many men would make up the crew of Lyman's ship," she asked Cordelia in a low whisper.

"Too many to think that an outright assault would have any hope of—"

A clattering in the entrance foyer caused all of them to look to the door. It opened an instant later as McClellan shouldered her way into the room.

"I know you asked me to stay at the house and keep the Weasels there if they returned home, m'lady," announced the maid. "But I thought it imperative that you see this."

She slapped a note down atop the chart. "Riche received this and, given the recent murders, he took the liberty of reading it. He then sent it on to me, in case I knew where you and the earl had gone." A huff of relief slipped from her lips as she spotted Wrexford. "Thank heaven you're both here."

Charlotte quickly unfolded it and read it over. "It's from Moretti. He says he just recalled who was asking questions about Becton's work." A sigh. "Alas, it's simply telling us what we already know." To McClellan, she explained, "We already discovered for ourselves that von Stockhausen is the villain."

"How—" began McClellan.

"Sit down, Mac," said Wrexford. He poured a measure of whisky into a cup and carried it to her.

"Oh, bloody hell, what trouble has Tyler got himself into?" muttered the maid. "I'll wring his neck if he's put the Weasels in peril."

"First we have to free him from the villain's clutches—with

his neck intact," replied the earl. "And then you'll have to stand in line for your turn to rattle every bone in his body."

McClellan took a swallow of the malt. "I take it we have a plan?"

The question seemed to grow louder and louder as it echoed through the gloom. When no one answered right away, the maid stared meditatively into her cup. "That bad, eh?"

"Raven and Hawk have gathered a band of their friends and are searching both banks of the river to find where the ship is hiding until the tide turns." Charlotte hurriedly recounted all that had happened over the last several hours.

"So Daggett is friend, not foe," mused McClellan.

"We might not feel that way if he has the Royal Navy blow Tyler and the specimen to flinders," observed Wrexford. "So we need to rescue both captives before Lyman's ship reaches Greenwich, where an armed-to-the-teeth frigate is waiting. However, short of launching our own flotilla of warships and forcing the enemy's surrender, I'm not quite sure . . ."

He let his words sink into silence.

Charlotte tried to fight off a feeling of defeat. They had all been extraordinarily lucky in dodging terrible dangers in the past. But Lady Luck was notoriously fickle.

"You know . . ." Sheffield remained staring out at the river for a moment longer before turning to face them. "Those little wherries and lighters skim over the waves like water bugs . . ." He gestured out at the rippling currents.

Charlotte realized he was right. She hadn't really taken notice of it, but the river was teeming with the white sails of numerous small cargo boats plying their trade.

"And like bugs," he continued, "no one pays them the least attention."

"Surely, you're not suggesting we put together a fleet of them to attack Lyman's ship?" The earl made a face. "Even if we could man them with a force of experienced fighters, we would never get close. As a privateer, the ship is armed with cannons, and a crew who knows how to use them."

"An outright attack would, of course, be doomed to failure," agreed Sheffield. "However . . ." He rubbed two fingers against the point of his chin. "Growing up, I used to sail every summer with my cousins off the coast of Bournemouth."

"Kit, pleasant though they may be, now is not the best time to wax poetic on childhood memories," said Wrexford with a note of sarcasm.

"Bear with me, Wrex," came the reply. "I have an idea that I'd like to float by everyone . . ."

CHAPTER 27

"You're either mad or brilliant," murmured Wrexford, once Sheffield had finished sketching out his idea.

"Sometimes one needs to be a little of both," said Charlotte. She looked at Cordelia. "Can the logistics be arranged?"

"It so happens they can. Quite easily, in fact. One of our messenger lighters is tied up at the wharf just outside. And with the ebb tide adding assistance to the wind, it can bring you quickly to Limekiln Quay, where Mr. Linonia and his two sons handle moving our local deliveries up and down the river."

Cordelia fetched pen and paper from one of the cabinets and scribbled out a quick note. "Give him this and he'll lend you one of his wherries."

Seeing Charlotte's brow furrow, she explained, "Our Thames wherries are small sailing craft designed to haul cargo. They have broad-beamed hulls that sit low in the water, and are equipped with a gaff-rigged mainsail, as well as oars for maneuvering."

"Most important, they can be sailed by one man," added Sheffield with a smile.

Wrexford thought it over. It was risky, but, in truth, not overly so. However, he could see that Charlotte was apprehensive over one part of the plan. A child's presence would add a look of innocence to the wherry—

"Oiy, oiy!" Raven suddenly burst into the room, a look of jubilation shining through the streaks of mud on his face. "We found it—we found the bloody ship!"

"The little patch of water just above Mill Stairs?" asked Cordelia.

"No—it's tucked away in Duffield Sluice, right by Mariner's Stairs," answered the boy.

"Clever," conceded Cordelia. "It's such a tiny inlet, but now that I think of it, the warehouses fronting the river provide a perfect cover."

"Well done, lad," said Wrexford, shooting a glance at the clock on the bookshelf. "And we've plenty of time to get upstream."

"No rush at all," agreed Sheffield, his smile stretching wider. "We can't put our plan in motion until after the tide turns."

"What plan?" demanded Raven.

"We'll explain that to you as we sail upstream," answered Charlotte. She cast a critical look at Sheffield. "You don't look like a riverman dressed like that. Go find a bargeman down at the dock and negotiate an exchange of clothing—the shabbier, the better. The smallest flaw in our masquerade could scuttle our plan."

Her gaze moved to Cordelia. "When Hawk returns, please send him to the dowager. Tell him I'm counting on him to help my brother keep her safe. That should ensure that he does as ordered. It's imperative that he doesn't chase after us."

"I'm coming with you?" asked Raven, his eyes flaring wide with excitement as Sheffield hurried away.

"Yes—" began Charlotte.

"As am I," announced McClellan.

"Mac," said Wrexford. "There is an old adage, *Too many cooks spoil the broth . . .*"

"If all I could do was wield a soupspoon, milord, I would be forced to agree with you. But it so happens that I'm a skilled sailor, with a great deal of experience in navigating the tricky currents and eddies of a tidal river. So I may be of use to Mr. Sheffield," replied the maid. "And as you know, I'm an excellent shot."

"After sunset, the wherrymen often have a woman passenger aboard. Either their wife or . . . other companion," pointed out Cordelia. "It will add an excellent touch to the wherry and make your little band look even less threatening."

The earl looked to Charlotte, who gave a small nod.

Hell's bells. He surrendered his misgivings with a sigh, feeling he couldn't, in good conscience, forbid her from being part of her cousin's rescue party.

That is the trouble with all of us—we're too damnably loyal for our own good.

"You had better go and find a fishwife with whom to trade clothing."

McClellan allowed her normally stoic expression to soften for an instant. "You won't regret it, milord."

Darkness had settled over the river by the time they reached Limekiln Quay and finished making all the preparations for launching their plan. The wherry was now bobbing through the wind-ruffled currents, the *slap-slap* of the choppy waves beating against the low-slung hull.

Charlotte sat wedged between two canvas-covered crates in the belly of the boat and stole a look at Sheffield. Dappled in the scudding moonlight, he was perched on the fantail, the tiller in one hand, the mainsail sheet in the other, looking at ease as he skillfully navigated a course through the swirling water. McClellan was beside him, keeping a watch on the flickering lantern lights dotting the river. With the tide now flowing out toward the sea, quite a few merchant ships were beginning to cast off their mooring lines.

Raven was crouched in the prow of the wherry, ready to wave a signal when Mariner's Stairs came into view. The plan was to put into the landing there and wait for Lyman's ship to begin its journey to the sea. It wouldn't be long now. The breeze was freshening and the current was gaining speed . . .

Curling closer to Wrexford, Charlotte found his hand and pressed her palm to his. The steady pulse of warmth helped to steady her skittery breathing. And yet fear refused to relinquish its hold on her heart.

The earl feathered a kiss to her cheek. "There's little danger, my love—save for catching a chill from the freezing water." His appearance was that of a wraithlike shadow. He was dressed in black, from head to foot—knitted toque, jumper, trousers, and stockings—and his face was smeared with a coal-dark grease. He had left his boots behind.

An involuntary shiver skated down Charlotte's spine as she spotted the chisel, fine-tooth saw blade, and wooden mallet beside him. "What if they hear you?"

"A ship is alive with creaks and groans from its timbers," answered Wrexford. "Add to that the sounds of the wind in the rigging and the floating debris hitting up against the hull, and I promise you, my fiddling with the rudder will go unnoticed."

A sharp whistle from Raven signaled that the stairs were fast approaching. Sheffield steered the boat up to the stone landing and the boy jumped down to secure a rope around one of the stanchions.

Dark on dark against the night sky, the tips of a ship's mast poked up from behind a row of warehouses. They waited in silence, straining to hear any signs of its impending departure above the lapping of the water against the stone quay.

Charlotte shifted, feeling the weight of the pistol in her pocket. Sheffield and McClellan were armed as well. Gunpowder would be no help to the earl, but he was carrying a knife . . .

For all the good it would do him against a boatload of cut-throat killers and mercenary ruffians.

Another whistle, but she had already seen it, too. The masts were beginning to move. It seemed to take an eternity for them to disappear into the swirls of fog.

One, two, three . . . Charlotte began a mental counting of the seconds. Wrexford and Sheffield had calculated beforehand how long to wait before pursuing the enemy.

The *thump* of Raven's feet reverberated through the deck as he jumped back on board. She felt the wherry shudder and start to move through the water. As they angled out to the middle of the river, Charlotte saw their quarry up ahead, ghosting along through the tendrils of fog under her topgallant sails. The ship was moving sluggishly, as the tide had not yet gained its full force.

Sheffield pulled in the main sheet, tightening the sail, and the wherry picked up speed.

Wrexford lifted her hand to his lips and brushed a quick kiss to her knuckles before releasing his hold. She met his eyes and felt a sob well up in her throat.

He smiled, and then was gone, a dark shape wiggling quick as an eel over the floor toward the stern.

"Ready, everyone," called Sheffield softly. He shifted a large jug of spirits to the slatted seat beside him and started to sing a bawdy song in an off-key bellow. In response to his increasingly erratic tugs at the tiller, the wherry began to pitch and yaw, its prow swinging around toward Lyman's ship.

McClellan began to curse her good-for-nothing husband, with Raven adding his own mewling to her shrieks.

Charlotte winced. They were making enough noise to wake the dead.

Her own role was to fumble with the rigging, as if trying to help Sheffield change direction.

"Avast, you barnacle-witted fool!" Their cacophony had

drawn notice from the ship's quarterdeck. As they swooped closer, Charlotte saw a man was now standing at the taffrail, waving his arms. "Steer left! Steer left!"

Sheffield raised the jug in a friendly salute. "Y'wanna buy a woman fer yer journey. She be a shrew, but I'll sell her te ye cheap, ha, ha, ha!"

McClellan slapped him around the head, knocking the wherry farther off course. It was now aimed right for the rear side of the ship.

The thump of wood against wood rose above the shrieks and howls of the combatants.

"Sorry!" shouted Raven as he grabbed up the gaff pole and pushed the wherry free.

Out of the corner of her eye, Charlotte saw Wrexford slip over the side and into the water without making a sound. The ripples were quickly swallowed in the gloom.

"Move off, you lummox, or you'll soon be food for the crabs!"

Charlotte spotted von Stockhausen brandishing a musket. An instant later, another man appeared by his side and caught hold of the barrel.

"Now, now, there's no need for violence," called the newcomer, swinging the weapon's aim skyward. "However, madam, I suggest you take command of your vessel and head for safe harbor." A note of arrogant amusement colored his voice. "Before my compatriot orders for the cannons to be run out."

Raven let out a wail of terror and began a frantic paddling with his hands.

The newcomer—Charlotte guessed it was Lyman—began laughing. Wresting the musket away from von Stockhausen, he took aim and fired a shot that came perilously close to the boy, who wisely flung himself back into the scuppers.

"Monster," whispered Charlotte as McClellan hauled in the

sail and set the wherry flying for the opposite shore. Their part was done for the moment. They would circle back shortly and shadow the ship's progress.

But now, it was all up to Wrexford.

The water was colder than Satan's heart. The shock of plunging into its depth froze his muscles for an instant, but as the current pulled at his clothing, sweeping him away from his target, Wrexford forced himself to stay submerged and began swimming toward the ship.

As he rose to draw a gulp of air, the crack of the musket shot cut through the night. He swiveled around to see the wherry come about and disappear into the rolling bank of fog. Whether anyone had been hit was impossible to tell. But the bark of laughter that floated down from the quarterdeck sent a wave of fury pulsing through his blood.

Clutching the chisel and mallet, he ducked beneath the waves and kept moving. Buoyed by the current, he soon found himself deep in shadow, staring up at the Baltimore Clipper's graceful stern. The clank of rudder chains shifting in the waves filled his ears. At this point in the river, the helmsman had few obstacles to navigate. The fellow would need only a light hand on the wheel.

Which is all to my advantage, thought the earl, allowing a cold smile.

Kicking closer, Wrexford seized hold of the rudderpost, hauled himself into position, and set to work.

Charlotte and Raven fought to control the flapping canvas as Sheffield lowered the sail.

"Let it fall into the cockpit, then step aside," he directed, after wrestling an ochre-colored replacement out from the storage locker beneath the front deck. "I'll reeve the new sail onto its fastenings, then the two of you can roll up the old one and stow it before changing your jackets."

McClellan had already shed her garish mustard-yellow shawl and straw bonnet for the more subdued dress of a prosperous merchant wife. The jug of gin had gone overboard, along with Sheffield's shabby outer garments. Once he slipped on his new coat and hat, the drunken wherryman would be transformed beyond recognition.

"Let us hurry," urged Charlotte, though she knew Wrexford would need at least another quarter hour to finish. She hated to think of him alone in the treacherous waters. As she knew all too well from her work, the Thames was a notoriously dangerous place for a man adrift on his own.

Raven looked up from tugging the old sail out of Sheffield's way as he worked it free of the rigging, the creamy canvas casting a ghostlike pallor over his narrow face. "Wrexford won't come to harm, m'lady. He's . . ."

Immortal?

"Of course he won't," she replied, forcing a smile before looking away so the boy wouldn't see the fear flooding her eyes.

"He's a very good swimmer, Charlotte," said Sheffield as he quickened his efforts. "There was a prank we pulled during our Oxford days involving a very unpopular don. It required Wrex to cross the River Isis and . . ." He continued with a very entertaining story, which made Raven and McClellan laugh.

A smile—a real one—touched her lips as he finished. These close-knit friendships were a precious source of strength when her own nerve failed her.

"Thank you, Kit," murmured Charlotte as she edged past him to change her garments. He grasped her hand and gave a fleeting squeeze, which said all that needed to be said.

After tucking her hair under a different-shaped hat, she helped Raven finish storing the old sail.

"Ready, Mac?" called Sheffield as he grabbed a halyard to hoist their new colors.

The maid gave the tiller a push, nodding in satisfaction as the ochre-hued canvas billowed out to catch the wind. The transformed wherry now bore no resemblance to its original appearance. With all the other small cargo boats on the water, the enemy would have no reason to suspect that they were being shadowed.

"Hard a-lee," warned Sheffield, signaling to McClellan to bring the wherry about. "Now let us go ensure that those blackguards are stopped dead in the water."

CHAPTER 28

Wrexford paused for a moment, clamping the saw blade between his teeth in order to shake the numbness from his fingers. The lower half of his body, still submerged in the swirling currents, felt like a block of ice, and the chill was slowly spreading up his arms, but on close inspection, he saw that the job was nearly done. He had chiseled the wood away from the massive bolts holding the rudder in place, exposing just enough to saw away at the steel. Two bolts were cut through completely. In another few minutes, the third one would snap away and the rudder would sink into the river, leaving the ship unable to steer.

The villains would then have two choices: They could abandon the vessel in order to save their own necks. Or they could stay aboard and risk taking the time to make repairs, gambling that the authorities had no way of linking Tyler's disappearance to them.

Either way, the ship wouldn't be blown to smithereens by the Royal Navy frigate. Once it was helpless in the water, there was plenty of time to send word to Daggett, who could then make quick work of capturing the ship with a boarding party. Even if Lyman's crew wished to fight, they would have no way of maneuvering to aim their guns.

After blowing some warmth back into his hands, Wrexford resumed sawing. Even if von Stockhausen held Tyler as a hostage, he was confident that the scholar-turned-murderer would be willing to bargain. Avoiding the hangman's noose was an excellent incentive to make a deal.

The rasp of metal on metal was suddenly joined by a strange scrabbling at the far corner of the stern. Wrexford froze and cocked an ear. Something was scraping down the side of the hull. Perhaps they had heard him?

He quietly regripped the saw blade between his teeth and reached for the knife strapped to his leg.

The sounds grew a touch louder—and then came a soft splash, punctuated by a watery oath.

Bloody hell.

Shoving the knife back into its sheath, Wrexford then grabbed the saw blade from his mouth and let out a sharp hiss. A shadowy flutter of movement stirred the dark water. He couldn't make out any shape to it, but he heard a faint gurgling as it came closer.

"What the devil are you doing here?" whispered Tyler, who was struggling to keep hold of an inflated oilcloth sack.

"I could ask the same thing of you," retorted the earl. "Though I daresay, I have the better answer. I'm pulling your cods out of the fire . . . though I ought to have let them burn to a crisp."

"Granted, I misjudged Adderley. He's Lyman's cousin—and a brute—but he's got a very sharp eye." The valet had drifted close enough for Wrexford to see the nasty bruise on his face. "However, there is a bright side to my clumsiness—"

"Never mind that now. Hold the rudder steady while I finish sawing through the last bolt." Seeing Tyler struggle to control both the oilcloth and the slippery wood, Wrexford swore under his breath. "Ye gods, let go of the damnable sack. We need to disable the ship." Tempting as it was to let von Stockhausen, Lyman, and Adderley sail into a hail of cannon fire, there had been enough bloodshed. He wished to see them brought to justice.

"Seeing as we've all gone through hell to find what's in the damnable sack, I'd rather not let it float away."

"Becton's specimen?" demanded the earl.

"Of course," answered Tyler. "You didn't think I would leave the ship without it, did you?"

"Move behind me. I'll manage on my own. Watch out for the steering chains. They're likely to snap when the rudder falls."

Tyler dutifully paddled around to join him. "Might I inquire how we are going to keep from drowning, once we've sunk their chances of escape?" He grimaced. "The bloody river is a lot colder than I imagined."

Wrexford was already sawing away at the bolt. "Do you see a wherry with an ochre sail behind us?"

The current was starting to quicken, its whirls slapping bigger waves against the hull.

"There's some sort of small craft in the distance, but I can't make out the color," said the valet.

"I think we can assume it's our friends coming to our aid. Charlotte, Sheffield, and Raven will be delighted to see you . . ." The bolt emitted a low crackling. "Mac may be a trifle less—"

The rest of the earl's words were swallowed in a shuddering *crack* as the weighty rudder broke off from its moorings, tearing loose the chains—and disappeared beneath the water.

From high above them on the quarterdeck came the sounds of all hell breaking loose.

Wrexford grabbed Tyler's sodden shirt and indicated a thick swirl of fog off the right, its tendrils lying low over the waves. "Swim for cover before we're spotted."

The shouting grew louder. He recognized von Stockhausen's voice amid the cacophony. Someone lowered a rope with a lantern tied on its end, which clearly illuminated the damage.

Caught in the current, the ship yawed and started to drift toward them. The commotion quieted as the crew seemed to shift to the front of the ship. For several moments, the earl heard only the flapping of the sails. And then . . .

"How could the bloody rudder simply fall off, Reggie?" It was Adderley, his voice quavering with fury. "Everything was shipshape yesterday."

"A good question."

"That's Lyman," murmured Tyler. The wind had shifted in such a way that the voices floating down from the quarterdeck were clear as a bell.

"But it's not one we're at leisure to answer at the moment," added Lyman. "Come, let's lower one of the longboats."

"What about von Stockhausen?" asked his cousin. The navigation lanterns hung in rigging cast enough illumination for Wrexford to make out the two figures standing together by the rail. "And what about the ship?"

Lyman laughed. "Why would we take a plump pigeon with us, when he's ripe for plucking by authorities. As for the ship, there's no need to worry. I've a plan."

"You usually do," said Adderley with a nasty chuckle.

Wrexford batted at the fog floating around him, straining to keep Lyman and his cousin in sight as they moved to the stern of the ship.

"I learned a great deal about those devious dastards and their sordid plans during my interrogation," muttered Tyler as he and the earl continued to tread water. "And I can explain how the pieces all fit—"

"*Shhhh!*" hissed Wrexford as another figure appeared on the quarterdeck and accosted Lyman and Adderley with an angry shout and a flurry of curses and demands.

"Stop the crew from abandoning the ship?" repeated Lyman. "You're welcome to try, Herr von Stockhausen. But money won't do them any good in Newgate Prison."

"You, too, are like filthy rats, trying to slink away," cried von Stockhausen. "I'm paying you a king's ransom to partner with me, and you've only received half of it."

Lyman shrugged. "You're worth more to us here, taking the blame for everything."

"Even among thieves, there is a code of honor," protested von Stockhausen. He was clutching a small valise—valuable, no doubt—to his middle. "My money should purchase the short passage to shore. I demand that you take me with you."

Adderley snarled an oath and shoved him aside as he and Lyman set to work, rigging the longboat to a set of pulleys and tackles hanging from a set of davit arms, and swinging it out over the water.

The ship was drifting closer and closer to Wrexford and Tyler. Pushed by the waves, the stern was almost facing them.

"Stop—I order you to stop!"

The anger was gone from von Stockhausen's voice, noted the earl. Instead, there was an edge of cold-blooded calmness.

The other two men continued to ignore their erstwhile partner in crime. After positioning the longboat to a spot several feet below the ship's rail, Lyman climbed down into its stern and loosened one of the pulley ropes in readiness for lowering it into the river. Adderley moved to the bow and swung one leg over the rail.

"Stop!" repeated von Stockhausen.

"Or what?" sneered Adderley. "You'll cut my throat?"

Another laugh from Lyman.

"Poison is a pampered aristocrat's weapon. You're too lily-livered to do it, face-to-face." Adderley brought his other leg over the rail and turned his back on the Prussian, readying himself to drop down into the longboat.

A shot rang out. Limned in a shower of fire-gold sparks, Adderley toppled headfirst into the longboat, the impact of his weight sending Lyman flying out of his seat. He twisted in midair and just managed to catch hold of the outer gunwale with one hand to keep from falling into the river.

"*Ja,* I don't feel beholden to kill face-to-face," jeered von Stockhausen through the silvery haze of his smoking pistol. He dropped his spent weapon and drew another one from his valise. "I do whatever is most pragmatic."

"Holy hell," uttered Tyler, his eye widened in surprise. "Who would have thought . . ."

"Not I," admitted Wrexford. He darted a look over his shoulder, trying to spot the wherry through the mist that was beginning to rise from the river. At first, he saw nothing, but then suddenly a sail flickered in and out of the fog. The shift in the wind had slowed its progress, but it was creeping closer and closer.

His attention snapped back to the drama unfolding between the two conspirators. With unexpected agility, von Stockhausen leaped into the longboat and dumped Adderley's lifeless corpse over the side. It hit the water with a dull splash and began to sink.

Lyman spat out a curse. His face was streaked in blood—he must have struck his head on the combing while being thrown from the longboat—and he redoubled his efforts to pull himself back into the cockpit.

The click of the pistol's hammer caused him to freeze. "Be reasonable, von Stockhausen. In our world, there's always a deal to be made. You uncock your weapon, and I row you to shore."

"You think me too soft to wield the oars, just as you thought me too soft to spill blood? You stupid, stupid man—I spent a number of years exploring the wilds of Spanish America, and faced a myriad of dangers in the jungle that would make your hair stand on end. Trust me, I can fend for myself."

Bracing his legs for balance in the rocking longboat, he calmly took aim at Lyman's forehead.

"I'll return your money!" Lyman's arrogance had dissolved to a desperate wheedling. "I've a safe place where we can shelter from the authorities, and a network of smugglers who will get us out of the country."

"The time to make a deal is past."

Wrexford stared in shock as von Stockhausen pulled the trigger and Lyman's skull exploded in a sickening spray of shattered bone and brains.

"I suppose I should feel a twinge of pity . . ." He thought about the British troops betrayed by Lyman and shook his head. "But if ever a man deserved an ugly death, it was him."

"Amen to that," said Tyler, his breathing a little ragged as he labored to keep the oilcloth-wrapped specimen afloat.

"Our friends will be here shortly," said Wrexford. "I'll stay with you if you're tiring, but otherwise . . ."

A heavy splash indicated that von Stockhausen had worked the block and tackles to lower the longboat into the water.

"Otherwise, I'd like to make sure that our nemesis doesn't escape."

"Go!" gurgled the valet as a wave slapped his face. "I'm Scottish—a little cold and wet won't do me a lick of harm."

The oars thudded into the brass oarlocks. It appeared that the Prussian hadn't lied about his survival skills. He maneuvered the boat around with practiced ease.

"I shall count on that," replied Wrexford, keeping his eyes on von Stockhausen, who began rowing toward the south bank. "I would greatly miss your everyday insolence." With that, he drew in a deep breath and submerged beneath the rippling waves.

The Prussian's course was angling close to the floating fog in which they had taken cover. Propelling himself underwater with silent strokes, he passed the longboat and quickly pivoted and raised his head just enough to gauge the perfect moment to grasp the prow.

Wrexford heard a grunt from von Stockhausen as the drag of his own weight slowed the longboat's momentum. The currents in this part of the river were fitful, and he was counting on that to keep the enemy from becoming suspicious. Sure enough, he heard a low oath as von Stockhausen redoubled his efforts.

All the better that the dastard was fatiguing himself.

Keeping a grip on the longboat's front cleat, Wrexford took a moment to regain his breath. His plan was a simple one—rowing required von Stockhausen to face the rear. While the Prussian huffed and puffed over the oars, the earl intended to work his way down the railing until he was almost abreast of the center seat—and then to tip over the longboat with a sudden yank and spill von Stockhausen into the river.

In another few moments, Charlotte and Sheffield should swoop in and capture him as he flailed around in the water.

Hand over hand, Wrexford slid his way along the varnished railing. Closer . . . closer . . .

NOW!

The earl yanked himself upward with all his might. But his movements were sluggish from the cold and his fingers slipped. The boat rocked, but only enough to knock von Stockhausen from his seat. As Wrexford fell back into the water, he saw the Prussian scramble to his feet, snatch up one of the heavy oars, and lift it high over his head with a bellow of rage.

Damnation. There was no time to swim out of range. His only hope of avoiding a lethal blow was to dive—

Crack!

The oar fell harmlessly against the gunwales as von Stockhausen teetered for an instant before dropping like a stack of stones over the stern and disappearing beneath the water.

Wrexford blinked the brackish spray out of his eyes and looked up to see the wherry bearing down on him. McClellan was balanced on the bowsprit, one hand clutching a shroud, the other a still-smoking pistol.

Behind her were Charlotte and Sheffield, who were just lowering their own weapons.

"You should have let me shoot him," said Sheffield.

"No, better me than any of you," said the maid cryptically.

The earl was about to speak, but then all of a sudden, hands were reaching down and hauling him up into the blessedly dry cockpit.

"T-Tyler," he sputtered as Charlotte draped him in a blanket.

"Yes, yes, we saw him." Sheffield rushed to take the tiller from Raven. "We'll have him safely aboard in a moment."

"You bloody idiot," said Charlotte before wrapping the earl in a hug and kissing him full on the mouth.

Wrexford couldn't recall having ever tasted anything so exquisitely sweet.

"What the devil were you thinking?" she murmured, her lips now feathering against his cheek. "That madman had just shot two men. How could you be sure he didn't have a third weapon?"

"*Nobody* carries three pistols," he answered. "It defies logic—two hands, two pistols."

"Be damned with logic." She hugged him tighter. "Don't ever attack a ruthless murderer with naught but your bare hands again."

Raven peered over one of the crates, his look of concern giving way to a grin. "Oiy, you're supposed to be setting a good example for me and Hawk."

"Ahoy there," warned Sheffield, slowing the wherry as it approached Tyler.

McClellan leaned over the rail and lifted her cousin and his bedraggled sack into the boat.

"Are you injured?" she demanded after clasping him in a fierce embrace.

Tyler smiled. "Just a few scrapes and bumps."

"Good." The maid cocked a meaty fist and smacked him square on the tip of his chin, knocking him out cold. "Let that be a lesson not to draw the Weasels into danger in the future."

She caught him as he slumped forward and quickly wrapped him in a blanket before laying him gently on the cockpit floor, sheltered from the wind. "Now, I suggest we all return to His Lordship's townhouse as quickly as can be arranged . . ." She cracked her knuckles. "And break open a bottle of his most expensive Scottish malt."

CHAPTER 29

Alas, it quickly became apparent to Charlotte that the celebratory libations would be delayed for some time. On docking at Nereid and Neptune's wharf and returning to the company's office, they found the place crowded with a contingent of Bow Street Runners left by Griffin as reinforcements. The acting commander had no idea as to where the Head Runner had gone, but there was little time to ponder that conundrum in the frenzy of activity needed to bring the chase for the villains to an end.

Wrexford busied himself with dispatching a note to Daggett at Greenwich explaining all that had transpired. The American and the Royal Navy would need to stand down from the blockade and turn their efforts to retrieving the disabled Baltimore Clipper.

As for the dead bodies . . .

Charlotte shivered, thankful that she had only seen Lyman's skull shatter from afar. Wrexford's grim account of the details had been bad enough. Griffin's second-in-command hadn't been at all pleased that he and the other Runners were tasked with rowing out and searching for three corpses in the river. But that, she decided, was a skirmish for Griffin to face.

We have fought more than our share of the battle.

At last, the duties were done, and they managed to find hackneys to take them back to Berkeley Square. Cordelia, who hadn't let Sheffield out of her sight since his return, insisted on coming with them. Charlotte suspected part of the reason was because Cordelia wished to be sure that the dangers were truly over.

Given all the investigation's pernicious twists and unexpected villains, she didn't blame her.

"Welcome home, milord." Wrexford's butler didn't bat an eye at their little band's motley appearance. "Mr. Griffin is waiting for you in your workroom."

"Excellent," muttered the earl. "I'll already have a Runner present when I wish to report that a larceny has taken place in my larder."

Riche maintained a straight face. "He mentioned that he was feeling a bit peckish and that you wouldn't begrudge him a meal."

"Never mind the food," said Tyler, hurrying to open the workroom door. "As long as there's plenty of whisky."

"Don't count on it," rumbled a voice from one of the armchairs near the hearth. "Wrex's selection is far superior to my sheep swill," added Henning.

"Oh, we've left them a few wee drops." Griffin rose and gave a lazy stretch before turning and eyeing them over his glass. "Good Lord, you all look like death warmed over. Dare I ask what happened?"

"Not before I get a drink of my own damn whisky," growled Wrexford.

"And not before you and Tyler go upstairs and change into dry clothing," said Charlotte. "Which you will do before I allow any malt to be poured."

As the earl and his valet hurriedly retreated for the stairs, she looked at the Runner—thankfully, Cordelia had provided her with a change of clothing at the shipping office, so she was no longer wearing her urchin's rags—and, crossing her arm, fixed him with a scowl. "Do not make a jest of this, sir! Wrexford and Tyler are lucky to be alive."

"I didn't mean to do so, milady." All trace of ironic humor disappeared from Griffin's face. "I've been in a pucker of worry over His Lordship—and all of you. It's *my* duty to see that justice is done, not yours. It pains me deeply that you felt compelled to take such unholy risks."

Charlotte instantly regretted her sharp words, knowing that the Runner was a man of both honor and courage. "It's no reflection on your skills, sir, that we got involved. Your hands are tied by the government rules and regulations, while we have leeway—"

"To break whatever laws you choose?" suggested Henning.

"Let us just say, we use our imagination and intuition," she replied.

Stifling a snort, Sheffield moved to the sideboard and poured four measures of whisky.

Griffin raised a brow, but made no comment as Charlotte, Cordelia, and McClellan each accepted a glass and savored a long swallow.

"While Lord Wrexford and his valet attend to their sartorial needs, might I ask you for a summary of all that has occurred since this morning, when His Lordship left me eating breakfast here in his townhouse, saying he was merely making a short visit to your residence?"

"I . . ." Charlotte took another sip of her whisky and let its heat slide down her throat. "I hardly know where to begin." The first tranquil hours of the morning seemed so very, very far away.

"I suppose it all started when Wrexford noticed that Tyler

had disappeared without any explanation," she said, knowing she had to tread carefully, as Griffin knew nothing about her wards being part of the earl's band of urchins. Thankfully, Raven had been wise enough to hang back and take shelter in one of the shadowed alcoves.

"So, suspecting that he may have gone to do some sleuthing around the docks for the missing specimen, the earl and I decided to pay a visit to Mr. Sheffield at the offices of Nereid and Neptune . . ."

Griffin took a seat and listened without interruption to Charlotte's narration—helped by an occasional comment from Sheffield—of all the byzantine twists and shocking discoveries that had led them to the final dramatic confrontation with the primary villain.

The Runner then allowed a long moment of silence as he mulled over what he had heard. "Just to be sure my admittedly slow wits have comprehended the facts of what you told me," he said, "Captain Daggett is an official ally of our government."

"Correct," answered Charlotte.

"And the grand villain of all this was an innocuous scholar, aided by the infamous Reginald Lyman and his cousin?"

"Yes."

"And they are all now dead, and the missing plant has been found?" pressed Griffin.

"Your wits are working quite well," murmured Sheffield.

"That, too, is correct," replied Charlotte. "Your second-in-command and his men are out on the river looking to retrieve the bodies. But Wrexford and Tyler witnessed the deaths of all three of them, so they can confirm that the blackguards are dead."

The Runner nodded thoughtfully. "Just one thing puzzles me. If the other two conspirators were killed by the Prussian, then who shot von Stockhausen?"

"I can't say, Mr. Griffin," she answered with a hitch. "What with the fog and commotion—the crew of the ship was rowing away in the other longboats—it was all very confusing."

"Yes, I can well imagine it was. However—"

"However," interrupted Wrexford as he and Tyler returned, clad in clean and dry clothing, "we're all too damnably tired and thirsty to answer any more questions. Come back in the morning and you can pepper me with your queries over breakfast."

"Fair enough." Griffin rose and moved toward the door with his usual slow-footed gait. But as he passed Wrexford, he paused to place a hand on the earl's shoulder. "I trust it goes without saying that I'm very relieved to see you alive, milord."

"There was no need to worry," replied Wrexford. "As I said, I've bequeathed a meal stipend to you in the event of my demise."

"Yes, but who else would feed me a steady diet of sarcasm?"

Charlotte smiled as Griffin turned and made a surprisingly polished bow to the rest of them. "Good night, everyone. I'm not capable of fancy speeches, so I shall just say thank you."

Wrexford handed Tyler a glass of whisky before pouring one for himself. The glow of the lamplight accentuated the nasty bruising on the valet's face. He had taken a rough beating from his captors, and the earl could see McClellan eyeing him with concern . . . and what looked like a flicker of remorse for her own blow.

"*Slàinte*," said Henning, raising his own drink in salute. "I think the occasion calls for a formal toast of thanksgiving—"

"Wait!" The pounding of the dowager's cane punctuated her call from the corridor. Hawk darted into the room, several steps ahead of her and Wolcott.

"I sent word to Alison that we were all safe," said Charlotte, unwinding herself from Hawk's hug.

"I say . . ." Wolcott cleared his throat. "Has the solving of murders become a regular occurrence in this family? Alison seemed to take the news of your chasing a dangerous killer with remarkable calm."

"You had better get used to it," said Wrexford as he uncorked a fresh bottle of malt. "Your sister is no ordinary lady."

Her brother allowed an uneasy chuckle. "I've known that for years." He accepted a glass from the earl and gave it a meditative swirl. "Allow me to add an addendum to the original toast . . ." His gaze moved around the room. "To unconventional ladies, and their keeping us gentlemen on our toes." A pause. "God help you, Wrexford. But clearly you know that."

Once the laughter died down, the earl motioned for everyone to take a seat. "Before we all seek some well-deserved sleep, I'd like to fit the last few missing pieces of the puzzle into place, so that the picture is finally complete." He looked to Tyler. "And it seems to me that you managed to ferret them out, though at no small cost to your phiz."

"By the by, is your nose broken?" asked McClellan.

"No—just my chin bone," retorted the valet in an injured voice. "Why the devil did you hit me?"

"Because your running off half-cocked put the Weasels, along with Lady Charlotte and Lord Wrexford, in terrible danger." The maid huffed a sigh. "And, if you must know, because it scared me half to death when I heard you were captured."

"On the other hand, if he hadn't been so cork-brained, we wouldn't have learned all the gory details," pointed out Wrexford. "So without further ado, Tyler . . ."

"Right." The valet set aside his empty glass. "The key factor that kept us running in circles for so long was the fact that there were *two* sets of villains, each with a different criminal plan. And adding to the confusion was the fact that DeVere and Quincy were originally trying to wheedle Becton into partnering with them on his discovery. However, despite being despicable individuals, it appears they weren't willing to commit murder for it."

"Are you implying that they never intended to steal it?" asked Charlotte.

"Apparently not," said Tyler. "According to Lyman and Adderley, who lie at the heart of both nefarious plots, DeVere and Quincy came up with another plan to profit from Becton's discovery."

"One that involved the importation of enslaved souls," mused Wrexford. "But what is the connection between the two?"

"The plant!" replied Tyler. "Think about it. Quincy owned vast plantations in America, and had the botanical expertise in growing crops for commercial sale."

"And Becton's discovery would require his miracle tropical plant to be cultivated on a large scale," realized the earl.

"Precisely," said the valet. "Adderley, who as you know had been hired by Quincy for his botanical knowledge, explained that Quincy had a large tract of hot, swampy land, perfect for growing Becton's plant, but it had never been able to be used for anything because enslaved workers died in droves from malaria if put to toiling there."

"So the irony of the plot was that Quincy could grow the plant profitably because the new medicine would keep them healthy," said Charlotte, her face darkening with anger. "What a horribly ingenious plan."

"DeVere helped concoct it. His experiences in India helped inspire the idea," explained Tyler.

Sheffield frowned in thought. "So Quincy's purchase of the small shipping company based in Martinique likely had to do with transporting the plant specimens from Spanish America to South Carolina." He thought for a moment longer. "And probably the poor souls needed to cultivate the swampland as well. It would have been easier to land the original boatload of enslaved souls on one of the smaller islands, and then transport them in smaller ships to America, where the illegal entry could be done in one of the myriad tidal coves and rivers along the coast near his plantations."

"That's exactly what was planned," confirmed the valet.

"So why did Lyman and Adderley decide to turn on DeVere and Quincy?" asked the earl. "I'm sure they were being paid handsomely."

Tyler hesitated, glancing first at Charlotte and then at her brother.

Wrexford suddenly realized what the answer likely was. But Charlotte wouldn't thank him for trying to hush it up. It was best to get it out now. With Wolcott here, there could be no discussion about it, but he would deal with her in private.

"Go on," he said evenly.

Tyler's gaze now dropped to the dregs of his drink. "They were concerned about the stirring of public awareness concerning the shoddy maintenance practices of Quincy's shipping company. They feared that further probing into the business might reveal their involvement in the slave-trading side venture. Lyman couldn't afford that."

Charlotte's expression remained neutral, but Wrexford didn't miss the swirling of emotion beneath her lashes. *Guilt?* He clenched his teeth. Much as he admired her steely sense of right and wrong, there were times when he wished it could bend just a little.

"And it so happened that they got an alternative offer for their services, and decided it was a more attractive one," finished the valet.

Wolcott frowned. "By Jove, didn't that scribbler, A. J. Quill, do several drawings about how the company was risking the lives of their sailors and the property of their clients?"

Their friends all shifted uncomfortably. Charlotte's brother, of course, knew nothing about her secret identity.

"Yes—and Quill ought to get a medal for it!" Cordelia's emphatic voice broke the silence. "DeVere and Quincy were wicked men. Their plan would have shattered countless lives, enslaving poor souls and tearing them from their families and homeland." A martial fire blazed in her eyes. "Murder is an abomination, and vengeance is not a substitute for the rule of law. But in this case, I believe they got what they deserved. For me, there is a poetic justice to the fact that evil exterminated evil."

"I couldn't agree more," said Henning quickly, and the others all added their assent.

Wrexford fixed Charlotte with a meaningful look. He would keep his words for later.

To his relief, she nodded and murmured, "*Malum facit sibi malum.*" The lamp flame flickered, throwing her face in shadow for an instant. "*Evil begets evil,*" she translated. "Those who foment it must suffer the consequences."

"Amen to that." Henning rolled his glass between his palms. "And what of von Stockhausen, Tyler? Did you learn anything about how his plot took root, and how he came to make the connection with Lyman and Adderley?"

"Yes, von Stockhausen took pleasure in explaining that in great detail," said the valet. "We all knew that he was part of von Humboldt's first scientific expedition through Spanish America, and that Becton traveled with the main party for several months before striking out on his own."

"That's how the two of them became acquainted," Wrexford pointed out.

"Yes, but what we didn't know was that von Stockhausen also met Adderley on that trip," continued Tyler. "As we learned before, Adderley was part of an American naval mission to Granada, in Spanish America, and the Spanish viceroy had a reception for the American officers. As von Stockhausen and von Humboldt were both Prussian aristocrats, and happened to be passing through the city on their way back to Europe, they, too, were invited."

"And von Stockhausen and Adderley discovered that they were kindred souls with criminal minds," muttered Cordelia.

"That explains how Adderley and Lyman became connected to von Stockhausen," mused Wrexford. "But what interests me more is what turned an obscure Prussian scholar into a malevolent murderer."

"The answer is simple—jealousy and ambition," answered the valet. "Von Stockhausen apparently resented the fact that von Humboldt, his fellow Prussian, became famous for his scientific exploits, while his own scholarly papers garnered little notice. The anger festered over the years, and when he got hints from Becton about a momentous discovery based on a botanical specimen found in Spanish America—the two of them had kept up a casual correspondence—he again felt he had been cheated of fame and fortune. So, knowing Becton planned to keep it as a secret until he was ready to reveal it to the world here at the symposium, he began to plot how to take the discovery for himself."

"Good Lord!" exclaimed the dowager. "What a thoroughly despicable man. To think of murdering an old friend for money . . ."

"It wasn't just the money, as von Stockhausen is quite wealthy on his own," said Tyler. "It was the obsession with being lauded by his peers as a luminary in the world of science."

"No matter that it would be a fraud?" exclaimed Alison.

"A fraud, indeed," mused Wolcott. "I've read some of his papers, and while I am no expert in the field, his work struck me as mediocre."

"Men like von Stockhausen are delusional," responded Charlotte. "They are willing to betray the truth, as well as any other moral principle."

"Thank heaven that Wrexford and you—and all your friends—managed to stop him and his cohorts," replied her brother. "I'm . . . well, I'm deucedly proud of all of you."

Charlotte smiled. "I firmly believe that love and friendship is more than a match for the dark side of human nature." Raven and Hawk had quietly crept over to sit on the padded arms of her chair. She clasped their hands, twining the three of them together. "It's a never-ending fight, but surrender is unthinkable."

Wolcott looked thoughtful. And then, as he eyed the boys, his expression became uncertain. "I can't help but notice that the boys appear to have played some role—"

"I think we've had enough questions answered for one night," interrupted the dowager. "You'll have ample time in the future to become better acquainted with your nephews. But for now"—she raised her empty glass—"I suggest that Tyler pass around the bottle so we may raise another toast—and then toddle off home. It's way past my bedtime."

Henning waited for the libations to be poured before clearing his throat with a gravelly cough. "To upholding the noble ideals of truth and justice." He ran a hand over his unshaven chin. "We don't always make the fight look pretty, but we get the job done."

Tyler grinned, and then winced. His bruises were turning a very unpleasant shade of purple.

"I have just one remark to add," said the dowager, waggling her cane to get everyone's attention. "On no account are any of you allowed to trip over another dead body until *after* the wedding ceremony." The waggle turned into a warning swoosh. "Slay my plans for a festive celebration and it will be *you* who is going to the grave."

CHAPTER 30

The next fortnight passed in a dizzying blur. There were fittings for her wedding gown, menus to go over with McClellan and Wrexford's cook, and sketches for the decorative flowers and bridal bouquet to review with Hawk and the dowager . . .

"Lud, an elopement was so much simpler," muttered Charlotte as she tucked a loose strand of hair behind her ear and hurriedly added the last section of cross-hatched shadows to her drawing for Mr. Fores. "I wonder if Wrexford would consider . . ."

But the thought quickly yielded to a rueful smile. The earl would likely leap at the idea, but she wouldn't dream of disappointing Alison for a second time. The boys, too, had become increasingly excited by the idea of the pageantry. Indeed, they had taken it upon themselves to design a procession for leading her down the aisle.

A soft laugh tickled in her throat. The procession included Alice the Eel Girl, Skinny, One-Eye Harry, and Pudge—their urchin friends from the stews who now were part of the earl's country estate—carrying bouquets of flowers designed by Hawk.

Raven and Hawk were going to lead the way, with Harper, Wrexford's wolflike Scottish deerhound, walking between them, draped with a floral garland.

After putting the finishing touches on her drawing, the last one due before departing for the earl's estate, Charlotte consulted her list of the things left to do before their traveling party left for the country first thing in the morning.

"Good heavens." Her eyes widened in dismay. "Surely, there can't be *that* many!"

"M'lady, m'lady!" called Raven from the foot of the stairs. "Aunt Alison has arrived!"

"I'll be down in a moment . . ."

Dawn's pale light was just giving way to brighter sunshine as Wrexford helped Charlotte into the carriage. He quickly climbed in after her and closed the door, shutting out the shouts and laughter from the rest of their party, who were piling into the dowager's barouche. Tyler was bringing up the rear with the baggage wagons.

"I was beginning to fear that you had eloped," he quipped after sitting beside her and settling his shoulders against the soft leather squabs. They had hardly seen each other during the past two weeks. But thankfully, Alison had offered to have the boys and McClellan journey with her, allowing the two of them some quiet time together.

Her laugh warmed the still-cool morning air within the shadowed interior. "Oh? With whom?"

"Actually, I was thinking that the impending prospect of being leg-shackled to me might have made you run off on your own," he replied.

"Sorry, but I'm afraid you're stuck with me." Charlotte shifted closer, her body fitting comfortably—nay, perfectly—against his. "Alison would have both our heads on a platter if we didn't show up for the ceremony."

He brushed a kiss to the top of her head. "And heaven forfend that we displease the dowager."

"I let her down in the past," replied Charlotte softly.

"I think you've more than made it up to her, my love." He drew her into the crook of his arm. "I've missed you. What with all the demands on our time, we've had so little time together."

"And I have missed you." She slipped her hand beneath his coat, her fingers playing over the folds of his linen shirt. "Have all the complications of the murders been resolved with the authorities and the investigation deemed officially closed?"

"Yes," he answered. "The government was relieved that it wasn't necessary for Lyman to stand trial. It would have been awkward for them to admit America's involvement in bringing the miscreant to justice for his many crimes. In private, however, Daggett received a medal, and sails for home tomorrow with the assurance that the Foreign Office will redouble its efforts to make peace between our two countries."

"The captain should be pleased," mused Charlotte. "He is a hard man, but a fair one. I hope Lyman's demise helps put to rest his own personal demons."

"He sends you his best regards," said Wrexford. "However, had he made one more mention of how fetching you look in breeches, I might have had to darken his deadlights."

Her fingers stilled on his chest. "Oh, come, Wrexford, you don't have a jealous bone in your body."

"Are you quite sure?" He turned just enough to look down his nose at her. "I don't think you've explored my body thoroughly enough to come to an accurate conclusion."

Is that a blush darkening her cheeks? He smiled at the thought of it.

"Perhaps you're right." Her eyes were now twinkling with amusement. "After all, you've explained to me ad nauseam that the scientific method demands that assumptions must be proved by empirical evidence."

"There is much to be said for the scientific method." He pulled her into a long and lush kiss. "But first, I ought to finish telling you about the other developments concerning Becton's discovery. As we learned last week, Professor Murray did indeed receive the research papers, and has agreed to return them to the Royal Society."

"That seems the right decision, as they are the leading scientific society in the world, and the best qualified to decide how to proceed," replied Charlotte.

"As it happens, they've created a large endowment to develop the medicine," said Wrexford. "You see, I accompanied Griffin and his men when they searched Lyman's house for evidence of other conspiracies. There was, if you recall, a chest of gold delivered there from Quincy."

"A partial payment for illegally trafficking in enslaved men and women," mused Charlotte.

"I convinced Griffin and his superiors that it ought to be donated to the Royal Society so that the blood money could be put to a noble use. And they, in turn, created the endowment in honor of Becton." Wrexford couldn't hold back another smile. "I'm delighted to report that they appointed Dr. Hosack as its director, with authority to oversee the cultivation of the specimen plant and the continuing research to develop a medicine that will hopefully save many lives."

"What marvelous news, Wrexford! That was quite brilliant of you."

"That's not all that will please you," he murmured. "Hosack is very impressed with your friend Moretti and his scholarship. The doctor has offered him the position of chief researcher, and he's accepted. The two of them will sail to New York on the same ship as Daggett."

"Thank you," said Charlotte, her voice thick with emotion.

"In all fairness, I can't claim any credit for that decision." He paused. "But I'm happy to have been proven wrong about thinking him a fribble."

Charlotte touched his cheek. "You're not often wrong, Wrexford. Though I daresay, I'll regret telling you that."

"I make my share of mistakes." He took her hand and pressed a kiss to her palm. "But there's one elemental thing that I got oh-so-right."

Sunlight flickered through the windowpanes as the carriage passed Regent's Park and turned onto the road leading north.

She smiled, then her expression turned pensive. "As to getting things oh-so right . . . I am worried about Kit and Cordelia. Their attraction is clear to everyone around them, but—"

"But like us, they are grappling with their own inner demons?" suggested Wrexford. He settled back against the squabs. "Kit fears that she still sees him as naught but a charming wastrel. And Cordelia worries that she is too eccentric and independent to fit into the role of a wife. And much as we wish to tell them otherwise, it wouldn't help. They must muddle through their doubts on their own."

"For a man who claims to be ruled entirely by logic, how is it that you've become oh-so wise about emotions?" murmured Charlotte.

"Perhaps practice makes perfect," he replied.

The glow that lit in her eyes sent a shiver of warmth through him. "Perhaps you're right."

"Now, let us put aside further talk of murder, mayhem, and the romantic travails of our dear friends," he said, "and turn our thoughts to happier topics for the rest of the journey."

"Er, speaking of which," murmured Charlotte, "have the Weasels told you about their plans for Harper . . ."

The next few days passed in another whirlwind of activity. Wolcott and his family arrived, and the opportunity to reconnect with her long-estranged relatives and introduce them to her loved ones filled Charlotte with profound joy. Raven and Hawk took their younger cousins under their wing, the playful antics filling the stables with the sounds of merriment. And the manor house with copious amounts of mud. Their dear friends—Sheffield, Cordelia, and Henning—were also in residence . . .

And then, all of a sudden, it was the day of the wedding. Charlotte awoke early, her stomach too fluttery to seek anything other than a strong cup of coffee in the breakfast room before retreating to one of the side parlors to complete one last task before dressing for the ceremony.

"Charlotte?" The dowager poked her head into the room an hour later and let out an exasperated huff. "Good heavens, gel, what are you doing? You should be upstairs dressing!"

"Yes, yes, in a moment," she replied. "I've just finished."

"Finished what?" demanded Alison.

"A. J. Quill could hardly pass up the opportunity to satirize the infamous Earl of Wrexford's wedding." Charlotte made a wry face. "Besides, I owe it to Mr. Fores not to let James Gillray steal all the profits of making the public laugh."

The dowager crossed the carpet in a flash to take a look at the just-completed drawing . . . and let out a peal of laughter.

"At last!" she chortled. "Thank you, my dear! How delightful to have finally merited a caricature from the pen of A. J. Quill."

Charlotte had debated how to deal with the subject. She wasn't about to reveal the intimate details of the ceremony— the guests, the decorative flowers, the wedding breakfast. However, in a flash of inspiration, she had come up with the perfect way to entertain the public.

The drawing depicted the dowager, known throughout the beau monde as *The Dragon*, waving her cane and breathing fire at Wrexford, who was cowering behind his new bride. The caption, boldly lettered above the flames roaring out of Alison's mouth, warned that she would roast his cods to a crisp if he ever displeased her great-niece.

Raven and Hawk, who had been eavesdropping in the corridor, darted in to take a look for themselves.

A snigger sounded from Raven. "I don't mean to shock you, Aunt Alison, but that's a *very* unladylike word coming out of your mouth."

"My dear Weasel, I know exactly what *cods* means," replied the dowager primly. "Indeed, I daresay, I know far more bad words than you do."

Raven looked insulted. "Ha! I bet you don't!"

"Let us not put that wager to the test," said Charlotte as she quickly rolled up the drawing in a protective piece of oilcloth and held it out to Raven. "A special messenger is waiting for this in the kitchen. He needs to leave without delay."

As the boys scampered off, Alison fixed her with a martial look. "And now, my dear, off you go to begin preparing for your march down the aisle."

The march went off without a hitch, though there were a few tense moments when Skinny forgot to stomp the horse dung off his boots and was about to step into the chapel. But Alice the Eel Girl quickly corrected the oversight, and the only fragrance wafting down the aisle was that of Hawk's beautiful floral bouquets.

As for the bride, Wrexford felt his breath catch in his throat as he turned and saw Charlotte's radiant smile.

Love. His heartbeat quickened and its pulse seemed to thrum against the ancient stones and bring them alive with a golden glow.

"I do," said Charlotte softly in response to the chaplain.

And that was that—they were now man and wife.

The wedding breakfast was a gloriously festive affair. With all the laughter and champagne, nobody—save for Charlotte—noticed Harper had wolfed down half a platter of sliced ham that Hawk surreptitiously placed under the table.

She made a wry face and drew Wrexford through the open French doors and out to the terrace. "I fear that the Weasels are going to plead with you to let the hound come back to London with us."

"Our townhouse is already adding new residents," he drawled. "The more the merrier."

"Be careful what you wish for."

Chuckling, he took her arm and led her down the steps and into the gardens. They walked for a bit in companionable silence, the sounds of celebration giving way to the gentle flutter of the leaves in the breeze.

"You look pensive," he murmured after slanting a glance at her profile.

"There is much to think on," she said. "So many things are about to change."

"For the better, I trust." Wrexford smiled. "Think of our marriage as opening up a whole new realm of adventures."

"I daresay, we get into enough trouble as it is." Charlotte slipped her arms around his waist and pulled him close. "However, since you put it that way, I can hardly wait to see what intriguing things are going to unfold."

A laugh, low and husky, tickled against her cheek. "Well, then, let us start exploring our future. Heaven only knows what lies ahead . . ." He swept her up into his arms. "However, there's one certainty—whatever adventures come our way, we shall be facing them together."

AUTHOR'S NOTE

Those of you familiar with my Wrexford & Sloane series know that I like to weave in an important development in Regency science/technology as a main element in the mystery. In this book, I've focused on botany, rather than a "hard" innovation like steam engines or voltaic batteries.

Botanical medicine has, of course, been around for centuries, with traditional healers passing on their knowledge of local flora by word of mouth. But as the Age of Enlightenment encouraged scientific inquiry and empirical observation, a new breed of physicians were beginning to look past the traditional ideas on illness—many of them left over from the ancient Greek philosophers—in order to understand how better to treat maladies.

Building on Enlightenment advances in science—both in technology, like microscopes, and in empirical thinking—the Regency era saw the development of even more rigorous methods of analysis and logic within the field of botanical studies. David Hosack, who plays a fictional role in this book, is a real-life physician and man of science who founded the first botanical garden in America. An amazingly accomplished man, he had a profound effect on shaping a scientific approach to botanical medicine. He inspired a new generation of physicians to explore America's treasure trove of plants for healing medicines. Much knowledge was gained from Native Americans and incorporated into what Hosack and his peers were discovering on their own. Plant field guides proliferated, and new medicines were discovered through scientific study. I highly recommend *American Eden* by Victoria Johnson for further reading on Hosack and his innovative work in botanical medicine.

I also mentioned the real-life Alexander von Humboldt, who

today is considered the father of ecology. An international celebrity in his own time, von Humboldt studied the interactions of Nature, and man's effect on the environment. His early research trips through South America, where he collected countless plant specimens, inspired more new thinking about how the plant world might help cure human ills. (Today's botanists still explore Amazonia for yet-undiscovered "miracle" plants.) He also called for a uniform system for identifying plants, as there were so many different local names that botanists often found it impossible to engage in scientific discussions. This led to the Linnaean system of nomenclature, created by Carl Linnaeus in 1758, to be adopted around the world so that international scholars had a common language. *The Invention of Nature* by Andrea Wulf is a marvelous book on von Humboldt and the natural world. And *The Brother Gardeners*, also by Wulf, is a fascinating look at the Georgian/Regency-era individuals who were instrumental in starting the international interchange of botany specimens.

While my "miracle" plant in this book—and the nefarious plot that revolves around it—is entirely fictional, it was inspired by the "discovery" (they learned of it from the indigenous peoples of the region) of cinchona bark by the early Spanish explorers. Cinchona—often called Jesuit's bark—contains quinine, and was the only treatment for malaria at the time, which made very valuable both politically and economically. Malaria was a huge scourge in many parts of the world in the early 1800s, so a revolutionary new botanical cure, such as the one I imagined, would have been momentous.

I've mentioned the Royal Botanic Gardens at Kew in some of the previous books in this series, and I can't say enough about how important it and other early research gardens in various countries, like Hosack's Elgin Garden and the Old Physick Garden in Edinburgh, Scotland (now the Royal Botanic Gardens in Edinburgh and the place where Hosack studied as a student) were in disseminating invaluable knowledge on medicine, agriculture, and myriad other aspects of botany around the world. They shared specimen cuttings with each other, so valuable plants could be cultivated in non-native regions, and also shared their scientific research so that men of science around the world build on each other's knowledge. You can read more about both the Royal Botanic Gardens and David Hosack under the DIVERSIONS tab on my website. (andrea penrose.com)

As for the other subplot in the book, both Britain and America banned the trade in enslaved peoples in 1807—though America allowed domestic trade to continue until the Civil War put an end to it. Britain's Royal Navy was quite aggressive in patrolling the Atlantic coast of Africa to enforce the law, so I've taken the liberty of having the two countries create a secret joint effort to put a very nasty consortium out of business.

As my characters often point out in my stories, a world experiencing momentous changes in so many aspects of life offered exciting opportunities—both for doing good and doing evil. I hope you've enjoyed this tale!—*Andrea Penrose*

ACKNOWLEDGMENTS

Writing entails much solitary effort, which makes me even more grateful for all the wonderful people who help bring a book from that first faint glimmer of an idea to the printed (and digital) pages.

Many thanks go to my wonderful agent, Kevan Lyon for her guidance and encouragement in navigating the ever-changing waters of modern publishing. And I'm incredibly grateful to my fabulous editor, Wendy McCurdy, whose suggestions and counsel always make me a better writer.

I'm also sending heartfelt shout-outs to special friends . . .

To "Professor Plotto," whose astounding breadth of knowledge—from the esoteric to the sublime—is a source of constant inspiration . . .

To my amazing blog group, The Word Wenches—Nicola Cornick, Christina Courtenay, Anne Gracie, Susan King, Mary Jo Putney, and Patricia Rice—who are always there with a cyber crying towel and a virtual slug of single malt scotch! I'm extraordinarily lucky to have such wonderful brainstorming partners and Beta readers. But most of all, I'm extraordinarily lucky to have such wonderful friends . . .

To the Saybrook Fellowship, whose collective creativity and scholarship are constant reminders that books and ideas make the world a brighter place . . .

And lastly, hugs to all the PR, production and art staff at Kensington Books. You guys are the best!

Don't miss the next book in the Wrexford & Sloane
mystery series . . .

MURDER AT THE SERPENTINE BRIDGE

Beyond the glittering ballrooms and salons of Regency
London there are mysteries to untangle and murders to
solve—and the newlywed duo of Lady Charlotte and the
Earl of Wrexford once again find themselves matching wits
with a cunning enemy . . .

Charlotte, now the Countess of Wrexford, would like nothing
more than a summer of peace and quiet with her new husband
and their unconventional family and friends. Still, some social
obligations must be honored, especially with the grand Peace
Celebrations unfolding throughout London to honor victory
over Napoleon.

But when Wrexford and their two young wards, Raven and
Hawk, discover a body floating in Hyde Park's famous lake,
that newfound peace looks to be at risk. The late Jeremiah
Willis was the engineering genius behind a new design for a
top-secret weapon, and the prototype is missing from the
Royal Armory's laboratory. Wrexford is tasked with retrieving
it before it falls into the wrong hands. But there are unsettling
complications to the case—including a family connection.

Soon, old secrets are tangling with new betrayals, and as
Charlotte and Wrexford spin through a web of international
intrigue and sumptuous parties, they must race against time to
save their loved ones from harm—and keep the weapon from
igniting a new war . . .

Available in October 2022 from Kensington Publishing Corp.

Visit us online at
KensingtonBooks.com
to read more from your favorite authors,
see books by series, view reading
group guides, and more!

BOOK CLUB
BETWEEN THE CHAPTERS

Visit us online for sneak peeks, exclusive
giveaways, special discounts, author content,
and engaging discussions with your fellow readers.

Betweenthechapters.net

Sign up for our newsletters and be the first
to get exciting news and announcements about
your favorite authors!
Kensingtonbooks.com/newsletter

Praise for Andrea Penrose's Wrexford & Sloane Mysteries

"Compelling . . . an intricately plotted mystery set in Regency England. Its complex story line and authentic historical details bring the early days of the Industrial Revolution vividly to life. Bound to fascinate readers of C.S. Harris and even fans of Victorian mysteries."
—*Library Journal*, **STARRED REVIEW**

"Scientific discoveries combine with a complex mystery to provide an action-packed brain teaser." —*Kirkus Reviews*

"The author captures the Regency era's complexities in vivid settings, contrasting milieus, and a wealth of fascinating details . . . This thoughtful blend of derring-do and intellectual discussion should win Penrose new fans." —*Publishers Weekly*

"This book is very suspenseful and takes many turns, as the clues point first to one person, then another. Penrose is excellent at conveying the details of early nineteenth-century science and experiments with electricity. This was the era of Frankenstein, after all. The relationship between Wrexford and Charlotte is further developed in this book, and I am looking forward to seeing where it leads next."
—*Historical Novel Society*

"Andrea Penrose masterfully weaves the numerous plotlines of *Murder at Kensington Palace* into a scintillating whole."
—*Criminal Element*

"Charlotte Sloane and the Earl of Wrexford are a perfect crime-solving duo as headstrong and intelligent sleuths bucking the conventions of society." —*RT Book Reviews*

"The relationship and banter between the two stars of this series is incredible. Readers will look forward to seeing Charlotte and Wrex again (and, hopefully, very soon)." —*Suspense* **magazine**

"Thoroughly enjoyable . . . with sharp, engaging characters, rich period detail, and a compellingly twisty plot, Andrea Penrose delivers a winner . . . fans of C.S. Harris and Kate Ross will be rooting for Charlotte Sloane and the Earl of Wrexford. Devilishly good fun!"
—**Deanna Raybourn**, *New York Times* **bestselling author**